the GREAT ESCAPE FROM WOODLANDS NURSING HOME

Also by Joanna Nell

The Single Ladies of Jacaranda Retirement Village
The Last Voyage of Mrs Henry Parker

the GREAT ESCAPE from WOODLANDS NURSING HOME

JOANNA NELL

HODDER &
STOUGHTON

First published in Australia and New Zealand in 2020
By Hachette Australia
An imprint of Hachette Australia Pty Ltd

First published in Great Britain in 2020 by Hodder & Stoughton
An Hachette UK company

1

A CIP catalogue record for this title is available from the British Library

Hardback ISBN 978 1 529 34933 7
Trade Paperback ISBN 978 1 529 34931 3
eBook ISBN 978 1 529 34929 0

Typeset in Sabon LT Pro
Printed and bound in Great Britain by Clays Ltd, Elcograf S.p.A.

Hodder & Stoughton policy is to use papers that are natural, renewable
and recyclable products and made from wood grown in sustainable forests.
The logging and manufacturing processes are expected to conform to the
environmental regulations of the country of origin.

Hodder & Stoughton Ltd
Carmelite House
50 Victoria Embankment
London EC4Y 0DZ

www.hodder.co.uk

For my parents, John and Diane

'Hope' is the thing with feathers –
That perches in the soul –

EMILY DICKINSON, '"HOPE" IS THE THING WITH FEATHERS', 1861

Prologue

THE ANAESTHETIST'S BREATH SMELLED OF INSTANT COFFEE and skipped meals. A dormant surgical mask hung beneath his chin as playfully, he invited her to count backwards with him.

Ten.

Nine.

They were on *eight* when she noticed the doctor's missing tooth. When performing the pre-operative checks, he'd asked her to open her mouth and peered in as if appraising an old horse. Perhaps she should have done the same. Surely if he were any good, he could afford to visit a dentist? Or was he so good, so in demand, that he couldn't spare the time?

Seven.

This whole thing was terribly inconvenient. The ladder had seemed sturdy enough when she tested it, shaking the uprights against the russet trunk of the old Angophora tree. It had hardly been used. She remembered her father buying it to evict a possum from the roof. She'd begged him to let it stay. She didn't mind the scratching and the scuffling at night, she'd told him, found it a comfort even. But the following morning the bewildered creature was in the cage and sent off to be re-homed, or so she had been told. That was nearly eighty years ago. Things simply weren't built to last anymore. Ladders and hips alike. Both rotten and crumbling with age.

Six.

The bottom rung was mossy after several days of spring rain, and her leather-soled Oxford slid. Standing back on the damp leaf litter at the base of the tree, she took stock. The smell of petrol wafted through the broken fence slats as, out of view, the first of the chainsaws choked and stalled. She inhaled the cool, metallic fumes. She had to trust that the ladder would hold. Give it a second chance.

Five.

A cool breeze tickled up her forearm and her body drained away beneath her. A chainsaw whined in her ears, drowning out the gruff voices beyond the fence. Don't fall asleep, she willed herself. She had to stay awake. The birds were counting on her.

Four.

She pulled herself up, one rung at a time. Not much further now. But she was tiring, her arms trembling, legs leaden and unyielding. It was much colder up here, darker too.

Three.

Two.

As a small child, Hattie Bloom had dreamed of flying. She'd longed for the weightlessness of feathers, to fly out of her bedroom window and see the world as the birds did. To soar.

One.

'It's your age,' the surgeon had explained before he pinned the splintered shards of her femur back together. 'Your bones are thin and brittle. Like honeycomb.'

Hollow.

Like a bird's.

1

Hattie

NEVER ONE TO DWELL ON THE PAST, HATTIE BLOOM HURRIED from hers – the last few days of it, at least – and headed for the waiting taxi. She wouldn't look back, determined to put the whole unfortunate episode behind her. There were only so many sing-alongs, only so many games of carpet bowls and bingo that a sane person could endure. Legs eleven? If only. She'd settle for two that actually worked.

The taxi driver held the small plastic bag of Hattie's belongings and her walking stick while she wrestled her unyielding limbs onto the back seat. He was in his fifties, she guessed, or perhaps forties after a hard life, and smelled strongly of onions. With his sweat-stained shirt and open-mouthed breathing, he wouldn't have been her first choice, but Hattie couldn't afford to be picky when it came to getaway drivers. This was, after all, her one and only chance to escape from Woodlands Nursing Home.

Back in the driver's seat he addressed her via the rear-view mirror. 'Where to, love?'

She gave the address.

The driver started the meter. The little red numbers were already more than Hattie could afford, and they hadn't gone anywhere yet. Unsure of the correct protocol for tipping at a nursing home, she'd left a pile of small change – all she had – on her bedside table before she left. With her wallet and pockets emptied she hoped the driver would accept a cheque at the other end.

When the driver asked Hattie if she would prefer the windows open or closed and her choice of radio station, she shrugged that she didn't mind and pleaded silently for him to hurry. Her knotty fingers worried at the handle of the walking stick balanced across her lap. She risked a backwards glance as the taxi pulled out of the covered portico into the sun, past the ornamental fountain in the shape of a leaping fish and down the short driveway. So far, so good.

At the road, the taxi came to a halt waiting for a gap in the line of stationary traffic. From her bedroom window, Hattie had watched this daily procession of children to and from the nearby school. They walked scuffed-toed in ones and twos, or small untidy groups, staggering like turtles beneath their giant backpacks. A few rode bikes, but far too many were chauffeured to the drop-off point outside the main entrance. She had hoped to avoid the crush of traffic at this time of the morning, but an earlier sprinkling of rain had caused chaos and narrowed her window of opportunity. Dozens of parents fearing their delicate offspring might dissolve on the slightest contact with water now clogged Woodlands Road with their armour-plated people movers.

'I'm in a terrible hurry,' said Hattie, now gripping the seatbelt like a lifeline.

'Don't tell me you're running away?' The driver grinned into the mirror as if he had all the time in the world, drumming his fingers on the steering wheel in time to the music that sounded to Hattie's ear like the cries of a wounded animal.

Running away? Hattie scoffed at the irony. Only yesterday had she been given official clearance to walk, let alone run.

'I've been walking all my life without official clearance,' she'd tried to protest in a three-way tussle with the nurse and the physiotherapist. What she lacked in physical strength, Hattie more than made up for in steely determination, and she'd managed to bargain her way out of a four-wheeled walking frame in favour of a single walking stick.

'Can I have a wooden one?'

'They don't make wooden sticks anymore,' the physio had replied wearily. So, Hattie settled for one made from stainless steel. Her fingers traced the cool lightweight metal and she had the sudden urge to twirl it like a drum major with a baton. It might come in handy as a weapon too, should the need arise. You could never be too careful in the suburbs.

The driver's eyebrows twitched in the mirror waiting for an answer. Was he on to her?

'I've been on a short convalescence.' Shorter than planned. Plenty long enough.

'So, you're not escaping, then?'

'No, no. Nothing like that. This is a nursing home, not a prison.'

This was sufficient reassurance to turn the driver's frown into a crinkled grin. For a moment, Hattie worried he'd spotted the pyjamas under her coat.

It was true. Woodlands Nursing Home was not a prison. Technically, she was free to walk out the front door at any time. If she hadn't been doped up on morphine after the operation, she would have told the surgeon and the social worker where they could stick their 'respite' and discharged herself there and then. But things had snowballed.

The driver flicked idly between radio stations. Woodlands Road was in gridlock. A horn sounded, then another. Soon there was a cacophony of toots and beeps as somewhere out of sight, patience morphed into indignation. Hattie prayed the taxi driver was more restrained with his horn. The last thing she needed was to attract attention before they were even off the property. The meter ticked over, but by now Hattie was beyond worrying about the cost of her liberty.

'What's the hold-up?' Her mouth was so dry she could barely speak.

'Fender-bender in the kiss-and-drop zone,' said the driver with the nonchalance that suggested this wasn't an isolated incident.

Hattie's palms grew sweaty on the plastic handle of her walking stick. Pulling the seatbelt loose, she turned and looked back at the concrete building behind her. She counted the windows to the right of the portico until she found her room. Old Kent Road on the whimsical Monopoly-themed layout had been advertised as having a 'community view' – in reality this meant her room looked out onto the car park and the main road. The tiny silver lining was that she could watch the comings and goings from her window, which at least helped to alleviate the daily boredom. Nights were another matter. In the darkness, her window became a mirror reflecting the walls of the room that felt like a cell, and her face, a nightly reminder that she was old and for the first time in her life totally dependent. Even with the curtains drawn, Hattie had lain awake staring at the textured ceiling tiles and the air-conditioning vents that kept the entire facility at a constant twenty-three degrees. There could be a second Ice Age outside and none of the residents of Woodlands Nursing Home would be any the wiser. Night after night she had wrestled with sleep; her body dodged it, sparred with it and punched it away whenever it came close. The harder she struggled towards unconsciousness, the harder it fought back. Sleep was as out of reach as the ocean bed, and like a diver without a weight belt, she simply couldn't sink deep enough to touch it.

When she had finally managed to drop off, she'd been woken by the click of her bedroom door and a torch shined into her eyes. She'd cried out in fear.

'Just checking to see if you're asleep,' the nurse had said. Long after the woman and her torch had retreated into the darkness, Hattie had remained wide awake, alert and vigilant to every sound and shadow. It was easy to see why authorities used sleep deprivation as a method of torture. The staff were only doing their jobs, naturally, but she'd had enough. If she ever wanted to sleep again, she needed to get home.

'Isn't there another route?'

Ominously, the taxi driver turned off the engine. 'Sorry, love,' he said. 'No one's going anywhere until this gets sorted out.' He pointed towards the melee where two women in matching figure-hugging sports wear and tight ponytails spoke into their mobile phones, indifferent to the chaos they had caused.

Hattie picked at her thumb. She pulled loose shard after loose shard until she had a little pile of skin in her lap. If everything had gone according to plan she would be home by now. Once she'd made sure the Angophora tree was safe she could relax completely. Only when she saw with her own eyes the owls in their hollow would the nightmare be over.

She had been away from home too long. She had missed the familiar screech of the boisterous cockatoos and the kookaburras' cackle. She had missed the gentle *pock-pocking* of the frogs from their damp hollow at night and of course the *oh-woop* of her powerful owls. It was time to leave behind the plastic-wrapped mattress that puffed and sighed whenever she shifted position, surprisingly comfortable as it was. Beds, she was fairly sure, weren't meant to come with sound effects. She wouldn't miss the pillow; it made her feel as if she was being suffocated by a giant marshmallow.

Only a short taxi ride away, her own bed was waiting to welcome her home. She'd been conceived in that bed and then born in it. With Woodlands Nursing Home behind her, it was safe to assume she would one day die in it too. The idea of buying a new bed had never occurred to Hattie. Not that she could afford one. It wasn't so bad. The springs and what remained of the stuffing had settled around the contours of her body over the years. The mattress had moulded to her, and vice versa, her ageing spine was now curved and bed-shaped.

It was her pillow she missed most. Hattie couldn't wait to press her nose into the faded cotton pillowslip and inhale her own sleepy breath. Was there anything that smelled more of home than a pillow? If she listened too, ear against the feathers, she could still hear the echo of her mother's distinctive heartbeat.

The taxi was hot and stuffy in spite of the cool air blowing through the vents. All too conscious of her recent breakfast pushing up against her diaphragm, she took big gulps of air and clawed at the collar of her blouse. At the point she thought the smell of onions would claim her, the traffic started to flow once more. The wheels had barely moved when a hand slammed down hard on the taxi's roof, followed by shouting.

'Stop!'

If she were a Hollywood fugitive, this would be the cue for screeching tyres and the big chase. She would clutch her improbably light suitcase – suitcases always appeared empty in the movies – and make her getaway, only for the authorities to capture her again later. But this wasn't the big screen and Hattie didn't have a suitcase, let alone anything to put inside one. She had a plastic bag containing a spare pair of donated pyjamas, slippers, dressing-gown, and the clothes she'd been wearing when the ambulance arrived to find her broken at the foot of the tree.

'Mrs Bloom!' A face appeared at the window, a hand now motioning for the driver to lower the window. 'Where are you going?'

Hattie's door opened. Two smiling, uniformed women gestured for her to step out of the taxi and into a waiting wheelchair.

'Now come along, Mrs Bloom,' said one of the women, leaning in to undo the seatbelt. 'Why don't you come back inside and have a nice cup of tea?'

'But I need to get home.' Hattie clung to the back of the driver's seat with strong pale fingers but somehow, gently and skilfully, the two women managed to extricate her from the taxi into the wheelchair. The driver was appeased with a twenty but not before he'd mouthed a silent 'sorry' to Hattie. He was still standing, watching as the wheelchair headed back up the drive, past the ornamental fish. Hattie looked back and they exchanged a final wave as the morning sun bowed to the shade of the portico.

She hadn't noticed the sign over the entrance when she'd arrived: *Woodlands Nursing Home. Putting life in your years.*

As she slumped mute and resigned in the wheelchair, a high tide of pain returned to Hattie's hip. She'd run out of fight. For now. Her body might be a prisoner, but her mind and her spirit would remain free as long as she let them.

Instead of punishment or judgement, the women made breezy conversation as if nothing unusual had happened. 'The good news is you're still in plenty of time for carpet bowls, Mrs Bloom.'

'It's *Miss* Bloom,' Hattie protested. At least that was one shackle she had managed to avoid.

2

Walter

WALTER WAS RUNNING OUT OF HIDING PLACES. THE VOID between the back of his pressure-relieving cushion and the vinyl of his electric recliner had served him well but had reached capacity. Three empty Scotch bottles and a month's worth of medication now sat uncomfortably behind his buttocks, barely concealed by one of Sylvia's crocheted cushions. So far he had stayed one step ahead of the revolving door of care staff, but he would be found out eventually. Damn pills. He'd take the puffy ankles any day over the endless trips to the bathroom, each one a mini-marathon of effort followed by the disappointing dot–dot–dash sprinkled against the bowl. At least he was getting his money's worth – every trip made the expense of the en-suite more affordable.

He had a visitor. There was barely time to sit back down as a boy appeared in the doorway. Walter hastily disguised the clinking and crunching sounds with a cough.

'James! What a lovely surprise.'

It was difficult to see his grandson's face beneath that foppish fringe. Perhaps that was the idea. Walter felt a tug of sympathy for the lanky kid. He wanted to tell him to stand up straighter. There was plenty of time later on for that slouch. Walter pinned back his own shoulders, silently urging James to do the same.

'Hey, Grandpa,' said the boy.

'Where's your mum?'

James flicked his fringe towards the door. Walter saw his daughter standing outside in the corridor talking to the tea lady. Her passive-aggressive head tilt and thin-lipped smile suggested more than chit-chat. Walter could only make out snippets of the conversation. Something about biscuits.

Naturally he looked forward to visits from his family. More precisely, twice-weekly visits from Marie, who dragged James along at respectable intervals. When he wasn't busy with Taekwondo or Jiu Jitsu or whatever his latest thing was.

'How's school?'

'Good,' replied the boy, collapsing rubber-limbed into a chair near the window. The chubby toddler who'd always laughed at his grandfather's face-pulling was now an etiolated kid, growing as quickly as Walter was shrinking, all but oblivious to the world beyond his miniature screen. His eyes slid back to the mobile phone in his hand as it chirped a tinny tune that reminded Walter of a barrel organ at a fair.

Sylvia was the one who had insisted Walter write the cheque two Christmases ago for the latest piece of technology that the boy protested he was the very last of his friends to own, dismissing Walter's suggestion of a train set or Scalextric. 'I don't think they play with that sort of thing anymore,' she'd said. Sylvia had always made such a fuss of James, the late-arriving grandchild who'd been as much a surprise to the bewildered doctors as to career-minded Marie and her childless-by-choice husband. But Marie had risen to the challenge of parenthood, like every other task she'd set herself. The impatient little girl who'd cast aside the baby doll that wet itself had grown into a doting mother.

In turn, Walter had always wanted to be a good grandfather to his precious only grandchild. He'd planned to take the lad to the science museum, and teach him how to fish and whittle wood. Somehow the plans had stayed as just that. Once upon a time there had been all the time in the world. Somehow, he'd blinked and missed it, the days so slow, the years so fast.

'Am I going to have to confiscate that?'

Walter stiffened, trying not to move. Had she spotted his last bottle, containing only dregs, poking from beneath the skirt of his reclining chair? Marie stood with her hands on her hips. Glowering at her son. James's smile disappeared, as did the mobile phone into his pocket. 'Sorry, Mum.'

'Kids, honestly.' Marie leaned down to kiss the top of her father's head. 'I've lost count of the times I've told him to put that thing away.'

'What thing?' asked Walter. He tried to pull Marie into a hug. She pulled away.

'New mobile, Grandpa,' said James. 'Want to see?'

'No!' Marie interjected. 'He's obsessed with it,' she added. 'Can't help himself. It's like a compulsion for him.'

With that, she began her usual routine: tidying and straightening the newspapers, squaring up the tissue box and glasses case on the bedside table, then heading to Walter's wardrobe to repeatedly ball and un-ball pairs of identical black socks in the drawer. He'd noticed the wrinkles at the corners of her eyes, and white corkscrew hairs sprouting from her temples. His little girl was an ageing woman.

'Did they find your missing cardigan?' With a frown, Marie moved a single empty coat hanger to the exact centre of the hanging rail.

She had always been a tidy child, lining up her teddies and dolls, something Walter assumed she got from her mother. She'd become worse after Sylvia died. That was over twelve months ago now.

'It's only temporary,' Marie had assured him when she'd handed him the brochure for Woodlands Nursing Home.

He'd handed it straight back. 'You can't be serious,' he'd scoffed. 'I don't need a nursing home.'

It was true the past few months had been tough. He and Sylvia had been married six decades; he was simply going through a period of adjustment. That's what the counsellor had said. The truth was he didn't want to adjust. If he couldn't hold on to his wife, he could at least hold on to the pain and the nagging guilt that he could have been a better husband. Anything was better than the numb empty nothingness of loss.

'You're coping so well,' everyone had said at first. Like riding a bicycle with a slow puncture, Walter had battled on for as long as he could before he finally wobbled and fell off.

After several minutes of holding a conversation with his daughter's back, Walter said, 'Don't worry about the cardigan now, love.' No doubt she would order an immediate search party for the missing garment. Things had a habit of disappearing at Woodlands. Cardigans, socks, dentures and hearing aids alike, all vanishing into thin air. People too. Walter would get to know someone then they would disappear, never to be seen again. A laminated butterfly sign Blu-Tacked to their door at the point of no return and then a few hours – or days – later, *poof.* Gone. Sometimes Walter found himself staring round the communal dining table wondering who would be next to cark it.

'I'll buy you another,' said Marie. 'The one you're wearing is pretty tatty, Dad.'

Walter smoothed down the pilled wool on the front of his cardigan and tried to hide the hole in the pocket. It was his favourite, although it would never do to say so. Sylvia had had a habit of donating his favourite items of clothing in the name of charity. No sooner had a garment become comfortably worn in, than a stiff replacement would appear in his wardrobe. Marie became more like her mother with every visit, fussing and filling his living space with superfluous objects. What had begun with framed photographs, knick-knacks and ornaments soon progressed to small items of furniture. An entire carload of useless items that would only need to be lugged home again at the end of his stay. Fortunately this time she'd only brought in the carriage clock, the one he'd given Sylvia for their golden wedding anniversary. It was a lovely piece he'd found in a local antique shop. Remembering her wistful look he wondered now whether it simply represented all the journeys they hadn't taken together.

He gave up on Marie and turned his attention to the wall-mounted television. The sports channel had been extra, a concession he had insisted on when signing the agreement. His golf clubs might be gathering dust in the garage but he still had his imagination.

'Have you been watching the news, Dad?' Marie had shifted her scrutiny from the wardrobe to the television. 'It's important to keep up with what's going on in the outside world.' With that, she aimed the remote at the par three, seventeenth hole. When nothing happened, she shook the remote control, banging it against her palm before tutting and announcing she was off to find new batteries.

'Do you like golf, James?' Walter asked as Marie swept from the room.

James yawned. 'I guess.'

Golf, Walter supposed, like broccoli and whisky, was an acquired taste. But the boy was still young. His hand slid to his pocket and retrieved the phone. The music resumed, James soon a mesmerised cobra to a charmer's flute, his thumbs a blur over the controls.

'That's a pretty fancy piece of equipment you have there,' said Walter.

Without looking up, James listed the specifications, none of which meant anything to Walter.

'Mum only agreed to me having the phone for safety,' said James, now biting his lower lip in concentration as his thumbs twitched across the screen. 'So she can track me if I get abducted.'

Walter was dubious. At the same age, he and his mates would be untraceable for hours, off on some big adventure like explorers. Neither kids nor parents had been bothered by these wanderings. The world was smaller than ever for these youngsters, more connected, and yet most of them never ventured further than their bedroom.

Marie returned with AA batteries and immediately turned the green, the flag and the spectators into a blank screen on the wall. 'That's better,' she announced. 'Now we can chat properly.'

Marie's chats usually flowed in a single direction. About how Walter should eat less, move more, try to do things for himself. This was usually when they discussed biscuits.

'I saw you talking to Margery,' said Walter by way of a pre-emptive strike.

'Who's Margery?'

'The tea lady. Margery-with-a-g.' *Like the spread.* Parts of Margery's ample anatomy had certainly spread more than others. But since she controlled the rations of the sugar and caffeine, it paid not to draw attention to her unusual centre of gravity.

'Is she new?' Marie asked.

How little he and his only daughter knew about each other's day-to-day lives. When Marie left home, their weekly phone calls had invariably consisted of a brief exchange of pleasantries before Walter handed the phone to Sylvia.

'Here's your mother,' he'd say.

'Bye Dad, nice to talk to you.'

Mother and daughter could talk for hours. Now, the muted TV only amplified the awkwardness of the silence. Without Sylvia, it was as though the glue had dissolved from their relationship.

'How's Andrew?'

'He's having some "me time" this week.' Marie made quote marks in the air with her fingers. 'He's gone surfing with the boys.'

The conversation stalled. Walter knew nothing about surfing. How much better the two of them might have got on if his son-in-law had shown a penchant for spiked shoes rather than Lycra shorts, a wetsuit, or whatever unflattering wardrobe his latest midlife crisis had entailed.

'I read in the paper that we might have a storm later.'

'Yes, so I heard.' Marie's fingers fidgeted in her lap. Her eyes kept returning to the sock drawer.

Walter played his conversational trump card. 'How's work?' Strictly speaking, Marie had been to university and therefore had a career rather than a job, albeit one that left her stressed and tired and resentful. When Walter had pointed out that with Andrew's exorbitant salary she didn't really need to work she'd called him old-fashioned and sexist. Even after the lecture about gender equality, he still didn't really understand what she did. Another modern job that had been invented since his day. One that naturally came with its own indecipherable jargon.

'Busy,' she smiled, obviously happy that he had remembered to enquire. She wore her busy-ness like a badge of honour, like everybody nowadays. For all the time-saving technology society had invented, people were more time-poor than ever.

More silence. Walter sensed Marie scrolling her mental to-do list. As if reading his mind, she said, 'Sorry, Dad, we can't stay long. I promised James a poke bowl.'

'Sounds painful, mate,' Walter winked at his blank-faced grandson.

'Oh, before I forget, where's your calendar?' Marie flitted about, opening drawers and lifting old newspapers. She mumbled something about an appointment with an occupational therapist.

James leaned towards his grandfather and whispered, 'Mum says you have to pass a test before you're allowed to drive the Tesla.' He was looking in the direction of the shiny red mobility scooter charging in the corner.

'Piece of cake.' Walter puffed out his chest. 'I was a professional driving instructor for forty years. I reckon I can handle a motorised shopping trolley.' He was pleased to see the outline of a smile emerging between James's dot-to-dot pimples.

'Nevertheless,' Marie interrupted, 'the DON made it perfectly clear that Woodlands would only allow you to keep the scooter if you pass the proficiency test. Otherwise it has to go back to the showroom.' Then she added her favourite sign-off. 'We've already talked about this.'

How could he forget the frosty conversation with the Director of Nursing? In hindsight he should have thought to forewarn her about the delivery of the Tesla, but honestly – he and his brothers had made go-karts that went ten times the speed of the Tesla. In the end, the discussion involving Walter, the DON and the salesman had resulted in a compromise: a practical assessment by the occupational therapist.

'It's nothing personal, Mr Clements,' the DON had said. 'It's simply a matter of health and safety.'

Walter bristled at the questioning of his driving skills. For crying out loud, he'd made a living teaching others to drive. He barely recognised the world he was now living in. Everything had to be either healthy or safe. Things that human beings had been doing for millions of years now needed a risk assessment. You needed a certificate to take a piss in this place. No wonder the rainforests were disappearing; all those bloody forms.

At least he saw a way to get home again. Once he was mobile, he would have his independence back, and they would have to let him leave. After the incident in the car everything was still being finalised with the insurance company but it was the first step on the road to getting back on the road.

There would be many more obstacles in the way, not least Marie, even after the tests had failed to reveal a cause for his apparent blackout at the wheel.

The cardiologist had put it down to a heart arrhythmia and changed his tablets. The counsellor – a woman in her sixties with a soft voice and an equally soft body, who had listened while Walter clambered for the words he thought she wanted to hear – had implied that grief and depression had steered his front wheels towards that telegraph pole. He told her he wasn't the depressive type.

'Even men have emotions,' she'd said.

Naturally, Marie had put it down to age. Ninety was too old to drive, she'd implied, never mind that statistically it was teenage boys who were most likely to be involved in a crash. No one knew for sure what had caused the incident, least of all Walter and he'd been the one behind the wheel. He remembered nothing until the tow truck arrived, and after the humiliation of the roadside breath test and the once-over by the paramedics, the silent ride home in Marie's car.

'I've heard back from the insurance company and the car's a write-off, Dad,' she'd said a few days later.

A write-off. Walter had baulked at first, then settled into misery and hopelessness. What an ignominious end to his faultless driving career.

James was grinning now. 'Just think, Grandpa,' he said. 'If you pass, you can give people lifts on the back. You know, like Uber.' Walter must have looked puzzled because James clarified. 'It's like a taxi service where people use their own vehicle.'

Walter looked at the Tesla parked in the corner. 'Like a rickshaw, you mean?'

'Sort of. Only yours would be a scooter-Uber.'

'A scoober?'

James laughed. 'Yeah, you'd be a scoober driver.' James had abandoned his mobile phone and was examining the electric scooter's controls with interest. 'Can I take it for a drive, Grandpa?'

'Off!' Marie made them both jump.

'He's all right. Let the lad have a bit of fun.'

'You shouldn't encourage him. Scooters are not toys.'

'It won't be long before you're driving,' said Walter to his grandson. An idea had come to him, a way for the two of them to bond at last. 'I could give you a few pointers, if you like? Teach you a few of the basics, like hazard perception and road positioning.'

'Really?' James's eyes widened.

'Sure. I just need to get this stupid piece of paper first.'

'The OT is booked for Friday,' said Marie. She wrote it in CAPITAL LETTERS on the calendar, even though it was the only event for the entire month.

'Good.' Walter traced the T of the key ring with his finger. 'That leaves me plenty of time to practise.'

Marie swooped on the keys and snatched them away. 'Oh no you don't. I'm handing these in at the nurses' station for safekeeping. You can have them back when you've passed your test.'

As soon as his visitors left, Walter poured his jangled nerves a dram. Memories came flooding back of the tow-truck driver taking his car keys, while he insisted for the umpteenth time that he was unhurt and didn't need to go to hospital. Walter savoured the warm glow from his glass, the amber liquid stilling his tremor almost before it had reached his stomach.

There was still one thing he could do without a test. Walter Clements, founder of the 100% Driving School, was quite capable of pouring his own drinks.

3

Hattie

BACK IN OLD KENT ROAD HATTIE PUSHED HER BREAKFAST away, untouched. The toast was cold and soggy in its own sweat. Outside, the road was once more empty of cars, the children all now safely in class. Her prime position overlooking the outside world meant she was now finely attuned to the way the school day mirrored that inside Woodlands Nursing Home only a short distance away. The school bell comically heralded the serving of morning tea. At midday, the school principal kindly alerted the nursing home that it was time for lunch.

It was easy to see how nursing-home residents became institutionalised. After a lifetime of living by her own rules Hattie had assumed she would simply maintain her daily routine, albeit within set mealtimes, and yet she already sensed the irresistible tug, a hidden undertow in an otherwise tranquil-looking stream.

Like one of Pavlov's dogs she had become conditioned, listening intently for the sound of the breakfast trolley that carried the satisfying crunch of Corn Flakes in cold milk and the sugary hit of jam on toast, then a mere few hours later licking her flaky lips as the tea trolley approached. Like the broken key on the typewriter that always gave away the murderer, each trolley had a unique signature: the tea screeching like a black cockatoo, the sorrowful koel of the medication.

At Woodlands, time moved differently for the staff and the residents. To work here meant to rush, to chase the second hand of the clock. There was never enough time to do what needed to be done. To live here meant watching the hour hand trudge wearily around the clock face.

'Not hungry, Mrs Bloom?'

Miss Bloom.

It was the smiley Assistant in Nursing, a slight girl with glossy black hair that smelled of fruit, tied back in a pony-tail that nearly reached her waist. At first Hattie had found the AIN's cheerfulness reassuring, a welcome change from the tense faces of some of the overstretched employees. Hattie liked to watch the staff as she'd watched her birds: sitting silently, unseen. She came to recognise their calls and their favourite roosts. They wore the same uniform but she noticed their individual personalities. Some flocked together, others were more solitary. Like birds, they had a pecking order too. Some, Hattie knew, saw beyond the frailty of the residents and recognised each as an individual. But some did not. That was the nature of human beings.

'The toast is cold,' said Hattie. 'Like the tea.' She waved a hand towards the muddy-coloured liquid in the cup and milky scum that had already marked a ring inside the rim. Tea should be hot. It didn't get much more fundamental than that.

'You must try to eat. You're all skin and bone. You must get your strength back.'

I was perfectly strong before I came to this place, Hattie wanted to say. The longer she stayed here the more her muscles wasted. Another reason to get home as soon as possible.

Sensing her dissent, the smiling AIN tried to motivate Hattie with the promise of meals in the communal dining room, which did nothing to improve her appetite. It was another two hours until the school bell signalled a dreary morning tea. Another four hours until the disappointment of lunch. The passage of time was marked in weak tea and uninspiring biscuits.

The plastic bag of belongings taunted her from the chair, a reminder of yesterday's failed escapade. It was hardly even worth unpacking them. Every morning the same question: What would she like to wear today? Every morning the same response: She didn't mind. A brown woollen suit that was a touch too warm for twenty-three degrees, or the borrowed cotton blouse and canvas skirt that were slightly too chilly? Her clothes didn't belong at Woodlands, and neither did she.

So far no one had actually mentioned the taxi. Hattie had heard the word 'feisty' uttered as the two uniformed women wheeled her back to her room. Up until the fall, 'feisty' had kept her out of places like Woodlands. Now that she was inside, it was an unwanted label. One that could potentially prevent her from leaving again.

The AIN removed the breakfast tray and began to unpack the plastic bag, inspecting each item before inserting a hanger and transferring it to the narrow rail. Hattie had never been one for clothes. Modern clothes especially; they smelled of plastic, as if they were held together with glue rather than stitches.

Birds owned the one set, a uniform of sorts that identified them as part of a group. They took great care of their attire, preening and fluffing up their plumage. When feathers became old or tatty, they simply shed them and grew new ones. Always in the same colours and patterns. There was no need to worry about the season's fashion or making a statement.

'Everything is *brown*.' The AIN's smile slid when she stood back and perused the contents of the wardrobe.

'I happen to like brown. It's a very practical colour.'

'Don't you want to look nice?'

Nice? If she were a sparrow, brown would be considered the height of sartorial elegance. *Haute couture.* At home there was no one to judge her tastes. Free from scrutiny, she had adopted a utilitarian style. She had never before had to dress to impress. Female birds coloured for camouflage rather than display. It made sense for them to sit on their eggs unseen. Unfortunately, the appraisals didn't stop at her clothing. It had never occurred to Hattie to feel ashamed of her naked body. It was simply a body, a collection of useful organs and appendages, none of which had invited judgement or evaluation until now. She was more interested in what it could do than what it looked like. To undress under the gaze of a complete stranger was unsettling, to say the least.

At first she had politely declined her compulsory daily shower, pointing out that it seemed a waste with water such a valuable commodity. Besides, people were simply too clean these days, she explained to the AINs – both the smiling and unsmiling ones – since the lathering of manmade chemicals stripped the natural oils from the skin. When her aversion to bathing reached management level, Hattie gave in, tiring of the daily battle. She had asked the smiling AIN for a bar of soap, only to be told that Woodlands didn't allow soap.

'Use the body wash in the plastic container on the wall,' the AIN had shouted into the steam-filled bathroom.

'I'd rather have soap.'

'Too dangerous,' the AIN replied. 'A resident could slip on it, or a staff member hurt their back bending over to pick it up.'

The AIN made the bed and tidied up the wet towels as an exhausted Hattie sank into her reclining chair and closed her eyes. Her sudden reliance on others made her feel more vulnerable than all her years of living alone ever had. She'd always taken her independence for granted. Like trust, independence was fragile and at times, a heavy burden to carry on such narrow shoulders. Once lost, it was almost impossible to regain. On the plus side, the pain in her hip was slowly improving, though a little too slowly for Hattie's liking. Her foray in the taxi had stirred things up in that area, added stinging pulses of pain to her bone-deep aches, but it had been worth it for the modest sense of achievement. She consoled herself in the knowledge that this was nothing new; she had endured pain somewhere every day since she turned fifty and she counted herself lucky that it never lingered too long in one spot.

There was a woman standing over her. The AIN and cold toast were gone and Hattie's glasses had slid to the very end of her nose.

'Sorry to wake you,' the woman said. She introduced herself as The DON.

'Are you Italian?'

'I'm from Queensland,' the woman said before her confused frown relaxed into a smile. 'It stands for Director of Nursing.'

The DON wore her hair like a platinum helmet, and her eyebrows were as severe as the creases in her uniform tunic. A pair of silver-rimmed glasses hung from a chain around her neck. The DON's eyes were kind and she had an all-purpose smile that made Hattie feel both reassured and slightly uneasy.

Of course, they had already met, briefly. The DON had been part of the welcome committee when Hattie arrived at Woodlands clutching a sick bag. The journey from the hospital was one she never wanted to repeat. Perhaps she should have asked to sit in the front seat, looking straight ahead rather than in the back. Though judging by how urgently the hospital had wanted her to vacate the bed, she was surprised the patient transport vehicle didn't have lights and sirens. She had been in no mood for niceties that day and too overwhelmed to take much in.

Woodlands came as a welcome change from the bright lights of the ward where she'd lain behind paper curtains in a perpetual state of mild alarm after her operation. The nursing home was gentler on the senses, a softer-focus version of the hospital. It didn't smell of boiled cabbage or stale urine as she had feared. Indeed, there was no odour, unpleasant or otherwise. The manicured front gardens, elaborately arranged flowers on the reception desk and neatly coordinating furniture were reminiscent of a luxury hotel. Strangers smiled as they passed, and soft department-store music wafted to every corner. There was, however, no escaping that this was still a facility. More than the smells or the sounds, it had been the looks of resignation on the faces of the other residents that struck Hattie as the stretcher rumbled along the corridor towards her allotted room.

The DON arranged a chair beside Hattie's recliner and, making sure she was exactly at eye level, said, 'It's wonderful to see how well you're settling in, Mrs Bloom.'

Miss Bloom.

There was a white lever-arch file in her hand. Hattie braced herself for an official dressing-down. The DON pulled out a series of blank forms and rested them on her lap. 'Paperwork! One or two questions,' she said. 'Won't take long.'

Hattie was wary of incriminating herself. 'Do I need legal representation?' Like the doctor she never needed, she had a solicitor, in name only. With her meagre income, she simply couldn't afford to be in trouble.

The DON laughed and fanned herself with the forms. 'No, you have the right to remain silent, Mrs Bloom, but we have an accreditation coming up, so we have to make sure we have all our I's dotted and T's crossed.'

'Good. About the tea, it's never hot enough—'

'Not that kind of tea, I'm afraid,' the DON interrupted. 'I'm more interested in the I's and T's in your life story.' She gave a nod of encouragement. 'In your own time, Mrs Bloom.'

Miss Bloom. Hattie folded her arms.

'When you're ready.' The DON circled the ankle of her crossed leg.

'What do you want to know?'

'Here at Woodlands we like to get to know our residents as individuals. We like to know their story.'

'I don't have a story.'

'Everyone has a story.'

Did she? She'd knocked a jug of milk from the kitchen table with her skipping rope when she was five. Was this what the DON wanted to record in her white file? Or was it how the sound of the crockery smashing on the stone floor had left her father quaking and shielding his face with his arms. She'd never thought to ask why until she was old enough to read the harrowing accounts of Wilfred Owen, Sassoon and Graves, and later, Vera Brittain's *Testament of Youth*. Did the DON want to hear how Hattie, aged six, had found her mother in floods of tears after the possums had eaten the lettuces in her vegetable patch? Or that she was seven before she realised she was different from other children. It never occurred to her to ask questions when she was growing up, much less turn what she'd never understood into a story. Instead of trying to make sense of her parents' wounds, she had learned to retreat to a place deep inside herself, time and time again until it was the only place she felt safe.

Sensing her hesitation, the DON said, 'Okay, why don't you start by telling me where you were born.'

'Angophora Cottage.' That one was easy.

'Good. Excellent.' The DON scribbled on her piece of paper, sounding out the words as she wrote.

'Parents?'

'My mother died when I was eight, my father when I was twenty-three.'

'Excellent, Mrs Bloom. Now we're getting somewhere.'

'Actually, it's *Miss* Bloom.'

The DON looked confused. She rustled through some papers and looked over the top of her glasses.

'Are you sure?' she asked, scanning a document. 'It says here . . .'

Surely Hattie would have noticed if she had been sharing her bed all these years. 'Quite sure.' Hattie sucked in her cheeks.

'In that case, I'll amend the record. Thank you for letting me know. So, you're single?'

Single. The term suggested wanton, sexually indiscriminate, unrestrained. 'A spinster,' Hattie corrected, which instead made her sound frigid. She had been none of those things.

'S-p-i-n-s-t-e-r,' the DON spelled it aloud as if hearing the word for the first time. Surely Hattie wasn't the only one in here? Although the Second World War had somewhat depleted her generation of eligible men, it had never occurred to Hattie that she had missed out in the tombola draw of potential mates.

'Do you have any animals?'

'Birds,' replied Hattie.

'Birds. Marvellous.' The DON's pen skated across the paper. 'What kind of birds?'

'*Gymnorhina tibicen.*' Her father had taught her the Latin names of all the birds that visited the large tree the cottage was named after. 'Translated it means bare-nosed flute players.'

'Hmm?' The pen stalled.

'Magpies.'

'Oh, yes, m-a-g-p-i-e-s. Good.'

'Myna birds. Cockatoos.'

'Right,' said the DON, struggling to keep up.

'Corellas, lorikeets, king parrots, butcher birds . . .'

The DON looked up from her form. 'I'm running out of space here, Miss Bloom.'

'Pity,' said Hattie. So were the birds. Almost daily she woke to the hungry whine of a chainsaw that saw ancient trees hacked to pieces and fed through giant shredders. She rubbed the healing scar over her hip. Her skin was still numb from the slash of the surgeon's knife.

'Oh, I see, you're talking about *wild* birds.' The DON smiled with relief. 'Well, you'll be pleased to hear we have our own bird here at Woodlands, Miss Bloom. His name is Icarus and he lives in the day room. I'll introduce you later.'

Hattie thought it best to be honest with the DON, before the situation got any more out of hand. 'Look,' she said. 'I don't want you to waste too much time on my I's and T's. I'm not going to be here very long.'

'Aren't you happy with your room?' The DON spread her arms and looked around as if showing off the presidential suite. 'It's been renovated.'

'It's not that.' Indeed, apart from the oppressive tree-trunk wallpaper that made her feel like a babe lost in a wood, the room was so tastefully neutral as to discourage any sort of feeling, favourable or otherwise. It did, however, beat the paper dividing curtains that had made her feel as if she were lying inside a wrapped parcel for days on end.

'If you want to go on the waiting list for a garden view, we can discuss it. We're anticipating availability in Trafalgar Square or Fleet Street soon.'

Hattie pulled her brown cardigan around her. The DON took the hint and put away her pen. It wasn't that Hattie was ungrateful. Woodlands was a perfectly nice facility with perfectly nice staff. In fact, she could hardly fault the place. In many ways, not least the comfort of the mattress, it was far more impressive than her shabby little cottage.

'There's nothing wrong with Woodlands as a nursing home. It just isn't *my* home. Please let me go home.'

'It's not that simple,' said the DON.

'I feel a fraud being here.'

'You're eighty-nine.'

'But I don't feel eighty-nine.' Hattie sensed this wasn't the first time the DON had had this conversation, judging by the deep breath she'd just inhaled.

'You've had a nasty fall and you've barely recovered from the surgery. That hip is going to take several weeks to heal. You live on your own, apart from the birds, obviously. It's not safe.'

So far, the DON hadn't actually told her she couldn't go home. Indeed, she'd tried once already yesterday, and had come tantalisingly close to freedom, only to be reeled back in by the irresistible tug of Woodlands' invisible umbilical cord.

'When *can* I go home?'

'When your hip has healed,' said the DON.

'Solid as a rock.' Hattie knocked on her hip, trying not to wince. There was enough Meccano holding her shattered bones together to keep an entire Cub Scout troop occupied.

'You'll need a few weeks of rehab,' said the DON.

'How many weeks exactly?'

'Four to six weeks on average.'

Four to six weeks? Hattie let out a whimper. She felt as if she'd reached the front of a long Post Office queue only to hear that the person ahead wanted to renew their passport.

Taking advantage of Hattie's silent affront, the DON closed her file and leaned in. 'I wasn't going to mention this yet but now seems as good a time as any,' she said. 'The council have been in touch. They've received complaints from the neighbours about your cottage. Apparently there are some urgent repairs that need attending to. And something about a tree.'

~

The new neighbours had arrived bearing a torte.

'Did you say a tart?' Hattie inspected the teetering stack of berry-topped cream and chocolate in the box.

'No, it's a torte.'

'Can you spell that?'

The young couple had exchanged glances before the man obliged, pausing to confer with his wife that there was indeed an e on the end.

'Is it French?' Hattie had asked.

The woman replied, 'I don't know. It's from the shop down the road.'

Hattie scoffed silently. A loaf of bread from that place cost a week's pension. Even introducing oneself to one's next-door neighbour could apparently now be outsourced. Her mouth watered at the elaborate creation.

'Does it contain nuts?' Hattie tended to err on the side of caution where her teeth were concerned rather than risk a trip to her rapacious dentist.

The man was in a hurry to move the small talk past patisserie goods. 'Have you lived here long, Mrs Bloom?'

'It's *Miss* Bloom,' corrected Hattie.

'Sorry,' they apologised simultaneously.

They were the fifth set of new neighbours she'd had in a decade. People rarely stayed in one place long these days, always looking to upsize, or downsize, tree change or sea change. No one was content with where they lived for long. Thankfully, the neighbours mostly kept themselves to themselves, offering little more than a friendly wave over the fence. This couple were different. They already knew her name. And they'd brought a torte. A ginger tomcat appeared, weaving between the couple's legs. It was wearing a tiny bell in its pale blue collar. Hattie wasn't fooled. They eyed each other warily.

'I was born in this cottage,' said Hattie, squaring up to the couple and their cat. 'And I intend to die in it,' she added.

The couple looked uncomfortable. 'Oh,' said the woman. She cradled what looked like a baby bump. Either that, thought Hattie, or she'd eaten too much torte.

'But don't worry,' said Hattie lightly, 'I'm a tough old bird.'

The couple laughed awkwardly. Then the young man cleared his throat. 'While we're on the subject of birds, I'd like to have a word about the tree.'

'Which tree?' Hattie narrowed her eyes.

The pregnant woman took over. 'The big one on the boundary.'

'The one with the overhanging branch,' the husband clarified.

Hattie drummed her fingers on the torte box. 'Yes? What about it?'

The man continued, 'Just letting you know that we've had an arborist round to inspect it.'

'And?' Hattie's fingers started to crush the cardboard.

'He says there's a lot of dead wood in that tree. It needs to be pruned back.'

'Pruned?'

'Yes,' the woman looked warily at her husband as if to say, let me handle this. 'To encourage new growth.'

Nature had been doing a good enough job of keeping that tree in shape for the past hundred and fifty years. Up until the view to the water became real-estate gold. She was no fool.

'We are perfectly within our rights to trim any branches that encroach on our property,' said the husband.

It's our right.

Everyone was so aware of their rights these days. In better times, rights had gone hand in hand with duty.

'I'd prefer it if you didn't touch my tree,' she said.

'Our *shared* tree,' the woman corrected.

'Regardless of who the tree technically belongs to, it's dangerous.' The man patted his wife's pregnant belly.

'There is a family of owls nesting in that tree. They're sitting on the eggs at the moment. If you disturb them, they will abandon the nest.'

The couple looked at each other. 'It's not safe, Miss Bloom. We park under that big overhanging branch.'

Hattie looked incredulously from one to the other. Could people really be that stupid?

'The car is already covered in bird droppings,' said the man.

'That'll be the male, bringing food to the female on the nest. It's only whitewash,' she said. 'The pellets come out the other end.'

'What pellets?' The woman looked confused.

'Bits of fur and bones. They vomit them up.'

'We've tried to be reasonable Miss Bloom,' the man said in a noticeably less reasonable tone.

The woman looked close to tears. 'We brought you a torte.' Her lip quivered and her husband put his arm defensively around her shoulders.

'I'm merely asking you to wait until after the babies have fledged,' said Hattie.

'I think you're making this whole thing up,' said the man. 'We haven't seen any owls. Only a few cockatoos.' The cat licked its lips.

'Of course you haven't seen them,' said Hattie. 'Owls are nocturnal. They're shy birds. Just because you can't see them doesn't mean they're not there.' She was worried she had raised her voice. She was even more worried they were about to take back the torte. Her fingers tightened around the box.

The pregnant woman made a plaintive sound and leaned into her husband's protective arm. 'We were only trying to do the right thing.'

'The right thing would be to leave the owls in peace.' If Hattie didn't stick up for them, no one would.

The man's nostrils flared. 'In that case, you'll be hearing from the council. And our solicitor.' With that, the new neighbours left, picking their way along the overgrown front path towards the road. The cat had other plans, however, and followed Hattie instead. At the door she had to use her foot to keep the cat from following her all the way inside. She never let strangers in.

Hattie carried the torte through to the kitchen and paused for a moment before heading out onto the patio, where she opened the box and threw the over-priced cake onto the grass for the waiting magpies.

4

Walter

'GOOD MORNING, MR CLEMENTS. MY NAME IS ANDREA. I'm the occupational therapist.'

Having never met an occupational therapist before, Walter wasn't sure what he'd expected but it wasn't Andrea: barely five feet tall, with bright blonde hair neatly scraped back, her blue eyes shining as she introduced herself. Her voice was high-pitched and reached the limits of his comfortable hearing but her hand was so soft and kitten-like that he had to fight a sudden urge to stroke it.

Woodlands had a very active Allied Health scene. It was one of the things that had impressed Marie on their tour of the facility. Physio, podiatry, aromatherapy, massage. All complimentary, they were told, the cost conveniently buried in the exorbitant daily rate. Given that he would be going home soon and as a man who was open to trying anything once, he had tried them all, to get his money's worth. As it turned out, he'd liked the idea of a massage more than the actual massage itself, given by a masseuse named Nigel. An hour of gritted teeth and clenched buttocks later, Walter was a mass of knots.

Walter suspected that the various therapists were all part of one giant cartel. A visit from one usually ended in a referral to another, leaving him feeling as if he were following some complementary-medicine treasure hunt. As long as he was able to go home at the end, he'd go along with it. Besides, apart from Nigel, most of the therapists were young and female. He enjoyed the banter with the girls. Walter liked to think he provided a bit of entertainment for them with his witty repartee. His repertoire might be a little old-fashioned but good comedy never dated. He'd already worked his magic on the aromatherapist and dietician but he was yet to crack the physiotherapist, an outdoorsy girl with a raspberry-ripple complexion. The perfect opportunity had arisen during the timed Up and Go Test. Armed with a stopwatch, she had explained that the number of seconds it took Walter to get out of his chair, walk three metres and return to the chair was a good indicator of his future life expectancy.

Panting back in the chair, Walter had asked how he'd done.

'Not very well, Mr Clements.'

'It's not my fault,' said Walter feeling the thrill of holding the punchline in his hands. 'All my get up and go has got up and gone.'

She wasn't laughing. 'It took you thirty-five seconds.' A frown.

'That's not even time for a final cigarette!'

When the physio remained straight-faced and offered to refer him to a hypnotherapist to help him quit smoking, Walter was disappointed but not defeated. There was still the occupational therapist. He was quietly optimistic about his chances with Andrea. What's more, she'd brought the Tesla keys with her.

'I never thought I'd need an occupational therapist,' he said. 'I've been retired twenty-five years.'

Nothing. She didn't even look up from her paperwork. Was he starting to lose his touch? He reached for the keys, but the OT moved them out of his reach.

'Not so fast,' she said. 'There are a few checks we need to do before the practical test.'

'Of course,' he said. 'We wouldn't want to run before we can drive, would we?'

'I get the impression you're not taking this very seriously, Mr Clements.'

This whole thing seemed a little unnecessary. No, it was more than that. The idea of having to take a test was an insult. Trying to keep his tone light, Walter tried to explain. 'I was a professional driving instructor with a one hundred percent pass rate,' he said. He felt the next line building inside. Wait for it. Wait for it. '. . . Even with the girls.' He always chuckled at that. Even now.

The OT's cheeks flushed. 'You do realise this is the twenty-first century, don't you?'

Walter cleared his throat. 'Sorry, my dear.'

'I'd prefer it if you called me Andrea,' said Andrea.

Fair enough. Everyone was so casual when addressing each other these days. He was even on first-name terms with the urologist. It was strangely disconcerting, not least because the urologist, Brian (a bow tie–wearing man in his early sixties who rarely made eye contact), always hummed

'Hickory, Dickory, Dock' while performing Walter's annual prostate exam.

Andrea sat on the edge of the bed, resting the clipboard on her lap. 'Medical history?'

'Only the usual,' replied Walter. 'I think you'll find I'm not a bad age for a man of my shape.' He sucked in his belly, raised his chin to slim his neck.

'How far can you walk? The actual distance?'

'It depends if the wind's in the right direction.' He winked at Andrea, who recoiled as if he'd blown her a kiss. This was much harder than he'd imagined. His humour was usually catnip for the ladies.

Andrea tested his upper limb function, asking him to put his arms above his head, behind his back, then squeeze her fingers and finally to resist her downward pressure. She was stronger than she looked.

'Do you lift weights, Walter?'

'Only the Sunday paper,' he quipped. 'You need a truss to lift the sport section.' When this failed to raise even the corners of Andrea's mouth, Walter slumped, tired and defeated under the weight of the mounting bureaucracy. The only thing he had ever bothered to check before his students were allowed behind the wheel was the correct spelling of his name on the cheque.

With the paperwork finally completed, Andrea handed Walter the keys to the electric scooter.

'Time for the fun part,' she said, without smiling.

'Prepare to be impressed,' said Walter, struggling to get out of his recliner chair. He knocked another six weeks off his life expectancy with two failed attempts at standing but he didn't care. His legs might be failing him, but his wheels never would. Walter considered himself something of an ace behind the wheel. Would it be immodest to describe his driving as masterful?

Andrea insisted he wear proper shoes for the test, but after so many weeks of schlepping around Woodlands in slippers, it was like walking in flippers, his swagger more of a sashay. It was just as well the Tesla had handlebar controls rather than foot pedals.

'I take it you've read and understood the instruction manual, Walter?'

'Three-horsepower engine, fourteen-inch alloy wheels with pneumatic tyres, rear coil spring suspension and a top speed of twelve kilometres per hour.' Walter patted the armrest of the Tesla's swivel seat with pride.

'I was thinking more of the safety features, actually.'

'My last car was a V8,' said Walter, assuming this would offer sufficient reassurance to Andrea.

'As I'm sure you're aware, in Australia an individual using a mobility scooter is classified as a pedestrian and must obey the relevant road rules at all times.'

'Does that mean I can't be breathalysed?' A whole world of possibility suddenly opened up before him. The bar at the RSL, the golf club, the bottle shop, all within scoot-able distance of his house. Sure, the boys might pull his leg when he parked the Tesla amid the Beamers and Mercs but soon enough they'd be begging him for a Scoober ride home after a skinful.

Andrea knitted her brows. Could she smell the Scotch on his breath? He closed his mouth and tried to breathe through his nose.

'In the wrong hands, an electric scooter is a lethal weapon, Mr Clements,' said Andrea. She watched him pull the charging cable out of the socket with a wary expression. 'Do you know how many injuries these vehicles cause each year?'

'Being ninety is dangerous, Andrea.' Walter sighed. At his age, sneezing could be fatal. 'Last month, Edna Petersham choked on a piece of lamb shank and was dead before they'd wheeled in dessert.'

At Woodlands they were all heading for the edge of the cliff.

5

Hattie

HATTIE'S WALKING RECUPERATION WASN'T PROGRESSING AS fast as she would have liked. She was nothing if not determined and believed that the four to six weeks the DON had enforced could be shortened to one or two with the right attitude. Everyone was entitled to parole. As an only child she had never needed to learn the art of patience. Every day that passed at Woodlands was another step in borrowed shoes. She only hoped she could make it home before she got blisters.

It wasn't so much the pain that held her back. Already the muscles around her hip were wasting away, and persuading them to do what they had been doing all her life now required conscious thought and effort. Working out when and how to place the walking stick added an extra layer of complexity to what should have been second nature. It was like trying to walk with three legs. Things would be so much easier if she were a bird. An image of her friend the one-legged myna bird sprang to mind. It flew perfectly well but its touchdowns in the Banksia tree were more precarious, like a jumbo jet with only half its landing gear. The bird had no choice but to carry on if it wanted to survive. *Acridotheres tristis*. The common myna. If it was in pain, those little yellow eyes didn't show it.

Having set herself the target of being home again in a fortnight, Hattie put her mind to the task. Walking was the key. Every footstep was a step closer to home. The first circuit of the four long Monopoly-board corridors took her an hour, the second only forty-five minutes. Her room, Old Kent Road, opened next to a brightly lit corner stacked with bookshelves holding dozens of dusty books that no one appeared to ever borrow. The adjoining corridor housed the more upmarket north-facing rooms – Mayfair, Park Lane, Bond Street and so on – that looked out over the garden and, beyond that, pristine bushland. Each time she reached the book corner having completed another circuit, Hattie mentally collected her salary for passing GO. The circuits got quicker and her imagined bank balance grew. Yes, the hip ached, but less and less as the days passed.

'Come and join us for morning tea, Miss Bloom, before you make us all dizzy,' shouted Margery the tea lady, as Hattie trundled past the day room on her third lap of the morning. 'It's a choice of lemon syrup sponge or millionaire's shortbread, though if you're after the shortbread, I'd hurry.'

Hattie would have preferred a quiet cup of tea alone in her room but Margery had other ideas. Like the other staff who handled food or beverages in any form, Margery wore what looked like a paper operating-theatre hat as she dissected the lemon syrup sponge with surgical precision.

'Come and sit here between Eileen and Fred,' said Margery. 'The good news is that Fred's wearing the right dentures again, so we're hoping for the best. Aren't we, Fred?'

Sit between two complete strangers? It was like mixing parrots and pigeons, or pelicans and penguins. They might all have feathers but they each sang their own song. Fred's wizened face reminded Hattie of a dried apple. Eileen was singing to herself, her orange lipstick – which was worn mostly on her lips – mouthing some familiar tune. Would Hattie be expected to make small talk? The weather, the food . . . she'd soon run out of topics to discuss. What would happen when the conversation stalled? It was so much easier to revert to old habits and let others talk about themselves.

'Eileen was a big name on Broadway in her day,' said Margery, returning with a cup and saucer for Hattie. 'Weren't you, sweetie?' It was hard to imagine this insubstantial woman commanding an audience. She hummed the rest of the song and then smiled, her shimmery blue-shadowed eyes closed as she basked in the adulation of her imagined audience.

'I'm Fred Carpenter,' said the dried apple with a thick nasal accent, extending his hand to Hattie. 'Carpenter's Antiques.'

Hattie shook his hand and introduced herself in a quiet voice. She would be going home soon but that was no excuse for rudeness. Good manners cost nothing. 'Have you been here long?' She angled her body towards the man's chair and smiled. She could do this. With a little effort.

'Fred Carpenter.' The man smiled and offered his hand a second time. 'Carpenter's Antiques.'

A hunched woman appeared, pushing a walker. She was a strange shape around the lower half but in this place Hattie had learned not to stare.

'Ada, dear, there's a spare seat over here,' shouted Margery.

'What *are* you wearing, Ada? It looks like you've stuffed a couple of chicken Marylands down your drawers,' said a woman with tight white curls that gave her head the appearance of a cauliflower, her voice appearing to bounce off the far wall.

'They're hip protectors,' Margery clarified. 'Ada's been designated a high falls risk.'

'That's Judy,' said Eileen *sotto voce* for Hattie's benefit, indicating the woman with the cauliflower head. 'She's a narcissist.' When another woman entered pushing a walker, Eileen added with a knowing nod in her direction, 'That's Laurel Baker. She's had work, you know. Oh yes, our Laurel's no stranger to the knife.'

Hattie stared at the woman's stretched skin and rigid hair, then back at Eileen's clown face. Eileen, Laurel, Judy and Ada were her cohort. Was this what women of her age were supposed to look like?

Fred leaned over. 'Where are my manners,' he said, extending his shaky hand again. 'I'm Fred Carpenter. Carpenter's Antiques.'

Any minute now, thought Hattie, the Mad Hatter and the March Hare would arrive, shuffling on walking frames and wearing cardigans and sofa cushions. She looked around for an escape route. Enough was enough. There was a bus stop outside. Why hadn't she thought of it before? It was less obvious than the taxi and downhill to boot. Depending on the timetable, she could be home by lunchtime.

The cup and saucer toppled from Hattie's lap and landed on the carpet at her feet, a deep stain of lukewarm tea soaking into the weave. She tried to get up but her legs wouldn't move.

This was all some horrible dream. The kind where you need to run but you can't, or scream for help but no sound comes out. It had to be a dream. With luck she would wake up in her own bed, a child again, in Angophora Cottage with her mother asleep beside her. *I had a horrible dream*, she would tell Mother. *I dreamed I was old and alone in a nursing home.* And Mother would pull her close and whisper a lullaby with her soft warm breath on the back of Hattie's neck. But Mother was long dead. This was no dream.

'There, there, Miss Bloom. Take some big breaths now.' A hand clamped her shoulder. It was Margery. 'Don't you worry about a thing. I'll fetch you a fresh cup. Sit back and enjoy André Rieu.'

André who? On the muted television screen, a man with paradoxically scruffy hair and an immaculate suit played a violin for a thousand overdressed people who looked as if they'd been paid to smile.

Ada and her hip protectors were now wedged between the arms of the chair opposite, mesmerised by the violinist. 'He's quite a dish, isn't he?'

Judy replied, 'He's not my type. I like them a bit more rugged. Give me a man who smells of engine oil and I go weak at the knees.'

'Your knees go weak at the smell of lavender oil, Judy,' Eileen replied.

The ladies tittered into their teacups, and as Hattie wavered between deigning to smile out of courtesy and the temptation to withdraw as quickly as her body would allow, a chirping sound caught her attention. She turned to see a tall domed Crystal Palace–shaped cage in the corner of the day room. How marvellous! A little feathered friend. Company at last.

When she went to investigate she found a small blue bird cowering at the back of the cage staring into a small mirror beside a dish of untouched seed. The bird was missing several tail feathers, its wings folded by its side, redundant, conjuring the image of a fragile little heart beating inside a spindly ribcage.

Melopsittacus undulatus. The budgerigar.

Hattie put a finger through the bars of the cage. 'Hello,' she said. The bird didn't react. 'You must be Icarus.'

The budgie chirruped a response, flapped its wings a couple of times and then returned to staring at its own reflection.

'He's getting on a bit,' said a voice. Hattie turned to see the DON standing behind her.

'They can live to a ripe old age, you know, birds.'

'So I hear,' smiled the DON. 'No one is quite sure how old Icarus is. He was here when I arrived.'

Margery chimed in from the tea trolley. 'That bloody bird will outlive all of us.'

Looking around the day room, Hattie didn't doubt it. Most of the residents looked like they had already donated their organs.

'I've been thinking,' said Hattie. Now seemed as good a time as ever to bring it up. 'If I agree to the repairs on Angophora Cottage, can I go home sooner?' No point coming on too strong. Hattie didn't want to appear difficult. She was rather rusty with people but common sense told her she was more likely to get her own way if she asked nicely.

The DON had a look on her face that Hattie couldn't read. 'It's not that simple, you see.'

Hattie didn't see.

'The list of defects is quite extensive, Miss Bloom. Apparently there's a hole in the roof.'

'It only leaks when it rains,' Hattie said, truthfully.

There followed a long and convoluted explanation of why it wasn't possible for Hattie to go home. In addition to the hole in the roof, the DON reeled off a defect list that left the century-old Angophora Cottage barely standing. Hattie's home was a death trap, boasting an impressive range of potential obstacles and trip hazards: uneven pavers, loose rugs, steep stairs and an overgrowth of vegetation that belonged in a Grimm fairy tale.

Beaten down by the onslaught of potential hazards, Hattie finally relented. There was no point mentioning the owls. No doubt she would be labelled batty as well as feisty. Once again, she had been skilfully placated. Bamboozled. If she wanted to get out of here, she would need to be clever, to use all her cunning and guile. Create the illusion of compliance. It would cost her what little savings she had put away. But what choice did she have? Freedom wrote its own cheques.

Inside the birdcage, Icarus flapped his wings.

6

Walter

'WHAT DO YOU MEAN, I FAILED?' WALTER'S HANDS TREMBLED as he attempted to push the charging plug back into the socket on the side of the Tesla's tiller column.

Andrea pushed his walking frame towards him and took over. 'You failed the assessment.'

'I don't understand.'

'Failed, meaning you did not pass.' She retrieved the keys from the ignition and slipped them into her pocket. 'I'm afraid you are not allowed to drive the scooter.'

'Surely there's been a mistake,' said Walter leaning on his walker. 'I've said I was sorry about your foot.'

'It wasn't just my foot,' said Andrea, examining the tyre marks across her white lace-up shoe. Perched on the edge of the bed she untied her shoelaces, wincing as she exposed her bruised and rapidly swelling foot.

'If it's about the statue,' said Walter, 'I've already said I'll pay for the damage. A bit of superglue and no one would know the difference.' It was a stupid statue, the kind of froufrou that Sylvia used to collect. Since dusting was the sole indoor domestic task with which he had been entrusted, he had developed a particular enmity for the Spanish dancers and cherub-faced children. If he'd had his way, he would have lined them up on the driveway and mown them all down in his V8.

'It's not only the statue.'

'That table was too old-fashioned anyway. It's time the furniture was updated. Management should be thanking me.'

'It was eighteenth century, according to Fred Carpenter. It was a rare piece, very valuable apparently.'

What a shame people didn't increase in value when they got older and rarer. 'Ridiculous place to put a piece of furniture,' he muttered. On the plus side, it would give that lazy handyman something to do beyond stealing chocolates from the nurses' station.

Walter was torn between wanting to comfort Andrea and get rid of her. With any luck, there was a brand-new bottle of Johnnie Walker Red Label waiting at the back of his wardrobe, in its usual spot inside an empty slipper box. His change would be hidden in an envelope behind the bottle, minus a small commission. No need to count it. He trusted his supplier implicitly. The arrangement suited them both perfectly.

The test had started so promisingly with an exaggerated repositioning of all the mirrors, just as Walter had always taught his students. He'd spent several minutes adjusting and readjusting his seat height and position to Andrea's satisfaction. He'd even remembered to pull out the charging cord before driving off; a rookie mistake he wasn't about to make. After that, things hadn't gone quite so smoothly, starting with a mix-up over the foot pedals. Or rather, the lack of foot pedals.

Walter's right foot searched impatiently for the accelerator before he remembered the smarmy scooter salesman demonstrating the correct use of the handlebar throttle. The speed could be preselected and therefore controlled from a dial on what passed for the dashboard. Andrea's idea of a suitable speed was a walking pace, which Walter felt defeated the purpose. He adjusted the dial accordingly, prompting Andrea to step in and dial it down again. The poor scooter was confused, and they eventually compromised, Andrea breaking into a half-jog to keep up.

Ahead, he had correctly identified his first hazard: Fanny Olsen. She was in a hurry to nowhere as usual. For a frail-looking old lady she was surprisingly nimble on her feet and Walter imagined tiny sparks of static as her slippers scuttled over the high-traffic nylon carpet. She was carrying what looked like a large yellow torch under her arm. Another item for her eclectic collection. Fanny Olsen was renowned as the Artful Dodger of Woodlands Nursing Home, and the staff always turned a blind eye to her harmless pilfering.

Out of habit, Walter shouted a warning. 'Fore!' Hauling the handlebars to the left at the last minute, he avoided Fanny Olsen but made contact with Andrea's foot instead.

'Ooh, lucky,' he said when Andrea's face had returned to a normal colour. 'That could have been nasty.'

The official obstacle course had been carefully set out in the dining room, the furniture moved to the perimeter leaving several strategically placed chairs. Andrea limped around the course, demonstrating the required sequence of chairs. It was more Monza than Monaco, but Walter was quietly confident as he navigated the tight turns in the Tesla. He could feel Andrea's critical eye following him and, unaccustomed to an audience, he oversteered at the final hairpin, toppling a dining chair that in turn felled a plastic palm. Nevertheless, Walter remained cautiously optimistic. It wasn't as though he'd knocked over another resident. Walter snuck a glance at Andrea but if she was impressed by his driving prowess, her poker face gave nothing away.

By the end of his third lap, Walter had the hang of the controls. Pull back on the right-hand throttle lever to go forward, release to brake. Same with the left hand to reverse. Andrea was growing restless, not bothering to right the chairs as they tipped over, one after another. When she pointed out that he had attempted to use both indicators at the same time, he argued that it was better to be safe than sorry. The same went for his liberal use of the horn.

'I think I've seen enough, Mr Clements,' said Andrea, as the last of the dining chairs crashed to the carpet. He swelled and returned a warm smile. *Still got it, old man.*

On the way back to Walter's room, Andrea hobbled behind the scooter clutching the official paperwork protectively against her chest. Ahead, steam rose from the urn on the tea trolley, which stood idling in the hallway like a locomotive at a station. Spying an unguarded plastic container of biscuits, Walter leaned towards the trolley to avail himself of a sneaky ginger nut. Before he knew what was happening, the Tesla lurched forward, his right hand spasmed around the forward throttle. The three-horsepower engine picked up remarkable speed, the pneumatic tyres eating up the patterned carpet as the scooter careered down the corridor.

'Stop!' Andrea's squeaky voice rose beyond the limits of Walter's hearing and conveniently disappeared. The fingers of his right hand relaxed from the spasm and the Tesla slowed momentarily before he clenched them again. He had the hang of this now. He pictured himself as Steve McQueen on a stolen motorcycle heading for the snow-capped mountains of Switzerland, a thumping rock anthem playing in the background.

As he passed Murray's room, Walter pipped his horn and waved. His friend would be trying to finish the crossword in the paper as he did every day. Walter hoped it was a short puzzle; there was no knowing how much time the old boy had left now the cancer had emigrated from his prostate. Walter had heard the doctor and nurse discussing his prognosis in hushed voices. The palliative drugs were apparently written up on his chart but so far the stubbornly stoical Murray was resisting his butterfly sign.

Walter ignored the voices in the distance. The engine hummed beneath him. Man and machine, in perfect synchrony.

Top speed now, the dial fully clockwise, the walls a watery blur of tasteful landscapes. Up ahead, a right-angled corner loomed. He released the throttle, slowed a fraction outside Laurel Baker's room where the podiatrist was filing away Laurel's big toe like a lead violinist while Laurel selected chocolates from a large box.

What happened next was officially recorded in Andrea's shaky handwriting on her form, and later by the DON in an official incident report. Walter remembered shouting to Laurel asking her to save him the hazelnut whirl but apparently not the scream and the sickening sound of crumpled metal.

Surely he should have been awarded bonus marks for bringing the vehicle to a controlled emergency stop without skidding? His prompt action in cutting the engine had, after all, prevented further casualties.

The silence stretched out like India rubber. Then the commotion began. People ran from all directions. He hadn't seen the staff congregate that quickly since they'd opened the champagne at the Christmas party.

Naturally, the DON was first on the scene, followed by an ashen-faced Andrea who hopped towards them. Ignoring Walter, they gathered around a frail-looking woman in brown who lay crumpled on the floor next to a stainless-steel walking stick. The corridor was soon cordoned off. A crime scene. From nowhere, a nurse appeared with a gauze pad and bandage. Before he could take it all in, the unknown woman and her bleeding leg were whisked away to the treatment room, Woodlands Nursing Home's equivalent of landing on GO TO JAIL.

7

Hattie

THE DON SUCKED AIR THROUGH HER TEETH AND SHOOK her head like a builder giving a quote. The registered nurse swabbed away the congealed blood. They winced in stereo. When the third person to enter the room also grimaced, Hattie knew it must be serious.

'Nasty,' was the general consensus. The skin on Hattie's shin was split and curled back like a boiled tomato. Worse still, it was her good leg.

The nurse carefully lifted the loose flap of skin with a pair of blue plastic tweezers and unfolded the corners, stretching the wafer of skin back into place.

'It all happened so fast,' said Hattie, replaying the moment she hadn't seen coming.

'Such bad luck,' said the nurse as if Hattie had thrown a one instead of a six, then muttered something about the place going to the dogs.

The DON began to fuss. Hattie wasn't used to all this attention and she didn't particularly like being poked and prodded, meanwhile her leg throbbed beneath what she was assured was Woodlands' most expensive dressing. 'It's impregnated with silver,' said the nurse. 'It'll heal much quicker with silver.'

Woodlands already cost her most of her pension and was eating into her savings faster than a nest of ravenous termites through a fallen log. Hattie wanted to ask if the silver-level treatment was included but thought better of it in case they assumed she couldn't afford it and relegated her to bronze.

'How long will it take to heal?' Hattie asked.

There was some umm-ing and aah-ing accompanied by thoughtful cheek tapping and chin tugging. 'Several weeks.'

'How many weeks?'

'Four to six weeks,' replied the nurse.

Was this included in the four to six weeks her hip would take to heal, or in addition? Hattie wondered. Could her body cope with two insults at once or had her time at Woodlands just doubled?

'Assuming it doesn't become infected,' said the nurse.

'Is that likely?'

'It's unlikely,' the nurse replied.

'But possible?'

'Possible but not probable,' said the DON.

Hattie didn't like these odds. Time was running out for her to get back to the cottage. She had managed to inadvertently stall the first tree-trimming efforts by summoning the emergency services – all three, apparently – when the ladder collapsed, taking the rickety fence with it and revealing Hattie's spreadeagled body to the astonished tree-loppers. She was running out of bones to sacrifice to save the tree and the owls. The chainsaws would be back.

The registered nurse tore off a piece of white tape and secured the loose end of the bandage, then stood back to admire her handiwork. 'That's you finished,' she said, clearing away the dressing things.

With the evidence now discreetly hidden, Hattie's thoughts turned to the unfortunate incident itself.

'Who was that man on the scooter?' she asked. She couldn't picture his face, having registered only the movement towards her and then the carpet at close range.

'That's Walter Clements,' said the nurse.

'Which room is he in?' So she could be sure to avoid him in future.

'He's in Whitechapel Road. He's your next-door neighbour.'

So, this was the Walter Clements of the blaring television. Walter Clements who assumed he owned the entire corridor. Typical. Humans, and their sense of entitlement.

The receptionist appeared at the back of the audience, hand darting up and down as if she needed to be excused from class, alerting the DON to an urgent health-and-safety situation in the craft room. Apparently the hot-glue gun had malfunctioned and there was mayhem. The DON apologised and disappeared. The nurse was still admiring her efforts, angling her head one way, then the other.

'We'll need to keep a close eye on that leg,' she said, leaving Hattie to wonder how that was possible given that the leg was bandaged tighter than Tutankhamun's. 'Otherwise you could end up with an ulcer.'

'Ulcer?'

'Don't worry, Miss Bloom, Woodlands sent me on a course recently. I'm really good with leg ulcers,' she said cheerily.

8

Walter

WALTER STARED AT THE BROWN LIQUID IN HIS BOWL. ALL the food was brown in this place, including most of the greens. Brown breakfast cereals and toast, brown biscuits or slices for morning tea, brown soup for lunch, more brown soup followed by well-cooked meat in a brown sauce for dinner. His sense of taste and smell had long since deserted him. Apparently so too had his colour vision.

'My wife was the most marvellous cook,' he said wistfully. It was Walter's turn to fill the silence at the communal dining table. No one answered, his lament lost in the clink of cutlery. It was true that while Sylvia's repertoire was limited, her offerings in the kitchen – and the bedroom – while lacking imagination were always wholesome and gratefully received. Walter could barely boil his own egg.

'Is it rissoles again?' It was Laurel Baker from the far end of the table holding the menu up to the light. 'Didn't we have rissoles last night?' She was too vain to wear glasses, or, according to the rumours, use a pillow at night lest she disturb her elaborately set hairdo.

'Last night was sausages, Laurel. You're getting confused again.' Judgy Judy was the head-girl type, undoubtedly an eldest sibling. A stickler for trivial detail, Judy could always be counted on for the latest in playground gossip too. 'Don't you remember, you didn't finish yours?'

'I could have sworn it was rissoles,' said Laurel, lowering her cutlery to her plate to emphasise her certainty.

'No, Laurel. It was sausages and you turned up your nose. Such a waste of perfectly good food.'

Judgy Judy had been gunning for a fight all evening. It had started with a skirmish over the croutons and gone downhill from there.

'But we always have sausages on a Thursday,' said Laurel.

'Today is Friday,' Judy scoffed.

'Are you sure?'

'It's rissoles tonight,' said Judy. 'So it *has* to be Friday. Last night was chicken sausages. Thursday.'

Laurel paused for a moment, until something dawned on her. 'Oh, I do remember now,' she said with a shudder. 'It goes against all the rules of nature. Sausages should be made from pork, not poultry.'

'Not if you're Jewish,' Judy countered.

'Lamb or beef, then,' snapped Laurel.

'Hindus don't eat beef,' said Judy. 'On account of cows being sacred.'

'The last time I looked, there weren't any Hindus or cows at Woodlands.'

The table fell silent as the residents looked each other up and down.

Walter piped up. 'What about Sameera?' He had a soft spot for the young AIN who usually worked nights and pronounced his name in a way that made it sound exotic. Having had the same name for ninety years, he felt reinvented.

'What about her?'

'She's vegetarian.'

Laurel found a convenient stepping stone back into the conversation. 'My Derek's Presbyterian.'

'You mean pescatarian, Laurel,' Judy corrected. 'He eats fish.'

Another mealtime. Another incarnation of the same conversation. Walter wasn't sure how much more he could take and yet he hated to eat alone. Even Sylvia's twice-yearly visits to her sister up the coast used to make him miserable. During the day he would be content to potter about the empty house but then, overwhelmed by loneliness as he reheated the meal Sylvia had left for him on a plate, Walter would head off to the pub or club for a schnitzel instead.

At Woodlands, he was always going to be outnumbered by the ladies. His saving grace was Murray. The two men had struck up a friendship after they'd moved in around the same time. Walter liked to tease Murray that his room, Bond Street, was at the 'top end of town'. In return, Murray used to pretend to wipe his feet on the way out of Walter's room.

Used to.

Murray hadn't made it to the dining room all week. In fact, Murray hadn't been out of bed for several days now. Walter had been forced to pair with Eileen for carpet bowls. He'd had high hopes when she assured him she won bronze for curling at the 1964 Winter Olympics in Innsbruck. Unfortunately, Eileen appeared to have lost her form and they came second last. Carpet bowls aside, it was at mealtimes that Walter missed his friend the most. Specifically, he missed their regular game of Guess The Soup.

After slurping the soup from the spoon he'd sieve it through his teeth like a whale eating plankton, searching for clues. After that, he'd swill the soup around his cheeks and declare it, 'Earthy, full-bodied, chewy with a hint of grass . . . linseed . . . and a suggestion of . . . pumpkin?'

Murray's turn. 'I was thinking more dense, toasty, jammy . . . with a flabby middle . . . and a cigar box aftertaste. To my mind this is a classic Woodlands Cream of Mushroom.'

They'd erupt into raucous laughter, provoking predictable disapproval from the ladies.

Laurel and Judy were still debating the merits of alternative sausage fillings when young Alex, who worked three evenings a week, arrived with the wine.

'It's the sommelier!' Walter waved his glass eagerly.

'Red or white?' Alex hovered with two bottles.

'I'll hedge my bets and have one of each,' said Walter. He scanned the table, his glance stopping at Fanny Olsen sitting opposite. He leaned across and availed himself of her empty glass. 'And I'll have one for Fanny too.' He winked at her. She stared back blankly.

Alex was doing something with computers at the university he rarely seemed to attend. As far as Walter could tell, he spent most of his time behind the drive-thru window at McDonald's, or serving at Woodlands.

'Leave the bottle here, son,' said Walter with a knowing look. In exchange for a small donation towards his education fund, the lad usually left the wine unattended within Walter's reach.

'Righto, Walter,' said the lad, obliging.

'Growing a beard?' Alex looked as if the bottom of his face had been dipped in iron filings.

'Nah, this is designer stubble,' he replied, stroking his chin with his long fingers.

Designer stubble. Whatever next? Apparently a whole new industry had sprung up around male grooming. Oils, waxes, pomades, balms. Walter had read about it in a women's magazine he found at the nurses' station. Body hair was out. Facial hair was in. Unfortunately, Walter's hair follicles had mixed up the message. On his last visit, the barber had trimmed his ears and ran the clippers halfway down his back.

Dessert arrived.

'Are you having ice-cream, Ada?' Judy had to tap Ada on the shoulder to get her attention. 'Ice-cream,' she mouthed.

'No, the discharge has gone. Doctor says the infection's all cleared up now.'

'Not eye cream, Ada. *Ice-cream.* Where's your hearing aid?'

Walter drained the dregs of his red wine. Not a bad drop, that. At least it made the meal more bearable. Made the ladies more bearable. From the other end of the table, he heard Judy regaling the captive audience with her eyewitness account of Walter's scooter test.

'She went flying!'

'Poor Miss Bloom.'

'He's a menace.'

Walter waved. 'I'm right here, Judy.' If only his wingman, Murray, were here.

Judy offered a derisive snort. 'I hear it on good authority that Miss Bloom is heading for a leg ulcer,' she said between mouthfuls of rissole.

Walter took the last of the bread rolls from the basket. 'The steering was faulty,' he said. 'Luckily the scooter is under warranty.'

'But what about poor Miss Bloom?' said Laurel, now siding with Judy against a common enemy. '*She* doesn't have a warranty.'

'You need to be more careful, Mr Clements.' It was Judy again. 'What if you'd knocked poor Laurel over? She suffers from brittle bones.'

Laurel looked smug. Here came her party piece. 'I'm riddled with arthritis too,' she said proudly. 'The doctor said it's a miracle I'm still walking. He said I should be a cripple, with a backbone like mine. Worst X-ray he'd ever seen.' She manoeuvred a piece of gristle with her tongue and transferred it to her waiting napkin.

You're a miracle all right, Walter wanted to say, but instead he smiled indulgently. Laurel Baker was rather selective when it came to remembering her doctor's words. Whatever anyone else had, she'd had it ten times worse. She was a professional patient.

'I was a sickly child,' she'd once said within his earshot. 'I've always had a weak chest. And now I've got a crumbling spine.' Walter thought she looked rather robust for someone who'd supposedly barely clung to life for eighty-odd years. Her son Derek kept the staff on their toes too. Always hanging around, questioning every pill and prescription.

'He's a pharmaceutical representative,' Laurel liked to boast. She took enormous pride in her son's interference as well as his daily visits. No one could touch Derek Baker when it came to caring. The man was as bald as an egg, another fashionably hirsute hipster with a beard that looked like a fluffy bib hanging from his chin. He was always here. While sadly many of Woodlands' residents never had a visitor, Derek Baker may as well move in.

As dinner drew to a close several of the residents looked as if they had more food on their plates than when they started; others had polished off seconds. Walter was only relieved they didn't have to split the bill. He tried to match the shape of the woman who had toppled directly into his path to one of those around the long communal table. The woman, whoever she was, had given him quite a fright. A man of his age, with his heart condition – who knows what might have happened?

Walter shuffled out past young Alex, slipping a ten-dollar bill into his pocket in exchange for full custody of the cabernet sauvignon. The lad reminded him of James, in a few years perhaps. Sylvia had been so fond of that boy. An image of her planting lipstick on his cheek brought a smile to Walter's face. Cradling the bottle to his chest, he closed his eyes and floated towards the memory.

9

Hattie

HATTIE'S STOMACH FLOODED WITH ACID AT THE SIGHT OF the congealed offerings on the plate. She had survived a fall from a ladder and been knocked over by a motorised scooter, and yet it was possible that she might actually die from starvation.

'They're rissoles,' the young man explained as he laid the tray in front of her.

'They look more like owl pellets to me.' That raised a smile and an offer to find her a cheese-and-tomato sandwich instead.

What was wrong with something green and leafy? Outside, it was definitely salad weather. Inside Woodlands, however, it was perpetually meat-and-two-veg weather. Even the menu was climate controlled.

The lad returned as promised with the sandwich. By way of compensation for her accident, Hattie was allowed to eat in her room, a brief reprieve from the cacophony of crockery, cutlery, whistling hearing aids, gurgles and coughs of the communal dining room, as well as the inane chatter of the ladies who congregated at the far end of the dining table. To Hattie's relief they had barely noticed her, let alone invited her to join them.

The sandwich was satisfactory, and out of habit she saved the crusts for the birds. Not that she'd seen any birds since she'd been at Woodlands, besides the melancholic Icarus trapped in his caged prison.

Hattie's eyelids drooped more out of boredom than sleepiness. It was dusk, and soon the AINs would arrive to put her into her donated pyjamas. Old Kent Road was farthest from the nurses' station. Last for tea. First for bed.

Later, she lay awake listening to Walter Clements' television. It was hardly fair: he was clearly enjoying his evening's entertainment while she was trussed up like a mummy. At this very minute, hostile bacteria were gathering beyond the horizon like an army preparing to invade the gaping hole in her leg. Every person who entered her room was potentially teeming with millions of germs. Just one could make the difference between her going home and unknown multiples of four to six weeks incarcerated at Woodlands. Worse, four to six weeks could make the difference between the eggs successfully hatching and fledging, and the owls leaving for good. And that was assuming she didn't develop an ulcer. Potentially, she could be stuck in Woodlands for the rest of her life, the last sound she ever heard on this earth either canned laughter or the jingle of Walter Clements' game show through the dividing wall.

She turned onto her right side, her most comfortable position, but even rearranging her limbs between the layers of sheets – parallel, perpendicular, entwined – she couldn't find the release. After eighty-nine years of taking her body for granted, Hattie was now painfully aware of every stray hair that tickled her nose, every ache in every muscle. Her legs begged to move. Her hot feet searched for cool cotton. Her pulse was deafening against the pillow.

The usual tricks didn't work. She started with sheep but after counting an entire herd of Merino ewes was still wide awake. She tried humming the tune to 'Onward, Christian Soldiers' but, unable to recall all the verses, she repeated the chorus over and over until she was hoarse. She'd never been the church-going type, although at her age she knew she was taking a risk. The last time she had set foot inside a church the pews had been filled with grey heads. Should she play it safe and start believing in God again? When it came to falling asleep, however, Hattie found no more success with the Almighty than the sheep.

It was hardly surprising. Outside it was still light, the setting sun yawning around the edges of the blackout blinds. There was no fooling her body clock; it was the only reliable thing about her these days. She had to believe she would go home eventually. There was no point even thinking otherwise. Angophora Cottage wasn't going anywhere. If she closed her eyes it was there: the honey-coloured sandstone blocks; the writhing creeper that hugged the cottage, twisting and straddling the mortar joints like ligaments. The native hedge had long ago devoured the wooden picket fence and the mossy pavers were all but invisible after so many years. She remembered her father laying them – one of her earliest memories – when her mother complained about the gum leaves and red dust traipsed inside on dirty shoes. Hattie's father had built the cottage, the only property on what was then a cheap and undesirable sloping block miles from the city. The irony was that now, no one who had grown up in the suburb could afford to live in it.

For many years, her mother had tried to cultivate the delicate flower species of her English childhood. But the odds had been stacked against her from the start and in the end her tenacity was no match for the unforgiving climate. When Hattie's mother died, so did her garden. For a while, Hattie had tried to keep it alive but it wasn't long before the rubber hose perished, and without constant watering, the flowers soon wilted. Mother Nature reclaimed the soil, planting simple, hardy plants and weeds that were perfectly adapted to the harsh Australian conditions.

Hattie turned her head to a sound at the door. In the shadowy half-light she couldn't make out who was wearing the uniform. As Hattie's eyes adjusted, the woman stepped out from her apparition. Her tunic strained at her pillowy bosom. Her smile shone in the gloom.

'Can't sleep, honey?'

'Who are you?' It came out sounding sharper than Hattie intended. She pulled the bedclothes up around her chin to protect herself from this potentially germ-infested stranger.

'I'm Sister Bronwyn,' she said, her voice warm and musical. 'I'm the night nurse.'

At least she looked clean. Fifty-something, Hattie guessed, and past pretending. As she drew closer, Hattie looked at the skin on her hands: pink and dry, hopefully from frequent washing.

'Are you new?'

'Me? Goodness no. I've been on holiday. Brendan and I had a few dog-friendly days away. Queenie's too old for kennels now.'

'Queenie?'

'Labrador. She's ancient, can barely see. She sleeps most of the time. Stinks to high heaven but she's harmless. She's like an unofficial therapy dog. A very unofficial therapy dog, if you get my drift. I'll bring her round to meet you later.'

Hattie wasn't sure she wanted a dog sniffing around her leg. She wasn't any fonder of dogs than of cats, especially when it came to her birds. One noisy and stupid, the other potentially a clever and stealthy assassin.

Sister Bronwyn busied herself, straightening the bed-clothes and various nursing-home accoutrements Hattie had accumulated during her short time at Woodlands: boxes of tissues, water glass, water jug, the activities schedule, the Gideon Bible. When she'd finished, chatting continuously as she worked, Sister Bronwyn perched on the edge of Hattie's bed and pulled out a packet of brightly coloured jelly babies.

'I'm addicted to these. You don't get many skinny night nurses,' she laughed, offering the packet. Hattie politely declined.

'Do you only work nights?' What mortal sin had Sister Bronwyn committed to be punished in this way?

'By choice,' she replied and seeing Hattie's surprise added, 'I'd rather work nights than days. Less hassle, more freedom to get on with the job. No management looking over my shoulder every five minutes. I like to do things a little differently, and let's just say I don't always follow a strict protocol.'

Hattie understood. She glimpsed a wedding ring on Sister Bronwyn's fleshy finger and wondered what her husband thought about her working every night.

As if reading her mind, Sister Bronwyn said, 'Brendan works nights too. He's a wardsman at the hospital. It suits us both perfectly but Queenie hates being left alone.'

'I suppose you get used to it,' said Hattie. 'The staying awake all night, having to sleep during the day?'

'With a little help from my friends here.' Sister Bronwyn popped another sugary friend into her mouth.

Hattie sagged from weariness. 'I don't think I've slept a wink since I arrived.' She yawned until her jaw clicked.

'You're not alone there,' said Sister Bronwyn. 'What people, management included, don't fully grasp is that very few old people sleep a convenient solid eight hours at night. Most wake up at least once or twice, and many of the residents are awake all night. It's the big aged-care secret that no one likes to talk about.'

It explained why there were so many dozing residents during the day, in front of the television, propped up in armchairs after lunch and often at lunch itself. It was as if night and day were reversed. She had never travelled across time zones, never even been on a plane, but Hattie imagined life here was like existing in a state of permanent jet lag. If only Woodlands was on the other side of the world, everything would be fine. Could a long-haul flight cure them all?

Hearing a distant scream, Hattie's body tightened. A woman. The sound of pure terror, of pain and fear. Some terrible trauma relived. Hattie knew that sound. Her startled heart clattered like a stick along railings at a memory of her father calling out night after night from his own nightly torments.

Sister Bronwyn, on the other hand, appeared unperturbed. 'That'll be Fanny Olsen,' she said. 'Have you met her? She always looks like she's late for something. Wears a red bobble hat and a paperclip on her lapel.'

Hattie nodded. She knew the woman by sight only, either hurrying along a corridor, or other times still and watchful in a corner like a cat. Always with the red bobble hat. 'I've seen her around.' She would look out for the paperclip.

'Never utters a word to anyone. We were told she'd lost most of her English. It can happen at that age. Connections lost, wires crossed. Poor Fanny. Something happens when the sun goes down: screaming and calling out like she's being tortured. The day staff wouldn't believe me, so I don't bother recording it in her notes.'

Another scream, shrill and shocking in the dark. This time Hattie listened, trying to discern what sounded distinctly like a name.

'It sounds like she's calling for someone.'

Viga Ossicker!

'Someone from her past, I expect. I've checked her family's contact details and none of them are called Viga.'

'Is she all right?' Hattie wrinkled her forehead. 'Should someone go to her?'

'She's fine,' said Sister Bronwyn scrunching the jelly baby packet back into her tunic pocket and hauling herself to her feet. 'She'll be right as rain once she's in the day room with the others.' Then she added, 'You should come along.'

Hattie hated to point out the obvious. 'Aren't you supposed to be helping everyone get to sleep?'

A smile crept across Sister Bronwyn's face. 'I don't believe in drugging you all up to the eyeballs simply to keep you in bed. As I said, I like to do things a little differently.'

'How so?' Hattie sat up in bed.

'You'll see, Miss Bloom. Why don't you come along and join The Night Owls, and find out.'

10

Walter

WALTER COULDN'T UNDERSTAND IT. THE MONEY WAS EXACTLY where he'd left it, in the sealed envelope in the slipper box. He searched frantically for the new bottle, all reason and logic deserting him as he ransacked his wardrobe looking in the same places over and over again. Johnnie Walker was missing.

Bloody hell. His supplier was usually so reliable. There was his emergency bottle, stashed away at the bottom of the drawer. As long as Marie didn't insist on another clear-out, he was safe. But Walter hated to use his contingency supplies. Was this a true emergency or, like shipwrecked survivors in a life raft, should he not touch it for the first twenty-four hours? Nothing could beat breaking the seal on a new bottle. The joy that came from anticipation evaporated, and hopelessness settled in its place. He'd never get to sleep.

Walter blamed his GP. By refusing to prescribe a sleeping pill she had forced him to resort to a nightly medicinal dram.

She had literally driven him to drink. In fact, pleasant as she was, Dr Williams had a lot to answer for.

'You're ninety, Walter. For the record, your heart is ninety years old too,' she'd said when he'd enquired why, after more than a month of every therapy Woodlands had to offer, he was no better than when he arrived.

'Can't anything be done?'

'Try to make the most of what you have.'

Naturally the doctor had cushioned the blow with that lovely smile of hers. The trajectory of Walter's decline after Sylvia died would have brought him here sooner or later, he knew that. The longer he'd left it, the less chance he would have of ever getting out again. The truth was he had agreed to the move simply because there was no fight left in him. He was lost and empty. Every corner of his soul ached with sadness and every day without his wife was a prison sentence. Woodlands had given him time to reflect on his many shortcomings as a husband. He was finally coming to terms with his failings. Little by little, the fight was returning, and with it the sense of humour that had once won Sylvia's heart.

'Well, in that case I'm going to make an official complaint,' said Walter.

'About what?' The GP had looked worried.

'About my energy provider. It's not doing its job properly. I'm exhausted.'

She'd smiled at that, though Walter suspected mostly out of pity. In many ways he did feel better than when he arrived at Woodlands. His appetite had improved even if the food hadn't. He had always been a big man. Broad like his brothers. While the other residents struggled to hold onto their kilos, his big bones had refused to let his go. If he couldn't walk his way out of here, he could try eating his way out instead. Once he was home he could decide what he ate – and drank – and when. Back in his own bed, he would be able to sleep again too. He would take Sylvia's warm memory over a belly full of grog every time. Until then, he would have to make do with Johnnie Walker.

In its parking spot, the Tesla with its shiny red bodywork was already dulling beneath a layer of dust. Fully charged, the mobility scooter taunted him. The bottle shop was only a ten-minute ride away. There was a handy basket on the front, and the weatherproof compartment behind the seat could carry up to eight kilos. Five bottles of Red Label and still space for some salted nuts. They would play havoc with his fluid retention but it would be worth it. He briefly thought of the woman next door and the OT's crushed foot. The solution was obvious: he simply needed more practice.

Around the corner in Bond Street, Murray was lying in bed. Walter crept in, eyes adjusting slowly to the dimmed overhead LEDs. 'You awake?'

Murray turned his head and gave a weak smile. 'Always. Not keen on the alternative, my friend.'

'Mind if I join you?'

'Be my guest. Do me a favour and untuck the bedclothes, would you? I've got a cramp in my leg.'

Leaving his walker at the door, Walter shuffled forward and pulled the sheet and bedcover to the side. Murray's big toe was curled unnaturally, the muscles in his lower leg in taut spasm. It looked bloody painful, and without much thought Walter stretched the toe back and massaged his friend's shin.

'There you go, mate,' he said, withdrawing his hand as swiftly as possible. Besides the liver-spotted handshake they exchanged on first meeting, the two men had never actually touched each other. It wasn't what blokes like them did, they agreed without having to say it. Women were far better at that touchy–feely stuff.

Murray released a clenched breath. 'Thank you. You are a true gentleman.'

'I don't know about that,' said Walter, licking his lips. 'I'm here for purely selfish reasons. I'm feeling thirsty.'

'Bottom of the cupboard next to the bed.' Murray smiled knowingly.

'Just a drop. I'll leave the rest for you, don't worry.'

'Fill your boots, Walter.' Shadows disguised Murray's gaunt features but there was no escaping the wince.

'Why don't you just say yes to the pain medication the doctor recommended?' He twisted his dressing-gown cord around his fingers. Murray would know he'd been eaves-dropping. Not that there were any secrets in this place. He added, 'Geez, there are plenty of blokes who'd pay a fortune for that stuff on the black market.'

'No drugs,' said Murray decisively. 'Not yet.' A glimpse of the forthright teacher. Enough for Walter to drop the subject.

Walter wasn't so brave. The nurse had seen right through him when he'd complained about a lingering dry cough. A spoonful of codeine linctus might have helped him to sleep, given him a bit of a boost too, but then he'd hacked up a glob of phlegm by accident.

'That cough looks more productive to me, Mr Clements.'

He'd ended up with a spoonful of Senega and Ammonia instead, which made his guts ache and did little for either the cough or a good night's sleep.

Checking first that the coast was clear, Walter found the mostly empty whisky bottle hidden behind a pile of books in the bedside cabinet. He could hardly call up room service and order two whisky tumblers, so he emptied Murray's water glass into the bathroom sink and removed the toothbrush from a plastic container next to the tap. He divided the dregs of Johnnie Walker between the two cups and offered one to Murray.

'Go on, live a little.' Walter cringed but it was too late to take back the clumsy comment. Murray put up a hand and shook his head.

Perched on the seat of his walking frame, Walter swallowed the whisky in a single gulp. He wiped his mouth on the sleeve of his dressing-gown and closed his eyes as the amber liquor ran hot down his gullet and into his belly.

'Are you sure?'

'Yes, you take the bottle.'

Walter longed for the good old days of a month, even a fortnight ago, when he and Murray had slipped in and out of each other's room like two errant schoolboys.

Most of their conversations were now held in the past tense. They both knew that their time together was running out. He would be left with Fred Carpenter for company. The Wolverhampton Wanderer. A nice enough bloke, but holding a conversation with him was like listening to a record when someone kept nudging the turntable, and that's when he wasn't disappearing without warning.

Relaxing into the warmth of the alcohol, Walter regaled Murray with the day's events.

'I heard all the commotion,' said Murray.

'Did you know that Miss Bloom got dinner in her room tonight? Talk about favouritism.'

'You ran her over, Walt.'

Walter tapped the side of the toothbrush beaker thoughtfully. 'Well, that depends on your point of view. Strictly speaking, Miss Bloom was on the wrong side of the road.'

'Strictly speaking, if it's lined with carpet, it's not a road, my friend.' Murray tried to prop himself up on his elbows. Walter readjusted the pillows behind him until they were face to face.

'It's common sense to keep to the left.'

'Woodlands isn't big on common sense.'

'You can say that again.'

'Maybe you should have a man with a red flag walking in front of you,' chuckled Murray.

'What is this, the eighteen hundreds? I had a clean licence up until today.' If not a full no-claim bonus.

'You still have. Technically.'

They sat in silence for a while until Murray's head lolled backwards onto the pillow and his jaw slackened.

'Mate?' whispered Walter, leaning in. Was he asleep? Was he even breathing? Walter felt for reassuring warm breath against his cheek. Should he check for a pulse? His fingers hesitated over Murray's slack-skinned neck. He'd done a CPR course in the local community centre donkey's years ago but he couldn't remember whether he was supposed to check for a pulse or breathing first. What if he made a mistake? In the wrong circumstances, blowing into someone's mouth or pounding their chest without their permission could be construed as assault. On the other hand, doing nothing wasn't an option either. Walter hovered over Murray, almost touching him.

Murray's eyes snapped open. 'What are you doing?'

Walter jerked away, almost losing his balance. 'Checking you were still alive. What do you think I was doing?'

'I thought you were moving in for a kiss,' said Murray. A smile.

Walter cleared his throat. Dropped his voice half an octave. 'I'm not like that.'

'Like what?' Murray was having fun with him now.

'You know . . . dual purpose,' replied Walter.

'Don't worry, you're not my type,' Murray laughed. 'Besides, your breath stinks like a distillery.'

They were back on familiar ground now, more comfortable with insults than mutual affection. Walter often wondered if he and the gentle Murray Thompson, who'd taught geography to generations of ungrateful kids, would have been friends outside Woodlands. Would their paths have crossed except at parent–teacher nights? Teachers had always made Walter nervous – for good reason given his dubious record as a student – and he tended to overcompensate. Marie had often berated him for embarrassing her at school events.

Murray's laughter turned into coughs. He splinted his body against some unseen pain.

'That's it,' said Walter turning for his walker. 'I'm going to fetch Sister Bronwyn.'

'No, don't bother her. She'll be too busy.'

Sister Bronwyn wasn't too busy. Walter found her – or rather the drug trolley – outside Liverpool Street Station. She sent Sameera, the AIN, to microwave a heat pack and handed Murray a couple of paracetamol with a cup of water. Then she stood, hands on hips, ready to deliver a few home truths.

'There are no prizes for bravery in this place, Murray,' she said. 'But if you're going for the stubborn old bugger award, I'd say you're definitely in the running.'

'Thank you,' said Murray, adjusting the hot, corduroy-covered bag of beans at the base of his spine. 'You're an angel.'

'So I'm told.' She smiled and straightened the bedclothes. Walter fidgeted in the hallway by the door, not sure if he should intrude, whether his friend needed privacy, if there were such a thing at Woodlands. When he turned to leave, Sister Bronwyn called him back.

'Where do you think you're going, Walter Clements? I need you to talk some sense into this friend of yours. There is no need for him to put up with this pain. I have more drugs in that trolley than Pablo Escobar and if he won't take them I'm going to have to sell them on the street.'

Murray laughed, and Walter felt a twitch of envy. It wasn't that he begrudged Murray a chuckle – laughter was supposedly the best medicine, after all – it was more that he wanted to be the one to make his friend laugh. He was the funny guy. Funny was who he was. It was all he had left.

After Sister Bronwyn had gone, the two men settled back into their usual banter. Walter cracked a few gags. Murray laughed. Walter's shoulders dropped. He couldn't shake off the idea that his friend was only being polite. Was Murray only laughing out of habit? Walter could have read out the form guide and Murray would have found it hilarious. Would all that change once he started on the morphine? Walter pushed away the selfish thought. The reality was that he would soon lose Murray, as he'd lost Sylvia.

'What's up, Walt?' Murray was looking at him, his eyes huge in the after-hours light.

Walter swallowed and brushed a warm tickle from his cheek with the back of his hand. He reached for the remote control. 'How about a bit of Netflix before we head to The Night Owls?'

Murray rubbed his hands together. 'The usual?'

'On one condition,' said Walter.

'What's that?'

'Strictly one episode at a time. One and no more, you understand?'

'No bingeing?'

'No bingeing,' said Walter, wagging his finger at Murray. 'We'll savour each one and see how long we can make them last.'

11

Hattie

DISMISSING THE FUTILE BEDTIME CHARADE, HATTIE PUSHED her feet into her slippers and, fully awake, set off in search of something to do. She heard The Night Owls before she saw them and paused to take stock before she ventured in. She thought of the way the magpies often sidled up to her when she stood at the kitchen door, natural curiosity and the hope of a titbit eventually winning over fear. They would glance at her sideways, wary black eyes always on the lookout for danger, unlike the owls with their glowing raptor eyes that stared straight into hers.

The hallway was cosy, the dimmed electric lights reflecting the warm colours of the carpet while outside, the pale midnight moon cast cool, grey shadows over the courtyard. It was good to be out of her room, the blood flowing in her legs once more. It was slow going, with screws and metal plates in one and bandages like tourniquets around the other. But Hattie was in no hurry. She had all the time in the world, and then some. If anything, having two bad legs had evened her up and her double limp was more efficient than her previous hobble.

The day room had taken on a life of its own with the gentle thrum of unhurried conversation. Everywhere Hattie looked, residents were busy. Woodlands had its very own factory floor.

Ada half looked up as Hattie approached, smiling as she reached into the plastic laundry basket at her feet. Pulling another white fluffy Woodlands towel from the basket, she folded it with precision, in half, then half again, before adding it to the growing pile on the table. In the far corner, Eileen sat in her satin dressing-gown shelling peas into a bowl. Hattie saw Fred Carpenter of Carpenter's Antiques shining a silver teapot with such fervour she half expected a genie to appear from the spout.

A black dog creaked to its feet and sidled over to investigate. The dog's muzzle was peppered with white whiskers and its undercarriage – no other word for it, really – hung low and loose beneath its body. Her body. She sniffed Hattie's feet and wagged her tail slowly in approval.

'Meet Queenie.'

When Hattie looked up she saw Sister Bronwyn's upside down pear shape slaloming between the tables and chairs towards her. 'I'm so pleased you made it,' she said with her habitual open-mouthed grin. 'Welcome to The Night Owls.'

It was hard to believe this was the middle of the night. The place was a hive of activity. Sister Bronwyn introduced her to the others as she might a fresh arrival at a flagging party. Some were new faces to Hattie, others already uncomfortably familiar. With all the residents in dressing-gowns and slippers, it was like one giant pyjama party.

'Let me explain how this works,' said Sister Bronwyn, arm hooked through Hattie's as she led her around the day room. 'Eleven until midnight are what I call office hours. I encourage each resident to work on a job or task related to their old life. It helps to give people a sense of purpose again. That's as important now as it ever was in their younger lives.'

Around the room, a dozen other residents concentrated on their individual tasks – sorting loose coins by denomination, marking what looked like a handwritten essay in red pen, polishing a pair of shoes. So many faces. She hadn't bothered to commit any of their names to memory. There wasn't much point. A farmer must always resist naming his stock.

Sister Bronwyn continued. 'Midnight is cocktail and canapé time.' Seeing Hattie's eyes widen, she said, 'Don't worry I'm not running some illegal gin joint here. You'll get the idea. Then, one o'clock through till three is special request time. We had a silent disco one night, and another time we turned the day room into a haunted house. I had a hell of a job talking Ada out of Murder on the Orient Express but she saw my point eventually and we came to a compromise with a High Tea instead.'

The contrast with the sedate daytime gatherings couldn't have been starker. The energy in the room was palpable, the atmosphere as different as . . . well, day and night.

A man in striped blue pyjamas nodded his acknowledgement as Sister Bronwyn emptied a small bag of coins onto the table for him to count. 'Last week Fred suggested a poker night. He helped set it up and oversee things for the others,' she said over her shoulder in Hattie's direction. 'It was a huge success. Except that we used different flavoured rice crackers for the poker chips. It worked up to a point until Queenie helped herself. She ate a fortune!'

'Oh, goodness,' was all Hattie could say.

'Yes, just a word about Queenie here. If ever there was a breed that was going to eat itself into extinction it's the Labrador. She gets fed twice a day despite what she might tell you. Let me warn you too, she can be very persuasive.'

Queenie was sitting at Hattie's feet, pleading with her big brown eyes. It was quite disconcerting until something dropped from a table in the periphery of her vision and she dashed off to investigate.

'That's the one good thing about her,' said Sister Bronwyn chuckling, 'we don't have to worry about crumbs with the old girl around.' Behind her hand she whispered, 'Easier to cover our tracks, if you know what I mean.'

Hattie hadn't known what to expect. Not real owls obviously, but perhaps a bunch of dozing residents in dimmed light, maybe a sing-along and a cup of hot cocoa.

'Any preference for something you might like to do?' Sister Bronwyn asked, and when Hattie stared back blankly, she added, 'What was your occupation?'

How enlightened of her to ask, to not assume she'd been purely decorative in her younger years.

'I was a naturalist,' she said.

Sister Bronwyn's eyes widened and her mouth fell open. 'Really? You can do that for a living?'

'My father always encouraged me to follow my passion.'

'None of my business, love. We've had all sorts in here, I can tell you.' Sister Bronwyn took a tiny step backwards then looked Hattie up and down. 'Only, I'm not sure it's appropriate for The Night Owls, do you?'

Surely it was a perfectly respectable career? Hattie's face prickled as she searched for clues in Sister Bronwyn's wide-eyed scrutiny.

'My main area of interest was Australian birdlife, although I've covered trees and native wildlife too.'

Sister Bronwyn let out a hoot. 'Oh, *naturalist*,' she said, her bosom bouncing as she tried to get her breath. 'I could have sworn you said *naturist*! Imagine that!' She was still laughing as she led Hattie to a soft upholstered armchair away from the tables of busy residents. Sister Bronwyn promised to return for a chat once she'd found Ada some pillowcases.

Naturalist. She'd never really considered it a job before. It had never felt like work to Hattie, and although her published work had brought in a modest income, she had seen it as more of a vocation. It was her life. A fascination with nature was in her genes: a marriage of her mother's flora and her father's fauna genes. She'd spent her early years helping her mother in the garden, learning the names of the plants and trees, both native and the ones her mother had tried to cultivate with mixed success. Her father had introduced her to birds. She could never remember a time when she didn't know the names and recognise the calls of every species. He'd taught her about their behaviour and rituals.

'Forget the idea of "bird brain" as an insult. Birds are actually very clever creatures,' he used to say. 'They might appear to have tiny brains but they are intelligent enough to learn and adapt in harsh environments. Not many humans can do that.'

After he returned from the Great War, her father had done a series of low-paid jobs, none of which he stuck with for very long. Once the guns of war had fallen silent, he'd found solace in the quiet company of birds. They were the one constant in his life. Birds and booze.

When her father died, he bequeathed Hattie his most treasured possession: his 1891 edition of *The Birds of Australia* by GJ Broinowski. She'd read that book cover to cover, over and over until the spine detached and the pages were so dark and speckled with age that the words were barely readable. But like her father, those descriptions were enough to ignite a passion that had never waned. Birds had been her life's work: six volumes on bird behaviour (all now out of print), an acclaimed series of essays and the patronage of a number of ornithological societies. She was self-taught, like her father, serving what she thought of as an apprenticeship rather than following a formal academic pathway. Sadly, her father didn't live to see his daughter's accomplishments. He died only weeks before the local newspaper advertised for a weekly nature columnist.

The discarded paper had blown up the front path and when Hattie bent to retrieve it she noticed the advert. Seeing it as a sign, she wasted no time in writing to the editor. In her letter she admitted that she lacked any formal qualification in either zoology or journalism. Instead she wrote in detail about a pair of magpies in her garden and described how they not only sang a perfect duet but also learned to imitate Nat King Cole when she played his record on the gramophone. She annotated the description with the little sketches that would become her trademark and hoped for the best. The editor wrote back by return of mail and offered her the position. It wouldn't pay more than pin money, he warned. To Hattie, who at twenty-three already owned her own home and whose outgoings were negligible, the job was perfect.

Each Monday, after typing up her report on a second-hand typewriter, Hattie would walk down to the post office to buy her stamp and slip the envelope in the post box. Sometimes she attached photographs taken with her father's old Box Brownie and was always thrilled if the editor published them, although the film was expensive and the images so grainy it was difficult to make out the trees let alone the birds. Before long she had an invitation from a small publisher to turn her popular weekly column into a book.

Sister Bronwyn was back with a small footstool. 'For now, your fulltime job is to keep that leg elevated.' Queenie followed and flopped down next to the footstool. 'And to keep her ladyship here company.'

Taking in the giant wall-mounted screen directly in her line of vision, Hattie said, 'I'm not really a big television fan.' Perhaps fan wasn't the right word. The last time she'd actually watched television, it had been in black and white. The cinema was different, but the last time she'd paid to see a film, the screen had been all but obscured by cigarette smoke. Books had been her escape, a more satisfying experience all round.

'Give it a chance, Miss Bloom,' said Sister Bronwyn. 'This is slow TV. You'll love it once you get into it. Everybody does.'

The program was filmed in the outback, a dusty train travelling along a track. The blue of the cloudless sky and red of the dusty earth were so vivid they looked as if they had come from opposite sides of an artist's colour wheel. Every minute or so, the view would change, the camera filming either the view from a passenger carriage, a panning shot of the train passing by from the ground or a bird's-eye view of the entire train snaking below. The television, Hattie now realised, wasn't muted at all, the gentle *clackety-clack, clickety-clack* of the wheels on the track the only sound, mesmerising and strangely soothing. There was no commentary; no dialogue. Slow television was made for a place like Woodlands. As Hattie looked around, she realised Woodlands had its own real-life version. It made a pleasant change from the long-haired violin player.

Sister Bronwyn was doing the rounds with a tray of what looked like triangles of buttered toast. 'Canapé, Fred?'

'Thanks, love,' Fred replied. He popped one into his mouth and licked his fingers before returning to his task. 'I've got to get this finished and put it in the window. Nice piece, this. Should get a good price for it.'

'Jolly good. I won't hold you up.'

Next on Sister Bronwyn's round was a woman huddled over a pile of wires and electrical components concentrating on what looked like an old-fashioned Bakelite radio stripped down to its individual components. She was a study in calm concentration as her dexterous fingers worked first a pair of pliers, then a soldering iron.

'Hungry work, Fanny?'

Fanny? The same Fanny Olsen who only an hour ago had let out scream after bloodcurdling scream, calling for her long lost *Viga?* Hattie had watched Fanny pick at her meals in the main dining room, always sitting some way apart from the gaggle of garrulous ladies who congregated at the far end of the table. Sometimes it took her forty-five minutes to eat a single sandwich and yet away from the dining table she was restless, in a state of perpetual motion. No wonder she was so slight. It was a miracle she managed to consume sufficient calories to stay alive. Perhaps Sister Brownyn's canapés were more than party food.

Next out was a silver platter of 'cocktails', presented like champagne flutes. They looked more like cups of warm milk, others she could swear were cartons of the expensive high-energy drinks designed to build up the frailer residents. It occurred to Hattie that Woodlands could save a fortune simply by making the food they served more appetising and nutritious.

At the moment Ada's leaning tower of towels threatened to topple, a young AIN swooped in with a new basket filled with what looked like pillowcases. Seeing Hattie seated in front of the television, the AIN came over and asked if she would like a blanket for her legs. Apparently it could get quite chilly, the steady temperature feeling much colder in the early hours of the morning.

'Why do you think the night staff all wear cardigans?' She smiled at Hattie. Her name badge said Sameera.

Sameera. Hattie tried to forget the girl. It never paid to get too close to people. But like seeing a yellow bicycle when you're told not to think of yellow bicycles, Sameera and her smile were soon imprinted on Hattie's mind.

Hattie softened in the armchair, her leg growing heavy on the footstool. With the table lamps emitting a warm and soporific glow, the chair was comfortable enough for Hattie to feel her eyelids sag. She yawned until her eyes began to water. They were dry and irritated from having been open so long. In spite of the activity around her, sleep was almost close enough to touch.

Hattie wondered what Icarus made of all the nocturnal activity and, in particular, of Queenie. She had written about clever birds learning the names of their owners' dogs and calling them or issuing commands like 'sit' and 'stay' simply for the fun of it. But this dog and bird were oblivious to one another. The cage door was ajar and Icarus was nowhere to be seen, while Queenie's paws twitched as she slept at Hattie's feet, an occasional muffled bark escaping her billowing cheeks.

'Chasing cats again,' said Sister Bronwyn, pausing on her round with more canapés. 'She's scared to death of them in real life, but I suppose even dogs can be the hero in their own dreams.'

12

Walter

Remembering their agreement, Walter paused the television. How easy it would be to let the next episode roll on. How easily his friend could slip away without a reason to keep going.

'Rock cake?' Murray nudged the Tupperware box towards Walter as the credits rolled. 'Watch your teeth.'

'How is the lovely Joyce?'

'She's baking again.' Murray gave a knowing look. 'It's how she copes.'

Walter tried to chisel away a few crumbs with his front incisors. 'I might wait for the hot chocolate to come round. Soften it up a bit.'

'I can't bring myself to tell her I'm not even allowed a cup of tea let alone anything as solid as this.'

'They *are* verging on monolithic,' said Walter putting the rock cake to one side.

'Hey, that's my wife you're talking about!' Murray pretended to take umbrage.

'Seriously, how's she holding up?'

Murray sighed. 'You know my Joyce. She's dealing with it in her own way. With all this . . .' His hand swept an arc indicating the potted plants that now covered every horizontal surface. Some, tall and lustrous in decorative pots, looked as if they'd come straight from the garden centre; others were mere cuttings in old tin cans or ice-cream containers. Every shape and texture of leaf, some in full flower, others bearing optimistic buds.

'You could open your own nursery,' said Walter noticing several new arrivals even since yesterday.

Murray's brow wrinkled. 'I think she's working on the premise that if I can't go to my garden, she'll bring the garden to me.'

'She's a good woman, your Joyce.'

'There's no such thing as a bad woman, Walt. Only bad men.'

'That sounds like something my daughter would say. She was into women's lib or whatever they call it nowadays.'

'Feminism,' said Murray with the authority of a man who'd raised two daughters. 'And before you say anything, they haven't burned bras since the sixties.'

'Shame,' said Walter absent-mindedly.

'Men like you really are a dying breed, did you know that?'

'Marie calls me anachronistic. I'd always taken it as a compliment until Judy won word of the week and enlightened me.'

'It's not our world anymore.' Age and illness had pulled the corners of Murray's mouth down, but he still found the energy to turn them into a smile. 'We've all had our turn on the Ferris wheel. Time to hop off and let someone else have a go.'

They were running out of time. Just as Walter had run out of time with Sylvia. If he could turn back the clock, would he have done things differently? Would he have come home earlier, bought her flowers 'just because' or told her she looked lovely in that blue dress with the nipped-in waist? Regret was so self-indulgent. It was too late for whys and what-ifs. If he'd done things differently he wouldn't have been himself. He only hoped that he'd made it up to her in the end by going along with her wishes. It was the least selfish thing he'd done in their marriage, allowing her to depart this life on her own terms. Had it cost him his daughter? He would never know for sure. But it was the sacrifice he owed his wife. It was his penance for falling short as the husband he had vowed to be.

'I didn't deserve a woman like my Sylvia.' Walter tore at a strip of loose rubber on the handlebar of his walker and searched for a way to turn his worries into words. 'She was always too good for me.'

'Why do you say that?'

'She deserved better.' He'd given her a nice house with a double garage and all the mod cons. Had it been enough? Not to mention that as an older man he'd broken some sacred pact that should have seen him pop his clogs in a timely manner, leaving her to enjoy her unencumbered widowhood.

'No one is perfect, Walt. I think the best any of us can expect is to be human. To be good enough.'

Walter cleared his throat. This was where he cracked the gag. When the conversation was getting too serious, too maudlin. Lighten the mood. Break the tension. That's what he did. He'd always known how to turn Sylvia's tears to laughter and assumed that was the same as making up or saying he was sorry. When Marie fell over and scraped her knees as a little girl, he would scoop her up into his arms and tickle her. Walter had lived for his little girl's giggles and for the smile of the woman he loved.

For a while they stared at the paused screen on the wall. They had already watched six of the eight episodes. It wasn't even a particularly good show, but they had invested six precious hours. What was more important was that they had watched them together.

After a few minutes, a thought came to Walter. 'You know what this place needs?'

'I think I'm about to find out.'

'A vending machine.'

'An actual vending machine? I don't see the point. If you want something in here, you only have to ask.'

'I know, but how good would it be if we didn't have to ask? And then wait until someone wasn't too busy to fetch it? Give those poor girls five minutes for a breather every now and again.'

It wasn't the staff's fault. They did their best with what they were given. Places like Woodlands ran on the human equivalent of an oily rag. How much better for everyone if the residents could do things for themselves?

Murray's face lit up. 'So, what would your vending machine have in it? Bubble gum and condoms like the old days?'

'I wish.' Walter laughed. 'Safe sex in here means having a rail around the bed. No, I was thinking of useful items like hearing-aid batteries, or toothpicks. All the paraphernalia for old duffers like us.'

'How about corn plasters?' Murray wriggled his toes beneath the bedclothes.

'Now you're talking! Good old-fashioned fruit drops in tins . . .'

'. . . And bottles of hot sauce.'

'Johnnie Walker miniatures and antacid tablets.' Walter stifled a belch.

'Spare reading glasses! I can never find mine.'

'Nose-hair trimmers?'

Murray looked more animated than Walter had seen him in days. 'It would have to have the prices marked in large font,' he said, chuckling.

'And take small-denomination coins, fives and tens, especially to annoy Judgy Judy if she's behind us in the queue.'

Eventually the laughter petered out into silence.

'Icarus is on the loose again,' said Walter, absently.

'Oh yes?' Murray struggled to sit up. 'How far did he get this time?'

Walter rearranged the pillows behind his friend. 'As far as the nurses' station judging by the bird shit splattered down that hideous wall canvas.'

'But that painting over the nurses' station is modern art, it's meant to be abstract.'

'Well, now it's definitely a still life with bird shit. If anything I'd say the faeces enhances it.'

Murray said, 'I'd love to see that bird fly away one day. He always comes back. I think he feels safest in that bloody awful cage. Sad, when you think about it.'

'If he eventually got out – you know, properly out – do you think he'd be able to survive in the wild? After all this time living in a cage.' Walter tapped the rock cake thoughtfully against Murray's bedside table.

'I taught geography, not biology,' said Murray. 'I don't know much about birds.'

'Can birds like that live on their own, without a mate?'

Murray thought for a moment. 'We had this pair of king parrots that used to come to the balcony every day. Joyce used to feed them nuts and apple slices. They came for years, even brought their babies to meet us. We got to know them really well. Then one day, the female disappeared. She'd been starting to lose a few feathers in the weeks before, growing a bit skinny. The male looked completely bereft without his mate. He was grieving badly. You could see how lonely the poor old bird was.'

Walter rolled his walker closer, hanging on Murray's every word. 'Did he find a new partner? A new female friend?'

'Not exactly,' said Murray shaking his head.

'What happened to him?'

'Next door's cat got him.' Murray guffawed.

Walter didn't laugh. He'd wanted there to be a moral in the story, a happy ending. Perhaps that was the point. Life's end was full of loose ends. Unlike Netflix, there wasn't another episode waiting.

13

Hattie

THE TRAIN WAS IN THE MIDDLE OF NOWHERE. THE ONLY signs of life on the flat, empty plains were the low, scrubby bushes at the side of the tracks and the occasional spooked kangaroo bounding away. With her eyes focused on the screen, this was the most relaxed Hattie had been at Woodlands. Hypnotised by the real-time train journey, she had melted into the washable upholstery and at last, her bandaged leg had stopped throbbing.

'Is this seat taken?'

Hattie startled and tensed. Without waiting for a response, a white-haired man reversed his walker towards the adjacent chair then landed heavily beside her with a *whoomph*.

When he'd caught his breath he said, 'You're Old Kent Road, aren't you?' Extending his hand. 'I'm Whitechapel Road.'

This is it, thought Hattie, the next level of institutional-isation. Not quite reduced to a number but instead to the gimmicky name of her room. Far from conjuring a sense of playfulness, she found the whole thing deeply troubling. Almost as troubling as having Walter Clements now sitting beside her.

Reluctantly, Hattie shook his hand. The feeling of warm flesh under her fingers made her squirm. She tried to angle her body away but even shielding half her face with her hand, she could still see him in her peripheral vision.

'Good program?' Walter Clements angled his chair a degree towards Hattie's. After watching the train clatter on its route for a few moments he said, 'I've never understood why people pay a fortune to travel so far from civilisation. There's nothing there, is there?'

'I think that's the point,' said Hattie. 'Some people love the peace and quiet of it, that sense of space and emptiness.' She sighed, as if the breath were crowding her lungs.

'It'd be a bit boring though, with nothing to do but look out the window.'

Hattie dropped her head into her hands. He really was the most objectionable man. Her leg bandages were clearly visible poking out at the end of the blanket and he hadn't uttered a word of apology. She should be tucked up in her own bed listening to the *oh-woop* of the owls outside her window. Now, because of his reckless actions, she was sentenced to this perpetual twilight.

Sister Bronwyn seemed pleased to find the two of them sitting together.

'I see you've introduced yourselves,' she said. Then to Walter she said, 'I do hope you're going to behave, Walter.'

'Are you casting aspersions on my impeccable moral character again, Sister?' They laughed.

'I'm watching you.' Sister Bronwyn wagged her finger then she softened. 'No Murray?'

'He dropped off watching Netflix and I couldn't bring myself to wake him.'

'I'll check on him in a few minutes,' said Sister Bronwyn who, Hattie now noticed, was wearing what looked at first glance to be blue hotpants decorated with white stars and a red-and-gold burlesque corset. Seeing Hattie's eyes widen, Sister Bronwyn smoothed down her comical apron. 'Wonder Woman. What do you think?'

'You're my Wonder Woman,' said Walter Clements with a grin.

The light-hearted familiarity between this unrelated male and female was intriguing. Hattie twisted her mouth in concentration as she tried to make sense of it in the only terms of reference she truly understood. She supposed it represented some form of social bonding within the species. Not a breeding partnership obviously, but to enhance the cohesiveness of the flock. The more she witnessed of human behaviour, the more fascinated she became. She was still very much a novice and for now, happy to remain an observer.

Sister Bronwyn brushed flour from her cheeks and removed her apron. 'For tonight's activity, we're baking,' she said. 'Apparently Eileen used to work as a pastry chef in Paris, and she's supervising pastry rolling in the craft room. We're starting with jam tarts but she promises we'll be making *croquembouche* in no time.'

'Jam tarts,' said Walter. 'My favourite!'

Hattie couldn't quite picture Eileen in a white chef's hat and tunic. For someone who had lived such an eclectic life,

Eileen appeared very settled with her lot here at Woodlands. Hattie buried her doubts.

The smell of burning wafted through the day room. 'I think that's my cue,' said Sister Bronwyn turning on her heels. 'The last thing we need is the sprinklers going off again. I don't think I could cope with Gene Kelly singing and dancing and poking any more eyes out with that umbrella. Too much paperwork.' With a hearty guffaw, she hurried away.

'She's one in a million,' said Walter with a deep sigh of admiration. 'Like my dear late wife, Sylvia. She was one in a million too.'

'If your wife was one in a million and Sister Bronwyn is one in a million, haven't you just relegated them to one in half a million each?'

Walter rested his hand on the arm of Hattie's chair. 'You are so delightfully droll,' he said. 'A breath of fresh air.'

Hattie had never been anyone's breath of fresh air before. The moment passed before she could decide whether to be flattered or offended. The ambiguous exchange ended when a ruddy-cheeked Sister Bronwyn returned bearing a tray of jam tarts between two oven gloves. She transferred them to a platter and began to serve them. Sensing the arrival of potential titbits, Queenie woke and moved in for a closer look, giant pink tongue hanging like a piece of shaved ham from the side of her mouth. To Hattie's amusement, she aimed straight for Walter Clements and greeted him by thrusting her nose into his groin. She sniffed and, satisfied, sat at his feet wagging her tail expectantly.

'Steady on, old girl,' he said running his fingers through the thick fur around her neck and releasing a cloud of undercoat that rose like smoke from a bushfire.

'Jam tart?' Sister Bronwyn offered the platter. The tarts were irregular and slightly burnt. They were the kind of thing Hattie's new neighbours would pay a fortune for at the fancy patisserie down the road. They'd call them 'rustic' or 'artisinal'.

Walter, without pretence of politeness, helped himself and shoved an entire artisinal tart into his mouth. Hattie declined but couldn't take her eyes away from a glob of red jam that dribbled onto his chin and then tumbled down the front of his dressing-gown.

Sister Bronwyn said, 'Did you know that women live longer than men because they have a superior immune system?' Then she leaned in and shielded her mouth with her hand. 'I caught Queenie having a lick in the kitchen, but they've had twenty minutes in the oven so they should be safe for the men too.'

Walter fired pastry crumbs from his lips like a Bren gun, leaving Sister Bronwyn helpless with laughter as she clamped him affectionately on the shoulder. Hattie had to admit that The Night Owls were turning out to be far more entertaining than she'd imagined.

'These remind me of my daughter, Marie,' said Walter pinching another jam tart before Sister Bronwyn moved out of reach. 'She used to spoon the jam straight from the jar. She had such a sweet tooth.' He stared wistfully into some distant memory. 'They grow up so quickly, don't they? Do you have children, grandchildren?'

'No,' said Hattie. 'I never married.' She'd never needed to.

She had watched generations of birds build their nests, lay eggs and fledge families from her tree, yet Hattie had never assumed she would one day marry or have her own family. It was less a conscious decision than a default state.

Of course losing both her parents so early had left a void but not one she felt compelled to fill with another person. She was self-sufficient and quite content with her own company. Her life had not been defined by the lack of a husband and children, rather by the richness of everything else that meant so much to her: her work, her books, her birds. In evolutionary terms she had fallen short, having failed to mate and procreate, meaning her family's genes were heading for extinction. She'd consoled herself with the knowledge that she'd trodden lightly on the earth and done her best to preserve at least one tiny corner of the planet.

'What exactly is the point of this?' Walter nodded towards the television screen.

'It's slow television,' replied Hattie.

'Yes, but what is it about?'

'Does it have to be about anything?'

'It has to be *about* something.' He fidgeted. 'A crime that needs to be solved or an imminent threat to civilisation, heroes and villains, the ultimate triumph of good over evil.' He threw up his hands. 'Otherwise it's just one long journey to nowhere.'

Hattie raised her finger to her lips. 'Watch. It's like the old silent movies. I'm sure you'll soon get the hang of it.'

The train *clickety-clacked* over a wooden bridge, skirted a lake then trundled through flat marshland, a flock of white-winged birds rising like steam in its wake. Walter leaned forward and squinted in concentration. Soon, he was transfixed.

After several minutes, he said, 'This is almost as good as *The Great Escape*.'

'Which great escape are you talking about?'

'*The* Great Escape. Don't tell me you've never heard of it? McQueen? Garner? Attenborough? Epic war drama from sixty-three?' He looked at her as if she had two heads.

'No,' said Hattie. 'I've never heard of it.'

Regrettably, Walter Clements went on to give a blow-by-blow account of the entire plot, suggesting he had seen the film more than once. His timing couldn't have been worse, coinciding with the exciting arrival of the train at a tiny outback station.

'The motorcycles used in the film were 1961 Triumph TR6 Trophies disguised as German BMW R75s,' he went on. 'Steve McQueen did most of the stunts himself.' Even when she failed to show the slightest interest, he continued unabated. 'Apart from the twelve-foot barbed-wire fence jump.'

When the train eventually pulled away from the station platform, Hattie asked, 'What was the point of risking their lives when the Allies were so close to liberating them?'

'They didn't know that. As far as they knew, they were all going to die in that camp. The men saw it as their duty. It was a matter of honour. They would rather die trying than simply rot away, waiting to be rescued.'

On the television the camera angle had changed. Hattie was now inside a coach, looking out at the bright blue sky and passing scenery. Trains gave the illusion of freedom but what if those wheels longed to jump the tracks and head off in another direction entirely?

They fell silent again. Hattie watched Walter scoop the jam from a buttonhole and transfer it to his mouth on a finger. 'Waste not, want not,' he said dabbing at the crumbs in his lap. She didn't judge. They were both from the waste-not-want-not generation. The last generation to live through a world war. The stoic generation.

On the television, night had fallen and there was little to see beyond the headlights on the track ahead as the train hurtled into the pitch black.

'Tell me something, Mr Clements,' said Hattie after a while. 'Did the prisoners all manage to escape in the end?'

Walter smiled ruefully. 'Only the lucky ones.'

14

Walter

WALTER DREAMED HE WAS ON THE CAROUSEL AT THE FAIR with Sylvia and her bespectacled best friend, Lynne. The girls were still teenagers while, in his twenties, Walter had the square jaw of a young man who'd filled out early and a job that paid just enough to create the illusion that he was a good catch. Not that he had any intention of settling down. As far as Walter was concerned, he still had plenty of wild oats left to sow. Or so he'd thought until he'd laid eyes on the vision that was Sylvia. Showing off, he'd bought them each an ice-cream and was slowly plucking up the courage to ask her to a dance the following Saturday. He was working out how to get rid of Lynne when the sound of the barrel organ woke him.

'Dad?'

His eyes adjusted to the daylight. For a moment it was Sylvia standing over him and his heart leapt. No, not Sylvia but someone who looked just like her.

'Hello sweetheart,' said Walter. 'I must have dropped off for a moment.' Long enough to take him back to Sylvia, not quite long enough to hold on to her.

'Are you okay?' Marie frowned. 'Should I call the nurse?'

'I'm fine, Marie. I'm a little tired, that's all.'

Walter dragged himself away from his cosy stupor and tried to look alert. It would never do for Marie to find out he'd been awake most of the night in the company of a woman who wasn't her mother, however innocent their hours side by side on the slow train had been.

'In that case you need a blood test,' she said. Marie was a firm believer in blood tests, insisting the doctor cast the net wider and wider in the search for a simple deficiency of some key vitamin or mineral that might reverse the inevitable.

As far as Walter was concerned, a blood test was the last thing he needed. The results would merely confirm what he already knew: his body was tired, his insides a mess. His kidneys had grown lazy, working at barely half-speed, and his liver was simply bored of cleaning up after his excesses. It was only his heart that was working overtime feeding his ungrateful organs with blood.

'There's not a lot more the doctor can do,' he said to his daughter. Even the registered nurse raised her eyebrows at the number of multi-coloured pills she handed him three times a day, each designed to counteract a symptom that was no doubt a side effect of one of the other pills prescribed for the side effects of yet another pill. And so it went on; a game of pharmaceutical dominoes. When he'd wondered aloud what would happen if he refused to take them, if it was all worth it for a few extra years in a nursing home, the doctor had merely upped his antidepressant.

They'd had their differences – mainly over the sleeping tablets – but Walter didn't mind Dr Williams. She was a harassed-looking woman approaching retirement age, who appeared to be ageing faster than most of her patients. She was softly spoken and so far, apart from questioning why his liver-function tests could be so deranged, hadn't put two and two together. He was a social drinker, he told her when she enquired about his drinking habits. An extremely social drinker. She had given him a wry smile that told him she'd heard it all before.

'You'd be surprised how many of my patients drink two standard drinks three days a week,' she said. 'I always double what they tell me.'

Young James was skulking behind Marie, fixed on his mobile phone. It emitted a tinny tune that Walter recognised. The carousel music. A new game perhaps? It struck Walter as odd that although every kid had their own phone nowadays, none of them used them to speak to each other. Apparently it was all messages and photographs now. What would these kids reminisce about when they were old? Would they show their grandchildren the photo of their breakfast, or of themselves pouting into a bathroom mirror when they talked about the good old days?

James slouched in the spare chair. Even skeletons were redundant in this day and age.

Marie began her ritual of tidying, lining up the papers and pens on the table, squaring the telephone and smoothing out a wrinkle in the bedspread. He braced for today's object. Seeing him eye up the large carrier bag she'd brought in, Marie said, 'I thought you might like this.' From the bag, which Walter recognised was from Sylvia's favourite dress shop, she produced a large ceramic urn.

Walter's heart sank. He hated that urn. Sylvia had bought it from a bric-a-brac stall at the local fete. The sides were decorated in a mosaic of broken ceramic tiles and it had a brass lid with a tiny handle. At the time he had suspected it was a recycled cremation urn, but knowing Sylvia, if he'd spoken his true feelings about the ghoulish thing, it would have become her favourite piece and been given pride of place. So, Walter had remained nonchalant and his patience was rewarded when after several years, the urn ended up on the top shelf in the laundry.

'Thank you,' he said forcing a smile.

Marie tried the urn in several spots before settling on the chest of drawers beneath the television. Directly in Walter's line of sight.

The tidying and arranging had taken up most of the visit. 'We can't stay long,' said Marie. What would it be today? 'James has Latin at eleven.'

'Latin?'

'It's a new thing,' said Marie. 'It's all the rage.'

'On a Saturday?'

'It's more of a club, really, an ancient-languages club. It's a lot of fun apparently,' said Marie on her son's behalf. James looked like he would rather be in bed.

Boredom was good for kids, Walter had always maintained. Twenty-first-century kids' lives were crammed with extracurricular activities disguised as 'camps' or 'clinics' as if they were all prisoners or patients rather than kids. No one wanted their kid to be ordinary anymore. Even James, an average kid achieving average grades, had been trotted off to a series of specialists to discover why he wasn't sufficiently 'gifted' or 'talented' to warrant his extortionate school fees.

Walter scoffed. 'It's all Greek to me,' he said.

James sniggered.

'Then,' said Marie, 'James is going for a haircut.' She ran her fingers across his fringe like a pair of human scissors. 'I said I'd treat him to a re-style at the trendy new place in town.'

James squirmed and pulled away. 'Mu-um.'

Seriously, was this what lads did for fun these days? Latin club and a trip to an expensive barber? In his day, boys had real fun. They built dens, shot air rifles, passed around French postcards of pictures of naked women.

'You should be setting fire to things at your age, James. Your great-uncle Bill and I had some fantastic bonfires. And blowing things up too. It's quite easy to make explosives if you know what you're doing.'

'Dad!'

James looked up from his phone, his lips now spreading into a grin. 'Oh yeah?'

'Don't get any ideas,' said Marie. 'Your grandpa is only joking.'

'When are we going for that ride, Grandpa?' James looked over at the electric scooter, still charging in the corner.

'On the Tesla? Soon, mate. Soon.'

'About the scooter,' said Marie pulling the charging plug symbolically out of the wall socket. 'I've asked the rep to come and pick it up next week.'

'No! Whatever for?'

'It's on a thirty-day trial, Dad. If we return it in the next fortnight, we'll get our money back.'

My money, he wanted to add. Or what little was left of it, put away for a rainy day. He took in his latest purchase. The motorised pushchair wasn't quite the rainy day he'd envisaged but it was his way out of here, his ride to freedom. He wouldn't let it go without a fight.

'It's a shame that this place didn't come with a thirty-day trial,' muttered Walter.

'Mum said you ran over the OT's foot.' James smirked.

Walter harrumphed. 'People's feet are too big these days. They used to be much smaller.'

James had put the phone back in his pocket and was hanging on Walter's every word. 'And she told Dad you ran over an old lady in the corridor,' he said with relish.

'I didn't *run over* her; technically I only *knocked* her over. There's an important difference. Don't worry though, son, it's like that Whack-a-Mole game in here,' said Walter. 'You knock one over and another one pops up.'

James laughed in the background. Walter swelled a little. He was finding his comic stride once more.

'Dad, really,' said Marie. Walter thought he saw the shadow of a smile pass across his daughter's face before she turned her attention back to some frenetic sock-pairing.

'Don't you worry,' Walter whispered to James. 'I promised you a ride on the Tesla and I'm a man of my word.'

Marie swung round, an identical black sock in each hand. She waved the right-hand sock at Walter. 'You shouldn't make promises like that. Peter is coming to collect the scooter. I'll mark it on your calendar once he's confirmed the day and time.'

Walter winked at James. He wouldn't let his grandson down. The possibility of a second chance was still warm. It had a faint heartbeat, and Walter would do everything to see that he kept his word. The Tesla was charged and ready, in pole position on the starting grid. If they wanted to take it away, they would have to drive it over his cold, dead body.

A vision of Miss Bloom crumpling under his front wheel made Walter flush. No, not flush. Blush.

15

Hattie

HATTIE COUNTED DOWN THE HOURS UNTIL THE NIGHT SHIFT
arrived. Far from the dread that usually accompanied the end
of the day at Woodlands, tonight she found herself looking
forward to the hours of darkness. She'd read a few pages of
her book while Sister Bronwyn and Sameera went through
handover, finished the late drug round and checked all the
residents were, if not already asleep, then safely tucked up
in their beds. When her door opened and Queenie trotted
in, Hattie threw back the covers in eager anticipation. She'd
always thought dogs rather gullible in their doe-eyed devotion.
In theory, she should have identified more with cats who were
far less needy and content with solitude, but she followed the
slobbering, panting animal without a second thought.

The residents were already congregating in the day room,
assuming the positions and activities of the previous night.
Hattie claimed the same comfortable armchair in front of
the television, and in the absence so far of any distracting

crumbs, Queenie chose her company. The dog presented Hattie with a steady stream of soft toys and squeaky rubber shapes, responding with tail wags when each was thrown or wrestled to her satisfaction. Hattie couldn't help but feel she was the one being trained. The dog's favourite toy was a fluffy goose that gave a convincing *Honk!* when squeezed. The sheer delight in those big treacle-coloured eyes melted away any misgivings Hattie had about either the smell of rancid cheese coming from the old girl's ears or the black fur that clung to everything.

Last night's visit to The Night Owls had been rounded off with Sister Bronwyn's promise of 'something very special' for the following night's entertainment. It was first light when she and Sameera escorted the last of the residents back to their beds, where the early shift would find them, tucked up as if they'd been sound asleep all night. Walter Clements had insisted on walking Hattie back to her room. According to the physiotherapist, her hip was coming along nicely; so nicely, in fact, that in spite of her walking stick, she had to pause several times to let her galumphing neighbour and his walking frame catch up, leaving her wondering who was walking whom home.

'Ladies and gentlemen, boys and girls,' shouted Sister Bronwyn, creating silence with a clap of her big pink hands. 'I promised you something very special tonight and I know you will not be disappointed.'

Someone appeared next to Hattie, and as she turned to tell them the seat was taken she saw the white wavy hair, and the thick ankles spilling over paisley slippers. The tiny thrill of recognition was quickly overwhelmed by awkwardness as Walter Clements sat uninvited beside her.

'What have I missed?' he said, puffing. 'Damn nearly dropped off after dinner.'

Hattie put a finger to her lips to shush him.

'Ladies and gentlemen, I give you *Midnight at the Oasis*.' Sister Bronwyn backed away and immediately plunged the day room into darkness with a flick of the main light switch. The grumbles had already started when a spotlight (Hattie recognised the examination light from the treatment room) lit up a makeshift stage in front of the drawn curtains. Music sprang from a CD player, an exotic fantasia of drums, pipes, castanets and some kind of stringed lute. There were no words, only the occasional call or human wail. Then, from out of the darkness of the makeshift Bedouin tent, a shape appeared.

Shimmering.

Sparkling.

Edging into the light, a rhythmic tangle of pale arms and chiffon scarves.

Hattie didn't dare breathe. Walter Clements, rendered speechless, watched as Eileen twisted and writhed into the spotlight. The spotlight picked up the sequins on the scarf tied around her hips, nearly blinding Hattie. She squinted as if into an eclipse, unable to look away.

The music grew louder, Eileen's gyrations more daring. Her undulating hips were mesmerising; she circled her wrists in one direction, then the other. Next she began to hula-hoop her upper body and sidle towards the audience. All eyes were on Eileen's routine. Even Queenie was sitting to attention, panting with that big pink tongue.

Sister Bronwyn started to clap in time to the non-existent beat. One by one, the others joined in, including a bemused

Walter. Eileen slid towards him and released a shimmy of her hips so vigorous that Hattie thought she might do herself actual harm. Walter leaned as far back in his chair as possible, but Eileen moved in until she was almost in his lap. The music exploded and Eileen lunged one hip towards him as if she were trying to close the car door with her arms full of shopping.

Hattie could not tear her eyes away. Where had Eileen learned to dance like this? She remembered Margery the tea lady saying that Eileen had been a big name in her day. A big name where, exactly? In a harem? She was quite the chameleon.

Hattie was the last of the audience to join in the clapping. By now Eileen was looking her age again, wincing at some unseen pain and Sister Bronwyn placed a chair to the side of the stage just in case. When it appeared Eileen might need that sit-down, Sister Bronwyn pressed stop on the CD player, bringing the music to an abrupt halt. The lights came on and the desert oasis was gone. Once more they were back in Woodlands Nursing Home, the spell broken.

Eileen collapsed into the chair and fanned herself with one of her chiffon scarves. Her eyes were dark and heavily made up, as if she'd fallen into a coal scuttle. She'd really gone to town.

'Well, well,' said Walter Clements. Then, still struggling for superlatives, added, 'Well, well.'

'Can everybody join me in thanking our very own Eileen for that enthusiastic and authentic demonstration.' Sister Bronwyn led the applause. Most of the audience looked bewildered rather than impressed but joined in the applause regardless. Fred put down his silver teapot and folded his polishing cloth, lest any other apparitions emerge from behind the curtain.

While Sameera brought Eileen a glass of water and offered to fetch an ice pack for her rapidly swelling knee, Sister Bronwyn went on to detail the rest of the night's events. Continuing the Middle Eastern theme, there would be mint tea accompanied by baklava all round, and a special screening of *Casablanca*.

'Why would we need to wear a balaclava indoors?'

Sister Bronwyn chuckled. 'Not balaclava, Ada, *bak-la-va*. It's a kind of sweet pastry with honey and nuts.'

Ada pointed out that this was unfair, given that she was a diabetic and not allowed sugar lest she lapse into an instant coma.

'Don't you worry, Ada,' Sister Bronwyn assured her, 'I'll check your blood sugar before I go off duty and give you an extra shot of insulin if you need it.'

'Is she allowed to do that?' said Hattie to Walter.

'She's a registered nurse, she must know what she's doing,' he replied.

'But she's taking some risks, don't you think? The Night Owls is meant to be a strictly covert operation. Take Queenie, for instance – she doesn't have the official paperwork. She's not allowed to be here. And all the residents are supposed to be in bed.'

'No one is going to find out,' he replied. 'Not unless someone spills the beans, and I can't imagine anyone here wanting to make a fuss. Look, they all love her.'

It was true. The usually sour and expressionless faces greeted Sister Bronwyn with smiles and nods of appreciation as she flitted from resident to resident like a honeybee pollinating flowers, a kind word and gentle leg-pulling for each. She never gave the impression that there was somewhere more important she needed to be. Or would rather be. Sister Bronwyn alone embodied the philosophy of Woodlands. *Putting life in your years.*

Laurel and Judy were notable absences from The Night Owls. Perhaps they were good sleepers, Hattie mused. She couldn't imagine Judy wanting to miss out on a chance to critique Eileen's belly dancing. None of The Night Owls signed anything like a non-disclosure agreement; rather, it was implied. An unspoken code of conduct, and as long as Queenie hoovered up every last crumb and Sameera hoovered up every last dog hair, no one would be any the wiser.

'So, Eileen made pastry in Paris, sang on Broadway and even danced in a harem. What do you make of that, Mr Clements?'

'And don't forget the Winter Olympics! I'd say she's either led a far more interesting life than the rest of us, or she's making the whole lot up,' he replied.

Hattie thought back to the DON's verbatim recording of her I's and T's. It hadn't occurred to her to embellish the facts, to add colour or to stretch the truth even an inch. She, like every other resident, had entered Woodlands with a clean slate, the past no more than the words recorded on a form. It had never crossed her mind that she could have experienced anything different from the perfectly satisfactory life she'd chosen to live, or that here, within these neutral-coloured walls, she might re-invent herself.

16

Walter

WITH DAWN APPROACHING, THE NIGHT OWLS WERE WINDING down and the day room was bathed in a pale lustre. Fred Carpenter had dropped off with a jeweller's loupe wedged in his eye socket, and an exhausted Eileen was now snoring like a masonry drill in her armchair. Walter couldn't wait to report back to Murray. There was no such thing as a former member of The Night Owls, and Walter's blow-by-blow account of the evening's events would allow his friend to feel he was still part of things. He was also a man who now, more than ever, needed his precious sleep. Walter doubted he could do justice to Eileen's provocative convolutions, but he would try. Murray had a good enough imagination and was a man who would see the comic in the erotic.

In the chair next to him, Miss Bloom was trying and failing to attract Queenie's attention with an oversized tennis ball, but her frenzied waves were no match for the last of the baklava crumbs. Walter recognised a pang of jealousy, not at losing the dog's attention, but at losing Miss Bloom's. Was he wrong to assume that travelling side by side from Alice Springs to Darwin had meant the same to her as it had to him? They had exchanged barely a word beyond her pithy remarks about the scenery interspersed with his witty one-line observations. She hadn't exactly collapsed helpless with laughter but nor had she moved away to sit elsewhere. From what he was learning about Miss Bloom, he took that as a good sign.

'Here,' he said, reaching for the fluffy goose on the carpet beside his chair. 'Let me try.' He would show Miss Bloom how it was done. Walter reckoned he knew a thing or two about dogs since he knew a thing or two about most things. Queenie was over in a shot.

'The secret is to let them think they've won,' he said pulling on the goose's head while Queenie tugged the tail. The dog let out a playful growl as she leaned back, hindquarters tensing as she dug her paws into the carpet. Her jaws were stronger than Walter expected. Not wanting to lose face, he said, 'Watch this,' and suddenly let go. Queenie was thrilled at her win and wagged her tail furiously. Walter grasped the goose a second time and growled. Queenie's tail wagged faster. Walter growled and tugged. The tail thrashed against a small side table, sending a plate and Miss Bloom's cup of mint tea flying. It was revolting stuff, tasted more like mouthwash than tea. She wouldn't miss it. He risked a glance in her direction. Miss Bloom's eyes were the size of the saucer. He could tell she was impressed.

Miss Bloom wasn't his usual type. She was different from most women he'd met. She was anything but the delicate woman she first appeared, indeed she was surprisingly robust and capable. Her look was mid-century English teacher. Her outfits were mostly brown and hardwearing. *Fustian* was the word. Yes, Miss Bloom was built more suitably for the Middle Ages. Sylvia would have described her as 'natural', meaning plain.

Sylvia.

He remembered being attracted to her because she was different too, a brunette amid a crop of bottle blondes, slim and pretty with a nice smile that she used sparingly. He'd used all his boyish charm to see that smile. His jokes had proved a reliable aphrodisiac too, guaranteed to bring a grin to both their faces. But Walter's repertoire had staled for Sylvia and the laughter grown more elusive. What he would give to hear his wife's musical laugh one more time.

By now, Walter's antics with the goose had attracted an audience. When Queenie dropped the slobber-basted toy at his feet he stood and teased her by dangling it above her head. The dog danced on the spot in spite of her heavy set, the corners of her pink jowls drawn up into what was unmistakably a smile.

'Ready?' Walter stood and backed up a few steps to give himself room. For one glorious moment he was back playing cricket with his brothers using an old wooden crate for a wicket. He'd always fancied himself as a bowler, but being the youngest of four meant he was more often relegated to leg gully – the patch of long grass and weeds that surrounded the washing line. Without thinking, Walter shined the goose on his dressing-gown pocket.

Eyes on the toy, Queenie quivered with anticipation. Walter placed his fingers around the fluffy bird's head in the familiar grip he'd practised over and over in his youth, ready for a spinner. Miss Bloom's brow wrinkled in admiration.

Prepare to be impressed, he wanted to say. Instead, he circled his bowling arm at the shoulder until it loosened. Queenie was already on her feet, coiled like a spring. Walter had neither the space, nor frankly the energy, for a run-up. Instead he placed his feet side-on on an imaginary crease, extended his arm behind him and circled it overhead like a windmill. He'd planned for this to be a practice run but his arm had gained such momentum that at the top of the arc the goose took flight across the day room.

Whichever way Walter later replayed the event, he came to the same conclusion: the fall was simply a matter of being in the wrong place at the wrong time. Laurel Baker saw things quite differently.

Usually a solid sleeper, she had been woken by a bout of heartburn and when her buzzer had gone unanswered she went in search of Milk of Magnesia. Finding no one at the nurses' station, she followed the sound of voices. Queenie, leaping to catch Walter's leg spin, had collided with Laurel when she entered the day room at silly mid-off, sending her somersaulting over her walking frame. She landed awkwardly, tangled up in her dressing-gown cord. There was a *Honk!* as she rolled onto the goose, then silence.

Laurel Baker lay sprawled across the carpet in a classic murder-victim pose – the reverse of the recovery position. Her right arm, however, was bent at a peculiar angle and she had lost a slipper. Queenie, oblivious, trotted triumphantly back to Walter and dropped the goose at his feet.

On seeing Laurel, Sister Bronwyn turned deathly pale.

'Call an ambulance, Sameera. Lights and sirens.' As the AIN rushed to the door, Sister Bronwyn added, 'Leave her son to me. I'll call Derek once the ambulance is on its way.'

Walter had to admire the way Sister Bronwyn took charge of the situation, and the speed with which the paramedics arrived. It helped having the ambulance station serendipitously close to the nursing home, though no one could quite remember which was the chicken and which the egg.

The paramedics were an entertaining double act when they arrived. The two men had their jovial introductions down pat and took control of the situation with the same practised nonchalance they might have used to order lunch in a cafeteria. They gave Laurel a little green pain-relieving whistle, and by the time she was loaded onto the stretcher she was sucking away happily, one arm in a white sling and a bandage wrapped like a turban around her head.

Naturally, Judgy Judy made an appearance. Never mind that Park Lane was two sides of the Monopoly board away.

'What have I missed?' She elbowed Walter aside for a better view.

'Laurel's had a fall.' Eileen had woken at the sound of the commotion and pieced together the scenario.

Judy did a double-take at her charcoal eyes. 'I can see that, Eileen, but who caused it?'

Eileen looked at Walter. Was she about to dob him in? Dob them all in – Sister Bronwyn, The Night Owls, Queenie the unofficial therapy dog? Was there anything to dob, or had this been, like every other freak accident at Woodlands Nursing Home, a freak accident? 'You know Laurel,' said Eileen, 'she's got two left feet.'

'Excuse us, ladies and gents,' said the first paramedic.

When Sister Bronwyn assured Walter there was nothing he could do to help – indeed, his offers of assistance were dismissed as inappropriate under the circumstances – Walter backed away. It was the duty of a driver to assist at the scene of an accident. He'd drummed it into all his students. Meanwhile, Queenie had made a timely exit and was nowhere to be seen.

The jolly paramedics continued to crack jokes as they wheeled the stretcher down the corridor. Laurel was laughing by now, which might have had more to do with the little green whistle than the calibre of the jokes.

'Can you still feel your legs, Laurel?' Judy started to fuss. 'Do you need your coat, dear?'

Laurel laughed and waved. 'Bye everyone! Au revoir. Auf Wiedersehen. Adieu!' she shouted between sucks. As the stretcher rounded the corner, Walter heard her break into song.

Sister Bronwyn, conversely, was ashen, all her contagious joy gone as she tried to disperse the crowd of onlookers.

'Sameera, the early shift will be arriving soon. You help everyone to bed and I'll wait here for Derek.' She wrung her hands.

Walter knew when the party was over. There was nothing more he or anyone else could do. He would walk Miss Bloom back to Old Kent Road and wait to hear the latest on Laurel Baker's condition from Margery at morning tea.

Sameera pulled the plug and the slow train vanished. She did her best to tidy the day room but it was too late to hide all the evidence. Striding towards them was a man with a familiar beard. His eyes were on Sister Bronwyn.

Walter lingered.

'Hello Derek,' said Sister Bronwyn, her hands still twisting and turning on themselves. 'I'm so terribly sorry about your mother's fall.'

Walter watched Derek Baker bend and pick up Queenie's goose from the floor. Instead of unleashing a torrent of abuse, Derek Baker squeezed the toy in his thick hand until it emitted a terrified *Honk!*

17

Hattie

SHE'D THOUGHT IT BEST TO MAKE A HASTY EXIT AND LEAVE the staff to their work. Pausing for a breather at Marylebone Station, Hattie had come face to face with a man who had appeared from nowhere. His deep, determined strides had devoured the carpet and he nodded briefly as he passed. This was Laurel Baker's son, all right. Though Laurel tried to disguise hers with her scaffolded hair, and her son with his bushranger beard, they shared the same unmistakable low-set ears. As Hattie watched him approach Sister Bronwyn, she saw the scene through his eyes.

Queenie, animated by the comings and goings, bounced around like a puppy. She'd found the giant tennis ball and, mistakenly hopeful that the newcomer might be up for a bit of a game, had dropped it at Derek Baker's feet. She sat to attention looking alternately at the ball and then pleadingly up at his face. Even from her distance Hattie could see the ring of black dog hair on the carpet.

Equally hard to ignore were all the residents who should rightly be tucked up in their beds but who were very much awake. Eileen in her harem outfit was particularly conspicuous, as was Fanny Olsen, who was trailing the electrical cord from a soldering iron in one hand and a large wooden circuit board in the other. Walter Clements hovered nearby, pretending to admire the watercolour on the wall. Evidence of the night's activities was everywhere: piles of linen on the table, plates of leftover baklava and a dozen residents wandering in bewildered circuits as Sameera tried to herd them back to their rooms.

Derek had missed his mother being wheeled out only minutes before with her arm in a sling and a bandage that did little to disguise the pink rinse of blood in her hair. Sister Bronwyn had done her best to make Laurel look presentable for the ambulance and placed a chair discreetly over the bloody spot where she'd fallen. If anything, the chair simply signposted the ominous dark stain on the carpet.

Not wanting to add to the chaos, Hattie tore herself away from the unfolding drama and continued back to her room. She could hear Walter Clements calling but she didn't turn around. His wheezy shouts soon faded. Laurel Baker's blood was on his hands. He was the one who'd thrown the goose for Queenie. His apologies hadn't exactly deafened them all, in the same way he still hadn't apologised for knocking her over with his electric scooter. Walter Clements seemed genuinely oblivious to the consequences of his actions; he had gone out of his way to be friendly towards her, charming even. Were all men this contrary? According to her observations, the cock bird was driven purely by the basic desire to find food, to mate and to defend its territory from other males and predators. Its needs and wants made logical sense, enough to fill six volumes of her books on bird behaviour. But Walter Clements wasn't an easy bird to read.

Her eye registered a pulse of bright blue overhead moments before she saw the flurry of feathers as Icarus landed on the top of a bookcase near the nurses' station. The bird's eyes locked on her and it trilled a soft greeting.

'Hello, little fellow,' said Hattie. 'What are you doing all the way down here?'

Icarus made soft clicking sounds then preened a wing feather with his tiny grey beak. Even in her brief time at Woodlands, she had noticed him travelling further and further from his Crystal Palace cage. His nightly forays were becoming more daring, although he always returned safely by morning. So far no one seemed to have noticed the number of surfaces already adorned with his droppings. It made her smile. In Icarus, she sensed a kindred spirit.

Hattie pursed her lips and made soft kissing sounds as she approached the bird. He'd lived in captivity all his life, was tame and yet at the same time, the budgie appeared wary of people. He often looked as if he were sizing them up. If only she could get him to come to her. She inched closer and held out her hand. Would he trust her enough to fly to her?

'I won't hurt you,' she said softly.

Icarus flapped his wings. Hattie held her breath as he hopped along the bookcase towards her. She moved closer. The bird hopped. Patience was the key. Birds couldn't be hurried. It was all about overcoming their fear, and that took time.

Suddenly she heard voices, and sensed movement behind her. Hattie turned, her eyes drawn away from the little blue bird to the carnival procession heading towards her: Sister

Bronwyn, Derek Baker, Walter Clements and a shimmering Eileen, with Queenie galloping circles around them, barking. The last thing the chaotic situation needed was a budgie flapping around as well. But it was too late. Spooked, Icarus tensed and took off, flying over Hattie's head. Not away from the commotion but straight towards it. Hattie held her breath as the bird swooped low enough that everyone ducked. It was only when Derek Baker's fingers explored his bare scalp that she noticed the splattering of green and white trickling down his forehead.

18

Walter

EVERY MORNING THE SAME FACES. EVERY MORNING THE same expressions of faint relief at the dawning of another day. There had only ever been one face Walter wanted to see across the breakfast table, but that face was fading as time passed, sadly no more than a sun-bleached Polaroid in his memory. He would have to make do with these ladies instead.

The ladies were seated in their exclusive positions at the dining table, making Laurel's absence all the more obvious. The empty chair was not offered to Walter, nor did he make any advances towards it. Instead, he chose to sit alone at one of the smaller tables a safe distance from Ada's whistling hearing aid and Eileen's soprano humming, though not far enough to avoid the conversation. This morning's topic for discussion was coffee.

'Young folk are all completely addicted. They walk round like babies sucking on beakers,' said Judy.

Ada joined in. 'I blame the Italians. They're the ones who got us all hooked on the stuff.'

'It was the Greeks, Ada,' Judy corrected. 'They brought coffee here after the war.'

'I thought coffee came from Brazil,' said Ada.

'You're thinking of nuts, dear,' Judy said.

'During the war,' said Eileen, who, Walter had noticed, managed to steer almost any conversation towards the war, 'we had to make do with ersatz coffee. It was made from all sorts of things, except real coffee of course. Chicory, barley, acorns—'

'They made coffee out of unicorns?'

'Acorns, Ada. Not unicorns. Are your hearing aids in the right ears?' Judy tutted.

On cue, the tea lady appeared, pushing her steaming urn. 'Good morning, you lucky people. Welcome to another day in paradise.'

'About time,' someone muttered.

'Tea or coffee?'

'Would you settle a debate for us, Margery?' Judy was never one to back down when there was a point to be made. 'Was it the Greeks or the Italians who brought the coffee culture to Australia?'

'I think it was Nescafé,' Margery replied. 'Speaking of which, is everybody having the usual?'

The broad-bottomed tea lady had memorised everybody's preference for tea or coffee, Greek, Italian or ersatz. Margery remembered who took milk and who didn't, and the right number of sugars to keep each resident sweet. In a system designed to homogenise an entire generation into a one-size-fits-all solution, she recognised the little things that made life bearable. It mattered that Judy liked black tea with lemon, and that Fred preferred his with a dash of milk. It was her job to ensure that Eileen took two sugars, while Ada was only allowed sweetener.

Walter's ears pricked up when the conversation inevitably turned to last night's events.

'Poor Laurel,' said Judy, sprinkling psyllium husk on her cereal. 'She was airborne, you know.' The ladies joined in with a chorus of disapproving tongue clicks. 'Bruised like a week-old banana.' More tongue clicks.

'But you weren't there, Judy,' Ada challenged. 'You always sleep through.'

'I have it on good authority, Ada.' Judy leaned across the table for the milk jug. 'Sister Bronwyn will have a case to answer.'

'It wasn't really Sister Bronwyn's fault.' Eileen looked over her shoulder at Walter.

'I'm sorry,' Judy said, not looking in the least bit sorry, 'it was bound to happen sooner or later with a dangerous animal on the loose. This is a home for people not animals. Besides, that dog makes the whole place smell like a rabbit hutch.'

'But everyone could see it was an accident,' said Walter skidding into the conversation.

Judy gave Walter her famous look. 'If you ask me it was an accident waiting to happen.' As usual no one had asked her. 'There'll be consequences, you mark my words,' she said. 'Derek Baker has contacts.'

'What sort of contacts?' Ada swabbed the corners of her mouth with her napkin.

'You know, people who are high up.'

'High up where, exactly? The RSPCA, you mean?'

'No. I'm talking about high up in the right places, Ada. Derek is well connected.'

Walter pushed away his bowl. Not even an extra swirl of honey on his yoghurt could take away the sour taste in his mouth. After last night, Queenie's cover was blown, and Judy was right about one thing – there would be consequences. Good intentions were no defence when things went wrong; he must wear at least some of the responsibility for what happened. He doubted he would be the only resident to miss Woodlands' unofficial therapy dog. Queenie would be out on her smelly ear and The Night Owls wouldn't be the same without her.

Leaving the ladies to their conspiracy theories, Walter helped himself to toast.

'Here you are, handsome,' said a smiling Margery as she placed a fresh jar of marmalade within his reach. 'Your favourite.'

'Are you trying to sabotage my figure?' Walter patted his belly. 'I'll have you know that in here is the body of an elite athlete. And very tasty he was, too.'

Margery always laughed at his jokes. Unfortunately, Margery laughed at everybody's jokes.

'There's a seat over here, Miss Bloom,' she suddenly shouted. 'Walter won't bite.'

Miss Bloom stalled, looking between the empty chair at the ladies' table and the one that Margery had that second pulled out at Walter's. The ladies appeared in no hurry to invite her into their clique. After several moments of weighing up the two options, she joined Walter, inching her cutlery a fraction away from his. It was as though the slow train had never happened.

Margery filled Miss Bloom's teacup. 'You'd better watch this one,' she said with a wink. 'He's a bit of a ladies' man.'

'Now then, that's not fair. I'll have you know I've always been a one-woman man.' He added solemnly, 'If that.' It was enough to raise a titter from Margery as she tonged more toast into the rack.

'Any chance of a croissant today?' It was worth a try, while she was in a good mood.

'I wouldn't get your hopes up, sweetheart. Management have vetoed croissants. On account of the wastage.'

'What wastage?'

'The crumbs, pet. Same thing goes for anything in filo pastry.'

Walter tried to catch Miss Bloom's eye but she was busy scraping out the contents of a plastic butter container with a frown.

'They never put enough in these things,' he said, spreading his own butter like a coat of render. 'They either need to make the toast smaller or the butter bigger.'

She considered this and returned what might pass for a smile. You're a tough nut to crack, he wanted to say. He would get there, eventually. One day he would make Miss Bloom laugh. Above the collective crunching of toast, Walter once again tuned in to the ladies and the conversation that would no doubt play on an endless loop for days to come.

'Woodlands has a duty of care,' said Judy, stabbing between her rear molars with a toothpick. 'Remember the unfortunate electric-bed malfunction in Northumberland Avenue? Poor Mr Renfrew.'

There was a collective shudder at the table. Ada made the sign of the cross.

'This is a nursing home, in case you'd forgotten, Judy.' Walter accentuated his point with his butter knife. 'It's where people come to fall safely.'

'And poor Mrs Paterson from Pentonville Road?' Judy continued without missing a beat. 'She caught a chill in her bladder on the bus trip and was never the same again.'

'Mrs Paterson broke her wrist snapping off a piece of Toblerone,' scoffed Walter. 'That's my point. We're all past our use-by date in here.'

'I prefer to think of it as a "best before" date.' Miss Bloom looked as surprised as anyone to hear her words spoken aloud. The ladies paused mid-debate to stare in her direction.

Walter raised his teacup in a toast. 'Well said, Miss Bloom. It's a shame to throw out perfectly good food. Or people.'

Having assumed that her frostiness was a sign of contempt or haughty superiority, he now wondered if it was merely a façade. What if, having never married, she simply didn't know how to relate to people, especially men? He'd been born into a house of boys, and the only women he'd known growing up were the ones he'd dated; sadly, he could count those on one hand. They were both very much beginners in the art of platonic friendship. Walter was more intrigued than ever.

Margery was back with the teapot. 'Anyone for a top-up?'

Walter proffered his empty cup. 'Are you sure you won't marry me, Margery?'

'Too late, lover boy,' said Margery pointing to her wedding ring. 'How about I leave you the teapot, by way of consolation?'

When she'd gone, Walter counted the teabag tags hanging over the edge of the pot. 'Shame there's no such thing as tea-leaves anymore. My mother was quite the clairvoyant, she used to swear by them.' A wave of nostalgia broke over him as he remembered his mother emptying the dregs onto a saucer and her tightly knit brow as she tried to interpret the random pattern of dark specks clinging to the bottom of the china cup. Suddenly Walter was on a road-trip through the past. 'And whatever happened to ice-cream vans? I haven't heard one of those in years.'

'Corrugated cardboard too,' said Miss Bloom, to Walter's delight. 'You don't see that anymore.'

'Have you noticed that no one has an Adam's apple these days? Nor dandruff.' Walter let out a sigh. 'Things aren't what they used to be.'

'Will she really be in trouble, do you think?' Miss Bloom was biting her lip. 'Sister Bronwyn? After last night?'

'It's out of our hands, I'm afraid,' Walter replied. 'Sadly, most things are.'

19

Hattie

AT FIRST, SHE THOUGHT IT MUST BE TINNITUS. HIGH-PITCHED, unwavering, annoying. It was the wrong season for mosquitoes, the nights too cold. Besides, what free-willed living creature would venture inside a place like this? She held her breath and listened again, eyes scanning the half-darkness like searchlights.

This time when she listened she heard only the unanswered telephone sounding to her ear like a currawong that had stumbled across a fruiting tree and was broadcasting its good fortune. No, she must be imagining it.

Bzzz.

The sound was loudest in her right ear now, an off-key clarinet. She swatted away what she couldn't see and for a moment all was quiet before she heard an identical buzzing in her left ear.

Hattie turned the light on, bringing instantaneous silence.

She searched the ceiling for the dark speck to hover across her field of vision, waiting for its tiny movement to register.

Nothing.

She turned the light off again.

Bzzz-zz-zz.

Insects had never bothered her before. Every living thing had a purpose, if only to provide a nutritious meal for another creature further up the food chain. The bedroom windows at Angophora Cottage didn't close fully, the frames swollen with rot. Natural ventilation, Hattie liked to think. It meant that winged insects were free to come and go as they pleased. Largely, the bloodsuckers left her alone. Not so her vocal new roommate.

'You're wasting your time in here,' she told the insect she still couldn't see. 'I'm not very juicy, I'm afraid.' Hattie ran her finger along one leathery forearm. Good luck to them.

Mosquitoes couldn't afford to waste time. The male only lived a week or so. The females fared better and lived most of their lives without a mate. Several weeks on average. *Four to six weeks.* What a shame to spend it in here.

She parted the curtains. In the darkened glass she saw an old lady with her mother's dark, private eyes. It filled Hattie with sadness, not for what she herself had become, but for what her mother would never be.

The window opened barely a fraction but it was enough to bring in the dark outside air, scented with jasmine and the petrichor of distant rain.

'There you go,' she said. 'Time to head home.'

The insect was invisible, resting somewhere. It would leave when it was ready.

Hattie decided to walk off her restlessness. The staff would still be having handover; too early to discover if Queenie would be allowed inside after last night's debacle. Laurel's fall had dominated every mealtime, the incident discussed and dissected until in the tradition of Chinese whispers, no one was entirely sure of the facts. One thing they all agreed on, however, was that Woodlands Nursing Home was on the verge of a constitutional crisis.

At the nurses' station Hattie was taken aback when she saw a youngish woman sitting in Sister Bronwyn's swivel chair. As she approached, she got a better view. Not so youngish close up. Her hair a shade too yellow and her face obscured by thick make-up that gave her the appearance of an overworked painting. She had precise eyebrows that looked as if they'd been drawn on with a calligraphy pen, and conspicuous lips that looked as if they'd been caught in some sort of suction device.

The woman glanced up briefly. 'Good evening, Mrs . . .'

'Bloom. *Miss* Bloom.'

'What can I do for you?'

'Nothing. There was a mosquito in my room.'

'I'll send somebody with the fly killer in a minute.'

'That won't be necessary.'

'But if it woke you up—'

'I wasn't asleep. I'm not sleepy.'

The woman frowned. 'Do you need a sleeping tablet?'

'No, thank you, I'll wait until the mosquito leaves of its own accord.'

'We can't have insects flying willy-nilly round a facility like Woodlands,' said the woman.

'But why not?'

'Health and safety. Mosquitoes carry diseases like malaria, dengue and yellow fever.'

'Not in the suburbs, surely?'

'We simply can't take any chances. At the last place I worked we had a flu epidemic one winter, and scabies the summer before. It was carnage. What with the gastro outbreak that was splashed across the front page of all the newspapers . . .' The woman shuddered at the memory, then asked rhetorically, 'Now, where do we keep the fly spray?' She opened the cupboards one by one, searching.

Hattie stiffened. She couldn't allow an innocent creature to be euthanised like this.

'Have you worked here long?' she called, trying to distract the woman.

'I'm from the agency,' the nurse replied over the bang of cupboard doors.

'Sister Bronwyn not on duty tonight?'

'No.'

Hattie tried to keep her tone casual, conversational. 'I thought she always worked weekends.'

'Not anymore. I'm taking over her shifts.'

'For how long?'

'Until further notice.'

Hattie's walking stick wobbled in her hand and she grasped the handrail for support. It was worse than she'd imagined. Far worse. No Queenie, no Sister Bronwyn. And no Night Owls.

The nurse emerged from behind a cupboard door with a triumphant look on her face and a red aerosol can in her hand.

'Is that really necessary?'

'The mosquito must die.' The woman's puckered lips thinned a fraction.

Hattie was getting desperate. 'I'm terribly sensitive to insecticides, you know,' she pleaded. 'My head swells like a melon.'

'In that case I'll record the allergy in your notes when I get back.'

In the unlikely event her doctor might accidentally prescribe an insecticide? Hattie blocked the nurse's path with her walking stick. 'Please. Isn't there another way?'

The nurse sighed and pushed past the stick as if passing through a turnstile. 'It's a mosquito. It doesn't really serve any useful purpose. It won't be missed. And there are plenty more where it came from, I can assure you.'

With perfect timing, Fanny Olsen began to scream, a rising wail like an air-raid siren.

Viga Ossicker!

The nurse hurried off towards Fanny's room, leaving the aerosol on the desk. When she was out of sight, Hattie hid the can in the bottom of a swing-top bin next to the sink and covered it with scrunched-up paper towels. Left alone with a pile of confidential files within her reach, curiosity got the better of her and she searched through the pile until she found Fanny's unsmiling photograph. The sheer mischief of what she was doing was intoxicating. Her clammy fingers leafed through the pages. Unsure what she was even looking for, Hattie skimmed the pages of doctors' notes and old drug charts.

As a child, she had never been in trouble. At school the other children were scolded and punished for disobedience and disrespect, apparently taking it in their stride. On the other hand, as a child Hattie had always preferred the path of least resistance in all things. She simply couldn't see the point in flouting the rules, nor the logic in risking punishment if it ended in confrontation. But a different Hattie Bloom had emerged from the general anaesthetic. One that realised how much time she'd already wasted.

At last, her eye settled on Fanny's I's and T's. She'd struck snooping gold.

Fanny Olsen. Born in 1924. Place of birth: Bergen, Norway.

According to the details recorded on her arrival at Woodlands three years previously, she was a widow. No children. Her next of kin was a distant cousin in Norway. She was under public guardianship as a result of diminished capacity and was not permitted to leave Woodlands without official clearance. There was something about her fleeing to Australia after the war, but Hattie, on hearing someone approaching, quickly closed the file and buried it in the pile.

They had not exchanged a single word and had grown up on opposite sides of the world. On the surface, she and Fanny Olsen had nothing in common, and yet in many ways they shared the same predicament. Neither of them could escape, nor expect to be rescued. They were both completely alone in the world.

20

Walter

THE LATE-NIGHT TRAFFIC HAD GROUND TO A HALT. ON seeing the tangle of red walking frames outside the dark, deserted day room, Walter pictured blood corpuscles trapped in one giant blood clot. The softly spoken Sameera was struggling to be heard, let alone understood.

'The council really need to widen this intersection,' said Fred Carpenter. 'It's not good for business.'

'Is this the queue for the bus?' asked the woman from Marlborough Street wearing a pink dressing-gown.

From the middle of the melee, Walter's heart sank. He'd heard the rumours but needed to see it with his own eyes. The day room was in darkness, the birdcage covered with a blackout sheet. Sister Bronwyn wasn't here.

Sameera was getting nowhere, and the ensnared residents were growing increasingly restless. Somewhere out of sight, Fanny Olsen was tuning up and Woodlands was in danger of a full-scale meltdown. Attempting a three-point turn, Walter locked wheels with Ada's walker, resulting in a *do-si-do* that merely returned them to their respective starting positions.

'Please everybody, go back to your rooms,' shouted Sameera.

Walter nudged his way to the front of the clot. 'What's happening with The Night Owls? Where's Sister Bronwyn?'

Sameera shook her head. 'I'm sorry, Walter, she's not coming back. There won't be any more Night Owls.'

'You mean they're extinct?'

'I'm afraid so, and unless I can get everybody back to their rooms before the agency nurse finds out, I'll be extinct too.'

Walter buckled at the news. His walker groaned as the metal frame strained to keep him upright. At worst he had imagined that Sister Bronwyn might be cautioned, and Queenie banned. But gone? Forever? How was he going to break the news to Murray? Sister Bronwyn was Murray's favourite nurse – everyone's favourite nurse – and he now faced his last days in the hands of a stranger. Walter looked around the other residents; without The Night Owls, their dusk-till-dawns would be filled with fear and confusion and loneliness. Dark hours were like dog years – they lasted seven times as long as daylight hours.

'Can't we let everyone in? You can do the catering and I'll take care of the entertainment,' said Walter, but he could already see his answer in Sameera's expression.

'No, Sister wouldn't allow it. I've worked with her at another facility and she's very strict about the residents staying in bed.'

It was a blow, and not only for the sleepless residents. Walter had briefly pictured himself on the makeshift stage running through the new routine he'd been quietly putting together. He'd always wanted to have a stab at stand-up.

Woodlands Nursing Home wasn't exactly the big time, and at ninety his performance in front of Fred, Fanny and the other ladies would hardly launch his comic career, but he wanted to experience the thrill. Just once. Miss Bloom might be there too. Not that he expected her to laugh at his jokes; he would be content if she didn't fall asleep or walk out halfway through.

'Ladies and gentlemen!' he shouted, impressed by the projection of his voice. 'Your attention, please. Night Owls is temporarily postponed. Everyone needs to go back to bed and await further instructions.'

The clot shifted in response but failed to disperse. Weary and overwrought, some of the frailer residents began to wilt. Even Walter's dressing-gown seemed to have shrunk around his tight chest. He pressed his palm to his breastbone, suddenly remembering.

'Time is heart muscle,' the cardiologist had told him when he had his first heart attack. Walter, always a man who maintained that if a job was worth doing, it was worth doing properly, was secretly impressed when the cardiologist informed him he was lucky to be alive.

'It's called a "widow maker", the most dangerous kind of blockage in the worst possible place. It was only millimetres from blowing up the entire fuse box.'

Walter pictured a trail of gunpowder and a bomb going off leaving Sylvia and Marie floundering in the debris. The specialist had gone on, in the same manner M might explain a new bagpipe flamethrower to James Bond, to describe how he had used special equipment to suck the blood clot out backwards and leave a stent inside the narrowed vessel. Walter pictured a collapsed sewer, relined. On this occasion he hadn't needed the full bypass – the entire drain dug out and replaced. That was to come, a few years later.

Now, Walter had an idea. 'Here's what's going to happen.'

Ada, Eileen, the lady with the pink dressing-gown, Fred Carpenter. One by one, the residents followed Walter's instructions and reversed out of the muddle. Little by little, four wheels and two slippers at a time, the clot dissolved. Sameera promised everyone a hot chocolate back in their rooms and thanked Walter, her face full of relief.

He'd done his best to keep those stents open, even buying an exercise bike he used all of twice. Sylvia bought a heart-smart cookbook, forcing Walter to make clandestine stops at the bakery between students for his favourite donuts. The doctor had seemed as disappointed as Sylvia when Walter's weight refused to budge, and suggested bariatric surgery.

Sylvia, no fool, had said, 'What's the point of having his stomach stapled shut if his mouth still opens?' The subject was dropped.

Fanny had finally stopped screaming and the other residents were heading back to their rooms. It wasn't exactly Dunkirk, but as a driving instructor, Walter had had his fair share of close shaves on four wheels. Including his own. For once he could stand a little straighter, a cameo of the man he'd always aspired to be.

21

Hattie

SOME WEEKS, ESPECIALLY WHEN THERE WERE BILLS TO PAY, Hattie's pension wouldn't stretch to a full bag of groceries. At these times she simply bought a loaf of bread and a slab of butter and made do. The following week, if finances allowed, she would treat herself to a box of chocolates, with a strict daily allocation. She justified the extravagance by calculating the money she had saved by her years of exceptional frugality. Her conscientious avoidance of other human beings had always left her free of their germs too, meaning Hattie's experience with the medical profession was limited.

She had inherited a family doctor from her parents, neither of whom ever visited him, preferring to trust good old-fashioned stoicism to keep them in good health. Up until their premature deaths, that is. He was their doctor in name only. Selecting a new GP, therefore, was rather like picking a chocolate from a new box. Hattie stared at the list of names, none of which revealed anything about their skills as physicians. For obvious reasons, it was Dr Robin Sparrow's name that caught her eye.

'They're all very good,' the DON had said, waiting patiently for Hattie to make her decision.

'I need to be certain,' said Hattie. Was he a truffle heart or a perfect praline? She couldn't very well put him back into the tray having taken a bite, and swap him for a fudge duet instead.

Dr Robin Sparrow, it turned out, was an orange fondant of a physician. He would have to do. His straight nose at least gave him a reassuring air of authority, which was just as well, because his wrinkled shirt and trailing shoelaces suggested he'd recently climbed out of bed.

'Lovely to meet you, Mrs Bloom,' he said, addressing the bandage on her leg.

Miss Bloom.

'Are your hands warm?' Hattie enquired. There was still time to swap him.

He laughed, rubbing his palms together as if to spark a flame.

'I hear it's a bit whiffy,' he said jovially.

Hattie imagined he'd be a bit whiffy too if he'd been bandaged up tightly for days. She didn't say so. It was important to keep on the right side of Dr Sparrow. Theoretically, he was all that stood between her and home.

'Sister, would you mind . . .' Dr Sparrow motioned for the nurse to remove the layers of bandages and gauze. Hattie was already conditioned to the second-daily dressing routine, her leg beginning to throb the moment she even heard the dressing trolley's squeaky wheel. She gripped the sides of the big PVC chair in the treatment room so hard that a casual observer might believe she was about to be executed in it.

The nurse peeled away the final rectangular dressing using a pair of plastic forceps. She worked slowly and carefully, as if defusing a bomb. The pristine white square that had been so carefully applied only days ago was now covered in an unattractive green stain.

Sister and Dr Sparrow recoiled simultaneously, burying their noses in their elbows.

'Good grief,' said Sister.

'Oh dear . . .'

'What does that mean?' Hattie's eyes stung as the strong earthy smell filled her nostrils.

'Well, it's . . .'

The nurse took over. 'It means you won't be going home anytime soon, Mrs Bloom. Your leg is infected.'

'It's *Miss* Bloom.'

'Either way, this leg is going to take a long time to heal.'

With not the slightest attempt to disguise the mountain as a molehill, the nurse packaged up the dirty dressings and used gloves at arm's length, tying a knot in the white plastic rubbish bag as if they were radioactive.

Hattie didn't need to ask exactly how long. She already knew the answer.

'I can do the dressings at home,' she said. There was a perfectly good bottle of Dettol in the cupboard somewhere and a bag of bran that would make an excellent poultice.

'As your doctor, I wouldn't recommend . . .'

The nurse crouched next to Hattie's chair and with a sympathetic smile said, 'That's not possible. You see, the leg needs to be dressed in a sterile manner.'

'But if it got infected in here, then Woodlands can't be very sterile.' Hattie folded her arms. This place was one huge Petri dish and the sooner she got out of here the better.

'You do have a point . . .' offered Dr Sparrow.

'It's not just the leg,' said the nurse as she straightened up again with a creak from one of her knees. 'I'm sure the DON talked to you about the work that needs to be done to make your home safe.'

'My home is perfectly safe, it was the ladder that was rotten.'

'There's also the hole in the roof, the front door is jammed shut, and none of the windows close.'

'They've all been like that for years. I only fell recently.'

The doctor whispered something to the nurse before pulling up a chair. At eye level, he was more intimidating than when he'd been towering above her.

'This is not just about repairs,' said the doctor, obviously trying a new tack. 'Some of the staff have raised concerns.'

'What sort of concerns?'

'Non-compliance with medication . . . resisting personal care . . . withdrawn . . . wandering . . .'

'If I were at home, this would be perfectly normal behaviour,' said Hattie. It was Woodlands that was the problem.

The doctor continued. 'Your behaviour has been recorded as withdrawn, suspicious, even a little paranoid.'

'Paranoid?' If she wasn't paranoid before, she certainly was now.

'Have you been hearing . . .'

'Voices?' Only yours, thought Hattie, and she'd heard enough of that. 'What no one here seems to comprehend is that I need to get home as a matter of urgency. It's no exaggeration to say it's a matter of life and death.'

'Life and—'

'Death.' It was time to get to the point. 'There's an endangered owl nesting in my Angophora and the new neighbours want to cut the tree down. Not the entire tree, only the overhanging branch, but the result will be the same if I don't stop them. The parents will abandon the babies.' She didn't trust the cat either but refrained from voicing this out loud, not knowing for sure whether her healthcare providers were cat people or dog people.

'I see,' said the doctor. 'Well, all I can say is—'

'I'm running out of time as well as patience, Dr Sparrow. If I'm not allowed home I will discharge myself. I'd rather take my chances in my death-trap of a cottage than let the owls perish.'

'It's not that . . .'

'Simple?'

'Straightforward. That decision is only yours to make if you have full capacity. Otherwise a guardian will have to be appointed on your behalf, and since you have no next of kin . . .'

Hattie sighed. 'All right,' she said. She didn't need the doctor to spell it out. They'd been gathering ammunition. This was the brick wall. If she was going to get out of this nursing home she needed to use her brain rather than her rapidly diminishing brawn.

The tea trolley arrived, and Margery poked her head around the door. 'Tea?'

'I'll leave you to it, Miss Bloom.' The doctor backed away like a courtier. 'I'll be back on . . .' He was gone.

Margery placed the cup and saucer on the table next to Hattie. 'There you go, lovely.'

'Is it hot?' Hattie tested the side of the cup. Lukewarm.

'Now, you know as well as I do, I'm not allowed to make it too hot,' said Margery. 'It's against health and safety.'

22

Walter

Shucked from his bed each morning like a reluctant oyster, Walter spent his days trying to avoid the organised activities at Woodlands. He preferred company to being alone; he just didn't want to feel like he was in primary school again. The main foyer was his preferred spot to while away the hours. Here he could chat, socialise, and watch the to-ing and fro-ing of staff, visitors and fellow residents. Sylvia had often accused him of getting under her feet. Perhaps he'd been too clingy, too needy, but Walter hadn't seen it like that. He'd simply wanted to be with other people, especially the woman he loved.

No one paid much attention to him settled into his favourite chair next to reception. He blended in, more likely to be noticed by his absence than by sitting with his notepad, scribbling down random thoughts and ideas as they occurred to him. Some of his notes were material for his new comedy routine, others observations or musings. Sometimes, Walter fantasised he was a detective on a stakeout, disguised as an old man with a walking frame. Hiding in plain sight.

'Morning, Walter.' It was the lifestyle coordinator with a clipboard. 'Shall I put you down for the bus trip? The alternative is Twenty Questions at ten-thirty.'

'It's a veritable choose-your-own-adventure in here, isn't it?'

The lifestyle coordinator, a softly spoken man in his sixties, clapped him on the shoulder. 'That's the spirit,' he said.

'While you're here, can I make a request for tomorrow afternoon's movie?' If he had to sit through *The Sound of Music* one more time, the hills would be alive with screams not do-re-mi.

'What did you have in mind?'

'I thought we could have something we can all relate to. How about *The Longest Day* or *The Land That Time Forgot*?' He delivered his lines with a grin.

'I'm sorry, Walter. I'm afraid the ladies have requested Patrick Swayze again.' The lifestyle coordinator raised one eyebrow in sympathy.

What he wouldn't give for a good old-fashioned war movie. If he was ever going to watch *The Great Escape* again, he would have to wait until Netflix added it, or kill off all the ladies. Tempting as it was, he simply didn't have the energy for mass murder.

'Cheer up,' the lifestyle coordinator patted his shoulder. 'We're going to Sunrise Point this morning. Why don't you come along for the ride? The fresh air and change of scenery will do you good.'

Walter pretended not to hear. He wasn't one for the bus. He hated being a passenger of any kind.

'There'll be a picnic . . .'

'All right,' huffed Walter. 'But only if I get to sit near the window.'

'First in, best dressed,' replied the lifestyle coordinator. 'If I save you a window seat, the ladies will accuse me of favouritism.' He ticked his clipboard and added, 'Make sure you go to the bathroom beforehand.'

This place was more like a kindergarten than an old folks' home, Walter thought with a sigh. Craft time, story time, finger food, an afternoon nap. None of them were allowed out to play unless they were wearing sunscreen and a hat. Ironic considering most of the residents had already had more skin cancers removed than they'd had skin. Walter's dermatologist could have bought a nice new BMW by now on the proceeds of Walter's annual barnacle scraping. After scooping out each crusty cancer with his miniature melon-baller, the eerily milky-skinned man delivered his grim yearly reminder about staying out of the sun.

Having allowed adequate time, Walter still managed to be late for the bus. He blamed his agoraphobic prostate that seemed hell bent on confining him to dribbling distance of the toilet. Not for the first time he wished his bathroom floor was sticky with spilled beer rather than drops of pee. The bus queue snaked across the foyer, headed by Judgy Judy. The chances of a window seat were looking slim.

'Ladies and gentlemen,' Sally the fresh-faced receptionist with sparkly nails called from behind her telephone. 'Can I have your attention, please? We're anticipating a short delay in embarkation as Len is having trouble with the clutch. Your patience is appreciated.'

Time was malleable in Woodlands. 'In a minute' could mean anything from sixty seconds to never. Like white-goods deliveries, most things in this place came with a vague time-frame. Even Murray didn't know how long he had left to live.

'The doctor told me I only had four weeks,' he'd told Walter one night after a couple of Johnnie Walkers. 'The only problem is, I can't remember how long ago he told me.'

Walter had laughed at that one and added it to his notebook. He was sure Murray wouldn't mind him stealing it.

With no sign of the minibus, the crowd was growing restless. Sensing a potential situation, Sally suggested a sing-along. She was clearly out of her depth, though, and Eileen hijacked her valiant attempts, leading the crowd in a spirited chorus of 'Why Are We Waiting?' instead.

Walter noticed Fanny Olsen standing in front of the aquarium wearing her signature red bobble hat, incongruous amid the array of sun hats. This time it wasn't the hat that caught Walter's attention. Behind Fanny, the water in the aquarium was bright red. Swimming about in the blood-coloured water, the bewildered fish looked like they were trying to make sense of their new environment.

Red? Walter wondered if he'd burst a blood vessel in his eye – both eyes – until he noticed that Fanny was still human coloured. Her expression, as always, gave away nothing.

Before he could form a question, a gush of air blew in as the automatic doors swished open. There was a collective groan at the arrival of a visitor rather than the eagerly anticipated minibus, a tiny woman, comically dwarfed by an enormous pot plant. It was the Tupperware in her spare hand that gave her away.

'Worried Murray's not getting his greens, Joyce?' Walter nodded to the giant peace lily tucked under her arm.

Joyce's face appeared between the long glossy leaves, like a panda emerging from bamboo. 'Hello Walter, I didn't see you there,' she laughed. 'I'm bringing a bit of nature inside. Did you know that plants improve the quality of the air? I thought it might help him breathe easier.'

Something about the way she said it worried Walter. Anyone could see that Murray was past the point of no return. There was no breathing easier. No getting better. Perhaps this was Joyce's way of coping. Everybody was different. Walter had descended into a brief period of helplessness after Sylvia was diagnosed a second time, followed by a state of heightened activity in which he'd orchestrated every aspect of his wife's care according to a rigid timetable. He would do whatever it took to let her die at home as was her wish. Walter had overseen and coordinated the army of carers and nurses, ticking boxes on his clipboard for every task completed. Ticking boxes was how he coped. But not everyone had been happy with the arrangement.

'You have to fight it, Mum,' Marie had urged, pleading with her to have the chemo and the radiotherapy.

Taking Marie aside later, Walter had delivered a quiet word and asked her to go easy. It was unfair to put so much pressure on her mother, he'd told her. She'd been through enough already and was tired of fighting. *She fought bravely but lost her battle with cancer.* Cancer didn't play fair. It would win in the end, an unconquerable adversary.

'He certainly loves his plants, Joyce.' Murray was always talking about his garden. The only plants in Woodlands were either dried or made from plastic – another win for health and safety.

Joyce sighed, the plant suddenly looking too heavy for her. 'I know. I feel so guilty about him being in here. It's just that I couldn't manage on my own. Not until he's stronger. Once he gets his appetite back he'll be able to put on some of that weight he's lost. His face looks so gaunt.'

Walter winced. It wasn't his place to contradict Joyce. 'He's well cared for in here,' he said, unable to meet her eyes.

'Murray is lucky to have a friend like you. His only other male friends are the husbands of my friends. It's good that he's found one of his own. Men need to talk sometimes too, don't they?'

Walter nodded. Along with a little ribbing, name-calling and assorted insults.

A series of triumphant horn toots heralded the arrival of the minibus. The grumbling resumed, some residents unhappy about the wait, others about the noisy arrival. Taking this as her cue, Joyce headed off towards Bond Street, telling Walter to help himself to the muffins when he returned. One by one, everyone shuffled forward and climbed aboard the waiting minibus using the side door. Walter waited for the crush to die down and for the woman from Marylebone Station to be loaded in a wheelchair through the back on what amounted to a motorised parcel shelf.

Last in, first out.

The last of the passengers were boarding when the DON appeared, flanked by a serious-looking middle-aged couple clutching a Woodlands brochure.

'As you can see, we encourage our residents to go on outings,' Walter heard her say. 'The bus is a popular activity and we visit a number of local attractions as well as hosting picnics and morning teas at various beauty spots.'

You'll love it, Mum, Walter imagined them saying. *Give it a chance.*

It was the DON's turn for a double-take when she saw the aquarium, her gaping mouth and bulging eyes comically mirroring the fish on the other side of the glass.

'Is the water meant to be that colour?' The middle-aged man removed his glasses for a closer look.

'It looks like something has died in there,' said the middle-aged woman.

Sally came to the rescue, darting out from behind the desk. She straightened her Woodlands name badge and clasped her hands.

'It's the new theme for this month,' she said, nervously glancing at the horrified DON.

'Yes,' said the DON, catching on in the nick of time. 'We like to choose a different underwater seascape for the aquarium. This month it's the Red Sea.'

'How original,' said the middle-aged man arching his brows.

'I've called the aquarium company,' said the receptionist smiling broadly. 'They're coming out straightaway to check we have the right shade of red.'

'Jolly good. Now I'm going to show Mr and Mrs Parmington the dining room. Call me when the fish people arrive, would you, Sally?'

Walter was last onto the minibus, having to make do with the fold-down aisle seat. It was a small price to pay for an unobstructed view of the proceedings as the DON tried to explain away what looked like a giant tank filled with blood.

23

Hattie

'I DON'T SEE WHY I HAVE TO GET UP SO EARLY EACH MORNING.'
Hattie's words turned into a yawn. She'd been so close to
dropping off again after her doctor's early-morning visit.

The AIN, who must have been a quarter of Hattie's age,
tutted disapprovingly. The smiley one must be having a day off.

'Routine is important, Mrs Bloom.'

Miss Bloom.

'But I've had the same routine for eighty-nine years. I can't
suddenly change the habits of a lifetime.'

'No excuse for laziness,' the young AIN chastised. 'All the
other residents are up.'

'All of them?'

'Except for the ones who are dying.'

'They're allowed a lie-in?'

'Of course. But you've only broken your hip.'

'I've got an infected leg too,' Hattie pointed out, hoping
it might buy her a few extra minutes in bed.

The AIN shook her head. 'It's ten o'clock and you're still not dressed.'

'I *am* dressed,' Hattie replied. 'In my pyjamas.'

'How about a shower and then you can choose what you want to wear today.'

'Today I *choose* to wear my pyjamas.' And why not? They were comfortable and cool. A most practical outfit in the circumstances and one that saved everyone the upheaval of getting changed. The staff should be thanking her, not chastising her.

The AIN gave up and turned her attention to the bed instead. The sheets were tangled like a knotted handkerchief where Hattie had rotated rotisserie-style throughout the night.

Later, out in the sunny courtyard, Hattie was more sanguine. There was more blue than cloud in the sky and enough breeze to lift the loose hems of her cotton pyjamas. In the brochure, the square of concrete in the centre of the Monopoly board was referred to as a garden. The stacks of CHANCE and COMMUNITY CHEST cards were missing, though there was a sense that anything could happen out here in the unfiltered, unconditioned outside air, the next move as likely to be a SPEEDING FINE as winning SECOND PRIZE IN A BEAUTY CONTEST.

Hattie's optimism dimmed when she headed for the patch of suspiciously green lawn that on closer inspection turned out to be made of plastic. Her slippers gripped the faux lawn like Velcro, real grass presumably too abrasive and grass pollen too toxic for elderly lungs.

Hattie found the perfect spot at the far end of a wooden bench. Sitting in the dappled shade of a vine-covered pergola, she opened her top button to feel the sun's warmth on her chest and rolled her pyjama bottoms over her knees. Sunbeams danced in her unfocused vision. When she moved her eyes the sunbeams followed, though she conceded that given her age, they were more likely to be floaters. The floaters followed a myna bird that swooped in over the top of the wall and landed on the plastic grass close to her feet.

'Hello, little fellow,' she said.

The bird eyed her suspiciously but inched closer, overcoming its fear. The myna was soon joined by a pair of rainbow lorikeets, a squabbling mass of brightly coloured feathers. A timid king parrot landed on the armrest of the bench but didn't approach. The jealous lorikeets took immediate offence and all three took off in a flurry of red and green.

Hattie smiled at their childlike antics.

A rock dove walked like an Egyptian towards her.

'Hello,' she said.

Co-roo-coo-coo, it replied tilting its head.

The sun caught the dove's iridescent purple–grey neck feathers. Even the humblest birds could shine in the right light. Like the myna, the dove wasn't a native species but had made its home here and even thrived. The dove pecked without judgement around her tatty slippers, unfazed by her bandaged leg.

Each species had its common traits: some living in social groups, others solitary. Likewise, each bird had its own personality: some timid, some bold. The corellas with their blue-grey eye sockets reminded her of her perpetually hungover father, while the kookaburras brought to mind Walter Clements, always laughing at his own jokes. There were squabbles over food and territory. Allegiances shifted and mates competed over. Even monogamous partners enjoyed the odd dalliance. From years of careful observation Hattie had worked out how birds interacted. She'd learned their social hierarchies and their peccadilloes. She could read birds, and for decades had reported their behaviour in what was essentially an ornithological gossip column or society page. Humans, on the other hand, remained an enigma.

The sunshine was deliciously warm through the thin cotton of Hattie's pyjamas. She imagined her attire would be mentioned at staff handover. Not that she minded. In fact, she was disappointed the ladies weren't here to see it. With no news on Laurel's condition, it would give them something to talk about. Walter Clements too. He would no doubt find it very funny, and she liked his laugh. The man could be an insensitive oaf but at least he was entertaining. Time passed faster in his company, and with another four to six weeks *at least* until she was allowed home, that was no bad thing.

Hattie turned her face to the sun's rays and let her muscles loosen. She rolled up her sleeves. It was still too early for her skin to burn, and with the bus not due back for another couple of hours she could enjoy the peace and quiet with the birds. In fact, she vowed to make this part of her daily routine from now on. Maybe she would even steal a handful of seed from Icarus's cage for the parrots. She knew she shouldn't feed the wild birds; that she risked them becoming dependent on the human handouts, but the occasional crust wouldn't do any harm. Since humans were systematically destroying both their habitat and food sources, she owed them the odd meal. Besides, Icarus was off his food, more moody and withdrawn than ever without Sister Bronwyn. The residents weren't the only ones missing her.

Hattie's head nodded. She folded her arms loosely and stretched out her legs. Sleep was there, shimmering on the horizon, almost close enough to touch. She headed for the mirage. Step after weary step.

'Shoo!'

Hattie returned to consciousness with a jolt. The DON was standing over her with cartoon outrage sketched across her face. She clapped her hands and stamped her feet in a bird-scaring Flamenco. Walter Clements would be sorry he missed this.

The dove regarded her lazily and didn't move. Behind the DON, a middle-aged couple wore his and hers versions of the same horrified expressions.

'Here at Woodlands we believe that contact with nature is important to the wellbeing of our residents.'

With impeccable timing another dove landed at the DON's feet, followed by another and another. Soon, the courtyard garden was full of *coo-coo*ing grey bodies. The couple, clearly having had quite enough interaction with nature for one day, backed away.

'This is all a little too Hitchcock for me,' said the middle-aged man, shielding his face.

'Let me introduce you to Miss Bloom,' said the DON, rattled but doing her best to project a sense of corporate calm. 'She's one of our newer residents. She's making excellent progress with her rehabilitation.'

'How long have you been here?' The visiting man edged warily between the doves. 'If you don't mind me asking?'

'Since breakfast,' Hattie replied obtusely.

This was the most fun she'd had in ages. Having spent the past eighty-nine years behaving, it was high time for a few shenanigans. With one pyjama leg still rolled over her knee, the other at half-mast, she gave the end of her bandage a tug to free it as she stood.

'Well, it's lovely to meet you, Miss Bloom.' The middle-aged man smiled, rather more than was warranted. 'I'm sure my mother will enjoy meeting you. Her name is Cynthia Parmington. I think the two of you would get on like a house on fire. She loves birds too.'

'I'll be sure to look out for her.'

'You'll have so much in common,' said the middle-aged woman.

Hattie felt the satisfaction of the bandage unfurling and the dressing falling to the ground; what had been hidden beneath it now tingling in the fresh air. She only hoped Cynthia Parmington had a strong immune system.

24

Walter

THE MINIBUS DROVE TWICE AROUND THE CAR PARK AT Sunrise Point like a dog circling a blanket. Walter's hungry stomach fidgeted at the promise of the picnic. He certainly hadn't come all this way for the conversation. Margery, minus her tea-lady shower cap, had come along for the ride, making up the appropriate healthy and safe numbers for the trip, as well as young Jennifer, the lovely lifestyle assistant.

First off the bus, Walter turned and smirked at Judy. 'Last on, first off,' he said under his breath. The lady from Marylebone Station was next, alighting from the rear entrance. The minibus looked as if it had given birth to the wheelchair as it was lowered to the ground. One by one, Jennifer matched the residents to the corresponding walking aid as they emerged. Margery was dispatched with an advance party to set up the morning tea while Jennifer implored the stragglers to stay together. By the time they reached the picnic tables, however, someone was missing.

'Is it Fred?' The lifestyle coordinator was completing a breathless circuit of the picnic area in pursuit of the roaming resident. Walter helpfully drew the staff's attention to a pale blue figure heading off into the bushes.

Walter had always loved picnics; those summer days sitting cross-legged on a tartan blanket with Sylvia. She even had a special dress she liked to wear on their early picnics, a blue gingham sundress with a nipped-in waist. Sadly, their picnicking days were long gone. Now, the tartan blanket was as likely to sit on him, keeping his knees warm.

It was good to be out and about surrounded by trees and, in the distance, the ocean catching the sun like a carpet of tiny crystals. Walter had never been a big one for the great outdoors, golf course excepted. He only wished Murray could be here.

A white minibus decorated in primary colours pulled up in the car park. The doors were barely open when a stream of giggling, chattering children, each wearing a wide-brimmed red hat bearing the logo of a local preschool, spilled out onto the pavement. In all, Walter counted fifteen children, some holding hands, others sucking thumbs, one firing an imaginary rifle towards the Woodlands table. With one clap of her hands, the teacher – wearing an identical hat – had all the children lined up like soldiers on parade. In single file, the children marched to an adjacent picnic table where a helper was already setting up a morning tea of fruit and cheese slices. Meanwhile, another helper set to work building what looked like an obstacle course on the grass nearby, a series of orange plastic cones, balls, buckets and beanbags.

Back on the Woodlands table, Margery had prised the lid from a giant plastic container and produced a pile of paper plates with napkins. For the same reason Walter looked forward to deciphering the soup at lunch and dinner, guessing the 'cake of the day' was another form of cheap entertainment.

Ada, clearly enjoying her own version of the game, leaned in front of Walter to get the first peek. 'Banana bread?'

Judy tutted and elbowed her out of the way. 'It's lemon drizzle cake.'

'Are you sure? I thought we had that last week at the Botanic Gardens.'

'No, Ada,' said Judy as if she were rebuking one of the neighbouring preschoolers. 'That was carrot cake with cream-cheese frosting. Remember?'

Back from his private woodland excursion, Fred wolf-whistled. 'Does it come with whipped cream?'

'And a free stent,' said Walter under his breath. He half expected Marie to pop up out of nowhere and remind him of his triglyceride levels. She'd read about cholesterol on the internet and considered herself quite an authority on inter-mittent fasting.

'You should try it, Dad,' she'd said on the way back from his last appointment with the cardiologist.

'I do fast intermittently,' said Walter defensively.

'When?'

'Between breakfast and morning tea. Then I fast again between morning tea and lunch.' That one had come to him on the spur of the moment. One of his better attempts, and one that would go straight into the notebook.

'Seriously, Dad, it's really good for your metabolic profile.'

'There's nothing wrong with my profile,' Walter had said, sucking in his waist as he fastened his seatbelt. 'You heard the doctor, he said there was nothing else he could do for me.' He hadn't been quite sure how to take the news when the cardiologist discharged him from follow-up. He'd spent the entire journey home weighing up if he should be relieved or very worried.

'Sandwich, Walter?' It was the lovely Jennifer. She was all the medicine a man needed.

'Thank you, my dear.' He helped himself to a sandwich.

Walter wasn't the only one now eyeing up the preschool morning tea, a rainbow of fruit slices, plates of miniature sandwiches with trimmed crusts and a pyramid of mini-muffins. It was all a bit Alice in Wonderland but Walter couldn't take his eyes off the children, each waiting patiently for their turn to fill their plate. The children too had noticed the old people sitting nearby and were watching with equal interest.

When Walter helped himself to some cake, he heard Judy snort derisively.

'You should try cutting down a bit,' she said, licking lemon drizzle from her fingers. 'All those calories will put a strain on your heart.'

'I'll have you know that my cardiologist says my heart is one of the largest he's ever seen,' said Walter proudly, dabbing at his crumbs with a moistened index finger, although judging by the specialist's tight frown, he gathered this wasn't necessarily a good thing. He refrained from adding that the urologist had said the same thing about his impressive fifty-gram prostate. On the plus side, at least his prostate hadn't gone rogue like poor old Murray's.

Meanwhile, it was Fanny Olsen's turn to go AWOL. While the lifestyle coordinator set off on a new search Jennifer tried to distract the remaining residents with more tea. She held the cups while Margery poured.

'It's not looking good for Bronwyn,' Walter heard Margery say quietly. He cupped his ear.

'I can't believe they've sacked her,' Jennifer replied.

'On what grounds?'

'Something to do with duty of care.'

Walter leaned closer.

'I heard it was Laurel Baker's son who reported her to management. She'd been bringing her dog into work without official clearance.'

Jennifer screwed up her face. 'Derek Baker? You mean the creepy one with the beard and that funny rash on his hands?'

'It's called pompholyx . . .'

Ada chimed in. 'Who's got pumpkin lips?'

'It's rude to eavesdrop on other people's conversations,' muttered Walter. He wished she would shut up; it was hard to hear what they were saying.

The two women returned to the tea pouring, lowering their voices.

'It'll be this new health-and-safety thing,' said Margery in barely more than a whisper. 'You know, with the accreditation coming up.'

Walter shuffled along the bench, cupping both ears now.

Margery harrumphed. 'You'll soon need a parachute to fart in that place.'

Fanny Olsen had relocated and was helping herself to strawberry halves at the preschool table. In exchange, a little boy who introduced himself as Lachlan had arrived at the Woodlands table and was showing a keen interest in the grown-ups' cake. Fred wandered over to join Fanny, and a red-headed girl called Chloe joined Lachlan. Soon, the two tables had become one, curiosity eventually winning over fear. Young and old alike enjoyed watermelon chunks and lemon drizzle slices, mini blueberry muffins and ham sandwiches. The adults stuck with cups of tea while the youngsters sipped from brightly coloured water bottles. There wasn't much the helpers could do besides join in. Before long, they were all enjoying one big picnic in the sunshine.

When it was time for the obstacle course, it was only natural that the Woodlands residents would be invited to take part. Fred was game and paired up with Lachlan. Judy, never wanting to miss out, persuaded Chloe to be her partner. Some of the less mobile residents like the woman from Marylebone Station and Ada, who claimed her knees were playing up, were happy to spectate. A shy boy with long dark eyelashes sidled up and slipped his tiny and slightly sticky hand inside Walter's. Walter melted, his lonely skin relishing the child's touch. It was official. He and young Harry were an item.

Forty-five laughter-filled minutes later, it was time to pack away the balls and cones and beanbags and buckets. Judy and Chloe had been clear winners on points ahead of a flushed and breathless but delighted Walter with a doting Harry. Fred, who could barely find his own room at Woodlands, had skilfully negotiated the course alongside his plucky little friend Lachlan to come in a respectable third.

It was all about teamwork, the youngsters were told as the teacher called them to order at the end, cleverly turning the fun into a useful life lesson. Teamwork indeed, thought Walter. A team was more than the sum of its parts. Sometimes the most unlikely combinations could come up with surprising results.

An idea was forming in Walter's head.

THE GREAT ESCAPE FROM WOODLANDS NURSING HOME

'I think we should be getting back,' said the lifestyle coordinator after the prizes were handed out. Judy wore her plastic medal as if it were Olympic gold.

'Listen up, ladies and gents!' shouted the harried-looking lifestyle coordinator as they headed towards the bus. 'Could everybody please stand still while I do a head count?' He paused, and turned to Jennifer. 'Remind me: how many did we bring?'

25

Hattie

'CAN YOU RATE YOUR PAIN ON A SCALE OF ONE TO TEN?'
The new night nurse considered Hattie over the top of
bubble gum–coloured reading glasses that matched her
lipstick. 'I'm trying to work out how many painkillers to
give you.'

It was a harder question than it sounded and not because
Hattie's maths was wanting. 'I'm not really in a lot of pain.
It's very manageable.'

'I need a number, for the paperwork.' Growing impatient,
the night nurse added, 'Zero is no pain and ten is like having
your leg chopped off without an anaesthetic.' She mimed a
sawing action with her ballpoint pen.

Hattie had never had any part of her anatomy sawn off
before, with or without an anaesthetic. An image of the
chainsaws hacking through the limbs of the Angophora filled
her with more pain than the orthopaedic surgeon had when

he drilled through her bones. She imagined the amber sap bleeding from a tree surgeon's clumsy incision.

The nurse was losing the battle to hide her irritation. Hattie noted that she hadn't even introduced herself properly yet, nor was she wearing a name badge like Sister Bronwyn always did. Hattie had asked Walter Clements if he'd met her yet and whether he knew her name.

'Sister who?' he'd replied. And so *Sister Who* she became from that moment on.

'Can I think about it and let you know?' Hattie replied. She hated to be rushed.

'I'll wait.' Sister Who drummed her pen.

Hattie closed her book and tried to concentrate on the pain. Hip. Shin. Which hurt, and how much? The problem was that it varied, so it was difficult to quantify. No pain at all while sitting in her recliner reading *Jane Eyre*. If she got up to walk, then a two or a three, but it wore off once she got moving. Another thought occurred to her as she was about to give her answer. Did everyone feel pain the same way? Was her two the same as someone else's two? There were as many two out of tens as there were residents in here. A Murray two would be different from a Judy two, and as for a Laurel Baker two . . .

'Two,' she replied, hoping this would satisfy the need for a ticked box without being too modest.

Sister Who looked triumphant and returned from the medication trolley with a plastic pot containing a single white pill. 'Here you are,' she said.

'What is it?'

'A painkiller, of course.'

'I don't need it.'

'But you're in pain. Pain can keep people awake.'

In other words, she wanted all the residents asleep on her shift, thought Hattie. Remembering Dr Sparrow's warning about non-compliance and the looming threat of guardianship, she tipped the contents of the plastic container into her mouth and took a sip from her water glass.

Satisfied, Sister Who wished Hattie goodnight and left. As soon as the squeaky drug trolley wheel faded into the distance, Hattie pulled a tissue from the box beside her, spat the white pill into the tissue and threw it into the bin. She pulled her candlewick dressing-gown around her and tied a knot in the belt. It would be another hour or so before anyone checked on her, more if she arranged the pillows under the covers convincingly enough.

Late night was her best time, when she felt most alive and energised, and now, most inconveniently – as far as the new nurse was concerned – awake. She had never been a morning person, something that was unlikely to change now. At home, she would listen to music on the gramophone or tune in to the World Service on the radio in the dark. There were dozens of books on the shelves that she never tired of reading, either curled up in front of the open fire in winter or in the shade of the Angophora's wind-twisted branches in warmer months. Hattie had never been bored. Until now. The rigid routine and endlessly timetabled activities at Woodlands had left her in a state of restless agitation that she could only assume was boredom.

Shielding her eyes against the darkened window, she could make out the faint glow of the bus shelter, and beyond it the parked cars that lined Woodlands Road. She imagined that one or two belonged to staff members, others to the houses opposite. One vehicle in particular caught her eye. It was parked in the shadow between two streetlights, a long car that Hattie's Australian father would have called a station wagon, and her English-born mother an estate. There was nothing particularly remarkable about the car, other than there was someone sitting in the driver's seat, illuminated by the dim interior light. What's more, Hattie could swear that the same car had been parked outside the night before too.

When no one emerged, Hattie lost interest. She wasn't even tired, let alone sleepy and couldn't face another seven hours watching the bedside clock count down to morning. She marvelled at how each number could assume two columns and three rows. The digital semaphore told her it was nearly midnight. Time for a walk.

Hattie passed several residents who, without the distraction of The Night Owls, were roaming the corridors in search of something or someone. Inside The Angel, Islington, a lady cried out for her mother. Northumberland Avenue was calling for a nurse. Fanny Olsen emerged from the laundry cupboard trailing a long white sheet and headed back to her room.

The deserted foyer had a rather mystical atmosphere tonight. Hattie had heard talk of the Red Sea aquarium and hadn't quite believed it until she stepped into its eerie pink glow. Apparently the aquarium people had narrowed it down to ink or harmless food colouring; sabotage rather than mindless vandalism. The mysterious perpetrator remained at large and Hattie took comfort in knowing she had a co-conspirator somewhere amid the ranks of nodding grey heads. Meanwhile, the phlegmatic fish appeared unfazed in their psychedelic tank, gulping and gawking at the outside world, their bulging bug eyes all-knowing and all-seeing. One or two, Hattie noticed, were lying motionless on the sandy bottom, half hidden in the artificial weed. Were they asleep or dead? It was hard to tell the difference unless a tiny scaled body floated to the surface where it was hurriedly scooped out before anyone noticed. Like wilting plants in a doctor's office, floating fish were never a good sign in a nursing home.

The doors at the main entrance were locked, as was to be expected after hours, preventing the outside from getting in and the inside from getting out. Depending on how you landed on this particular Monopoly square, the foyer and reception area represented either IN JAIL or JUST VISITING. In theory, loved ones were free to visit at any time with permission of the nurse in charge. After-hours visits were not encouraged. Nor were after-hours excursions. Tonight, however, Hattie wanted to see the stars, if only for the reassurance that the universe was still infinite. Woodlands was crushing her, squeezing her chest like a pair of giant hands around her lungs. She had to hold on to the idea that life would return to normal, that one day all this would be behind her. She would get home, not just for the owls, but for her own sake.

Residents weren't privy to the security code for the keypad next to the front door. The four digits were whispered, and departing visitors reminded to check who was following them. For all of Woodlands' sophisticated security, Hattie's first guess at the number sequence – the four-digit suburb postcode – followed by the worn # button, saw the doors whizz open. Not so daft, then. Pulling her dressing-gown tightly around her, she headed out into the velvety blackness.

Overhead, the stars lit the sky like a sprinkling of icing sugar. The further she headed down the driveway and away from the foyer, the brighter they shone. Looking back over her shoulder, she saw Woodlands lit up like the golden windows on a Christmas card. It was strange to see it from this angle rather than inside looking out through her bedroom window. She had arrived from the hospital via the back entrance, at the same time as a delivery of commercial laundry. When she left, Hattie vowed she would walk proudly through the front doors. Assuming, that is, she could generate sufficient momentum to escape the nursing home's gravitational pull. And when she did, she wouldn't look back.

26

Walter

WALTER SACRIFICED A BRAND-NEW PAIR OF SOCKS TO DUST the Tesla. With an entire drawer full, he could afford to be extravagant. Cleaning his car was an activity he had never tired of. Until one day he was too tired to do it anymore. Age was like that, closing every avenue of pleasure, one at a time. His dusting revealed a tiny ding where the shiny red paintwork had made contact with Miss Bloom's metal walking stick. Regardless of which party had been at fault, the chivalrous thing to do would be to apologise. He was working up to it but was reluctant to jeopardise their fledgling friendship, relationship, or whatever it was, with a clumsy defence. Until then, he would act sorry, which was essentially the same thing as saying it. Besides, there was plenty of time to find the right words; she couldn't leave Woodlands until her leg had healed. Was it selfish of him to hope Miss Bloom was a slow healer?

Marie had often accused him of being selfish. She had always taken her mother's side, verbalising the things that Sylvia would only think and stew over for days. He wished that once, just once, he and his wife could have had a proper row, the kind they showed on the television. A bit of shouting and screaming, a smashed vase even, followed by tears and kisses. And of course, sex. Sylvia, on the other hand, held on to her silent resentments like a safety blanket, refashioning them whenever she was unhappy. At times like these she was impenetrable, pulling her little arms and legs inside her shell, leaving Walter to decipher her insistence that she was 'fine'. Fine. *Fine.* FINE.

When he was sure the coast was clear, Walter hauled himself aboard the black padded seat and swivelled round towards the steering column. The handlebars were solid in his grip. Surely one little ride round the block wouldn't do any harm? Even less harm if no one knew about it. Every bloke deserved a second chance.

Hanging on the wall, directly in his line of sight, was his calendar. Only a couple of days until Peter from All-Electric Scooters arrived to collect the Tesla.

The tip of Walter's finger circled the empty ignition slot on the dashboard. There must be a way of hot-wiring the engine into life, but electrics weren't his strength. He had an idea the keys were locked away in the treatment room, or at least that was the direction in which Andrea had headed after she'd confiscated them. It was time to stretch his legs.

The more casual Walter tried to act, the more visible he felt, his presence merely amplified by his laboured breathing. Fanny Olsen always managed to draw far less scrutiny. She was by anyone's standards unremarkable – a generic little old lady, the kind you'd struggle to pick out in an identity parade. Perhaps it was her unexceptional appearance that allowed her to acquire all manner of random objects. Umbrellas were a favourite and nowhere was apparently off limits to Fanny, as the chef discovered when an entire set of wooden spoons turned up under her mattress. On one occasion Walter had even seen her trailing a knotted rope.

Passing Sameera in the corridor, Walter greeted her cheerily. 'Good evening, my dear.'

'Good evening, Walter,' she replied. When Woodlands seemed to be one giant revolving door of temporary and agency staff, it was reassuring to see a familiar face. He only wished he could see Sister Bronwyn's too. As expected, Murray hadn't taken the news well. If it were possible, his face was looking even more haggard and his energy was at an all-time low. Murray was sinking fast.

'I'm exercising my heart,' said Walter. 'Like the doctor told me too.'

Not a complete lie, nor was it the whole truth either. Sameera gave him a half-smile. It was past midnight.

At the nurses' station he pretended to read tomorrow's menu long enough to be sure that there was no one around, then he stepped into the hallowed territory behind the desk. It was like peeking through the door into the school staffroom as a kid. There was no time for a stickybeak through the confidential files and papers stacked on the desk; the agency nurse might return at any moment.

One of the staff had left a box of chocolates unattended next to the phone. Only three left. Walter helped himself. Then couldn't resist a second. The final chocolate looked so forlorn Walter ate it and hid the empty box beneath a gossip magazine. The nurses' station was a smorgasbord of pilferable items and he debated stealing a pen too but changed his mind on discovering it bore the name and logo of a local funeral director. Searching for the elusive Tesla keys, Walter rummaged through the remaining items on the desk.

Three pairs of reading glasses.

A dark blue cardigan.

A set of dentures.

No keys.

He stopped to think. The keys were hardly likely to be stored somewhere they could be lost or stolen. The only lockable cupboard was the one in the treatment room where the controlled drugs were stored, the ones that Murray so stubbornly refused. And yet here, no doubt violating every health-and-safety regulation known to aged care, the treatment door was wedged ajar with a cardboard box of incontinence pads. How careless. How fortuitous. Seizing the single piece of good fortune since he'd backed an outsider called Guilty Pleasure in the 3.15 at Kempsey, Walter abandoned his walker and squeezed past the box.

He was no stranger to the treatment room, having suffered the full remit of minor ailments and injuries like any self-respecting man of his age, and yet Walter had never taken much notice of the layout, even sitting back in the big padded treatment chair once a month while the blood pressure cuff strangled his arm. If you took away the desk and chair, the room looked more like a kitchen with a sink, bench tops and rows of wall-mounted cupboards. The question was, where to start?

The first drawer contained syringes and needles, cotton wool, Band-Aids and a tourniquet. The next drawer down was full of dressings and bandages, while the bottom held laxatives, enemas and ominous sachets of lubricating jelly. Walter closed it quickly. All the wall cabinets were locked. One of these was the controlled-drug cabinet but he couldn't tell which. The official ledger in which the staff recorded each dose they administered sat closed on the work surface. If any of the residents were addicted to illicit substances, the chances of them helping themselves unnoticed were slim, if not zero.

Outside, someone called, 'Sameera.' It was the agency nurse, her voice not far away. 'Ada's buzzing in Fleet Street. Could you see what she wants?'

Walter's flabby heart tightened. He'd charmed his way out of a few pickles in his time, but this one? Even if the agency nurse didn't suspect what he was looking for, being caught inside the treatment room could jeopardise his chances of going home early. Walter had to keep his nose clean to make parole. If he wanted to avoid detection, he would have to make a run for it.

Halfway through the door, Walter clipped the cardboard box with his foot. The box shifted and the heavy door clicked shut. This was it. He pictured his hero being marched back to the Cooler in *The Great Escape*. The Cooler King. *Think man, think*. To escape before he was discovered, or stay and have one last attempt to find the keys? What would Steve McQueen do?

The first rule was to stay calm. Walter tried to rein in his breathing but it was impossible to override his body's hunger for oxygen. He'd heard Marie chant to herself when she got stressed: 'In through the left nostril, out through the right.' He stared at a spot on the wall and concentrated very hard on his nose.

The spot Walter's eye found was a small cupboard that looked like a miniature fuse box, partially hidden beneath a tatty-looking eye chart. The bottom right-hand corner of the door was warped, leaving a gap. Could it be? Risking his last remaining seconds, Walter reached for the cupboard door and could hardly believe his luck when it opened towards him. Inside, he found a row of assorted keys, each bearing a plastic labelled tag.

DVD cupboard.

Games cupboard.

Workshop.

Minibus.

Hanging at the very end, he saw the distinctive T-shaped key ring.

'Walter Clements retains his one hundred percent pass rate', he chuckled to himself as he slipped the Tesla keys into his dressing-gown pocket.

27

Hattie

AT FIRST, HATTIE ASSUMED SHE MUST BE HAVING SOME SORT of traumatic flashback. The red scooter was heading straight for her. With no time to scream, she simply closed her eyes and braced for the impact, but instead of cutting her off at the shins like a combine harvester, the scooter came to a standstill a safe distance away.

'Miss Bloom, how lovely to see you!'

Hattie opened her eyes. Walter Clements beamed as if they were long-lost friends.

'What are you doing?'

'Getting a few practice laps under my belt,' he replied.

'At this time of night?'

Walter leaned over the handlebars towards her. 'Better when the roads are clear, if you know what I mean.'

'We'd better get back to our rooms before Sister Who sees us,' said Hattie.

'Ah, *She who shall not be named.*'

'Where have you been? Didn't I see you coming in through the main entrance?' Walter gave her a sly sideways look as they kept pace, taking the long way around.

Is this what it would have been like if I'd had a husband? Not for the first time, Hattie was relieved she had never married, never had to account for her whereabouts. How anyone maintained their independence within a marriage was a mystery, let alone balance the needs of a partner with her own need for space and solitude.

'Getting some fresh air,' she said. A little white lie. Perhaps marriages were built on a series of little white lies.

'At this time of night?'

Touché.

Hattie huffed. 'What are they going to do, shoot us at dawn?'

'Too much paperwork, I imagine,' chuckled Walter.

'Perhaps they might shackle me to my bed. I hear they can do that, you know, if the relatives give permission.' Luckily she had no relatives.

'Even worse,' said Walter, 'they could force you to sit at the ladies' table.'

She relaxed her scowl. Perhaps this congeniality was as much of an apology as she was ever going to get and it was time to lower her expectations. Hattie had every reason to be furious with him, but it was as if a faint current ran between them, two opposite charges. Side by side with Walter, Hattie had the oddest feeling, and not an altogether unpleasant one. She wished she could turn back the clock; that they could be back at The Night Owls on the slow train together. She wanted to know more about *The Great Escape*, and find out what happened to the prisoners after they left Stalag Luft III. How many of them actually made it home?

'Uh, oh, don't look now.' Walter gestured to the large hoist emerging from a room further down the corridor.

'Quick,' said Hattie already retreating. 'This way.'

The scooter hummed behind her. 'Lead the way, Miss Bloom!'

'Keep your voice down. And do hurry.' Hattie ducked into the empty day room and gestured with her walking stick for the scooter to follow.

There was an undeniable degree of the ridiculous about the whole thing, sneaking around like a couple of naughty kids in a geriatric Malory Towers adventure. Sensing company, Icarus stirred in his cage beneath the blackout cover. Hattie heard a flap of wing feathers and the tinkle of his tiny bell. Would he squawk and give them away?

Walter whispered. 'What's our alibi?'

'We don't need an alibi unless we've committed a crime,' Hattie replied.

'Have you?'

'Have I what?'

'Committed a crime?'

'Keep your voice down, Mr Clements, otherwise homicide is a distinct possibility.'

She heard him chuckle again. 'Murder in the dark. My favourite game.'

Hattie listened for voices or footsteps but all she could hear was heavy breathing.

The voices were growing louder.

'Can't you breathe any quieter?'

'It's my heart.' Walter Clements patted his chest.

'What's wrong with it?'

'It's easier to say what's right with it.'

'Valve or arteries?' Faulty valves killed her mother; a faulty artery hastened her father's demise.

'Would you like the list in alphabetical order? A is for aortic regurgitation, B is for bundle branch block, C is for cardiomyopathy . . .'

'Shh, someone's coming.' Hattie heard the squeak of soft-soled shoes on the carpet. She tried unsuccessfully to hook and close the open door with the handle of her walking stick. Instead she shrank back into the shadows and held her breath. To her surprise and relief, Walter held his too.

Icarus was growing restless. Hattie made soothing kissing sounds with her lips. When this only made him more restive, she tiptoed towards the Crystal Palace cage and removed the blackout cover from the cage. The budgerigar calmed and angled his head, eyeing them curiously.

'Please, little fellow,' she whispered, 'be a good boy.'

The shoes squeaked past without stopping. It was only Sameera with the hoist, but even she might question why they were skulking about at this time of night. It would be a miracle if she hadn't seen them. Even in the dark the scooter was bright red. When the oblivious Sameera disappeared into a room, Walter let out a held breath in a giant gush as if he'd been punctured. Hattie's leg ulcer was pulsing with spent adrenaline.

'I've been thinking,' she said when they finally reached Old Kent Road. 'Would it help Sister Bronwyn if we went to the DON and explained what happened?'

'Explained what, exactly? That she encouraged Eileen to dress up as a concubine, fed sugary pastries to a diabetic and used residents as slave labour to do the laundry?'

Put like that, Hattie's idea would have been more evidence for the prosecution than the defence. The less said about The Night Owls, the better.

28

Walter

WHEN WALTER PASSED FRED'S ROOM ON THE WAY TO BREAK-
fast, he noticed a butterfly sign Blu-Tacked to the door. Poor
Fred. Walter wasn't sure if he should knock and say ... what?
Goodbye, so long, farewell old boy? Maybe after breakfast.

Unfortunately, he was too late. In the time it took him to
butter two pieces of toast and drink a cup of tea, the sign
had disappeared. And so had Fred. Walter hovered in the
doorway, watching two AINs strip the bed.

'Sorry, Walter,' one of them replied, arms full of balled-up
sheets. 'Fred passed away in the night.'

Passed away? Fred Carpenter of Carpenter's Antiques, the
Wolverhampton Wanderer, gone? There was no point asking
how or why. The details didn't matter. What mattered was
that Fred had seemed fine at dinner and now he was dead.
The implications were unavoidable. If it could happen to
Fred, it could happen to any of them.

Walter shuffled off, pushing his walker. It felt heavier than usual, or perhaps he did. Residents died all the time. This was a nursing home. It was where people came at the end of their lives. A collective melancholy had settled over Woodlands by morning tea. It was a sobering reminder that they were all mortal and the trapdoor could open under any one of them. For that he wanted to thank Fred. *Time to go home and enjoy what little time you have left, Walt.*

To honour a fallen comrade, Walter crossed his name off the list for the morning's bus trip. Pleasant Valley Gardens would hold little pleasure for him today. He and Fred had exchanged few words beyond an almost daily introduction, but a good bloke was always a good bloke in Walter's book.

Miss Bloom was sitting alone in a corner of the day room playing cards.

'Morning,' he said, trying and failing to sound cheerful. He sank into the other chair at the card table. 'What are you playing?'

'Solitaire.' She didn't look up.

'In that case, I'll keep you company,' he said.

'Don't feel you need to on my account.' She continued sorting the cards.

'It's no trouble.' He rubbed his hands together in anticipation. Her eyes narrowed in response. Good sign? Bad sign? Now he wasn't so sure.

Miss Bloom laid down her cards and sighed. 'Do you play?'

'Not exactly.' Sylvia had enjoyed cards. Walter had preferred his TV shows. Neither of them had been prepared to compromise. Looking back, he should have made the effort to learn. Would a quick game of canasta have even resulted in a trail of discarded garments all the way from the lounge to the bedroom? 'I'm more of a Monopoly man myself.'

He'd meant it as a joke, but before he knew it, Miss Bloom had packed away the cards and unfolded the green Monopoly board on the table. She offered him first choice of tokens. He chose the racing car, naturally, while she opted for the wheelbarrow. Next, Miss Bloom counted out the money while Walter arranged the CHANCE and COMMUNITY CHEST cards in the centre of the board.

'I used to play with my brothers,' said Walter. 'It always ended in a fight.' He chuckled at the memory of split lips and kicked shins.

Miss Bloom, having rolled the highest score with the two dice, went first, her pinched features a study in concentration.

'You know, in the Second World War, the British Secret Intelligence Service used to smuggle maps, compasses and real money to prisoners of war inside special edition Monopoly games,' she said. 'They were distributed by fake charities.'

'Very interesting.' Walter decided to be impressed rather than threatened by the extent of this woman's general knowledge. She had hidden depths. Miss Bloom's waters ran surprisingly deep.

They took turns, shaking, rolling and counting. Miss Bloom's forehead was still creased in concentration as she built houses and read out her CHANCE cards. Walter remembered the endless games he and Sylvia had played with Marie when she was young. *Monotony*, he called it when she wasn't around. Marie, a fidgety little girl, could paradoxically concentrate for hours, ruthlessly building her real-estate empire. Sylvia, he noticed would frequently disappear to put the kettle on and not return, leaving Walter to fake excitement at yet another of Marie's miraculous double sixes. What he would give to have that time all over again.

As the game progressed Walter tried to catch Miss Bloom's glance but she only had eyes for the board. If he had hoped they could take up this morning where they left off last night, he was disappointed. Darkness and daylight each owned a different version of Miss Bloom.

'Did you hear the news?' Walter spoke gently, as he parked his racing car on Trafalgar Square. 'Fred passed away last night.'

Miss Bloom nodded soberly but looked far away. To Walter's frustration, she made even Sylvia look like an open book. He had eventually learned to decode his wife's silences, her daily disappointments expressed in the words she avoided rather than the ones she spoke. Walter liked to think that he was attuned to her feelings, to women in general. But then, he'd always prided himself on being able to read a situation.

29

Hattie

FOR THE SECOND NIGHT IN A ROW HATTIE SPAT OUT THE little white pill and disposed of it. Peering through the curtains she saw the long car parked on Woodlands Road. The same every night, arriving as the staff changed shifts, and gone by morning. Same car, same spot.

Three nights, and still no sign of Sister Bronwyn. Sister Who's words played on a loop. At Hattie's age, 'until further notice' was unnervingly permanent.

On cue, Hattie heard Fanny shout for *Viga*. A buzzer sounded in the far distance, unanswered. The AINs must be busy and Sister Who still on her drug round. Above the usual cacophony, however, Hattie noticed a new sound.

'Hello. Is anybody there?' It was hard to ignore the plaintive cries that seemed just for her.

A man named Murray lived in Bond Street. Usually he was quiet and undemanding, and Hattie, not wanting to intrude on his privacy, had only waved politely on passing. She had noticed how the staff spoke with soft voices around him. Their movements too were gentle and unhurried. His wife visited him every day. Hattie had heard them chatting, puzzling over crossword clues or reading aloud snippets from the newspaper. They were a devoted couple by anyone's standards.

Moments later, Hattie found herself at Murray's bedside. Up close, his pinched cheeks and emaciated limbs looked waxy and yet his eyes were bright and he smiled when she approached.

'Are you all right?'

When her eyes adjusted to the dim light she saw what was a mirror image of her room. The furniture was equally bland, walls covered in the same tree-trunk wallpaper. She imagined all the rooms were identical. Alien to the confused people who lived in them, not one resembling the decor of the homes they must have left behind. No wonder people were confused. But there was something different about this room. The air smelled fresher, cleaner, easier to breathe, even a fraction of a degree cooler than the uniform twenty-three. Unlike every other room, Bond Street was full of plants. The room was alive.

'How lovely to meet you at last.' Murray's slack cheeks stretched into a broad smile. 'I've heard so much about you.'

Heard *what* about her? The generosity of the welcome threw Hattie. 'Did I disturb you? I'm sorry if I woke you.'

'I'm sorry if I woke *you*.'

Hattie shook her head. An understanding passed between them.

'Can I get you anything? A drink of water, or fetch the nurse for you?' She picked at her fingers. Yet again she was alone in a darkened room with a strange man. She felt a frisson of excitement at the sheer inappropriateness of it. Perhaps it wasn't too late to be wanton after all.

'No,' he replied. 'I'm a little lonely, that's all. Sometimes I mistake it for pain.'

'Strange to feel lonely surrounded by all these people,' thought Hattie and said it out loud.

'Do you ever get lonely, Miss Bloom?'

She considered it for only a moment. 'Surprisingly, not until I came here, with all these people. I'm a bit of a recluse, you see. I prefer my own company. Is that wrong?'

'Nothing wrong with that. It takes all sorts. In fact, I read somewhere about a village in Austria that ran a competition to find a replacement when the village hermit moved to the city. The job came with its very own hermitage nestled on the side of a cliff. Nice views, apparently, but very isolated with no heating or running water.'

It sounded like Hattie's idea of heaven. Did that make her a freak? To want to be alone went against human nature, didn't it? It was fine for professional hermits, but for a woman to want to live alone her entire life . . . It made other people uncomfortable. They treated her differently from, say, a widow or a divorcee. To have chosen such a cloistered life was still considered abnormal. Eccentric. Selfish, even. And yet it was duty, a solemn promise to her mother that had sealed her fate as her father's carer. After he'd released her from that burden she'd remained alone, first out of habit, and finally by choice. Solitude had been her destiny all along. But to Hattie, solitude was freedom.

Murray beckoned with a stick-thin arm. 'Would you stay a while?'

He waved towards his empty reclining chair. Hattie was reluctant to deny herself a quick getaway but seeing the grateful smile on his drawn face, she sat. She was soon lost in her thoughts and Murray in his. Neither of them spoke. It didn't feel in the least bit awkward, unlike the silences that Walter Clements appeared programmed to fill.

After several minutes, Murray's breathing changed. Slow and deep and regular. He was asleep. Should she stay or go? Just as she decided to return to her room, she noticed one of his eyes was open. As she moved, the other snapped open.

'Sorry,' she said. 'I thought you were asleep.'

'No, no. Not yet.'

'Do you know that owls sleep with one eye open?'

'Hmm, fascinating.'

Hattie leaned back in the recliner and traced the PVC piping around the armrest with one finger. 'Yes, they sleep with one half of their brain at a time.'

'Makes sense, I suppose. Always on the lookout. Wise old owls.'

More silence. Blissful silence.

Hattie ran her hand through the fine leaves of a potted fern on the windowsill. The leaves tickled her hand and triggered a rush of pleasure. Ferns were such uncomplicated plants. They had changed little since prehistoric times, impervious to fads and fashions or the latest gadgets like flowers or seedpods. They were hardy and adaptable, yet many gardeners pulled them out like weeds. The first plants to spring back after a bushfire. Resilient.

'Did your wife bring in all the plants?'

'She knows how much my garden means to me. I believe she's working on the premise that if I can't get out into my garden, she'll bring the garden to me.'

Perhaps it was her imagination but he seemed to sink deeper into the pillows. Hattie listened as they toured his beloved garden, pointing out his favourite flowers and the names of the bushes and trees. He took her to a painted wooden bench where they sat in the shade of a tall ironbark tree. Murray talked about his plants as she might about her birds.

'I miss my garden too,' said Hattie eventually. It wasn't really a garden now, more of a habitat, but it was hers.

'With a name like Bloom, I dare say you have green fingers.'

'I leave the guesswork and the heavy lifting to Mother Nature,' she said. 'I love discovering what she plants and where. She has quite the knack.'

Murray was staring at the ceiling, smiling. 'I miss pottering. A bit of digging, pulling a weed here or there. Watering is my favourite pastime of all. I'm never happier than when there's a hosepipe in one hand and a hot mug of tea in the other.'

'I think I can understand that,' said Hattie, an image forming of her mother watering those fragile flowers with a look of utter serenity on her face.

'Sadly, I'm no longer even allowed the tea. I have trouble swallowing, you see. They're all afraid it'll go down the wrong way and end up in my lungs. It could kill me.'

'Even the lukewarm dishwater they call tea in here?'

Murray laughed. 'Apparently so. They have to add thickener to all my liquids. It's like drinking wallpaper paste.'

He told her about his family, his beautiful and accomplished daughters. Both now living overseas, one a lecturer in European history at the University of Oslo, married to a

Scandinavian with a pair of flaxen-haired teenagers – his grand-Vikings, he liked to call them – the other running an orphanage in Sierra Leone.

'The irony of teaching them geography from an early age,' he lamented. 'On the plus side, how many people can claim they have eighty-three African grandchildren?' Amid the foliage, his beautiful but distant family smiled back from an array of picture frames.

Next he talked about Joyce and the job he'd loved.

'When I met Joyce, I was fresh out of university. It was my first proper teaching job. She worked in the school office. It didn't take long for the principal to work out why I was always running out of stationery but Joyce barely noticed me. It took me three years to work up the courage to ask her out.'

It occurred to Hattie that the odds of two people finding each other in a world of several billion were infinitesimally small. Especially two people who were alike enough – and at the same time different enough – to stay together for life. Finding a suitable mate must boil down to convenience, of finding someone receptive at the right time. Hattie had never considered that she might have missed out on a relationship. She had enough worldly wisdom to know that there were plenty who settled for the wrong person. In that respect she counted herself lucky. Having never experienced romantic love, she'd never been forced to endure the pain of its loss.

30

Walter

HAD JAMES GROWN AGAIN, OR HAD WALTER SHRUNK? THERE was a shadow now above the boy's top lip and a fresh clutch of pimples sprouting like pink molehills from the pale skin of his forehead. Last week, his grandson had been a child, with long silky hair flopping in his eyes. Today he was a young man, his hair cut short around his neck and over his ears, his fringe now stiff and slicked to one side with what looked like pomade. The trendy new barber had paradoxically given James an old-fashioned short back and sides. Everything old is new again, hummed Walter to himself.

'No school today?' A hug turned into an awkward hand-shake instead.

'School holidays, Grandpa.'

'How was Latin club?'

'Good,' came his grandson's non-committal reply as his fingers worried away at his mobile phone. This was his default, Walter had noticed. Everything was good: his new school, his friends, the expensive ski trip his parents paid for, his first surf lesson, his birthday party, his newly decorated bedroom. Good. All good. If anything, James appeared to exist in a state of perpetual boredom. Nothing wrong with that. The lad needed to loosen up a bit, that's all.

'What do you boys do for fun these days?'

James's face lit up. 'We play Fortnite,' he said.

Walter was about to ask the rules of the game when Marie appeared. 'Dad, have you seen the keys for the scooter?' she said, giving him a perfunctory kiss on the cheek. 'The DON can't find them anywhere.'

Walter's cheeks prickled with heat. He did his best to look confused. 'Keys?'

'Never mind,' said Marie. 'This place . . . I swear . . .'

Marie disappeared again.

'Mum feels really bad about you being here,' said James, not looking up. The phone was in his lap now, his fingertips exploring its edges like a rosary. 'After all that stuff in the papers.'

'What stuff?'

'I don't really know. Something about secret filming with hidden cameras showing old people being mistreated.' With his fringe slicked to one side there was no disguising the crease between his sprouting brows.

Walter was taken aback by the sudden display of insight. 'Not here, mate,' he said with bravado. 'This place is marvellous. The best.'

James looked relieved.

Marie reappeared with a triumphant grin. 'Ta-da! Look what I found,' she said, holding Walter's lost cardigan out as if it were trimmed with ermine. Peter, the vinegary-breathed scooter rep whose hair was a shade too dark, was right behind her.

'Don't worry about the keys,' he said. 'I've got a spare set here.' He jangled them for effect and flashed Marie a smile before striding over to shake Walter's hand. 'You're looking well,' he said. Walter crushed Peter's hand bones in return. Shaking hands with another bloke was always like that, an unspoken duel of hand muscles. A test of character. The measure of the man. Relishing the wince on the younger man's face, Walter recalled the night Marie's first boyfriend turned up to take her out.

While his sixteen-year-old daughter fetched her coat, Walter had run a full safety check on the lad's car, including the pressure of all four tyres, and demanded he show his licence and insurance details. They'd finished with a quick-fire round of road-safety questions that had brought Marie's date out in an unattractive sweat but left Walter satisfied. He'd clapped the boy firmly on the shoulder and wished them a pleasant night. The relationship petered out after a handful of dates, to Walter's – and possibly the young man's – relief.

When they'd exchanged sufficient small talk Peter said, 'Let's get this show on the road, shall we?'

Peter put the keys into the ignition and released the charging cable from the scooter's tiller column.

Marie was busy rifling through Walter's sock drawer, her back turned to him. Had she slipped in extra pairs again? She had wanted for nothing as a child, her feet always cosily clad, so where on earth had this sock fetish come from? It was the elephant in the room in their relationship. But even elephants only had four feet.

'How about a photo?' Walter was on his feet now. 'James, could you take a picture of me on the Tesla one last time? To keep as a memento.' He tried to look suitably solemn, while inside he was fizzing with excitement.

The DON had appeared at the door, sniffing out a potential health-and-safety violation with all the efficiency of a Normandy truffle sow. There was a moment where the pros and cons hung in a litigious thought bubble above her head, before she smiled and said, 'I don't see why not.'

Walter took his time, taking care not to look too familiar with the scooter's set-up. While pretending to adjust the seat, he surreptitiously turned the key in the ignition. James was at the ready, only too eager to use his mobile phone.

'Ready when you are,' said Walter, feeling the steering handles fit into his palms, as familiar as the leather steering wheel of a sports car.

'Smile, Grandpa.'

A broad smile threatened to betray him.

'Back up a little, James,' said Walter. 'Make sure you get the whole scooter in.' James took a step backwards. 'A little more . . . A little more.' With James safely next to the bed, Walter released the handle and the scooter inched forward.

'Steady on, Mr Clements,' said Peter nervously.

'Three, two, one . . .' James leaned backwards, framing Walter and the Tesla.

The mobile phone did an ironic impression of an old-fashioned camera shutter. Walter did his best impression of a confused old man who had accidentally aimed his scooter towards his bedroom door, weaving around the corner of the bed, the chest of drawers bearing the cremation urn and finally, the DON's feet. Peter took evasive action into the open wardrobe taking Marie with him. Walter shot him a warning look as he passed, aiming for the freedom of the open corridor.

'Chocks away!' he shouted. He paused in the doorway to check his wing mirrors. The DON stood rigidly with her hands over her face, trying not to see the paperwork that she would need to fill in. Peter looked as if he'd missed a clear shot at goal, his hands either side of his head. With her arms full of socks, Marie froze, her mouth gaping.

'Go Grandpa!' shouted James, still aiming his phone at the Tesla. Walter vowed to remember forever the grin on his grandson's face.

Flicking his indicator on, Walter looked left, right and left again before pulling out into the corridor. The next two or three minutes passed in a blur. Twelve kilometres an hour felt like the speed of sound, as he accelerated away from the cacophony of calls behind him.

'Walter, come back.'

'Dad, what are you doing?'

'Mr Clements!'

With James's whoops of encouragement ringing in his ears, Walter surged on towards the corner. He braked, chose his line and accelerated out of the bend. The prison guards were hot on his heels. The tasteful landscapes blurred into a single watery mural along the bland white walls, in his imagination the rolling green foothills of the Alps.

Room by room, curious residents peered out. Walter saluted Ada, who screamed. At Bond Street he slowed and called out to Murray, pretending to rev his handlebars when his friend looked up. Murray waved back from his bed, the empty skin flapping on his thin arm like a loose sleeve.

By Fenchurch Street Station, Walter had lost the pursuing posse. The entrance foyer was dead ahead, and beyond the automatic doors, freedom. He had a fully charged battery and nothing else on his calendar. The barbed-wire fence between him and Switzerland was nothing more than a figment of his imagination. He might be circling life's plughole but he wasn't going down without a fight.

31

Hattie

HATTIE WAS MAKING EXCELLENT PROGRESS WITH A FAMILY of magpies when the commotion began. She'd slipped out of the main entrance while the receptionist was restocking the brochure holder and had found a lovely spot on the bench overlooking the ornamental fountain. The youngest magpie, its breast feathers still more grey than black, yodelled a greeting. *Quardle, oodle, ardle, doodle, wardle, doodle.* Alas, her quiet nature encounter wasn't to last. The bird's long beak was millimetres from the crust of breakfast toast Hattie had been patiently holding when the automatic doors burst open to reveal Walter Clements astride his red mobility scooter wearing the jubilant expression of a conquistador.

'Morning, Miss Bloom.' He waved as he passed her.

Without thinking, Hattie waved back. 'Morning, Mr Clements.'

Startled, the magpie flew away. Hattie, on the other hand, settled in to watch the entertainment, nibbling the crust herself.

'Mr Clements, please be reasonable,' shouted the DON who was heading up a sweaty entourage. She looked as if she'd suddenly aged a decade.

'Dad, listen to her,' pleaded a harried-looking woman. His daughter?

Walter Clements, to his credit, remained unruffled. After a full circuit of the ornamental fountain at a comically funereal pace, he stopped and turned to face the slowly assembling crowd.

'Every man deserves a second chance,' he shouted. 'All I'm asking is to be allowed to retake my test.'

Faintly amused, Hattie's fingers found the loose edge of her leg bandage. She poked it back inside. By now, a number of residents had congregated in the out-of-bounds garden. With her front-row view now impeded by grey hair and red walking frames, Hattie stood and elbowed her way to a better vantage position.

'I'm sorry, Mr Clements,' said the DON, who didn't look in the least bit sorry. 'It's a matter of health and safety.'

Never one to waste an audience, Eileen conducted the booing, using a knitting needle as a baton. Like an orchestra tuning, the residents joined in one by one until they were booing in close harmony.

'Down with health and safety!' someone shouted. More boos.

Ada clapped her hands in delight. 'There should be more anarchy at Woodlands, don't you think, Judy?'

'It certainly beats decoupage,' replied Judy, relaxing her customary glower.

'I will not part with this scooter until I'm given a second chance. I want a re-test.'

Re-test. Re-test. Re-test. The crowd chanted.

'Dad, please. You're making a scene.' Walter's daughter wrung her hands, pleading.

The DON inched forward, as if to disarm a terrorist. 'Mr Clements. *Walter.* Give me the keys, and we'll forget this ever happened.'

Out on the road, a bus pulled up at the stop and inquisitive passengers gawped at the unfolding scene.

'Peter needs to take the scooter back to the showroom,' said the daughter, trying a new tactic. 'He's in a hurry, Dad.'

The scooter man looked sideways at her and licked his lips. 'Not in that much of a hurry actually.'

Hattie watched the passengers' heads swivel like owls' heads as the bus pulled away from the stop. A police car slowed to take a closer look. No one was making any progress. It was a Mexican stand-off. Walter Clements versus Health and Safety.

'There will be consequences,' the DON warned. 'For everyone involved.'

Eileen stepped forward. 'What sort of consequences?'

Ada piped up. 'Are we all going to get detention?'

'Or be fed nothing but gruel for a week?' Judy sniggered.

The crowd broke into ironic laughter.

'I wouldn't mind a bit of gruel,' said Ada.

'It would make a pleasant change from rissoles,' said Eileen.

The DON look flustered at the growing unrest. 'This is not an official meeting,' she shouted, struggling to make herself heard above the mounting list of grievances. 'Please keep any comments or suggestions about the food for the catering committee.'

Judy cupped her mouth and shouted, 'We demand pineapple rings on our gammon steaks!'

The crowd began to chant. *Pineapple rings. Pineapple rings.*

Hattie noticed a teenage boy standing on a garden bench with a huge grin on his face, holding a mobile phone aloft. She carved a passage through the walking frames and grey heads to get a better look. The device was some way from his face and thus allowed Hattie to see what he saw, the moving pictures playing on a tiny screen. Walter Clements was starring in his own action adventure.

The DON held out her hand. 'If you please.' This time she sounded like a camel whose back had finally broken under that last straw. The crowd shrank a fraction and a hush descended as residents reconsidered the protest. With a click of her fingers, the DON could change the cream-filled wafers into plain milk biscuits.

'The keys . . .'

Hattie held her breath. Walter Clements had run her over on that damn scooter. He'd sentenced her to four to six weeks of fancy dressings that cost the GDP of a small Pacific nation. He was rude and insensitive, crass and completely oblivious to the most obvious of social cues. And yet she silently clenched her fists and willed him to resist. In that moment, this unlikely hero represented the triumph of age over tyranny.

'The keys, Dad . . .'

To Hattie's horror, Walter Clements turned the key and pulled it out of the ignition.

No. Don't do it.

'All right,' said Walter, a mischievous grin corrugating his face. 'They're all yours.' With that he thrust the keys down the waistband of his trousers.

Sniggers now from Judy, Ada and Eileen. Hattie weaved to the front. She didn't want to miss a second. The impasse continued, the stakes – and potential official paperwork – reaching unprecedented levels.

A new round of placation and cajoling began without any real signs of progress. The DON tried to bribe her way out of the situation with morning tea and extra biscuits for everyone if Walter handed over the keys. A low trick. Seeing straight through it, Judy folded her arms and harrumphed. The DON quickly raised the stakes to tea and *chocolate* biscuits. Ada and Eileen folded their arms too.

Finally, the DON delivered her trump card. 'Happy Hour will be brought forward to four-thirty!'

There were several minutes of consultation culminating in a murmur of approval. The less committed of the crowd began to disperse, leaving only the ladies and Hattie. Walter, however, refused to budge and no one seemed game enough to crash-tackle him to retrieve the hidden keys.

Hattie turned to the teenage boy and said, 'Is that your grandfather?'

The boy grinned broadly, his eyes twinkling. 'Yep,' he said. 'That's my grandpa.'

'He's quite a character.'

'He's awesome,' replied the boy, now holding the phone above his head for a final aerial shot.

Hattie watched him manoeuvre the phone, noticed where his fingers tapped and how he could finish and start a new video with a couple of clicks. It was incredible. She had never seen anything like it and asked the lad to show her one more time. He was so adept. His generation were so at ease with technology, unlike hers. Had technology evolved in response to humans, or was it the other way around, she wondered. Was this evolution in progress?

In exchange for the DON's assurance that he could re-sit his test the following Friday, Walter finally handed over the keys. The teenage boy, wearing the same expression of faint jubilation as his grandfather, handed over his phone to his mother. Sensing an anticlimax, the ladies grumbled among themselves. When it looked as if the show was over, and with everyone resigned to head back inside, someone remarked on the bubbles in the fountain.

The cortege halted in its tracks. The ornamental fountain was indeed full of bubbles. Like Vesuvius, foam frothed from the mouth of the big leaping fish and tumbled over the edge like champagne.

There were bubbles.

A lot of bubbles.

No one apart from Hattie, who had based her life's work on her powers of observation, appeared to have noticed Fanny Olsen hidden in the bushes. No one noticed because at that very moment, a Patient Transport vehicle pulled into the driveway, followed closely by a sporty black car with darkened windows and the number plate DER3K 1.

32

Walter

AT NINETY, LIFE WAS A BLEND OF TINY WINS AND LARGER unforeseen losses. A game of existential snakes and ladders. It was important to celebrate the former while not dwelling on the latter. Walter toasted the Tesla's stay of execution with a sneaky pre-lunch Tim Tam. It was his last, but the news that he could re-sit his driving test was worthy of a little indulgence. Fortunately, he wiped the final crumb from his cardigan seconds before a figure appeared in his doorway. 'Can I steal a moment of your time, Mr Clements?'

How long would the doctor's moment be this week? On the one hand, she was always in a hurry to get back to the surgery, which would leave him with at least a fighting chance of making it to the dining room in time for the soup. On the other hand, when she went to the trouble of finding his medical file, which he could see clenched in her hand, it usually meant a longer visit. Never quite long enough to deal satisfactorily with all his complaints but long enough to risk missing out on the main course.

Walter stood up to greet her. 'Had a busy morning, Dr Williams?' he asked as she stepped into his room. She looked very nice today, but Walter had a vague suspicion it was un-PC to mention it.

'Dr Wilson,' she corrected, already flicking through the loose-leaf pages inside his file.

Walter looked her up and down, wondering why she'd changed her name since last week.

'Right,' said Dr Wilson. 'Have a seat.'

It seemed strange, being invited to sit in his own chair. Another reminder that Woodlands Nursing Home was not his home, however many material items Marie tried to fill it with. There had to be a better way than this. Instead of taking people out of their homes to be nursed, shouldn't it be the other way round? Wouldn't it even be cheaper in the long run?

'Everything all right, doctor?' Worryingly for Walter, she'd pulled up the spare chair and even gone to the trouble of taking his blood pressure herself. He could kiss dessert goodbye.

'Not all right,' replied the doctor when she eventually removed the stethoscope from her ears and unwrapped the Velcro blood-pressure cuff.

Walter frowned. Not more tablets. 'You mean it's too high?'

'Yours is fine, Mr Clements.' But before his sigh of relief was properly expelled, she continued. 'It's the staff who've got the high blood pressure.'

'Really? I'm not surprised with all those chocolates.'

'It's not the chocolates. It's you.'

He smiled broadly. 'I've been known to raise a few blood pressures in my time.' He risked a wink then regretted it when the doctor's eyes widened.

'I've been asked to talk to you about this morning. About your inappropriate behaviours.'

'Behaviours, plural? You mean I have more than one?'

The doctor nodded. 'Apparently they're becoming difficult to manage.'

When he was a lad, his behaviours were easy to manage. A belt across his backside from his father; a ruler across the palms from his teacher.

'In my defence, it's not my behaviour that's inappropriate,' said Walter. 'It's my age.'

'A facility like Woodlands has to have a structure and a code of conduct. The rules are there for a good reason. It's all to do with—'

'Health and safety.' The DON appeared, her jaw set.

She looked less polished than usual, her newsreader hair uncharacteristically frizzy at the ends. It must be the stress of the accreditation coming up.

Dr Wilson and the DON exchanged a few words out of Walter's earshot.

The doctor then appeared to start all over again. 'How have you been feeling lately, Walter?'

Walter wasn't sure how much she wanted to hear. Did she want a detailed account of his physical complaints? Was this social chit-chat, or a potential trap?

'Mustn't grumble,' he replied.

'Appetite good?'

He noticed the doctor glance at his middle. 'Mustn't grumble,' he repeated.

'Are you sleeping well?'

Here, he was perfectly entitled to grumble. 'I'm glad you brought that up. I don't sleep a wink.'

'That's not what the staff report.' She opened his file and produced something called a sleep chart. *Exhibit A.* 'Look,' she said, waving the piece of paper in front of him and pointing to the hours when he was supposedly tucked up in bed asleep over the past month.

Walter wasn't sure how to respond. On the one hand, he didn't want to get Sister Bronwyn into trouble, given that hers were the signatures on the chart. Equally, he didn't want to get on the wrong side of Sister Who.

'I'd sleep much better with a tablet,' he said.

'I don't prescribe sleeping tablets, Walter. I've told you that before.'

'Laurel Baker's GP gives them to her.'

'Sleeping tablets are highly addictive and they have side effects.'

'I'll sign a waiver, if that's what you're worried about.' Honestly, what did it matter if he got hooked at his age?

The doctor seemed to soften. 'I believe in a more holistic approach,' she said.

Walter's throat stiffened. Was it too late to change to a less holistic GP? 'I reckon I'll be fine once I get home to my own bed.'

The doctor adjusted her skirt. 'You're nowhere near well enough to go home.'

'But I *feel* well.' Well enough for the sake of this argument.

'That's not what your test results show.' Dr Wilson brought out a sheet of printed numbers, many of which were marked with an asterisk. *Exhibit B.*

The blood tests. His arms were covered in a bouquet of blooming bruises where the young phlebotomist had stabbed him.

Dr Wilson reeled off a list of numbers that meant nothing to Walter beyond what he already knew: he was stuffed.

'It's the liver function that I'm most concerned about,' said the doctor.

Walter's ears pricked up. 'What's wrong with my liver?'

'Your gamma GT is off the charts.'

'That can't be true, I never drink gin and tonic.' That was Sylvia's tipple. He'd always made a point of serving her one if she was brooding over something he had or hadn't done. It turned her into a different woman entirely.

The doctor closed her eyes and took a deep breath. 'Not G *and* T, Walter. Just *GT.*'

'Excellent,' replied Walter picturing Steve McQueen's shiny 1968 Mustang 390 GT Fastback in his second-favourite movie of all time, *Bullitt.*

Dr Wilson drew her chair a little closer. 'How much have you been drinking?'

'Eighteen glasses of water a day.' Or was it eight he was supposed to drink?

'I'm not talking about water. I'm talking about alcohol, Walter. Booze, grog, the hard stuff. How much? Be honest.'

'On a good day?'

'Yes, on a good day,' she smiled encouragingly.

'On a good day I'd have three or four.'

The doctor frowned. 'And on a bad day?'

'On a bad day I'd only manage two or three.' It was all in the timing.

Dr Wilson wasn't laughing. 'This is no joking matter,' she said. 'Drinking to excess can damage almost every organ in the body, not only your liver.'

'I thought by pickling my organs I might get another twelve months out of them.'

Nothing. If anything, her frown deepened. He was definitely losing his touch. 'Your drinking might be one of the reasons you're not sleeping.' Now this was strange, thought Walter. Only moments ago she'd shown his supposed sleep chart as if she were exhibiting evidence at a murder trial. As if reading his thoughts, she added, 'I never pay attention to these things. Last week I saw a chart that showed a resident had slept peacefully all night.'

'And?'

'I'd signed their death certificate two days earlier.' Dr Wilson gave a wry smile, then a wink. Indeed, it was all in the timing. 'Look,' said the doctor, checking her watch, 'I really have to dash. I'm already late for afternoon surgery. How about we come to a compromise? Hmm?'

'What sort of compromise?' Walter narrowed his eyes.

'A glass of wine at dinner.'

'Come on. Have you seen the size of the wine glasses here? They may as well serve it in a sample pot.' The house white certainly tasted as if it had come from one. 'How about two at dinner? And a nightcap.'

Dr Wilson stood awkwardly in her heeled shoes. 'Look, Walter, my medical advice is not a buffet offering. You can't pick and choose or go back for seconds.' She smiled in spite of herself.

Walter was confident he had the doctor wrapped around his little finger. At this rate, he would be home again in no time. What's more, to his relief, back in the dining room, the ladies were only halfway through their mains.

'Here you go, pet,' said Margery, who'd kept his lunch in the warmer.

'Any chance of more gravy?' Walter used his winning smile.

'It's a *jus*,' corrected Judy with the authority of someone who'd been on a guided coach tour of Europe.

Laurel's broken arm, encased in what looked more like quickset concrete than plaster of Paris, was impossible to miss. The AIN had cut up her meat into bite-sized pieces and she was chasing her food around the plate with a fork in a culinary speedway. She gave up and pushed her plate away.

'The doctor said it was the worst neck of humerus fracture he'd ever seen,' she said. 'It's a miracle my arm is still attached.'

Walter concentrated very hard on his lunch, trying to ignore the reproachful looks from the other table. Now more than ever, he was looking forward to dinner and Dr Wilson's official prescription glass of cabernet sauvignon. A win was a win.

33

Hattie

THE NIGHT STAFF ARRIVED ARMED WITH UMBRELLAS AND raincoats. Hattie had opened her window – as far as the safety catch would allow – to listen for the approaching storm. She loved rain. Loved to hear it on her roof as the frogs *pock-pock*ed in their damp hollows. Loved how it settled the dust and cleaned the air. Loved to watch the birds sip gratefully from puddles and bowl-shaped leaves. She wouldn't always be there to fill her stone birdbath. Hattie had to believe it would always rain.

Second thoughts had always held her back, like trying to swim against a strong current, but she vowed to act on first thoughts from now on. If there was one good thing about getting old it was that there was so little left to lose. A path of dutiful compliance had led all the residents to this low watermark in their lives, and nothing short of an uprising would get any of them out again. In theory, a full-scale mutiny or coup would be easy enough to incite, if a little tricky to pull off. The built-in power imbalance called for a more subtle approach; a coordinated strategy of civil disobedience that would only end when Sister Bronwyn was reinstated and The Night Owls were once again in residence. Walter Clements was waging his own war against oppression, and in Murray, Hattie at least sensed a sympathetic ally. As for the ladies, and Fanny Olsen, she couldn't be sure. Only time would reveal their true allegiance. Until then, she must act alone.

Hattie slipped her coat over her pyjamas and timed her exit to coincide with staff handover. The long car was parked in its customary spot. It was raining, not heavily but enough to shine the footpath. She watched the mist of fine droplets drift across the streetlights. At the bus shelter, Hattie stopped to catch her breath. The last bus had already departed and the road was deserted. So far everything was going according to plan. In a matter of moments, she would have her answer.

The raindrops grew fat and heavy, and in only three or four steps Hattie's hair and feet were sodden. Few things were as miserable as wet feet. She pictured her father in the mud of the trenches, his feet soaking for months. She pushed on, sopping-wet slipper after sopping-wet slipper. The rubber stopper at the end of her walking stick slid over the damp leaves on the slick path. A pause to steady herself, then she was almost level with the car, trying to ignore the cold trickle of water down her neck.

By now she was close enough to make out the voices of a talkback radio alternating with tinny modern music as the driver scanned between stations. She inched forward. When she was within touching distance, the car erupted into a volley of excited barks. A black head bobbed and weaved behind the long back window. Far from fear, Hattie was relieved.

The passenger window opened and a hand beckoned her towards the car. 'Is that you, Miss Bloom?'

Hattie bent forward until her head was level with the open window. 'Hello, fancy seeing you here,' she said nonchalantly.

The door opened and Sister Bronwyn invited her to get in. 'You'll catch your death out there.' She may as well have been offering Hattie a lift home from church.

'Bit wet this evening,' agreed Hattie, settling into the passenger seat with her walking stick between her knees. Queenie poked her broad black head between the seats and panted a fishy greeting, her tongue pulsing like a pink metronome. The front seat was covered in dog hair.

'We need it though, don't we?'

'Certainly do. The gardens need a good water.'

'My lawn is as dry as a crisp.'

'Is it Buffalo grass?' Hattie asked.

'Yes, it's meant to be more hardy. It'll spring back, even when it looks half-dead.'

Sister Bronwyn turned off the radio. She was wearing a navy cardigan over her Woodlands uniform, as if she had arrived ready for work. Only the shift had started an hour ago. And four shifts ago, she had been given her marching orders.

The women sat in silence. It was bizarre and yet not in the least bit awkward. They squinted in the headlights of a passing car, and then the sound of the tyres on the wet road faded. Hattie heard something in the distance, coming from the direction of the open bushland to the north.

Woop-woop-woop-woop.

Sister Bronwyn wound down her window a fraction and said, 'Can you hear the owl?'

'I think you'll find that's a tawny frogmouth,' said Hattie. 'Did you know that they aren't actually owls, they're more closely related to nightjars?'

'Well, well. You learn something every day.' Sister Bronwyn found a packet of jelly babies in the glove box and offered it to Hattie.

'*Podargus strigoides*,' said Hattie, chewing a yellow jelly baby. 'From the Greek word *podagra* meaning gouty.'

A jelly baby squelched inside Sister Brownyn's mouth. 'Gouty, you say?'

'On account of their little feet. They shuffle around as if they've got gout.'

'I could have sworn they were owls.'

'It's an easy mistake to make. They look very similar, until you observe them up close. If you're lucky enough to spot one. They can be hiding in plain sight.'

With a sideways glance, Sister Bronwyn replied, 'Appearances can be misleading, can't they, Miss Bloom?'

'It's easy to put up a front, and unless you correct them, people go on believing what they assume to be true. What they wish was true.'

The windows had begun to steam up and Sister Bronwyn opened all four windows just enough to keep the rain out. She unscrewed the lid of a thermos flask and poured tea into a small china cup, which she handed to Hattie. Pouring the rest into the thermos lid, she stared straight ahead as a volley of fat raindrops landed on the windscreen and coalesced into watery ribbons.

'Everyone knows that Laurel Baker's fall wasn't your fault,' said Hattie.

'Management think otherwise. Her son has an axe to grind.'

'I don't understand. All that fuss over a dog? She wasn't doing anyone any harm. All the residents love Queenie.'

'Not all of them,' said Sister Bronwyn. 'It's not the first time Queenie has been in trouble. When Brendan started doing nights, she hated being left alone. She used to howl all night and the neighbours called the council. The landlord threatened to evict us if it happened again, so I started bringing her in to work. No one objected until she left a puddle on – of all people – Laurel Baker's carpet. She's an old girl; she sometimes does it in her sleep. I was given a caution after Derek made a fuss. This time, Derek insisted they throw the book at me. My employment at Woodlands has been terminated.'

Sister Bronwyn looked crushed. It was true she had broken almost every rule in the book, even if with the best intentions. Unless Woodlands was prepared to re-write the book, there wasn't much anyone could do.

'I'm sorry to hear that,' said Hattie. 'We all miss you. And Queenie, of course.'

'I'll have to tell Brendan soon. We've been going through some financial difficulties recently. His business went under last year and the bank repossessed the house. Brendan had a nervous breakdown and he's only recently gone back to work. This wardsman job is a fresh start for him but we need my income to afford the rent. The lease is up soon and it's hard to find properties with a garden and landlords who'll accept a large dog.'

'So, you haven't told him yet?'

Sister Bronwyn looked into her lap. 'I'll have to, sooner or later. When the paycheques dry up. It's just that he's been doing so well, I don't want to risk him . . .' She trailed off.

It was easy to forget that the staff had lives too. But behind the uniforms, the nurses and AINs, and no doubt the managers, had worries of their own, sometimes even greater than the residents' complaints about the food and the tea and whether there was a pineapple ring on top of their gammon steak. They were human too, and that made them fallible. Everyone was doing their best. Like birds, they had to make do with what they had.

34

Walter

WALTER AND MURRAY KNEW THEY WERE TAKING A GAMBLE.
At least ten minutes had passed since Sameera gave them the
five-minute warning, and any moment now Sister Who would
be along on her round; she wasn't as tolerant as Sameera
when it came to their nocturnal activities.

There wasn't much to see from Murray's window at this
time of night, only the treetops silhouetted by the far-off city
lights. Earlier, from his own room, Walter had watched a
hunched figure head out into the rain, past the bus stop and
then climb into a parked car. He might have assumed it was
a late-night visitor heading home, except the car hadn't driven
away. He'd watched it for several minutes until eventually,
the car performed a U-turn then pulled into the Woodlands
drive and dropped its passenger under the portico at the
main entrance.

Murray's artificially thickened hot drink sat untouched
on the bedside table, a scum already clinging to the surface.

'You don't seem quite yourself tonight, mate,' said Walter. 'Everything all right?'

'I'm tickety-boo,' Murray replied.

'Tell the truth. You're in pain, aren't you?'

Murray's cheeks were as hollow as a sunken pie-crust. Each breath was weighed and measured. 'As long as I'm in pain, I know I'm still alive,' he said.

'Ma-ate,' said Walter. 'Why are you so stubborn? Say yes to the drugs.'

Murray turned his head away. 'It's nothing.'

'There is something rotten in the state of Denmark,' said Walter, 'and we both know it.'

A smile appeared between grimaces on Murray's face. 'So you did pay attention at school, then.'

It was Walter's turn to smile now. 'I'll have you know that I excelled at school. My report described me as "the worst by far of a very inferior bunch".'

'I never doubted it for a moment.' Murray's smile turned more serious. 'Isn't it time to drop the act? Be yourself for a change.'

Walter stared at his knees. 'What's the point? I think it's a bit late to change now. I'm too old.'

'Wait until you get to my age.'

'Now, don't you try to pull that one on me. We're both ninety and you know it.'

'It's just that my ninety feels older than your ninety. Let me remind you that however old you feel today, tomorrow it will seem young.'

Murray smoothed the bedclothes with one hand. The muscles had sunk between his knuckles, making his fingers appear unnaturally long and spidery. Walter had always had large hands, warm and fleshy. But his hands were lonely these days. They longed for human connection but at Woodlands, the only skin he was allowed to touch was his own. He recalled Harry's warm hand in his; a memory he would always cherish.

'I heard about your little scooter escapade today,' continued Murray. 'I overheard two AINs talking about it and Margery kindly filled in the details.'

Walter grinned. At least he was worth talking about. Some days he felt completely invisible. If that was what he had to do to get attention, then so be it.

'Getting a bit of practice before the big day.'

'What big day?'

'You'll see.' Walter tapped the side of his nose. 'It's time we shook this joint up a bit.'

'And that includes putting washing-up liquid in the fountain? You'd better watch it or you'll be in big trouble, my friend.'

'Nothing to do with me, mate.' Part of him wanted to claim the misdemeanour. What was the worst they could do? Throw him out of Woodlands? If only.

'If it wasn't you, then who was it? Apparently the big fish is still spewing Fairy Liquid.'

Again Walter toyed with the idea of taking credit. Secretly, he was peeved; there was only room for one maverick at Woodlands. On the other hand, whoever the mysterious aquarium-dyeing, fountain-tampering culprit turned out to be, it was good to know that he wasn't the only resident in Woodlands Nursing Home's underground resistance movement.

'I have my suspicions.'

'Is the enigmatic Miss Bloom one of them?'

Walter felt his cheeks colour. 'Why do you say that?'

'Come on,' Murray chuckled. 'She's an attractive woman. And single.'

'I'll have you know I'm a happily married man.' He paused. 'At least I *was* happy. And married.' Was that the same thing? He'd been lucky to find that once in his life. It would be greedy to expect another bite of the cherry. 'Sadly, these days I'm more of a trap than a catch,' Walter lamented.

They laughed as they kicked banter back and forth. Noticing that Murray had slid down the bed, Walter hooked one arm under his shoulder and helped him to sit more upright.

'I've been thinking,' said Walter.

'Careful,' smirked Murray. 'That could get you into trouble, my friend.'

Walter returned the smirk. 'I was thinking about how we could get Sister Bronwyn back.'

'And how do you propose to do that?'

'That's where you come in, Murray, old man. I will personally take on the role of operational commander but I'll need a second in command. You'll be responsible for strategy and intelligence.'

'Naturally.'

'We'll need to include Miss Bloom somehow too.'

'Naturally,' Murray raised his eyebrows suggestively.

'I think we'd work well together.'

Murray smiled. 'So, commander-in-chief, do share. How are the three of us – assuming Miss Bloom is receptive – going to pull off this master plan of yours?'

'Let's just say it's still a work-in-progress. Until then, you'll have to trust me.' Maintaining the right amount of confidence was the key. Timid drivers were as dangerous as the overconfident ones.

Murray tipped his head towards a Tupperware container on the windowsill. 'Help yourself,' he said. 'Made to be shared.'

It was the love in those burnt and dried-up offerings that made them special, rather than edible. Here, Walter actually could do something useful. Nibbling at the least concreted corner, he said, 'I had a dream last night.'

'Oh, yes,' said Murray. 'What about?'

'Steve McQueen. *The Great Escape.* I've watched him attempt to jump that fence again and again, hoping that one day he'd make it. Of course, no matter how many times I watch that film, he always ends up caught in the barbed wire and thrown back in the cooler.' Crumbs tumbled into Walter's lap as he took another bite.

'I'm listening.'

'Last night I dreamed that he made it. He cleared that fence at last. Do you know what this means?'

'That's an easy one. It's your subconscious desire to escape from your imposed incarceration in an aged-care facility.' Murray looked pleased with himself.

'Thank you, Dr Freud,' said Walter, 'I think I worked that one out for myself. No, that's not the strange thing. The most extraordinary part is not even that I remember the dream, it's that I actually had a dream.'

'I'm not with you, Walt.'

'To dream, I must have fallen asleep.'

35

Hattie

ON THE WINDOWSILL, HATTIE'S SLIPPERS WERE SOGGY AND stained. She left them where she hoped the AINs wouldn't ask too many questions, then she dressed and headed to breakfast. The dining room was bathed in the gentle apricot of morning sun. However, the ladies were already griping between themselves by the time she arrived. Their arguments always started like Newton's balls clashing backwards and forwards until the pendulum lost momentum and the bickering finally stalled.

Hattie took her customary place at a separate table and waited to be served. Walter Clements was late. As usual by the time it arrived, the toast was cold. Her late-night foray had left her with something of an appetite and she slathered the cold toast with butter. Or rather, she managed to butter two-thirds of the slice before running out.

Hattie managed to catch the AIN's eye. 'I'd like some

more butter please,' she said. The ladies exchanged looks, making her feel like Oliver Twist asking for more porridge.

The AIN nodded and disappeared.

'They never put enough in these things,' Hattie muttered.

Laurel was trying to scoop Weet-Bix using her left hand, while Ada poked about in her muesli as if searching for broken glass.

'Sultanas don't agree with me,' said Ada by way of explanation.

'But you eat grapes, Ada,' Judy pointed out.

'You're thinking of raisins, Judy.'

Laurel said, 'Sultanas and raisins are both made from grapes.'

'What about currants?' Eileen reached across Ada for the jam.

'What about them?' Judy sounded irritated.

'Currants are berries, surely? Red currants, black currants.'

Hattie spoke up without thinking. 'Sultanas and raisins are both grapes. And so are currants, small, red seedless grapes of the Zante variety. They came from Greece originally. But since grapes are technically berries rather than fruit you're both correct.'

Silence fell around the dining room as everyone waited for Judy's reaction.

The saliva dried inside Hattie's mouth. She could cope with being invisible, her presence unnoticed by this group of women. In fact it suited her just fine. But this morning was different. All eyes were on her.

To Hattie's surprise, Judy said, 'Thank you, Miss Bloom.'

The clink of cutlery on crockery resumed and Hattie could breathe again. One by one, the ladies glanced approvingly in her direction. The AIN returned with more butter packets and dealt them out like a croupier.

'I agree with Miss Bloom, they never put enough in these things,' Eileen looked over at Hattie as she said it and smiled.

The scraping and crunching and slurping fell silent. Hattie swallowed. She examined the empty plastic container. 'It's a terrible waste of resources to package something as simple as butter.'

Margery said, 'Don't you worry, Miss Bloom, these are all heading for landfill.'

'All that plastic! Can you imagine how many butter containers there are still in the ground?' Judy replied.

'It's destroying the environment,' said Hattie, finding her voice. 'Our generation invented plastic but now it's choking the planet.' She pointed to the discarded butter containers. 'We need to do something about it before it's too late otherwise that's how we'll be remembered.' Not for penicillin and air travel, sending man to the moon and ridding the world of smallpox, but by filling it with toxic materials.

The ladies began their own discussion about plastic, weighing up the usefulness against the travesty of everything from Tupperware to bin bags, yoghurt pots to polyester undergarments. The pinnacles of twentieth-century chemical engineering all now destined for a dubious immortality.

Eileen joined in. 'Remember Jacques Cousteau? What would he make of all that rubbish in the oceans now?'

'I prefer David Attenborough,' said Ada. 'He always wears that nice blue shirt.'

'But what about the French accent? I love a French accent.' Laurel swooned at the far end of the table.

Judy rolled her eyes. 'He's British, Laurel. He's good friends with the Queen.'

'I'm talking about Jacques Cousteau.' Laurel attempted to stand her ground. 'He's French.'

'*Was* French. He's dead, Laurel.' Judy pursed her lips.

Eileen rescued the conversation. 'What's your answer to the butter situation then, Miss Bloom?'

'I think they should serve it on washable crockery plates. Woodlands would save a fortune and it would be much better for the environment.'

Greeted by a unanimous nod of approval, the butter suggestion was a conversation stopper, in a good way for once. The ladies finished breakfast in silence. Once or twice Hattie debated bringing up the subject of Sister Bronwyn and her circumstances. To do that she would need to break Sister Bronwyn's confidence, but if she could only play on Laurel's sympathies, she might get Derek to retract his complaint, or even lobby for the return of the facility's most popular staff member. Sister Bronwyn was the cement that held Woodlands together. Without her, morale was at an all-time low. The Red Sea aquarium and foaming fountain were surely only a taste of things to come. With accreditation looming, management was understandably edgy but at the same time, Woodlands Nursing Home was hamstrung.

Back in her room, the tatty slippers had dried. There was a hole in the sole and it was almost impossible to tell what colour they'd once been. Comfortable and familiar as they had become, the slippers were hanging together by a thread.

36

Walter

THE PAINTING MARIE ARRIVED WITH WAS A STEP UP FROM the urn. It was one of Sylvia's favourites, a landscape in oils, not very valuable, the artist not well known, but as the interior walls of the house were his wife's domain Walter had dutifully banged in the nail.

'I thought it might brighten up your room,' said Marie.

'Thanks, love,' said Walter, accepting a kiss on the cheek.

James appeared next with a small side table. 'Where shall I put this?'

Marie fussed, placing the table first under the window and when that didn't work for her aesthetic eye, she moved it to a bare wall near the door. Standing back to admire it, she seemed pleased. It wasn't one of Walter's favourite pieces of furniture. Another of Sylvia's bargains.

The painting was a nice gesture but there seemed little point inconveniencing the handyman to come and hang it. Besides, it didn't really suit the cool white walls and grey carpet of his room. The decor at Woodlands had no doubt been chosen to neither offend nor appeal. More health facility than care facility. Why would Marie go to all this trouble to fetch things out of storage? Why now? Was there something she wasn't telling him?

Walter was almost relieved when Marie turned to the sock drawer and James took up his usual semi-recumbent position on the chair. He watched his daughter unwrap yet more black socks, pairing, balling and lining them up like soldiers in his drawer. She was getting worse. It dawned on him the whole thing had started when she pointed out that hole in his sock at Sylvia's funeral.

'Leave that for now,' he said. 'Come and have a chat.'

She was like a butterfly that refused to land on a single flower. Walter wished they could just spend time together, but every visit had its own agenda, a list of tasks that needed to be ticked off. It was exhausting.

'I will in a minute,' she said without looking at him directly. 'I need to have a word with . . .'

She was gone.

Walter studied his grandson. When the school holidays were over it might be weeks until he saw James again. The downy wisps of puberty had already darkened above his top lip. The hormonal juggernaut was unstoppable. Would he even recognise his only grandchild the next time he came?

'Thank you for carrying the table in,' said Walter. 'It was very thoughtful of your mum.' *Thoughtful*. And a complete waste of time. They'd only have to cart it back again when he went home.

'There's more stuff in the car,' said James.

More? 'What kind of stuff?'

'More pictures, a rug, that blanket that Grandma crocheted.'

Walter was uneasy. Even more so than when he looked at the urn taunting him from the chest of drawers.

James produced the mobile phone from his pocket, a grin hijacking his face and turning him into a little boy again. 'Want to see the video I took? Of you on the Tesla?'

The boy's thumbs flitted over the screen and as if by magic wound the clock back to Walter's moment of triumph. Together they watched the unfolding drama, heads close, giggling as Walter defied all attempts by the staff – and his daughter – to coax the keys from his hand. When the key ring disappeared down the front of his trousers, they both laughed out loud.

'This is even better than Netflix.'

'You watch Netflix? That's sick.'

Sick, Walter remembered, meant cool. 'Yes, my mate Murray has a subscription.'

James regarded him curiously, as if his grandfather having mates was even harder to believe than that they watched Netflix together.

'What did your mum say? About the thing with the scooter keys?'

'Not much,' said James. 'Here, look, this is the good bit.'

He held the phone for his grandfather as the shot panned out, taking in the fountain. Walter watched the frothing geyser of foam topple from the mouth of the fish and cascade down the stone plinth. He saw the smiles as the ladies scooped the bubbles and played like children seeing snow for the first time. James had captured their shrieks of delight, the laughter bubbling as brightly as the fountain. Then the video cut to a close-up of Fanny in her bobble hat, half-hidden in the foliage. What was that in her hand? Walter willed the camera to zoom in on Miss Bloom as she watched thoughtfully from the sidelines. Instead, the video came to an abrupt stop with Marie's distinctive voice, 'James! Put that thing away.'

'You've got quite an eye for cinematography, James.' The way he framed the shot, zoomed in to the action, panned around the crowd to capture the reactions – even Walter could see the boy had talent. 'Have you ever thought about being a filmmaker?'

James's face lit up. 'I'd like to,' he said. His mother reappeared and James's shoulders slumped.

'I was telling James he should study film,' said Walter.

'He's thinking about law or engineering,' she replied. James stared at the floor. 'He's getting extra maths tutoring every Wednesday.'

James tried to put the phone surreptitiously back into his pocket but it was too late, Marie had spotted it and swooped like a bird of prey.

'Mum! Please . . .'

'It was your last warning, James. I told you to delete that video. Grandpa doesn't want to be reminded about the whole embarrassing episode.' Marie confiscated the unnecessary reminder. 'One week. You know the deal.'

Scowling, James slid further down in the chair, his arms folded. Should Walter say something in the boy's defence? He didn't get the chance.

'We'll go and fetch the rest of the stuff from the car,' said Marie, placing the contraband on the bedside table. 'Won't be long, Dad.'

Walter interjected. 'Hang on a moment, what's going on?'

Marie looked sheepish. 'I thought you'd like a few more of your old things.'

Sylvia's old things. All Walter's things were either here in this tiny wardrobe or still hanging up in the garage.

'Tell me what's really going on. All this stuff.' He looked around, frowning.

'Dad,' said Marie rolling her eyes. 'Not this again.'

James shrank into his chair. Marie sat on the edge of the bed. At least she'd landed long enough for them to have a proper discussion.

'Once I've passed my scooter test, I'm going home,' said Walter. 'That's what we agreed.'

'What *you* agreed. We don't think it's a very good idea.' *We.* In other words, Andrew had put her up to this. She continued, 'You're still unsteady on your feet and the house is on two levels. You'd never cope with the stairs.'

'I could live on the ground floor.'

'The bathroom is upstairs.'

'There's a toilet and a sink downstairs.'

'In the laundry. Come on, Dad, be realistic. It's not suitable for your needs.'

What did she know about his needs? What he needed was independence, not a power shower and a dual-flush toilet. He could piss in a bucket and stink to high heaven as long as he was free to make his own decisions.

'I'm perfectly capable of looking after myself. I used to do a lot around the house. Ask your mother.'

It was too late to take it back. Marie looked away. 'I'm sorry, love,' said Walter, softening his voice. 'That was insensitive of me.'

'It takes more than mowing the grass once a month to survive on your own, Dad. It's obvious you can't go home. We have to talk about the options, realistically. Andrew has looked at your finances and it's not looking good.' So, Walter's instincts were correct. 'Your savings are almost gone. The house will have to be sold.' Marie wouldn't face him. When she eventually turned back, her eyes were red and puffy.

Sold? He and Sylvia had scrimped and saved to buy that house. It had taken them thirty years to pay off the mortgage; fifty years to add the little touches that made it their home. He'd laid the patio, re-laid it a couple of years later when Sylvia tripped over a wonky slab with the washing basket and broke her wrist. He'd painted every hard surface in that place, first in magnolia, then at Sylvia's insistence in Devonshire Clotted Cream, which to his eye was exactly the same colour. They'd conceived Marie in that house, brought her home in a carrycot through that front door, waved her off with her backpack from that doorstep. The only thing that had kept him going through the dark grief-stricken days at Woodlands was the constant assurances that he would go home one day. Once he'd recovered.

The words were lost before he spoke them. Mute, he watched the first tear tumble down his daughter's cheek.

'Come on, James, give me a hand with the other things in the car,' Marie said, now smiling bravely. 'I've brought your golf trophies, Dad. I thought they'd look nice on that little side table.'

She grabbed a handful of tissues from the box on the way out. James looked at Walter for a moment unsure whether to defend his mother or side with his grandfather. 'We'll be back, Grandpa,' he said. 'I promise.'

Alone, Walter listened to the sounds of another day at Woodlands. The squeak of a trolley somewhere down the corridor. A resident calling out. The infernal drone of unanswered buzzers. A bus pulling up at the stop on the street and then driving away.

His world was shrinking; about to shrink even more. He'd reached the pointy end of the funnel and there was only one way out. Marie had Power of Attorney and her husband was an accountant; the sale of the house was a fait accompli. She was only doing what she thought was right, what any daughter would do in a situation like this. But that didn't make it any easier for him to stomach.

Sylvia's painting looked small and insignificant leaning against the wall and the table incongruous amid the standard washable, wipeable Woodlands furniture. No, he couldn't let this happen. Things would change once he passed his scooter test; she would see things differently then. In the meantime he needed to hang on to his last thread of hope. It was time to take things into his own hands, to be the master of his own destiny. It was his duty to try.

Walter's eye settled on James's mobile phone. It was within reach and he was sitting on the perfect hiding place among the remaining empty bottles and Tim Tam wrappers. It would be a whole week before anyone would notice it missing. An idea had come to him. It was bold, audacious even, but it was time to think big. It was time to jump the barbed wire, if not on a Triumph TR6 Trophy disguised as a BMW R75 motorcycle, then on the next best thing.

37

Hattie

HATTIE LEANED ON HER WALKING STICK AT THE BEDSIDE, willing him to move, to take a breath. Murray's eyes were closed and his jaw slack. She hadn't heard him call out this evening and had gone to check on him, finding his silence more disconcerting than his shouts for company. Her fingers hovered above his pyjama sleeve. She wasn't ready for the same cool, unyielding flesh she'd recoiled from on the morning she woke to find Mother dead in bed beside her.

Her father's night terrors had terrified them all. The years had done nothing to soften the awful images that woke him nightly, sweating and screaming. Even the whisky was no match for the ghosts of the Somme. After dark, they came for him wherever he hid. In turn they came for Hattie and her mother too.

The moon was late to rise the night her mother's heart stopped, casting spectral shadows through the open bedroom window. The branches of the Angophora tree beckoned like ghoulish fingers.

'Why does Father have such bad dreams?' Hattie had asked.

Mother pulled her in close. 'Everybody has bad dreams from time to time. There were things that happened in the war, things he's seen that were upsetting.'

He was still fighting that war, many years after the guns had fallen silent, Hattie understood years later. It would defeat him eventually. 'We need to be kind to him, show him lots of love,' her mother continued. 'He fought the Great War to keep us safe and now it's our turn to keep him safe. Promise me you'll always look after your father. Even when I'm not here.'

'I promise,' whispered Hattie. It seemed an easy promise to keep when like every eight-year-old child she had believed her mother would always be there.

When Mother's breaths evened and her arm fell slack, Hattie lay awake, listening. Outside she heard the wind whistle as it caught the stiff gum leaves. Air was silent on its own, she realised, only heard when it came across an obstacle; a tree, a creaking window pane, or the damp insides of her mother's lungs as she slept. There were other strange nocturnal sounds that might have been frightening for a child of eight – owls hooting, possums hissing and rustling in the eaves – but Hattie found the sound of nature comforting after the manmade wounds that caused her father so much pain. She liked to think the birds and the frogs were there to protect them all. Daddy's birds, she called them. There was another sound that she found comfort in too. Her mother sounded different from her father.

Whoosh-dub. Whoosh-dub. Whoosh-dub.

Hattie turned her ear towards her mother's chest and listened for the sound of her heart. It was love rushing around her body, she'd once told little Hattie. 'You can hear how much I love you,' she'd said.

But in the morning, with the moon a sinking apparition and the sun setting fire to the Angophora tree, the love had fallen silent. Hattie's mother was cold and stiff beside her while her father slept, warm and drunk in the next room. A sore throat as a child, Hattie learned years later, that had led to rheumatic fever. Years too early for the new wonder drug penicillin. A generation too early for life-saving surgery that could have replaced those damaged heart valves.

Murray opened his eyes. Hattie released the breath she didn't know she was holding.

'Joyce?' Murray licked his lips.

'No, it's Miss Bloom. I'm sorry I woke you.'

He yawned. 'I'm glad you did. Plenty of time for that on the other side.'

Hattie hovered at the bedside.

'Would you like some company?' It wasn't a totally magnanimous offer. She liked Murray's room. Facing the reserve rather than the car park, Bond Street was quieter than Old Kent Road. With all the plants and greenery, it was fresher than hers. The more she got to know him, the more she liked Murray too. She enjoyed their conversations. Like her, he wasn't one for small talk.

Murray nodded and gestured to the chair. 'I'm afraid I did all the talking last time. Now it's your turn, Miss Bloom. Tell me something about yourself.'

Compared to Murray's accomplishments, his interesting career and family, her life had been unremarkable. She'd kept herself alive for almost ninety years. That was an accomplishment, she supposed. Beyond that, her world was small and to an outsider, she imagined, uninteresting. Hattie tugged at a loose thread and a tiny white button popped off her pyjama top and disappeared into the dark. She owed Murray something special, something she'd never told anyone else. She owed him a precious pearl, the essence of who she was.

'I have a secret,' she said, examining her lap. 'I've always preferred birds to people.'

Murray's eyes widened and he started to laugh. Seeing her face fall, he stopped. 'How intriguing. Do tell me more.'

'Birds are so much easier to talk to than people.' Hattie edged forward in the recliner and as she spoke, her hands joined in. 'I mean, most of them are fairly shy to begin with. It takes time to build up trust. But once you have that, you'll have it for life. They're my only family.'

'Tell me about your family, Miss Bloom.'

Hattie told Murray about the pair of pink galahs, the clown-cheeked corellas and the bossy rainbow lorikeets. She told him about the owls and the Angophora tree.

'When my father built our family home, we were surrounded by bush. One by one, other houses started to appear, and little by little, year after year, we lost our sense of space and privacy. My parents kept themselves to themselves and we never really got to know our neighbours. I began to see them as interlopers. I wanted to be left alone. I think they saw me as some sort of eccentric old woman and they left me alone too. That suited me just fine. I had the birds for company, you see. They are easy, uncomplicated. Basically they are only after food. There's no ulterior motive, no hidden agenda with birds. I could trust them in a way I couldn't trust people.'

'People can be trusted too, if you give them the chance,' said Murray.

Hattie considered his words. 'I'm beginning to realise that.'

'It's hard to make yourself vulnerable, isn't it? Feels wrong, I imagine. When you've been so independent all your life. Look at me. I was head of department at a high school. I am a justice of the peace, a father of two accomplished women and a grandfather. Now I need a twenty year old to wipe my backside. Even a cup of tea might kill me!'

'Oh, I'm sorry,' said Hattie. 'There's me going on about the stupid neighbours and you're . . .'

'Dying. It's okay to say it. It's the truth. And it's pretty easy, actually. All I have to do is lie here.'

Hattie winced, his parchment skin was pale and luminous in the dark. At least she could still look forward to going home, eventually. Murray had nothing to look forward to. He would never see his beautiful garden again. Never enjoy the refreshing taste of a hot cup of tea.

'I've told you all my secrets,' said Hattie brightly, rubbing her hands together. 'Now it's your turn to confess something.'

It struck Hattie that everyone who reached this age had secrets. She had been more honest with Murray than she had ever been with herself. Perhaps it was easier. She thought about Fanny and the secrets that made her scream in the dark and call out for the mysterious *Viga*. She thought about Sister Bronwyn, who would rather spend the night in her car than tell her husband she'd lost her job. Even Walter Clements, for all his superficial charm and joviality, was covering some deeper insecurity. No one got through life without a few scars. The exception might be Murray. He looked like a man who had made peace with himself. Woodlands had brought them all together, these people with nothing more in common than their secret pain. Perhaps it was holding on to that pain that made humans unique.

'I do have a confession to make,' he said. 'I'm so terribly ashamed of myself. I've been keeping it a secret for over sixty years.'

'What is it?' What could be so awful that he was only ready to utter it on his deathbed?

'It's to do with Joyce, my wife,' he said, unable to even look Hattie in the eye. 'She's the most terrible cook.' Murray appeared to melt with relief as he sank deep into his pillows.

38

Walter

TELEVISION WASN'T WHAT IT USED TO BE. NOT EVEN NETFLIX could match the great detectives and private investigators of the 1970s. *Starsky & Hutch*, *Kojak*, *The Rockford Files*, *Columbo*. He would often switch between channels to watch more than one at a time, much to Sylvia's annoyance. Her preference had been for antique shows and escaping to the country. Looking at the painting Marie had brought in, Walter wondered if he had ever really known what had gone on inside his wife's head.

Bored with second-rate celebrities lying about on hammocks in the jungle, Walter extinguished the television with the remote. He drummed his fingers on the arm of his chair, circled his thick ankles and yawned. Another nine hours before breakfast. Was it too much to expect to fall asleep two nights in a row?

The mobile phone lit up on the table. The thing had a life of its own, buzzing, beeping and flashing up messages every few minutes. Walter wondered how James could ever concentrate on anything else. How excited Walter and his brothers had been with their tin cans and string. Technology had come a long way since then.

His fingers searched for a tumbler filled with ice-cubes and found instead his water glass, filled with water. He missed the warm glow spreading through his veins with that first sip, the way his muscles loosened around his neck and shoulders as the alcohol took effect. The way his vision blurred and the world slipped into soft focus. He missed that. Rather than sit here and feel sorry for himself, Walter decided to walk off his lack of alcohol. Pausing as he always did outside Murray's room, he heard voices. It was too late for Joyce; her visiting hours revolved around the bus timetable and so she never stayed past five.

'Joyce doesn't drive,' Murray had told him. 'It's her eyes. Macular degeneration.' Two words that drove fear into the heart of everybody over seventy.

Walter listened, ear to the door straining to hear the woman's voice interspersed with Murray's. Could it be her?

'Knock, knock,' he said pushing the door with the front wheels of his walker.

His eyes adjusted to the dim light and his heart leapt. He was right; it was Miss Bloom sitting in the recliner while Murray lay propped up against a throne of pillows. A feeling Walter didn't recognise stabbed him in his guts. Jealousy? How ridiculous.

'I must be going,' she said, moving to stand. 'I'll leave you two to it.'

'No, please don't go on my account,' said Walter. Had that sounded too desperate? Too needy?

'Come in, Walt. Come and join the party,' Murray beckoned.

Walter parked his walker halfway between the bed and the recliner, and settled his backside onto the seat between the handlebars. Murray shifted position and his pressure-relieving mattress emitted a series of whooshes and whistles.

'You're looking better,' said Walter. It was a relief to see his friend sitting upright at least. People rarely died sitting up. 'You missed gammon steak at dinner.'

'Pineapple ring?'

'No, but I'm thinking of starting a petition,' said Walter.

'Giving democracy another stab?' Murray asked with a laugh.

'Assuming civil liberties apply to pineapple rings, that is.'

Murray's chuckle faded. 'What's happening with the master plan?'

Walter straightened up. He didn't want to look ineffectual in front of Miss Bloom. 'It's in the procurement phase at the moment.'

Miss Bloom weaved her fingers. She looked as if she wanted to say something but as usual kept it to herself.

'It's as if the usual laws don't apply in aged care,' said Murray. 'It's a case of out of sight, out of mind. Even prisoners of war have the Geneva Convention.'

'It's not as though we're completely helpless though, is it?' Both Walter and Murray turned to look at Miss Bloom. 'Everyone expects so little of us, expects us to be completely incapable. That's our secret weapon. Our disguise, if you like.'

'Go on,' said Walter.

'We could use it to our advantage.'

'To get pineapple rings, you mean?'

'No, to get Sister Bronwyn back,' said Miss Bloom with a look of faint exasperation. 'She's been given her notice.'

'How do you know?'

'I know. Trust me on this.'

'So, we're stuck with Sister Who,' said Walter.

'Unless we can get rid of her somehow,' said Miss Bloom. 'But even if we do, Woodlands will go straight back to the agency for a replacement.'

'Agency staff cost a fortune,' said Murray. 'The DON was complaining about it to Joyce the other day. The shareholders won't take kindly to the night-staff budget eating into their bottom line. That's why they'll want to make Sister Who permanent as soon as possible.'

No one spoke as they weighed up the consequences.

'Not if we can dig up the dirt on her,' said Walter eventually.

Miss Bloom frowned. 'What dirt?'

'I don't know yet. That's what we have to find out.'

'You've been watching too many cop shows, Walt,' laughed Murray. 'She might be a bit brusque but she doesn't strike me as a miscreant.'

'Nobody goes through life without breaking a few rules,' he said. 'It's a matter of finding which ones Sister Who has broken.'

'Even if we had her convicted of murder, it wouldn't bring Sister Bronwyn back,' said Murray.

'One step at a time,' said Walter rubbing his hands together. 'Let's work on Sister Who together and leave the rest to me.'

Walter produced his notebook from his dressing-gown pocket. After several minutes of intense thinking, they still hadn't come up with a plan. To all intents and purposes, the new night nurse was a model employee. She did her job swiftly and efficiently, and she was pleasant if not overly friendly to the residents. No doubt she had all her boxes ticked before she left each morning too. And it wasn't as though she brought a mangy old dog to work or entertained the residents with exotic dancing and poker nights. Maybe Murray had a point: Walter had been watching too many cop shows.

'I don't know if I'm imagining it,' said Murray tapping his chin thoughtfully with his finger, 'but I overheard two people talking.' He sounded hesitant, as if in two minds whether to even say it. 'I was stuck in the bathroom waiting for someone to help me back to bed. I didn't see who it was but the door was open and it sounded like Sister Who talking to a man. They sounded very well acquainted.'

'A man? There aren't any male nursing staff on overnight,' said Miss Bloom.

'What about Derek Baker?' suggested Walter. 'He's been hanging around this place like a bad smell since Sister Bronwyn left.'

'It could have been him, I suppose. They were saying something about "the usual arrangement". When he left I heard him say, "That's my girl."'

For several minutes, the three wrangled the possibilities. This should have been right up Walter's street but there wasn't much to go on. The clues weren't exactly showering down like they did for Magnum PI. Walter stroked his non-existent Tom Selleck moustache and just as self-pity threatened to get the better of him, he felt a pulsing sensation in his pyjamas. Then he remembered the phone in his pocket.

'What's that?' Murray asked when Walter retrieved the phone.

'It belongs to my grandson, James,' he said. 'His mother confiscated it. And I sort of confiscated it from her.'

'Can I see?' Miss Bloom held out her hand, to Walter's surprise. He handed over the phone, reluctantly.

'It's marvellous what technology can do nowadays, isn't it?' said Murray. 'Kids today are so comfortable with it.'

Walter thought about the satellite navigation in his car that he had stubbornly refused to use. It was bad enough having to accept directions from Sylvia sitting in the passenger seat – he was damned if he was going to let some young automated woman give him instructions.

'Yes,' Walter agreed, 'but have you met anyone under fifty who knows how to use a slide rule?'

Murray chuckled. 'Good point, Walt. Same goes for a map and compass.'

'Or an abacus,' said Walter.

Miss Bloom tutted. 'Abacus? Where did you grow up, Mr Clements, Mesopotamia?'

They all laughed at that. Walter said, 'My grandson told me there's something called an app on it that ages your face and makes you look old.'

'There's one of those in the bathroom,' chuckled Murray. 'It's called a mirror.'

Walter smiled but found himself staring at Miss Bloom, her face illuminated by the telephone screen.

She looked up and straight at him. 'Date of birth?'

He told her, buoyed by the fantasy that she might be planning a birthday surprise, or deciding that he wasn't too old for her after all. But she merely rolled her eyes.

'Not you,' she said. 'Your grandson. What's *his* birthday?'

He struggled to remember. He only had one grandchild – one child – and he'd forgotten his birthday. He'd missed Marie's most recent birthday too, he now realised. Eventually

Walter managed to recite the correct birth date and Miss Bloom unlocked the phone. He sighed in secret admiration.

'Where did you learn to do that?' Murray sat up taller, then shuffled his buttocks further back until he was sitting almost upright.

'I watched James do it,' Miss Bloom replied. Walter and Murray exchanged glances. 'While he was filming your scooter escapade. Honestly, don't you men ever pay attention?' The men grinned sheepishly.

'Well, well,' said Walter. 'There is no end to your talents.'

Her fine fingers danced across the screen. 'Here it is,' she announced, turning the screen for Murray to see. The scooter circling the fountain, the Mexican stand-off, Walter shoving the keyring down his pants, the DON's face. By the time the footage reached Eileen's spirited chorus of boos, Murray was laughing so hard he began to cough. Soon he was wracked by spasms that came from deep in his lungs. Walter didn't know whether to give him water or pat his back.

'Are you all right, mate?'

When he finally caught his breath, Murray said, 'I'm fine. In fact, I'm much better for having had a good laugh.'

When the video panned out to show the ladies covering each other with washing-up bubbles, Murray let out a great guffaw. 'It looks like someone has beaten us to it. We aren't the only ones waging a war of subversion,' he said on seeing Fanny hiding. 'I think we all have our suspicions as to who the culprit might be.'

The orderly arrived with the hot drinks trolley. If he was surprised to find three residents in Murray's room instead of one, he didn't say so. He poured them each a hot chocolate,

Murray's thickened with some form of gloop, and left with a knowing smile, shutting the door behind him with a soft click.

'Here's to the Underground Resistance,' said Miss Bloom raising her steaming cup.

'The Velvet Revolution.' Murray touched the side of the other cups then set his aside.

Walter joined the toast with his unsteady hand, spilling hot chocolate onto his favourite paisley slippers. He looked around at the three of them dressed in their pyjamas. They were an unlikely bunch of freedom fighters, undercover agents or whatever they wanted to call themselves.

'To the flannelette and velour revolution,' he toasted.

39

Hattie

It was past twelve when Hattie left the boys in Bond Street and headed back towards Old Kent Road. By now the hot chocolate was well and truly surging through her veins, the plucky little milk proteins no match for the sugar molecules. She wouldn't sleep for hours. It would take several circuits of the Monopoly board before she was even ready for bed. Serving anything beyond plain warm milk made no sense this late at night, especially when accompanied by a biscuit. Without Sister Bronwyn to corral the midnight wanderers, Woodlands was asking for trouble.

Dr Sparrow had visited again that afternoon. He had left her with his worrying frown and an addition to her drug chart. A new antibiotic. According to the doctor, her bug was unusual. Unprecedented even.

'We haven't come across this strain at Woodlands before,' he said. 'The good news is, it's not a superbug.'

Hattie was a tad disappointed. She'd never had a

super-anything before. She would have to make do with unusual. Uncommon. A rare bird.

Unfortunately, while she'd been plotting in Murray's room, she'd missed the late dose of the special antibiotic for her unprecedented bacteria. The doctor had been adamant she should take it regularly and although she abhorred the very idea of taking a chemical to destroy a living creature, albeit one that had claimed squatters' rights on her leg, she knew it was a means to an end. If her leg didn't heal, she couldn't go home.

'Two capsules every eight hours,' he had instructed the nurse.

'Wouldn't it be better to let the air get to it?' asked Hattie as Dr Sparrow ordered the dressings be reapplied straightaway.

He shook his head. 'Not in this . . .'

Hattie saw Sameera leaving Fleet Street with a bundle of soiled bed sheets under her arm. The AIN smiled but didn't say anything, seemingly content to deal with only one drama at a time.

Ahead, at the nurses' station, Derek Baker was leaning on the desk, chin resting on his hand, legs casually crossed. Hattie had noticed that his mother liked to listen to the radio at this hour but tonight the only sound coming from Laurel's room when she walked past was the rumble of snores.

Sister Who frowned on seeing Hattie. 'What are you doing out of bed?'

Hattie gripped her walking stick. 'I think I'm due my antibiotic.'

Sister Who looked irritated. 'You'll have to wait. I only have one pair of hands.'

The hands were a given. 'I'll wait,' said Hattie.

'It's easier if I come to you. Several of the other residents need medication too.'

So, Sister Who hadn't discovered Hattie missing from Old Kent Road. She hadn't even started the drug round yet. Which begged the question: What had she been doing?

Hattie sniffed the air around Derek Baker. The laboratory-created chemical molecules of his cologne cloyed in her nostrils. He looked in no hurry to leave, as if he had taken root. Hattie was in no hurry either.

'Well, then,' said Derek, the first to crack, 'I'll leave you to it.' He took a couple of steps then glanced over his shoulder. 'Goodnight,' he smiled, crookedly.

'Goodnight Mr Baker,' Sister Who called after him.

He stopped a little way down the corridor and bent down to tie his shoelace.

'Back to bed, Mrs Bloom, or I'll have to ask the doctor to prescribe much stronger sleeping pills.' She narrowed her eyes suspiciously.

'Remind me where my room is,' said Hattie, leaning more of her weight onto her walking stick than was necessary, making it wobble in her hand.

'Old Kent Road,' said Sister Who. 'How about I take you there?'

'No, that won't be necessary,' said Hattie. Walter was still in Bond Street with Murray. She couldn't do anything that would raise suspicion.

Everyone expects so little of us, expects us to be completely incapable.

'Old Kent Road, you say?' Hattie turned and headed off towards her room. 'Old Kent Road, Old Kent Road,' she chanted, as she deliberately weaved along the corridor.

That's our secret weapon.

40

Walter

LIKE ALL GOOD STAKEOUTS, WALTER WOULDN'T KNOW WHAT he was waiting for until it happened. Unfortunately, after two-and-a-half hours, whatever it was still hadn't happened. In his customary position in the main foyer, he patiently recorded every coming and going. The problem was that things simply came and then went again – a delivery man in a yellow shirt, the podiatrist, an engineer about the telephone black spot, and Ada heading off to the ophthalmologist with her daughter, then returning in dark glasses. None of it was comic material, and none of it would see Sister Bronwyn reinstated. Having lost interest, Walter heard the lunch bell and headed to the dining room, where he found Miss Bloom at her usual table, engrossed in a book while the ladies prattled on about the perils of a stray cauliflower floret that had evaded the soup blender.

'Am I disturbing you?'

She tore her eyes away from the page and gave him a weak smile. 'Hello Mr Clements. I didn't see you there.'

Abandoning his walker, he pulled a spare chair from the ladies' table and dragged it over, turning the table for one into a table for two. 'Do you mind?'

Miss Bloom placed her open book down on the tablecloth with a soft sigh.

'Have you seen Murray today?' he asked.

She told him she hadn't.

'I'm worried he can't hang on much longer.' Hanging on. Even the strongest wills couldn't hang on forever. 'Do you know what he said to me the other night?'

Miss Bloom shook her head.

'His only wish before he dies is to see his garden again. How sad is that? His wife bringing in all those plants.'

'Is he really too weak to go?' she asked. 'Can't Joyce take him for one last visit?'

'She had to give up her licence on account of her eyesight. I suppose there's a taxi – you know, one of those special ones that can take a wheelchair.'

'Poor Murray. I wish there was something we could do.' Then she looked around the other tables and, lowering her voice, said with not a small amount of conspiratorial interest, 'Laurel Baker's son was hanging around the nurses' station again last night.'

'The mongrel.' Walter tutted. 'Sister Who might not be my favourite person in the world, but she has the right to get on with her job without being hassled by the likes of Derek Baker. I've a mind to go and have a word with him. Some people have so little self-awareness.'

'That's the odd thing,' said Miss Bloom. 'She didn't look as if she minded him being there. In fact, they looked very cosy together. I wouldn't be surprised if Derek Baker's dutiful son act was merely a cover.'

Walter looked at her. 'You think they might be having an affair?'

'It's possible,' she replied.

Walter sat and digested this information more easily than he would digest the upcoming meal that the nervous new volunteer was ferrying awkwardly to the table. Then, as soon as the shy youngster had moved away, he said, 'I've got the answer!'

'I hate to disappoint you Mr Clements, but Alan Turing beat you to it a long time ago.'

'I've worked out a way to get Sister Bronwyn back,' said Walter, like a small child who had learned to whistle. Or a man who had cracked the Enigma Code.

He managed to raise only one of her eyebrows. He would have to try much harder if he wanted to impress the unimpressible Miss Bloom. Around them, the staff cleared away the plates and cutlery from the tables. One by one, the ladies walked past the table-for-two, exchanging suggestive looks and nudges.

'We need to catch Sister Who and Derek Baker in a compromising position,' said Walter.

'*In flagrante delicto?*'

'In where?' said Walter, confused. 'We'll take the evidence to management and Bob's your uncle.'

'And tell me again how we're going to capture this evidence?'

Walter reached into his pocket and pulled out the mobile phone. Remembering James's comments about the secret filming, he waved it next to his grinning face.

'There's not much battery left,' said Miss Bloom, taking the phone from his hand. 'See these little bars here? It's almost flat.'

Walter deflated a fraction. It was Sylvia and the off-grid camping trip all over again. What was it with women? Always finding a hole in the plan. He was a man and therefore a problem-solver. He would remove a couple of batteries from the TV remote and no one would be any the wiser. Women were always trying to complicate simple things.

Turning the phone over in his hands, he searched for a place to insert the AAs. Where on earth did they go? The whole thing was wafer thin. Even AAAs would be too big. Did they even make AAAA batteries? It wouldn't do to let the doubt show. As commander of this mission, it was his duty to instil one hundred percent confidence in his men. And woman.

'Now then, Miss Bloom,' he said slowly and deliberately, 'you leave the finer details of Operation Night Owl to me.'

'And in the meantime, Mr Clements, keep your eyes peeled for a phone charging cable.'

Typical woman. Always had to have the last word.

41

Hattie

THE RENDEZVOUS WAS SCHEDULED FOR 2200 HOURS, WITH Murray's room officially designated headquarters. It was important, she and Walter had agreed, for Murray to have a role, however vicarious. Indeed, he'd perked up considerably since they briefed him on the plan, offering solid encouragement between bouts of coughing. Yet another cup of wallpaper-paste tea had gone cold next to him. Meanwhile, as the operation's commander chattered and fidgeted like a child on Christmas Eve, Hattie began to harbour suspicions that he was some kind of fantasist. Was Walter Clements really a Walter Mitty in disguise?

They ran through the plan once more. Walter sketched a wobbly diagram on the back of yesterday's menu to illustrate their assigned positions. His hand was shaking, less than a few days ago but still enough to render the diagram little more than a series of meaningless squiggles. She didn't want to hurt his feelings, and neither it seemed, did Murray.

'Good luck,' said Murray, shaking them both by the hand. 'God speed.'

'Ready, Miss Bloom?' Walter and his walker were coiled in anticipation, like a horse and jockey in the starting gates.

'Ready,' Hattie replied, securing her leg bandage. They couldn't afford any mishaps.

Walter whistled his way to the nurses' station, every now and again glancing sideways to wink at Hattie.

'Do try to look less illicit, Mr Clements,' she hissed.

He stopped whistling and mouthed an apology. For all his self-proclaimed knowledge of detectives and private investigators, Hattie had never met someone less capable of nonchalance. He might as well wear a big sign round his neck spelling out what they were planning to do.

Sister Who was busy on the computer, and as they approached, Hattie considered aborting the mission. Having wasted valuable time trying – and failing – to agree on a safe word they were all happy with, they had no alternative but to keep going.

With Walter efficiently obstructing the view from the desk, Hattie eased into position, slipping behind the table and vase of twigs that passed for a decorative display. The bare branches and dried flower heads weren't to her taste but the scaffold of woody stems did provide the perfect tripod for the mobile phone.

Hattie's heart thundered in her chest and her hot skin prickled with anticipation as Walter apologised to Sister Who for interrupting her. They were on.

'Where exactly is the pain, Walter?'

Walter indicated the general area of his belly.

'Is it sharp or dull?'

'A bit of both, really,' he said.

Sister Who appraised his clinical condition over the top of her pink spectacles.

'Do you need the doctor?'

Walter shook his head. 'No, not really.' When she started to look uninterested, he added, 'Possibly. What would you suggest?'

To give him credit, Walter was excelling in his portrayal of an annoyingly vague old person, allowing Hattie to fiddle with the controls of the phone unseen. How had James started the video recorder? She ran her finger down the sides of the phone looking for a start button.

'I'm feeling it in my chest too,' Hattie heard Walter say. When she glanced up he was circling his breastbone with his fingers. Sister Who's eyes widened. What a stroke of genius. If there was one thing that was guaranteed to get the staff's immediate attention, it was chest pain. It was a gamble. Used sparingly, it was like dynamite. Overdone, and it could see Walter crying wolf. Or worse, whisked off to hospital.

The nurse suggested an ECG, prompting Walter to quickly add that the pain had moved to his knees. And possibly his elbows too. Well done, Mr Clements. He was doing well. A few more seconds.

'Good evening, Sister.' Hattie started at a voice. She shrank behind the vase of twigs as the target approached the nurses' station.

'Evening, Mr Baker.' Sister Who acknowledged him with what Hattie decided was a coquettish tilt of her head. 'Look, Walter, why don't we see how it goes. If you're still in pain tomorrow, we'll ask the doctor to visit.'

She shooed him away and turned her attention back to Derek.

'Mum asleep?' she asked.

'Like the proverbial baby,' he replied.

In Woodlands, they all slept like babies: waking up every couple of hours, screaming or hungry. Hattie imagined Laurel, drugged to the eyeballs, snoring on her back in her Mayfair penthouse so as not to disturb her hairdo.

Hattie sidestepped out of her hiding spot and into Walter Clements' shadow – for once, his considerable bulk was an advantage – and neither of them dared to look back until they were safely past Liverpool Street Station. If Sister Who was on to them, she didn't let it show, apparently too interested in her after-hours visitor. With any luck, Operation Night Owl would garner enough proof to see Sister Who hauled into the DON's office for inappropriate conduct. With Sister Who gone and Derek Baker seen for what he really was, Sister Bronwyn would have her job back straightaway. Admittedly, it was a long shot, bordering on complete fantasy, but Walter Clements had been so adamant it would work. And, well, neither Hattie nor Murray had come up with an alternative.

Rounding the corner they saw Sameera coming out of Bond Street. Perhaps Murray had simply needed a bathroom trip. She smiled almost apologetically and Hattie considered letting her in on what was going on; after all, she must be missing Sister Bronwyn too. But no, they couldn't risk implicating her.

When five minutes had passed, they reconvened. Murray would expect a debrief, and as this part of the plan hadn't been agreed to in advance, they needed to decide how long was long enough to discover what they didn't even know they were looking for.

'I'll go and check on progress,' Hattie whispered.

'No, I'll go,' Walter whispered in response.

'I'm faster than you. Less chance of getting caught.'

'I couldn't possibly put you in danger, Miss Bloom.'

'I was the one who planted it.' Never having had to negotiate the ownership of toys with siblings, Hattie was at a disadvantage. But she was catching on fast.

'It's my phone.' Did his chin jut out, just a little?

'Your grandson's phone, to be precise.'

'Exactly. My responsibility.'

Both still insisting they save the other the bother, she and Walter set off, as if the starter's gun had fired. Hattie's hip was sore but she was soon into her stride and overtaking her opponent. With great satisfaction she heard his heavy breathing fade behind her.

'I tell you what, Miss Bloom,' she heard Walter wheeze. 'You go ahead. I'll man the HQ and keep an eye out for Sister Who and update Murray.'

Not wanting to share her smug grin, she waved but didn't look back. Walter would claim it as his victory if all went according to plan, and if it didn't, she imagined he would shift the blame onto someone or something else. After a period of careful observation, Hattie was beginning to understand how the alpha male of the species operated.

42

Walter

WALTER BEAT A RETREAT TO BOND STREET AND WAS GLAD to sit down. All this cloak-and-dagger stuff was exhausting. Murray was coughing; it sounded as if he were trying to push one of Joyce's rock cakes up a steep slope. Would a manly slap on the back help him to dislodge it, or would he cause serious injury in the process?

'Miss Bloom won't be long now,' Walter said, drumming his fingers on the handle of his walker. 'The camera is in position and it's only a matter of time before we find out what they've been up to.'

'She's an impressive woman,' said Murray. He was giving Walter that look again. What were they, fourteen-year-old boys?

Unsure how to reply without giving himself away, Walter said, 'She's not bad on her feet, all things considered.' *All things considered.* At their time of life, everything came with a caveat.

They listened for the familiar shuffle of Miss Bloom's slippers on the carpet, returning with the phone. And, they hoped, the evidence they needed. But Walter's anticipation was edged with apprehension. He had been so carried away with phase one of Operation Night Owl that he hadn't stopped to consider what came next. As commander, however self-appointed, it was his job to keep up morale. He couldn't allow the slightest hint of self-doubt to show.

'She'll be back any minute now,' said Walter, as much to reassure himself as his friend. When Murray started to cough again, it was almost a relief to have a task. Walter helped him to sit forward, gently patting the human glockenspiel of ribs that was his back. Ever the gentleman, Murray turned his head away as if to spare Walter the disease that was slowly consuming him. The cough subsided, leaving Murray spent against the pillows.

'There you go, mate,' said Walter. When scalpels and drugs could no longer tame the snarling beast, only kind words were left.

Surely Miss Bloom should be back by now? Walter pushed his walker backwards and forwards around Murray's bed. Soon exhausted from the pacing he sat down and drummed his fingers instead. He shouldn't have let her go on her own. Yet again he'd backed down, as he always had with Sylvia. The thing with women was to use a bit of reverse psychology, to let them think that he'd thought it was his idea. It worked every time. Men weren't as stupid as women assumed they were.

'Joyce has made scones,' said Murray absently. He waved a spidery hand in the direction of a Tupperware container on the table.

'Cheese or fruit?'

'Difficult to say.'

They lapsed into silence again. Eventually Walter lifted the plastic container lid and helped himself, as much to give his hands something to do. Where *was* Miss Bloom with the phone? He should have insisted on staying and supervising. On the other hand, wearing her usual brown habit she was well camouflaged, hiding behind the vase of twigs while the video recorded.

Murray's breathing changed. Out of nowhere, he grasped at Walter's hand.

'I'm frightened,' he said.

Walter squeezed Murray's bony hand in return. It was an odd kind of a handshake for two men but it felt right. 'She can look after herself. As you pointed out, Miss Bloom is a very impressive woman.'

'Not that. There's been something on my mind and I don't know who to talk to about it.' The words caught in his throat, making him splutter again.

'I'm here, mate,' said Walter, his voice more breath than sound. 'Talk to me.'

'We've watched a lot of movies, you and me, haven't we?'

'Yes, not to mention binged several Netflix series together. I'd say that conveys a special status on our friendship.' Seeing Murray's eyes turn glassy, Walter was desperate to keep things light. He wasn't prepared for tears. Not yet.

'How many deathbed scenes have we watched in which the hero says all the things he's been meaning to say, how he's managed to put everything right and tell his family that he loves them? They're all like that, aren't they? Like the births on TV, all perfect and beautiful. Well, I've sat with Joyce through two deliveries and I know it's not reality. You'd be surprised by some of the words she came out with, my little Joyce. Well, what if it's not like that at the end? What if there isn't time for all those profound words because I'm drugged up and don't even know she's there? What if Joyce is stuck on the bus and doesn't get to hear that I love her? I may never get the chance to say goodbye.'

Walter squeezed Murray's arm. 'Trust me,' he said, 'everything you need to say in those last minutes will already have been said. In the years you've spent together, every night she's put her cold feet on yours, and in all the trinkets and scatter cushions you've pretended to like. Joyce knows you love her, and as a man who knows women, I can tell she loves you. If you can get to this point in your marriage without needing to say you're sorry, you are a lucky man. And Joyce is a lucky woman.'

'Thank you.' The tears slid from Murray's sallow cheeks onto the pillowcase.

'There's always more time to catch the bus than you think,' Walter smiled.

'When was the last time *you* caught the bus?'

'Me? About 1964, if I remember correctly.'

The moment ended when Miss Bloom burst in holding the mobile phone aloft like an idol. 'Ta-da!' It glowed in her hand and cast her in an ethereal light.

'Good girl,' said Walter.

Miss Bloom's triumphant expression changed to a scowl.

'You've done it!' said Murray. 'Well done.'

'Bring it over here and let's examine the spoils.' Walter tried to take the phone from Miss Bloom, but she gripped it tightly. Her prize. He relinquished his hold and they crowded around Murray's bed while she coaxed the technology to life.

'Watch this.' Miss Bloom pressed a tiny triangle and the video started.

There were muffled voices in the background, rustling sounds. The screen was pale, and the images blurred. Walter saw Miss Bloom frown as her own face came into focus, staring inquisitively at the camera. A moment later she was gone, the foreground lined with ornamental twigs and in the background, a simple white wall.

'I don't understand,' Miss Bloom began. 'Where is the nurses' station? The camera was pointed right at it.'

Murray looked from one face to the other as if watching an invisible tennis match. 'What does it mean?'

Walter remembered something. James had taken a photo of the two of them, holding the phone at arm's length before it was confiscated. By pressing a symbol, he'd turned the screen into a mirror. What had he called it again?

'Did you take a selfie, Miss Bloom?'

'A what?' Her face was blank.

'There's a button that turns the camera round. I think that's what must have happened.'

She sucked her teeth. 'Darn it.'

Walter swallowed hard to prevent himself saying, 'I told you so.'

Murray said, 'Never mind, there's always tomorrow night.'

'Tomorrow night,' Walter echoed. 'Same time, same place?'

It was a good sign. Murray was talking about tomorrow night. All he needed to stay alive day after day was a reason to. If anything, this was a good thing, though he would never say that to Miss Bloom.

Simultaneously, all three reacted to a noise from the corridor. An unmistakable *squeak-squeak*. The medication trolley. Sister Who. She was calling to Sameera, asking her to take Fanny to the toilet. That meant she had reached Oxford Street. The next along the corridor was Bond Street. Murray's room.

The door was ajar and Walter could already see the moving shadows. There was no way he and Miss Bloom could get back to their rooms without being seen by Sister Who, who was less accommodating than the other staff when it came to socialising after hours. Behaviours would be duly recorded, and strategies put in place. Another visit from the doctor.

'Quick,' said Miss Bloom, scuttling around the bed with her stick.

Walter could have done with more warning but struggled to his feet. Only his heartbeat was quick these days. Too quick to pump the blood where it needed to go, however, letting it seep from his lower legs like an overwatered pot plant.

Murray eyed the door. 'In the bathroom,' he whispered. 'I'll distract her.'

Walter allowed Miss Bloom to go first, holding the bathroom door open for her. They might be a bunch of renegades, but he was still a gentleman. For the second time that week, Walter experienced a frisson of excitement at hiding in the dark with this woman.

'You can have the seat,' he said once they were inside, indicating the closed toilet lid. Miss Bloom was having none of it.

'No, you sit,' she said.

'I insist.'

'Sit down, Mr Clements!'

He sat. Miss Bloom perched on his walker.

When the lights came on in Murray's room, Walter leaned forward and closed the bathroom door as much as he dared. Through the gap he saw Sister Who standing next to the bed.

'Evening, Mr Thompson, how is your pain?'

'No pain to speak of,' said Murray.

The lying bastard, Walter thought.

She studied him. 'Mmm, your face says otherwise. I've asked the doctor to prescribe a Fentanyl patch for you. It goes on like a Band-Aid and the drug is absorbed through the skin. Clever, really. No horrible tablets to swallow, no nasty needles, if that's what you're worried about. We used them a lot where I worked before.'

'Not yet,' said Murray. She really was insistent. Walter almost wished Murray would agree to the patch then conveniently lose it. Walter's multiple complaints of pain had fallen on deaf ears and he could do with a little pick-me-up.

'All right, then. If you're sure. In the meantime, let's try you with a plain Band-Aid, to make sure your skin doesn't react to the adhesive when the time comes. You won't even see it. I'll stick it on your back. Then I'll help you to the bathroom.'

Walter's heart just about exploded. In a whisper, Miss Bloom asked him if he was all right. Had she heard the clatter of his leaky valves billowing and collapsing like floppy sails? He shushed her, waiting for Murray to get rid of the nurse.

'I can manage on my own,' Walter heard Murray say.

Sister Who shook her head. 'Too much paperwork.'

'I don't want to hold you up. Send Sameera along later. I can wait.'

She relented. When Sister Who and the squeaky trolley had gone, Murray gave the thumbs up. Moving his walker to one side, Walter insisted Miss Bloom go ahead. It was quite a squeeze between the sink and the toilet and she pointed out it would be easier if he went first, but Walter wouldn't hear of it.

43

Hattie

ACCORDING TO THE DAILY ENTERTAINMENT PROGRAM, LOCAL singing duo The Melody Makers were returning to Woodlands by 'popular demand', and Hattie, against her better judgement, had agreed to attend.

'It's the Vera Lynn tribute or knit-and-natter, Miss Bloom,' the volunteer, a young woman with green hair and a sleeve of tattoos, had said. 'You can decide.'

'I'd rather finish my book,' Hattie had replied, assuming this would settle it.

'I don't blame you but it's accreditation this week,' the green-headed woman had replied. 'Management want all the residents to look busy.'

Hattie pointed out that she *would look busy. In fact she would be* busy. Busy reading her book. But the girl wouldn't take no for an answer and in the end it was easier simply to go along with it.

As Hattie was closing the door to her room, the handyman arrived with a ladder and a vacuum cleaner. He was here to suck out Hattie's air-conditioning vents, he explained. 'They get filthy,' he said in passing. 'You wouldn't believe the muck that collects up there.' Presumably the very same muck they all breathed on a daily basis. He went on, 'Do you know that Legionnaires' disease was named after an outbreak of a deadly bacteria at a convention of the American Legion? They traced it back to the air conditioning.'

'Really?'

'Yes,' he said cheerily. 'Thirty-four veterans died.'

Hattie picked up the pace, taking shallow breaths to avoid contamination as she followed the green hair towards the day room.

Brenda, one half of the popular duo that Hattie later discovered no one in the audience had actually heard of – let alone demanded the return of – was already at the microphone. She had the ample bosom of an opera singer and the fixed white smile of an entertainment veteran who'd never quite made the big time. She never would, thought Hattie, with a name like Brenda. To give the woman her due, she could still belt out a tune. Even Ada had to dial down her hearing aid.

Walter Clements, on the other hand, was sitting attentively in the front row. His wavy white hair was curled behind his ear. He was dressed in a new shirt and a new cardigan Hattie hadn't seen him wear before. Her fingers fussed at her own hair; wiry, haphazard. She tried in vain to smooth it.

Hattie imagined The Melody Makers – Brenda and a thin man wearing a sparkly jacket playing a keyboard – had been playing the same numbers for years. Most of the residents had been kids during the war, growing up listening to Elvis rather than Vera Lynn during their formative years. She looked around at the audience. In theory they would all know how to jive and do the twist. But rock 'n' roll was a health-and-safety disaster waiting to happen and with accreditation around the corner, they would have to make do with the forces' sweetheart instead.

During the interval, Margery served tea and slices while the ladies gossiped. All except Laurel, who, as well as being trussed up in so much plaster of Paris she looked as though she should be mounted on a plinth, was barely conscious. Her head lolled forward at an odd angle. A ribbon of saliva dangled from her chin and her unfocused eyes stared off into the middle distance. Had Laurel not been making a rumbling noise as she breathed, Hattie might have assumed the worst. The others carried on talking around her, oblivious.

Finally, Judy leaned across and addressed Hattie. 'She's on tablets, you know.'

Good gracious. What were they giving her, horse tablets?

'Is she all right?'

Laurel's slack lips quivered as she breathed out.

'Oh yes, Derek insisted she needed stronger painkillers,' Judy continued. 'And he's making a right hoo-ha about the fall.'

'Yes?'

'It's all very hush-hush,' Judy pursed her lips for emphasis. 'He's been in touch with a no-win-no-fee. He's planning to sue Woodlands.'

Eileen leaned in to add her penny's worth. 'Derek Baker's very au fait with the legal system.'

Walter turned around, catching Hattie's eye.

'Miss Bloom, I didn't see you there.'

The ladies exchanged glances. The heat rose in Hattie's

cheeks. Was it unusually warm in here? Stupid question. It was twenty-three degrees.

'How much do you think Laurel will get?' Eileen pondered.

'For a shoulder, you mean?' Judy replied.

'Not as much as a hip, I wouldn't have thought.'

'I'd have thought more. I mean, think of all the things she can't do now.'

'She couldn't do that much before.'

They talked across Laurel as if she wasn't there.

'I know, but what about her hair? It must be awfully difficult to spray the lacquer left-handed.'

With Laurel's right arm temporarily out of action, Hattie found comfort in the hope that the ozone layer might be granted a reprieve.

'She has to buzz for everything now.' Judy gave a knowing look.

The entertainment officer tapped the microphone. 'Ladies and gentlemen, let's welcome The Melody Makers back on stage again for the second half of the show,' he said. 'Come on, everybody, let's give them a clap.'

Ada adjusted her hearing aid again. 'Who's got the clap?'

Rapt in Brenda's breathy rendition of 'A Nightingale Sang in Berkeley Square', Walter Clements was oblivious when Hattie slipped away, leaving her seat empty. The angels had barely touched their entrees at The Ritz but over the far side of the day room, Hattie had noticed something amiss with Icarus. She found the frail bird pressed against the furthest bars of his cage, head hung low, dejected and unusually morose. He barely reacted when she approached, not even when she poked her finger into the cage. There were several bald patches on his body, and the bottom of the cage was covered with a carpet of soft blue feathers. His seed was untouched and he had his back to his favourite mirror.

'I think he's given up.'

Hattie turned to see Walter Clements directly behind her.

'Poor thing,' said Hattie. 'Cooped up all day in that tiny cage.'

'Apparently, he belonged to one of the residents. The old dear got the bird as a companion when her husband died, not realising that it would outlive her.'

'Do you know that there's a cockatoo that's been visiting my cottage for almost fifty years? If the kitchen door's closed, he'll knock with his beak and if I try to ignore him, he gets angry, tearing at the linoleum. He can get quite destructive, you know, he even picks the wood from the doorframe, and pinches the heads off the shrubs and flowers. We have a bit of a love–hate relationship.' She smiled and shook her head.

'Fifty years? That's a long time for a bird to live.'

Longer than many marriages, thought Hattie.

'They live even longer in captivity,' she said. 'Another twenty years sometimes.'

Was it the lack of predators that enabled them to reach a ripe old age, or the company? Hattie and Walter took awkward turns to look at each other. She had never inspected his face before. Not properly. She had an idea of the way his features were arranged, enough to recognise him in a crowd without committing them to memory, but not the details. How blue his eyes were. Film-star blue. He must have been a handsome man in his youth.

She remembered a column she'd written many years ago on how birds chose a mate. She'd noted that individuals generally picked a mate of comparable attractiveness. Being too choosy risked not finding a mate at all. Not choosy enough and the bird risked being a poor co-parent, a match ending ultimately in desertion. She hadn't worked out how the birds, without mirrors, gauged their own attractiveness compared to others. Apart from Icarus obviously, the little feathered Narcissus, who spent all day staring at his own reflection. Had he given up looking for a mate that met his expectations?

'Are you all set for tonight?'

Back in the moment, Hattie realised Walter Clements was talking to her. 'Tonight?'

'Operation Night Owl,' he said. 'Take two.'

She patted the pocket of her cardigan where the phone was safely hidden. The little battery symbol was down to only fifteen percent. This was their last chance.

'No selfies this time. You can trust me.' Hattie smiled gently, looking him directly in the eye. It wasn't as uncomfortable as she'd imagined. In fact, she experienced a tingle deep inside when she saw his lips part in surprise then close once more into a lopsided smile.

Walter headed back towards the music, where in the front row the ladies were staging a protest. They'd had enough of Vera Lynn. As usual, Eileen was leading the audience in a chant.

We want Michael. We want Michael. Eileen changed key. *Michael Bublé. Michael Bublé. Michael Bublé.*

Hattie stayed with Icarus, who hopped along his perch and wrapped his beak around one of the bars of the cage. The sound of scraped metal set her teeth on edge and she flinched. Icarus squawked in reply and flapped his wings sending more feathers seesawing towards the bottom of the cage where they joined bits of shredded newspaper.

44

Walter

THE MORE CASUALLY WALTER TRIED TO ACT, THE MORE self-conscious he became. Was it his imagination or was that actually a pain in his chest? He stopped outside Fred's old room, for a breather. The nurses' station was ahead. He rubbed his chest, trying to massage away the memories of the pain that had felled him on the fourth tee.

No, it wasn't really a pain; more of a pressure, as if something were sitting on his chest. Not quite the elephant the emergency department doctor had helpfully suggested all those years ago. This was more the size of a large family-sized dog. A retriever, perhaps? He pictured the hefty Queenie. No, maybe not that bad. A poodle. Was it even really a pain, or more of a discomfort? A poodle-sized discomfort. But the poodle grew heavier as Walter pushed his walker forward. He tried to breathe through it, slowing his pace, hoping the poodle would find another chest to sit on.

Derek and Sister Who were nowhere to be seen. The door to the treatment room was shut, and presumably locked. The decorative arrangement of branches and twigs hadn't moved. When he was sure he wasn't being watched, Walter searched between the stems for the phone Miss Bloom had planted only ten minutes ago. She'd worn him down with her insistence at a second chance and he'd buried his misgivings only because he couldn't remember how to switch the thing on. Not that he'd ever admit it. He'd consoled himself with the glorious image of returning triumphant, the conquering hero with the phone in his hand.

So far Marie hadn't mentioned the missing mobile and James wouldn't dare ask for it before the week was up. With any luck, she would assume she'd been the one who'd mislaid it and the two guilty consciences would cancel each other out. Neither would suspect Walter who'd never shown the slightest interest in technology beyond the TV remote.

At first he thought perhaps the phone had dropped into the vase. Walter delved deeper, his fingers finding only more stems. Had it fallen under the table? He leaned down but couldn't see anything. The poodle had returned and his heart fired off a volley of rapid beats as he raised himself back up. Where was it? Bewildered, Walter repeated the exact same search sequence. Between the stems, inside the vase, under the table.

Bugger.

Have you had a proper look? He could hear Sylvia now, pushing him aside, whatever he'd failed to locate invariably jumping straight into her hands. *Here it is!* Cue the free eye roll and bonus deep sigh. She would mutter something about why wasn't it women-only search parties sent to find missing hikers or planes.

Behind the nurses' station, Walter spotted an attractive pair of tortoiseshell reading glasses among the assorted lost property and nursing bits and bobs. Then he remembered that Fred had owned an identical pair. There was no sign of the mobile phone, and sadly, no unattended chocolates he could pilfer either. If he had to return empty handed, he needed something to sweeten the blow. A long white plastic-coated wire lay coiled on the desk. It was similar to the one James had wound round his hand and slipped into his pocket after demonstrating his new phone. It was a battery-charging wire. With the phone about to run out of power, it was a lucky find. He couldn't wait to show it to Murray. And Miss Bloom.

His excitement was short-lived.

'What good is a charger if we don't have the phone?'

It could have been Sylvia standing there next to Murray's bed with that faint look of exasperation on her face. However, to her credit, Miss Bloom didn't look heavenward as she said it.

The triumphant grin melted from Walter's face. 'I thought it might come in handy,' he said.

'Are you *sure* it wasn't there?' She continued her uncanny impression of Sylvia.

'We have to assume the worst,' said Murray. He dropped his voice. 'I think Sister Who might be on to us.'

'You think she found the phone?' said Miss Bloom.

Walter ran his fingers through the thick wave behind his ear. Had they been spotted? Had Sister Who known all along what they were up to?

'What now?' Miss Bloom wasn't addressing either of them directly. Clearly she no longer trusted anyone but herself. 'Without the phone, we have nothing.' She drummed the floor with her walking stick, but it was Walter's turn to be irritated.

'Was Derek *definitely* there again tonight when you planted the phone?' Had she mixed tonight up with last night? He knew he shouldn't have trusted her a second time. Women were good at spotting dresses on sale, but not as reliable as eyewitnesses.

'I know what I saw,' she snapped as if reading his thoughts. 'He was sitting in the swivel chair behind the nurses' station.'

'The swivel chairs are out of bounds,' said Walter. 'That proves he's up to no good.'

'I expect there's a training course staff have to do before they're allowed to operate an adjustable desk chair,' said Murray. 'Talk about a nanny state.'

Walter was about to mention the conversation he'd over-heard that morning but to his annoyance Miss Bloom beat him to it.

'I think Derek Baker's hanging around might have something to do with him planning to sue Woodlands. Think about it, his mother falls and now he stands to make – or at least inherit – a fortune on her behalf. And suddenly he's making decisions on his mother's behalf who is so conveniently drugged up she can barely speak. And all since Sister Who took over.'

'You think Sister Who put him up to it?' Murray's eyes widened. 'Are you saying this was no accident? That they staged the whole thing for some nefarious purpose?'

'But I was the one who threw the goose!' Walter blurted. He wanted to take at least some of the credit. He'd been the one doing the stake-outs. He was the one who'd watched all those cop shows.

The three of them slumped in collective defeat as the sheer ridiculousness of the situation hit them. Operation Night Owl was going nowhere. As it stood, they were nothing more than a bunch of nutty pensioners with vivid imaginations. The harder he tried to impress the unimpressible Miss Bloom, the more she shone in her own right. Perhaps Sylvia had been right all along; he did watch too much TV. He was a fraud. A phoney who made jokes that no one laughed at, least of all the impervious Miss Bloom. And yet . . . And yet . . . He was sure there was something they weren't seeing clearly, some vital missing piece of the puzzle. It was like playing Monopoly with only one die instead of a pair. The entire thing could drag on endlessly without a winner.

45

Hattie

'My door is always open,' the DON liked to tell everyone. Except when it wasn't. Seeing the closed door, Hattie dithered. Then she remembered her vow to always act on first thoughts. She knocked. Inside, she heard the DON punctuated by intervals of silence. A telephone conversation. The exchange had finished abruptly and the door opened.

'Yes?'

'May I have a word?' Hattie didn't wait for a response before crossing the threshold. This was important.

'Do have a seat, Miss Bloom.' To her credit, the DON managed a smile and looked as if she might allocate at least three minutes to whatever Hattie had to say.

Determined not to squander her audience, Hattie got straight down to business. She was surprised, therefore, when the well-prepared words in her head came out sounding rather different.

'Your hair looks nice,' she said, wondering if her tongue had been hijacked by a complete stranger. Woodlands was turning her in to one of the ladies.

The DON rearranged a few strands and looked genuinely pleased. 'Thank you.' Her smile soon faded. 'Was there anything in particular I can help you with today?'

'As a matter of fact, yes,' said Hattie, peeling strands of skin from her thumb like a banana, drawing blood. 'It's about . . .'

The DON pushed her glasses further up her nose and waited.

Hattie saw her glance at the clock on the wall. She had to hurry and yet her words were all muddled. She had rehearsed her suspicions until they sounded logical and comprehensively reasoned. There was no point worrying Walter Clements or Murray with her plan. They would only try to talk her out of it, or worse, try to take over as usual. It's what men did. This was her story, her idea. She was the one who'd spoken to Sister Bronwyn in her car. She alone had witnessed Derek's loitering, two nights in a row. She was the one who'd put two and two together. There was no one else she trusted to see this through.

Somewhere between her brain and her mouth, Hattie's powerful speech turned into a request for strawberry jam as well as raspberry with the scones at afternoon tea.

'Strawberry jam?'

'Yes, raspberry has far too many pips. It's off-putting to watch the other residents try to dislodge them.'

'I see,' said the DON, clicking the tip of her ballpoint pen.

Hattie would have kicked herself if her leg wasn't already crawling with uncommon bugs. Just say it, she told herself, just tell her what you saw.

'Proper whipped cream would be nice too,' said Hattie. 'Not that squirty stuff from a can. And a choice of plain or wholemeal.'

'Are we still talking about the scones?'

Hattie nodded.

'I'll look into those very helpful suggestions. Now, I do have a meeting starting very soon. Is there anything else I can help you with?'

It was Hattie's last chance to be useful.

'I think the individual plastic containers for the butter are wasteful,' she said. 'They're not recyclable. They go straight into landfill, you know. If you count the toast at breakfast, and bread rolls at lunch and dinner, that's three per resident per day. And that's not even counting the scones.'

The DON considered this. 'Here at Woodlands we do take our environmental responsibility very seriously,' she said weighing each word. 'We are actively working to reduce our carbon footprint. It's in twenty-four font on our website.' She straightened the papers on her desk. 'Now that we've discussed saving the planet, is there anything else you've come here to talk about? Apart from the scones?'

Hattie sucked the blood from her thumb. She should have written it down. Her thoughts were always more fluent and organised flowing through a pen onto paper than from her unreliable lips. Go on, she urged herself. Say, *I'd like to report that Laurel Baker's son, Derek, has been hanging around in the evenings, distracting the night staff. I am of the belief that he and the new night nurse are conducting a clandestine romantic relationship and that Derek Baker is planning to sue Woodlands when everyone knows his mother's fall was an accident. Furthermore, Sister Bronwyn deserves to be*

*given the benefit of the doubt given her many years of loyal
service. And Queenie is worth her not insubstantial weight in
gold as a therapy dog, whether or not she has the certificate.*

'Miss Bloom?' The DON was halfway to the door now.

'There is something else,' began Hattie. 'And it's nothing
to do with the scones or the environment. I feel I need to be
a spokesperson for the other residents. I really do have to
speak out. It's something I feel very strongly about.'

'What is it you feel so strongly about?'

In a matter of days, a week or two at the most, she would
be home again. Soon she would leave the birds to fend for
themselves again. It would mean saying goodbye to Murray
and Walter Clements, to the AINs and the ladies. In a funny
way she would miss Fanny Olsen too. This motley assortment
of old dears, each with their own set of unique foibles, were
the closest things to friends she'd ever had. In that respect,
Hattie realised, this was the only place she had ever really
fitted in. This was her parting shot. She could speak her mind
at last without fear of the consequences. Hattie Bloom was
the voice of the voiceless. She gripped the sides of the chair
and took a deep breath.

'Pineapple rings.'

'What?' The DON wrinkled her brow.

'The residents would like to see a pineapple ring on top
of their gammon steak.'

The phone rang before the DON could respond. Hattie
helped herself to a tissue from the box on the desk and
wrapped it around her bleeding thumb like a tourniquet. Her
heart throbbed in her neck and temples.

The DON stood up and covered the mouthpiece of the
phone. 'You'll have to excuse me. I have a family conference

booked for three o'clock. Thank you for your suggestions, Miss Bloom, I'll talk to the chef.'

Hattie shuffled from the office, the perpetually open door closing again behind her. The last five minutes summed up the collective failures of her life. Her body folded beneath the weight of disappointment. Perhaps it was time to stop spitting out the osteoporosis tablets Dr Sparrow had prescribed and grow a new backbone. Far from helping, she had let them all down.

A tiny woman carrying a Tupperware container smiled and made a beeline for her. Hattie recognised her from somewhere but was sure she wasn't one of the residents.

'Hello,' she said, extending her hand. 'You're Miss Bloom, aren't you? I'm Joyce, Murray's wife.'

Hattie shook her hand. A bloodstained tissue unwrapped itself from her thumb and fell to the floor.

'Oh dear, look, you're bleeding!'

'I'm fine, really,' said Hattie, hiding her hand in her pocket. 'It's lovely to meet you.'

'Murray talks about you all the time,' said Joyce. 'You and Walter. He calls you The Night Owls.'

'He talks about you all the time too. And everyone loves your rock cakes.' Hattie eyed the Tupperware, imagining the wonderful treat the birds were going to enjoy. Her parting gift to her feathered friends.

Joyce beamed. 'It's his birthday tomorrow. I'm planning to bake a special cake he can share with his friends.'

'How lovely.' Murray hadn't mentioned his birthday. She wasn't surprised. He wasn't the type to make a song and dance of it.

'I'm heading in there in a minute for a meeting.' Joyce nodded towards the DON's office. Her smile vanished.

'Murray's not a well man, as I'm sure you've realised. They've called me in for a chat. I'm worried he might need to stay at Woodlands for a few extra weeks.'

Poor Joyce. How long could she keep up this pretence, her out-and-out denial that her husband was dying? Hattie tried not to imagine Bond Street with a butterfly as Murray finally slipped away.

'I wish I could take him home.' Joyce's eyes glistened. 'But I can't manage him on my own. I'm not strong enough to lift him, you see. He was falling all the time before he came to Woodlands.' Her hand shot to her mouth.

Joyce and Murray were an unlikely couple, it seemed to Hattie. Joyce was a doll of a woman, tiny, petite. In the photo next to his bed she barely reached his ribs, even now when he was bent over by age and disease and possibly all the years of leaning down to kiss his wife. Hattie thought about those last few weeks caring for her father. She'd been a young woman, fit and strong and he little more than a frail shell at the end. Even they had struggled.

'He knows that. He's very comfortable here. The staff are excellent . . . Sameera is excellent.'

'I only wish . . . you know, for his birthday . . .' A sob escaped from behind Joyce's hand and then her face miraculously rearranged itself into a smile. Or at least a pastiche of one. 'Do keep the birthday cake a surprise, won't you, Miss Bloom. We've always loved planning surprises for each other. It's what we do.'

'I will,' said Hattie. 'I won't breathe a word.'

46

Walter

As usual, Miss Bloom was trying to take over. She had somehow got it into her head that the whole thing had been *her* idea, but he wasn't about to waste time arguing semantics.

'We'll have to hurry,' she said. 'The staff in-service only goes on for an hour. After that the place will be crawling with RNs and AINs.'

Walter wondered if the staff had been suspicious when Murray requested a collared shirt and his best pair of slacks after his shower that morning rather than a fresh set of pyjamas. His hair, what was left of it, was neatly combed and, unless Walter was very much mistaken, Murray was wearing aftershave.

'Very sharp, birthday boy,' Walter remarked, bringing a smile to Murray's face.

There had been no chance to rehearse; the timing of what they had planned held together like a daisy chain. Unlike the prisoners at Stalag Luft III, they had only the one Great Escape route. Instead of three tunnels named Tom, Dick and Harry, they had a corridor and a single elevator down to the basement. There was only one way out.

Compared to transferring Murray from the bed to the wheelchair, stealing the keys was the easy part. This time it was Miss Bloom's turn to create the diversion. She had put on a most impressive display, wandering along the corridor with her leg bandages unfurling like a kite tail. When they witnessed the ticking time bomb of wily pathogens, a nurse and an AIN had rushed to cover her bad leg, giving Walter the thirty seconds he needed to enter the treatment room, open the cabinet and retrieve the minibus keys. He'd been out again by the time the nurse led Miss Bloom towards the big PVC chair and swaddled her leg in fresh bandages.

'Are you sure you're up to it?' Miss Bloom had rested a hand gently on Murray's shoulder as he caught his breath, legs dangling over the side of the bed.

'It's not too late to back out, mate,' added Walter.

'Not on your life,' said Murray. His sapling arms shook from the sheer effort of lowering himself into the wheelchair. Miss Bloom helped him place his feet on the footrests.

'You go ahead and I'll push Murray,' said Walter to Miss Bloom.

'Don't be daft,' she replied with derision. Then she softened, perhaps reading his reaction. 'You'll need to direct operations from the front, Mr Clements.'

'Righty-ho.' Walter led the way. He was as ready as he'd ever been. Nothing was going to stand in his way, including the poodle that was still curled up on the centre of his chest.

Margery-with-a-g had cornered Eileen outside Liverpool Street Station and as usual was failing to cut a long story short. Meanwhile, Eileen was eyeing off the biscuit selection and, knowing her, about to claim first dibs on anything with chocolate. Margery, never one to let work get in the way of a good natter, remained oblivious to the goings-on in Bond Street.

Walter waved Miss Bloom forward with the wheelchair.

'I'll cover you,' he said, as he might a couple of commandos running into an enemy building rather than two grey-haired pensioners.

To his relief, Margery was barely out of the preamble, let alone approaching the point of her story. Eileen, however, was clearly impatient about the biscuits.

It was important not to arouse suspicion. Walter stopped every few paces to check on the seams between strips of wallpaper. Haring ahead, Miss Bloom had already reached the service elevator and was looking over her shoulder impatiently. Walter had watched her remarkable progress over the past few days with a mixture of emotions. Obviously he was pleased to see her out of pain, but her newfound mobility meant that she would be heading home soon. Just when he was about to lose Murray, it looked as if he would lose Miss Bloom too.

He was puffing when he finally caught up but stopped to straighten his shirt collar in the mirror while they waited for the elevator. He wasn't in bad shape *for his age*. From the neck up, at least. He had a full head of hair and full cheeks. Very distinguished.

Form an orderly queue, ladies.

Murray too had some extra colour in his face. Away from the white sheets that made everyone look like a patient, he was a different man. More alive. Happy even. If the entire mission went pear shaped, it would still be worth it to see Murray's smile.

After what seemed an eternity, the service elevator arrived with a ping that sounded deafening in the quiet surrounds. Luckily, neither Margery nor Eileen seemed to have heard.

So far so good.

Then the doors opened.

In the far corner of the elevator stood Fanny Olsen wearing her customary red bobble hat and, unless he was very much mistaken, a paperclip on the lapel of her blouse. Walter swore under his breath. What was she doing in here? Residents were strictly forbidden to use the elevator. There was even a number keypad for security. They'd been banking on it being the same four numbers as the front doors – the suburb's postcode, according to Miss Bloom – when all along, Fanny had been one step ahead.

'After you,' he said, motioning for Fanny to exit. She didn't move. He tried again. 'Here you are, Fanny. This is your floor.'

Walter caught Miss Bloom's eye. What do we do now? she seemed to be saying.

He'd heard of people who reverted back to their mother tongue when they developed dementia. If only they knew where she was born.

To his surprise, Miss Bloom said, 'Does anyone know any Norwegian?'

'Norwegian? Are you sure?'

'My daughter does, she's married to one,' said Murray.

No one moved, weighing up what to do next.

'Don't look now,' said Miss Bloom seeing something in the distance. 'Here comes Judy.'

Walter wasted no time. In a split-second all four of them were inside the elevator and the door was closing behind them. He had always prided himself on his reaction time, and even if his brain were now one step ahead of his body, they still worked as a team.

Murray pressed the buttons and they sank slowly towards the basement.

Miss Bloom whispered to Walter, 'What are we going to do?' Her eyes slid towards Fanny and her implacable expression.

'There's only one thing we can do,' he said. 'We take her with us.'

Fanny's eyes were on him now. When they reached the basement car park, she followed Walter, Miss Bloom and the wheelchair without a word.

Miss Bloom grasped Walter by the shoulder and stopped him in his tracks. 'We can't get Fanny into any trouble. Look, I'll help you load Murray into the minibus then I'll stay behind and take her back upstairs before anyone notices she's gone.'

'No!' said Walter sharply. 'We need to stick together.' If taking Fanny Olsen along for the ride was the price he had to pay to have Miss Bloom by his side, then so be it.

The minibus was parked in its usual spot in the corner of the underground car park. As Walter approached he could feel the heat radiating from under the bonnet. The engine was still warm from this morning's advertised bus trip to the Palm Farm. It was all he could do to refrain from rubbing his hands together in anticipation. This was it: his chance to get behind the wheel again. Forget the Tesla. He would show them all what he was capable of. Was once capable of.

When Walter pressed the button on the key fob, the indicators flashed and the doors unlocked.

'All aboard.'

'Hold on,' said Miss Bloom. 'How are we going to load the wheelchair in the back? It's parked right up against the wall.'

'I'll pull forward, wait here,' said Walter.

'It's too risky. If we muck about, they'll see us on the security cameras. We need the element of surprise.'

It was a good point and one he wished he'd thought of. If the receptionist happened to look at the screen and noticed the commotion, they would be discovered. As they were, the wheelchair was hidden from camera view on the far side of the bus. They couldn't risk it.

'I can walk,' said Murray. He kicked away the footrests and shuffled forward to the front of the webbed fabric seat. Murray's bones looked as though they might snap at any moment and it seemed to sap most of his energy, but after a couple of attempts he was standing. He looked pleased. The perfect birthday present to himself.

Fanny was already inside, in her usual seat on the second row next to the window, seatbelt fastened. Was she expecting a scenic drive followed by a picnic? Walter ducked as the doubts flew at him thick and fast. He hadn't given a single thought to how Marie might react. She would fume when she found out, not least because the last time he'd been behind the wheel, rather than a steering column, it had almost ended in tragedy. He'd only kept his licence because he promised Marie he wouldn't drive again, an easy enough commitment to make when his crumpled car was being loaded onto a recovery truck.

All that was in the past now; he was coming good again. Walter tried to picture James's grin when he heard about what his grandpa was about to do. Would this be the story his grandson told his mates at school? Would Walter finally get to be the hero of someone else's story?

Somehow Murray made it up the steps and into the minibus. He sat in the very first row, hands on his knees, chasing his breath. He coughed a couple of times and Walter was worried that someone might hear them. At the driver's door, he looked at his own walker then pushed it away like a discarded supermarket trolley. If Murray could do it, so could he. His legs felt as if they were full of quickset cement rather than excess body fluid but he managed to climb into the driver's seat and slot the key into the ignition. To his surprise and delight, Miss Bloom climbed into the passenger side next to him.

'Better fasten your seatbelt, Miss Bloom,' said Walter, gripping the steering wheel like an old friend.

In the first sign that she was not completely indifferent to him, she looked directly into his eyes and replied. 'Better fasten yours too, Mr Clements.'

47

Hattie

Hattie's exhilaration stalled with the engine. Twice. She watched Walter put the gear stick in neutral and try again after pumping the pedal. The engine roared to life, and so did the deep misgivings she had been secretly hoarding. This was all a huge mistake. They had allowed themselves to get carried away, like children on some make-believe adventure.

With the parking brake finally released, the minibus edged forward. Thank goodness they didn't have to reverse out. Walter Clements didn't have the most agile of bodies. The mobility of his neck was of particular concern. Contrary to popular belief, owls couldn't turn their heads a full 360 degrees. A little less than that in reality, but with their peripheral vision it amounted to the same. They were predators on the lookout for prey, but always risked becoming prey themselves. They were well adapted. Walter Clements was not.

Hattie hadn't even begun to worry about his eyesight. He *had* run over her on the mobility scooter, hadn't he? In broad daylight. It was one thing to take a chunk out of her shin but what if he crashed into an oncoming vehicle?

She held the sides of the seat as the minibus climbed the dark car park's shallow ramp out into the light. Her thoughts ebbed and flowed.

Finally they were doing something positive.

No, this was a bad idea from the start.

Good idea.

Bad idea.

'Everyone all right?' Walter paused in neutral at the top of the drive. He smiled into the rear-view mirror at Murray. 'Okay back there, birthday boy?'

The forced joviality was a concern too. By now, she had gleaned enough about human behaviour to see he was nervous and overcompensating. Humour was Walter's suit of armour but she had begun to suspect that behind the clown, there were tears.

'Onwards!' shouted Murray from the first row.

Walter looked left and right, swivelling his entire upper body and confirming Hattie's suspicions about his neck. 'I think there's a side entrance,' he said. 'I've seen delivery vans back up that way.'

Hattie had seen them too. Black, windowless vans. There had been one the day Fred passed away. Not only deliveries. Collections too. Goods in. Goods out.

'Quick,' she said. There was an AIN walking towards them, perhaps a late arrival. She was staring at her phone, and didn't look up. Hattie tried to shield her face with her hand as the AIN passed. How long before anyone noticed the minibus was missing? How long before anyone noticed four missing residents?

Walter steered the bus down a narrow lane that ran along-side the main building, past the industrial-sized bins that the council collected every Tuesday morning. Then, with only a minor skid, they were out on the road. Left then left again. At last they were on the main road. There was a tense moment when Walter stumbled through the gears but they'd picked up sufficient speed by the time the minibus passed Woodlands for Hattie to relax again. He was sweating, she saw, tiny droplets seeding his forehead. He ran his sleeve across his face, wiping them away, and began to hum tunelessly.

Past the bus stop, and the spot where Sister Bronwyn parked her car each night. Soon, Whitechapel and Old Kent Road were nothing more than a tiny speck in the wing mirror. The sky was especially blue, the leaves of the trees so unbelievably green. On the footpath, schoolchildren trudged home like Sherpas returning to base camp. There were prams, bicycles, dogs on leads. Everywhere Hattie looked, people were young and healthy and vibrant. After more than two weeks inside Woodlands it was easy to forget that not everyone was old and frail.

'Watch out for the school zones, Walt,' Murray warned.

Walter touched the brakes and the minibus slowed to a crawl behind a line of oversized cars as they vied for precious parking spots outside the school. It brought to mind the shiny black car Hattie's new neighbours insisted on parking under the overhanging limb of the Angophora tree. She hated being lied to. All along it had been about the view, not the car. She only hoped the owls had been saving up their ammunition for one last bombing blitz.

'Too much traffic on the road,' muttered Walter. His thick hands were fists around the steering wheel. 'It wasn't like this in my day.'

My day. Everyone spoke affectionately, nostalgically, about their day, some elusive time they would only recognise when looking back in years to come. For most, it was when they were too young or carefree to realise that this was as good as it got and to enjoy it. But what if her day wasn't already behind her? What if today was Hattie Bloom's day?

At the pedestrian crossing, Walter's hands released the strangled steering wheel for a moment. Noticing her watching him, he turned and winked. Fanny stared straight ahead, hands clasped loosely in her lap.

'Right then second left,' called Murray from the back. 'Then about a hundred yards on the left.' He was perking up with every passing milestone; a parched plant in the rain. He pointed out the school where he and Joyce had met; the church where they'd been married and their girls baptised. They even passed the spot where their first house had been bulldozed to make way for a supermarket in the early seventies. Joyce, always Joyce. She was his constant, the single reference point in his life. Was it hardest to be the one who was dying, or the one left behind? The years had been a salve on the pain of losing her parents so young. At least no one would suffer when her time came. She found the thought satisfying rather than depressing. She hated the idea of anyone wasting time grieving over her.

It wasn't far at all as the crow flew and yet Hattie suspected that to Joyce, Woodlands might as well have been on a different continent.

'White picket fence, roses round the front door,' he said excitedly, pointing with a shaky hand. 'There it is, there!' The house was exactly what Hattie had expected.

Walter indicated and eased the minibus to a smooth halt outside. All the houses were well maintained, if a little old-fashioned. Seventies' architecture. Many of the neighbours had concreted over their front gardens to make extra parking spaces but there was a lawn outside Murray's house. Hattie imagined how the suburb had grown up, young families moving into the new houses at the same time. She pictured Murray's daughters playing on the grass as children, and his Viking grandchildren coming to visit, imagining that every Australian home had a beach on its doorstep and koalas in the trees.

'Nice place you have here, Murray,' said Walter, turning off the engine.

'Lovely garden,' said Hattie.

Murray responded excitedly. 'Wait until you see the back.'

A wary Hattie was first out of the minibus. Had they been spotted? The surprise ruined? With the Woodlands logo emblazoned on both sides, the bus was hardly incognito. And neither were they.

Opening the sliding door, Fanny was already positioned to climb out. Murray was close behind. The colour had returned to his cheeks and the strength to his withered limbs. He was out on the nature strip in a flash.

'Ahh,' he sighed, inhaling the familiar neighbourhood air. 'That's better.' Hattie went to offer him her arm, but he brushed it politely away and stood tall. Exceptionally tall, she now saw. Walter was still struggling out of the driver's side. Suddenly he was the one Hattie was most worried about. The effort of hauling his heavy legs was etched on his pursed lips. It must be like walking with gumboots full of water, she thought, and yet he'd looked so at ease in the driver's seat. What a shame he had to make do with legs instead of wheels.

THE GREAT ESCAPE FROM WOODLANDS NURSING HOME

'Ready?' Walter opened the low white gate. It had sunk on its hinges and scraped a perfect arc in the moss-covered footpath.

'Must fix that gate,' said Murray.

Four aged pensioners headed towards the front door in single file, Murray at the front. Walter's steps were slow and measured as if he were walking across thin ice. Fanny's impatient feet took four steps to every one of his. Hattie brought up the rear.

Two cane chairs were angled conversationally, side by side on the front verandah. Murray paused at the end of the path and bent to pick a posy of lavender from the border.

The door opened on the first knock. Joyce appeared wearing an apron. The colour drained instantly from her face and she took a step backwards, hands rushing to her mouth. She let out a little gasp, then threw her arms around her husband's waist, nearly knocking him off balance.

~

Joyce served tea in the sunroom overlooking the back garden. Hattie sat next to Walter on the flowered sofa. Fanny Olsen had a chair to herself and Murray, sinking into his favourite armchair, looked like a man who had survived a shipwreck and collapsed onto a warm sandy beach. Joyce darted in and out of the kitchen, torn between preparing refreshments and not wanting to miss a single second with her surprise visitors.

The scent of jasmine wafted through the French doors. Hattie closed her eyes for a moment and listened for the birds, their twitters and tweets still audible to her ear above the human voices.

'You were right, Murray,' said Walter, sipping from a china teacup. 'It is a lovely garden.'

It was a small block screened from the neighbours on both sides by mature bushes and trees. The flowerbeds were a riot of colour. Silvereyes swooped into an ornamental birdbath on the tiny patio and bees hovered between the bright petals in planter boxes and terracotta pots either side of the open doors.

'It's a work in progress,' said Murray. Years of pain had slipped from his face and he looked relaxed and completely at peace.

Joyce returned with a fresh pot of tea. 'A garden is never finished,' she said. 'More tea everyone?'

'I was never much of a gardener myself,' said Walter. 'Sylvia, that's my late wife, used to enjoy pottering. I did the heavy work. She told me where she wanted a wall built or a hole dug, and I did as I was told.'

Hattie looked at the cup and saucer on the side table next to Murray's chair. Had Joyce remembered to add the thickener? She watched Murray move the saucer to his lap and clasp the delicate china handle between his thumb and fingers. Should she say something?

'Oh, I nearly forgot the cake!' Joyce scurried back into the kitchen.

Murray lifted the cup to his lips and took a sip. He closed his eyes, savouring what could have been the sweetest nectar. Another sip, then a sigh.

'Nice cup of tea, love,' he tried to shout to his wife in the kitchen but he began to cough on the last syllable and had to put the cup and saucer back on the table.

'Are you all right, Murray?' said Hattie.

He smiled. 'Never better.'

The cake arrived on a plate that matched what must have been the best china. The sponge was rather lopsided, reminding Hattie of the escarpment behind her cottage. It was still warm from the oven and the butter icing had melted and was trickling over the edge onto the plate. Joyce found some birthday candles and arranged a dozen on the top. They sang 'Happy Birthday' and when Murray struggled to blow out the candles, Joyce leaned in to help him. Fanny Olsen had drunk two cups of tea and eaten a large slice of cake but hadn't uttered a word. Joyce fussed over her as much as the others.

'Quick,' said Murray offering his plate to Walter while Joyce was showing Fanny to the bathroom. 'Either you have it or give it to the birds, will you?'

Walter patted his ample belly. Checking that Joyce was still occupied with Fanny, Hattie unfolded a napkin, wrapped the untouched cake and slipped it into her cardigan pocket.

When Fanny returned from the bathroom, Hattie decided it was her turn. On her way back, she ran into Joyce coming the other way with the empty cups and saucers. Joyce ushered her into the kitchen.

'Lovely cake, Joyce,' said Hattie, hoping she wouldn't notice the bulge in her pocket. The birds would love it.

'Thank you.' Joyce's bright face folded into a frown. 'I take it this isn't an official trip,' she said.

Hattie shook her head. 'Not exactly.'

Joyce put the cups and saucers in the sink. 'Our children grew up in this house. The girls, Maggie and Sarah. They're overseas at the moment, I expect Murray has told you.'

'He's very proud of them.'

'It's nothing fancy, but it's been a good home,' Joyce continued. 'A labour of love, you could say. He's fixed every leaking tap, broken window pane, squeaky floorboard and blocked drain in this place. At least twice. We chose all the furniture together. The wallpaper was on special, I remember that.' Tears pooled in the gutters beneath her eyes. 'I called the girls last night after the meeting with the DON,' she said, wiping her face with the apron. 'They both managed to get on flights first thing this morning. Should be home in a few hours.'

Hattie took Joyce into her arms. She had never hugged anyone besides her parents and yet it felt like the most natural thing in the world to draw this woman and her narrow shoulders against her body.

Joyce emerged after an avalanche of sobs, her eyes bloodshot. 'Leave Murray here,' she said. 'Let him stay the night. I called Bronwyn when I was in the kitchen and she's popping round later to see him. She's always gone above and beyond. Bronwyn is more than a nurse to us, she's like family. Murray thinks of her like another daughter. She gave us her personal phone number, you know. It was as though she half expected this to happen.'

Hattie wanted to tell Joyce that they would get Sister Bronwyn her job back. She wished she could promise that but Joyce, more than anybody, must realise the limits of false hope.

'Are you sure you can manage?'

Joyce nodded. 'Sure. Besides, knowing Murray, he'll want another slice of birthday cake!'

48

Walter

'I THINK SHE'S STARTING TO SUNDOWN,' MISS BLOOM SAID. The staff often used the expression. Walter knew it meant anything but watching the sunset with a nice cocktail.

They were saying goodbye to Murray and Joyce. A restless Fanny was busy dead-heading the roses in the front garden. Unfortunately, while they were still in full bloom. Joyce had intervened and cut her a bunch to take home, wrapping the stems in damp paper towel before covering them with a plastic bag.

'There you go,' Joyce said, steering Fanny gently towards the front gate. 'Do come and visit again soon.'

While Miss Bloom settled Fanny back in the minibus, Walter had spent a few shrinking moments with Murray.

'So long, old chap,' Murray said from his favourite chair, using what looked like the last of his strength to reach for Walter's hand.

Walter gripped it firmly and held it for a moment longer than was customary.

'You take care of yourself,' said Walter, his voice cracking. 'You hear me?'

'I will. You look after yourself too.' Murray's eyes, looking huge in his shrunken skull, were struggling to stay open. 'And thank you for everything you've done. This,' he looked around at his home, 'means everything to me.'

Seeing Murray there with his cup of tea, enjoying the view of his garden, Walter was sure they had done the right thing, whatever the consequences. Now it was up to him to get Fanny and Miss Bloom back to Woodlands.

It was late afternoon but the traffic was already crawling. Walter felt a sudden nostalgia for the good old-fashioned rush hour. Nowadays, the roads were in a perpetual state of gridlock. The emergency stop he'd rehearsed with his students was all but obsolete; chance would be a fine thing if a vehicle ever made it out of first gear on these roads. Before long, cars would drive themselves, making driving instructors obsolete too.

Ahead, Walter could see a yellow sign indicating the road was closed. Fanny was growing increasingly agitated in the back of the minibus. In the passenger seat Miss Bloom wondered aloud how long they would be. Walter decided to focus on his tiny victories instead of his myriad failures. For a moment he vowed to put aside the disastrous scooter test, Sister Bronwyn, and the defunct Night Owls. Instead he tried to picture Murray and Joyce, reunited. He would always remember his friend enjoying his garden. For a single night at least, Joyce was free of her guilt. And beside him, hanging on to her seatbelt, was Miss Bloom. He would keep on chasing that elusive smile, and one day turn it into laughter. He wasn't there yet, but Walter Clements might still retain his one hundred percent pass rate.

'I think Fanny might need a toilet break soon,' said Miss Bloom. In the rear-view mirror, Walter saw Fanny trying to undo her seatbelt. He hadn't planned for this contingency.

'Is she Caltex desperate?' he asked, seeing the sign for a grubby-looking service station in the distance. Sylvia's bladder was unpredictable, he remembered. She would be bursting one minute but then be able to hold on for hours if the facilities weren't up to scratch. How fussy were Fanny's waterworks?

'I don't think she can hold on much longer.' Walter craned his neck. Miss Bloom was weaving her fingers, mirroring Fanny's growing agitation. The police station was within walking distance, and Walter sensed she was weighing this up as an option. On the plus side, the police would have a toilet for Fanny. The down side was that they would probably also have a warrant for his arrest. Vehicle theft. Kidnapping. Not to mention the consequences of absconding from an aged-care facility. For once Walter didn't really care. Ninety and never been arrested. Maybe it wasn't too late to see how it felt. Would he make it into the papers? Onto the evening news?

A siren cut through the hum of idling engines and a police car whizzed past in a flash of red and blue. Some drivers were already doing three-point turns and accelerating back down the opposite lane. The minibus wasn't the most manoeuvrable of vehicles, however, even for a man of Walter's considerable prowess behind the wheel. It would be like trying to turn a super-tanker.

'I've got an idea,' said Miss Bloom. 'Turn left.' She gestured to a tiny lane a little way ahead.

'But it's a one-way street,' Walter said.

'Trust me on this, Mr Clements.'

By now, Fanny's face was contorted. It was one thing to take her on a joyride, it was quite another to see a lady lose her dignity. Walter checked his mirrors, flicked on his indicator and pulled into the bus lane. A horn honked as he edged forward.

'Go,' urged Miss Bloom checking the passenger wing mirror. Then, 'Now!'

Walter planted his foot on the accelerator and hauled the steering wheel to the left. Tongue tracing his upper lip in concentration, he managed to squeeze the wide minibus out of the line of traffic, around the corner and into the narrow street. Not a scratch on either wing. If only the occupational therapist could see him now.

So far, there were no sirens or flashing lights behind them, no startled drivers heading towards them. Following Miss Bloom's directions, he skilfully threaded the minibus through the back roads until there was more space than buildings and the ocean was just visible through the tree canopy.

49

Hattie

THE COUNCIL HAD RESURFACED THE TORTUOUS ROAD, THE familiar potholes repaired with Band-Aids of smooth dark tarmac and sad little pancakes of native road kill. They had trimmed the trees around the power lines too, the exposed branches shrinking back as if they had been electrocuted. Otherwise, little had changed in Treetops Road.

With every twist and turn along the narrow road she knew so well, Hattie's stomach shrank, squeezed by a mixture of nerves and excitement. This was the moment she had been waiting for. Thoughts of returning to her beloved cottage had sustained her through the weeks of pain and the long, unfriendly nights – and now she was almost there. It was time to see the work her chequebook had done to the cottage. A little pruning, perhaps. That wonky front step levelled. The fence repaired where the ladder had fallen. The repairs had cost far more than she had anticipated – everything did nowadays – and her savings were almost gone. From now on she would have to rely on her pension. Angophora Cottage was her only asset, along with her well-thumbed copy of GJ Broinowski's *The Birds of Australia*. It was a collector's item and worth a fair amount of money even in its well-worn condition, but parting with it would be a last resort.

'It's just past that lamppost,' she said, silently urging the minibus to hurry as it crawled those last few metres. Walter Clements swore as the front wheel clipped the kerb. 'Number sixty-three,' said Hattie.

He hauled on the handbrake and turned the key in the ignition. 'This is sixty-three,' he said peering at the numbers on the mailbox.

Suddenly Hattie wasn't so sure. The numbers were there: a shiny, pristine six and three. Hattie knew every telegraph pole, every tree and every hedge on Treetops Road but now she wasn't even sure they had the right house. The right road, even.

'Is this where you live?' Walter's knitted eyebrows registered her uncertainty.

Fanny Olsen was already out of her seat and hauling on the handle that opened the sliding door. Before Hattie could stop her, she had climbed out and was standing on the nature strip looking around. Hattie followed, her feet landing on the neatly mown grass surrounding her mailbox. Her *new* mailbox.

She tried to take in the wide-open space at the front of the cottage now lined with strips of freshly laid turf. Where trees and bushes had screened out the neighbours, neat borders now framed the lawn, rows of miniature lilly pilly bushes stood like pygmies. Hattie's eyes struggled to see everything at once, to register what was unfamiliar. The weathered sandstone had been blasted back to the original honeyed yellows and ochres. The afternoon sun reflecting off the clean windows made her squint. She had never seen the cottage like this. By the time she was old enough for memories, the paint was already starting to peel from the window frames and the sandstone blocks were dull with age. She didn't remember a time when the garage door didn't lean, propped shut with a wooden stake. Ironically, her father hadn't been one for maintaining the home he'd built, and Hattie had grown up with things the way they were; the loose pavers, the rot around the bottom of the front door, the bench entwined by creepers were all she'd ever known. But now, everything was different. Even the hole in the roof was gone, mended with closely matched roof tiles.

'Nice place you have here, Miss Bloom,' said Walter appraising the neat cottage and front garden. He whistled his admiration. 'Must be worth a few bob in this neighbourhood.'

Leading Fanny by the hand, Hattie crept towards her front door. She watched where each foot went, not trusting them to remember the way. It was a brand-new wooden door, far too modern for the era of the cottage. The wood stain was so . . . orange and totally incongruous amid the silvery greys of the surrounding spotted gums. Her hand hesitated where the old brass handle had once been. In its place was a lustrous new latch that had locked her out of her own home.

'Do you keep a spare key hidden somewhere?' Walter was puffing down the path behind them. The Woodlands minibus looked enormous parked on the side of the narrow street.

'Somebody's changed the locks,' said Hattie. Changed the door. Changed the entire property. Stolen her home.

Fanny marched impatiently on the spot, her fingers playing some invisible instrument.

'What do we do now?' For once, Walter Clements was happy to delegate responsibility.

'Quickly,' said Hattie. 'There's the outhouse.'

'You've still got a dunny out the back?' A smile crept over Walter's face. 'Well, I never.'

The path to the side of the cottage, once impenetrable, had been cleared. Looking now, Hattie wondered how the paramedics had managed to find her in the back garden and in turn been able to wheel the stretcher back out again. Her memories of that day were hazy, like a dream she was sure she would remember when she woke but was gone again by morning. The DON had mentioned a chainsaw, but the anaesthetic had erased every detail after the second rung of the ladder.

'Follow me, Fanny.' Hattie led the way towards the forgotten side entrance. No one had ever used the gate, which had rotted off its hinges decades ago and been consumed by a tangle of brambles and lantana. No one had ever needed to, so rarely did her parents leave home. After her mother died, her father had barely set foot outside the cottage except when the whisky ran low. Now, Hattie saw that the fence and gate had been mended, a new latch allowing the gate to swing open with ease. Any minute now, she expected to wake up on a plastic-wrapped mattress at Woodlands, hallucinating in a fevered dream. Maybe she was dying and her imagination was taking her home one last time.

To her relief, the outhouse was exactly as Hattie remembered it. The walls were made of the same sandstone as the cottage, though the sloping roof was a rusty corrugated iron. When Hattie had had a bathroom built indoors, with the meagre inheritance her father hadn't managed to drink away, she had kept the outhouse. The dunny, as Walter Clements had so colloquially referred to it. Every year a family of swallows nested in the eaves and she couldn't bring herself to evict them. While her neighbours built steel and glass extensions, cabanas and garden cabins, Hattie held on to her outhouse. She imagined it was quite an eyesore. At least she hoped it was.

The door was stiff and creaked on its hinges but Hattie knew exactly how to open it, lifting and pulling, then ducking when a bird flew out over her head. How marvellous! The swallows were still here. She swiped away the worst of the cobwebs and lifted the toilet seat to check for redbacks. Fanny Olsen didn't appear to be fussy and closed the door behind her with a look of relief.

'Give me a shout when you're done.'

Hattie left her to it, determined not to fuss and hover as they did at Woodlands. She was convinced it only encouraged dependency among the residents, as well as stage fright. Going to the toilet was treated as a health-and-safety risk, each call of nature potentially fatal.

So focused had she been in getting Fanny to the outhouse, it was only as she walked back towards the cottage that Hattie saw the rest of the garden. Her shadow on the path stopped her in her tracks. At this time of day, the sun should be sinking behind the giant Angophora tree, casting the back patio into a welcome shade. Instead, the patio windows were glinting, reflecting what Hattie could barely bring herself to turn round to see. Instead of the corkscrew limbs of the giant tree and the cool canopy of grey–green leaves, Hattie saw the rooftop of the house in front, further down the slope. Beyond that was the sparkle of sunlight on water and the white sail of a small boat. The tree had gone, reduced to a stump at the bottom of the block. She had read about a group of scientists that inadvertently killed Ming the Giant Clam, when they opened it up and discovered the clam was over five hundred years old. The world's oldest living animal. Hattie couldn't bear to count the tree's rings.

Skirting a brand-new boundary fence, she found more uniform beds dotted with hedging plants so small they would have been more at home in a pot on the windowsill. It would be ten years before they grew up tall enough to shut out the outside world and they would never live to offer a hundred-and-fifty-year-old nesting spot for the fussy owls. At the base of each plant, the soil was covered in a thick layer of mulch, as if each one had been tucked into bed with a blanket of chipped wood bark that exactly matched the warm coppery shades of the Angophora tree.

Hattie didn't notice Fanny emerge from the outhouse, her skirt tucked up into her underwear. Puffing, Walter caught up with them and immediately shielded his eyes.

'Here, Fanny,' said Hattie rushing to her aid. 'Let me sort you out.'

Fanny smiled gratefully. Never one for direct eye contact, she stared at Hattie, the smile becoming a frown. She lifted a finger to Hattie's face and traced a tear as it trickled down her cheek. It was almost a relief to discover that her redundant tear ducts, desiccated by age, still worked.

'Miss Bloom, are you all right?' It was Walter, his eyes full of concern. 'What is it?'

She had failed the owls too. She imagined the fragile eggs now crushed in the giant mulcher. The adults would have flown away in fear. Fight or flight. Hattie's fists clenched, the soft skin of her palms yielding to her jagged nails.

She must have swooned, because suddenly Walter Clements was there to steady her, his big warm hands grasping her upper arms. It was how he might hold an injured bird, strapping its wings against its body, preventing it from flying away.

'It's all right, Miss Bloom,' said Walter gently. 'I've got you.'

50

Walter

THE MOOD WAS SUBDUED ON THE DRIVE HOME. MISS BLOOM hadn't uttered a word since they left the cottage. A shadow had passed over her and he'd lost her again, a faraway look haunting her beautiful brown eyes. Miss Bloom was more inaccessible than ever. Fanny, perhaps picking up on something, was still and silent too. The afternoon had fallen flat on its face.

Walter wasn't surprised to see the police car parked next to the leaping fish fountain when they arrived back at Woodlands. It was time to face the music and this time it wasn't going to be 'The White Cliffs of Dover'. Accustomed now to its size and handling, Walter managed to negotiate the tight turn that led down the ramp into the underground car park and reverse the minibus to its customary spot without incident. The old solid confidence was returning too, and with it the sheer joy of being back behind the wheel. What with that second slice of birthday cake, the traffic jam and the detour to Miss Bloom's cottage, they had been gone for over two hours.

~

There was standing room only in the DON's office. Sally was dispatched to fetch tea and biscuits. Walter had been in the headmaster's office on many occasions as a boy. Refreshments were reassuring in the circumstances, he thought. The presence of two young police officers, Constable Wheatley and Senior Constable Morrissey, was more troubling.

'Now that we're all here I think we should get straight down to business,' said the DON. The arrangement of chairs suggested an inquisition.

The tea arrived and business was delayed while the DON, acting as mother, handed round the cups. Policing must have evolved since the 1970s when Kojak usually slapped on the handcuffs rather than poured the tea. Was now a good time to ask why the cops on TV always shielded the suspect's head when they put them in the back of the car? He would ask later. Once he and Miss Bloom were taken into custody.

With the biscuits shared around, the DON adopted her serious face.

'I have some good news and some bad news for you,' she said.

Walter dunked his shortbread finger into his tea, in case the bad news was that the police were here to take him away. He thought about prison and wondered what kind of biscuits they served, and whether the tea was hot. It was hard to say what thoughts were running through Miss Bloom's mind. She hadn't touched her tea or her biscuit. He wanted to tell her not to worry, that he had already decided to shoulder the blame. He was a man. It wasn't too late to be an honourable one.

Proceedings stalled yet again when there was a knock on the door and one of the constables leaned backwards on his chair to open it. Through the crack, Walter saw Fanny Olsen writhing with nervous energy. The DON picked up the phone to the receptionist and asked her to distract Fanny until the meeting was over. Walter consoled himself with the knowledge that at least they were treating her as an innocent party.

'The good news is that Woodlands will not be pressing charges,' said the DON. The constables looked disappointed. Walter's relief came in a sudden gush. He grinned at a stony-faced Miss Bloom. It was all over. Thank goodness for that. The Cooler King was back. But the DON hadn't finished. She raised her hand to curtail his relief. 'But, it will be recorded as an official incident. Your behaviour will be closely monitored from now on, Mr Clements, and your daughter has been informed.'

Marie. He doubted her sockets would be big enough to contain this eye roll. On the other hand, with the police involved, he imagined James would be impressed, even if he got away with a caution rather than incarceration.

There was another knock on the door and this time Fanny barged in.

Irritated by the interruption, the DON said, 'I'll come and talk to you when I've finished here, Mrs Olsen. Unless you've come to tell us that you'd like to press charges? Against Mr Clements and Miss Bloom here? For kidnapping?' The policemen sat up a little straighter.

Fanny was a wriggle of agitation.

'Are you all right?' Miss Bloom stood up and, as if waking from a coma, appeared to see everyone for the first time. She ushered Fanny to the chair with a hand on her back and gently rubbed the space between her shoulders until Fanny was calm.

'What is that?' The DON pointed to something in Fanny's hand. 'Let me see.'

Fanny handed over what she'd been carrying in her hand. Walter recognised it immediately.

'That's my grandson's phone,' he said.

'Where did you get this, Mrs Olsen?'

Fanny cowered.

'Are we talking about a theft here?' asked Constable Morrissey, getting his notebook out.

'No,' said Walter. 'I found it.' The constable narrowed his eyes.

'May I see it?' Miss Bloom asked.

The DON handed it over reluctantly, adding that the battery was flat.

Walter felt in his pocket for the battery-charging wire. 'Here, plug it in to the electricity, Miss Bloom.'

'I don't see what any of this has to do with the minibus,' said the DON. 'I think we can handle this ourselves.' She turned to the two constables and apologised for wasting their time.

Constable Wheatley hadn't finished his tea and looked in no hurry to leave. He helped himself to another biscuit. The DON began to clear away the tea things, clearly impatient to get rid of the incriminating police vehicle outside.

After a couple of minutes, the phone sprang back to life. And so did Miss Bloom.

'Wait,' she said, taking charge. 'This is important. There's something here I think you should see.'

Constable Morrissey's ears pricked up.

Walter added, 'There've been a few suspicious characters hanging around Woodlands after hours.'

Soon, everyone was crowding around Miss Bloom and the phone. 'Here it is,' she announced as if she had discovered a lost diamond ring. 'Watch this.'

The video played on an angle, as if shot from a listing ship, but this time it clearly showed the nurses' station and the treatment room. At first the comings and goings were unremarkable. The DON pursed her lips. 'What exactly are we looking at?'

'You'll see,' said Walter. What were they about to see? He had to put his trust in Miss Bloom as he had the second-hand car he'd given Marie on her twenty-first birthday. Nothing flashy, but solid and reliable, with just enough oomph beneath the bonnet to get out of a sticky situation.

Sure enough, a man with a dark beard entered the frame from the bottom right corner and walked diagonally across the screen towards the treatment room, glancing briefly behind him.

'That's Derek Baker,' said the DON, leaning her head on an angle to get a better look. 'What's he doing?'

With so many heads crowded together it was difficult to see. Miss Bloom, who had a front-row view, provided a helpful running commentary for those in the dress circle. 'That's Sister Who,' she said, pointing to a woman in a nurse's uniform who had appeared from the top left-hand corner.

'Sister Who?' The DON looked confused.

'The agency night nurse,' said Walter helpfully. *She who shall not be named.* On the video, the couple took a step backwards into the treatment room. He caught Miss Bloom's eye. They both knew what was coming next.

'What's she doing letting a relative into the treatment room?'

To his surprise and clearly Miss Bloom's too, Sister Who and Derek Baker did not fall into each other's arms in a tryst. Instead, the cupboard door opened, obscuring both their heads but not their hands.

'That's the S8 cupboard,' said the DON. It was hard to make out exactly what was going on, the camera was too far away, but it looked as if Sister Who was opening a box and counting something out into Derek's waiting hand. Individually wrapped squares, each the size of a large Band-Aid.

At that moment, the screen went blank. The DON took possession of the phone and played back the video. Meanwhile, everyone turned to look at Fanny. One mystery was solved at least: they now knew who had found the phone in its hiding place. At a glance, the phone might have simply been another of her randomly pilfered items, an eccentric habit of old age and feeble mind, but Walter suspected there was more to the story. An opportunist she was not. Fanny's acquisitions revealed the hand of a true professional.

Constable Morrissey asked to see the phone. 'Who took this video?'

'I did,' said Walter and Miss Bloom in unison.

A beat of silence passed when everyone looked at everyone else. Were they about to be charged with stalking too?

'Why exactly?' Morrissey unsheathed his notebook again then scratched behind one ear with his pencil.

Walter started to explain but Miss Bloom interrupted, correcting his version of events. It was like having Sylvia there, adding helpful but irrelevant details to the story he was trying to tell. Far from detracting from his recitation, however, Walter found that between the two of them, they provided a thorough and convincing case involving Derek Baker and his vexatious complaints about Sister Bronwyn.

'B-R-O-N—' Morrissey's pencil scratched the letters into his notebook, but the DON clearly had no patience for slow spellers.

'She's worked here for twenty years on night shifts. It was recently brought to our attention that she has been bringing her dog onto the premises. Animals are strictly prohibited. Her employment has been terminated as a result.'

'Seems a little harsh,' said Wheatley, who was clearly more used to wrestling hardened criminals than handling minor canine infractions.

'We've had a letter from somebody claiming to be Derek Baker's solicitor,' said the DON somewhat sheepishly, 'stating that he is prepared to waive his right to sue over his mother's injuries, provided Sister Bronwyn is not returned to night duty and that Queenie is banned from entering Woodlands at all times.'

Wheatley's ears pricked up. 'This sounds rather like blackmail to me,' he said.

'His mother's fall was an accident,' said Miss Bloom. Walter was relieved to hear it from her lips. Might it also mean she saw the scooter incident as that too? An unfortunate accident?

'I don't understand why Derek Baker would go out of his way to get rid of Sister Bronwyn,' said Morrissey, now twirling his pencil around his thumb like a baton.

Wheatley connected the dots. 'Presumably to move his girlfriend in.' He gave a licentious smirk.

Morrissey pursed his lips. 'This sounds more like an internal matter.'

'Hang on,' said Wheatley, wiping shortbread crumbs from his chin. 'Do you have CCTV? I recognise this bloke from somewhere. I've seen his photo up in the station.'

The DON nodded. 'In all the main areas, yes.'

'Is Laurel's son wanted?' asked Walter, his imagination limbering up.

'You think he's *that* Derek Baker?'

Wheatley nodded and turned to the DON. 'Have any of your controlled drugs gone missing?'

She shook her head. 'No, there's only one resident prescribed opiates at the moment, a Fentanyl patch every three days. But every patch has been accounted for and signed off in the S8 book.'

'Wait a minute,' Walter interjected. 'Are you talking about Murray?' She nodded, clearly surprised. 'Murray has been refusing his pain patches. Sister Who stuck a plain Band-Aid on his back instead, to make sure he wasn't allergic to the adhesive.' He blushed, worried he would be forced to divulge how he came across this information, revealing that he and Miss Bloom had been hiding together in the bathroom. In the dark.

The DON looked over the top of her glasses. 'Sister . . . Who has signed to say they've been given. And each dose was countersigned by the AIN.'

Wheatley stood up. 'I'd like to see the S8 book and the CCTV, if you'd be so kind. This might be our chance to catch the slippery Derek Baker. AKA "The Drug Rep".'

The collective gasp around the office was akin to the canned laughter of a TV sitcom.

The DON was agog. 'Are you telling me Sister . . . Who has been supplying Laurel Baker's son with Murray's Fentanyl patches and substituted a waterproof dressing for his cancer pain?'

Walter could have interjected again. He could have said that Murray had refused the pain relief because he was afraid of falling asleep and never waking up. Or because he was a stoical bastard. Walter said nothing. The case was stacking up nicely against Sister Who, and the likelihood of having Sister Bronwyn reinstated was enough for him to keep his mouth shut.

'Derek Baker is a dealer,' said Morrissey. 'Fentanyl is flavour of the month. You'd be surprised what people do with the patches to get a hit. Inject them, chew them, eat them. Some people shove them up their backsides to get a high or even make tea with them.'

The DON looked horrified and pushed away her cup and saucer.

Wheatley added, 'And your Sister . . . Whoever will have been taking her cut of the profit. She and Derek Baker are obviously in cahoots.'

Walter swelled with pride. Tom Selleck, eat your heart out.

The constables also looked very pleased with themselves, a promotion no doubt awaiting each of them once they secured the CCTV footage as evidence. The DON leaned on her desk, head in her hands. There was no sign of Fanny, Walter noticed. Once again she'd disappeared into thin air.

'Now all we need to do is to take a statement from this resident Murray,' said Morrissey, his voice now sounding deeper and more sergeant-like.

The DON's face dropped.

'I'm afraid that's the bad news I was going to tell you,' she said looking between Walter and Miss Bloom. 'Murray's wife, Joyce, phoned an hour ago. He passed away shortly after you left.'

51

Hattie

THAT EVENING AT THE DINNER TABLE, WALTER CLEMENTS' chair was empty. At first Hattie assumed that the excitement of the day's events must have simply worn him out or that he needed some time for quiet reflection after hearing about Murray. The two of them had been very close.

Later that night, there was still no sign of him. Beyond the thin partition wall, his television was silent and she heard only the low murmur of voices. On the pretext of walking off a convenient cramp, Hattie went to investigate. Outside Whitechapel Road, Walter's daughter Marie and his doctor were deep in hushed conversation. Not wanting to pry, Hattie withdrew. By the time the hot-drinks trolley squeaked around the corner, the doctor was packing away her stethoscope and there was a butterfly on Walter's door.

The news about Murray had been bittersweet. At least he had enjoyed a last cup of tea with Joyce and seen his garden. Although she was sure his ultimate dying wish would have been to see his daughters and grand-Vikings, Hattie knew they had done the right thing in taking him home.

The tea.

A chill ran through Hattie as she remembered that Joyce hadn't added the thickener to Murray's cup before he drank from it. Did he aspirate the hot tea into his lungs? Had the tea killed him? Hattie knew she could have said something, *should* have said something. A sin of omission was still a sin. If she'd been awake that night she would have heard the moment her mother's heart stopped. If she hadn't so selfishly fallen asleep, she might have been able to save her. Made that heart beat again. Brought her back to life. Her father had been beyond anyone's help but Hattie had carried the burden of her mother's death for eighty-one years, and yet the look of sheer undiluted pleasure on Murray's face as he sipped from the china cup was enough to assuage that guilt. She couldn't be responsible for what went on inside another human body. It was as simple as that.

The doctor acknowledged Hattie with a solemn nod. Hattie heard her on the phone telling someone she was leaving now and would be home in twenty minutes. The doctor probably had a husband and a family waiting for her. She looked as if she was wearing the emotional burden of her job like an extra decade around her waist and under her eyes. Old age was still far enough away, something she only saw in the crumbling minds and bodies of her patients. Did knowing what lay ahead make it any easier?

Marie was leaning back against the wall outside Walter's room, wiping her face with a tissue. She caught Hattie's eye and smiled through her tears.

'It's Miss Bloom, isn't it?'

Hattie nodded and walked towards her. 'How is he?'

'Dad is a stubborn old bugger,' said Marie. 'He's refusing to go to hospital.'

'Is it his heart?'

Marie nodded. Fresh tears spilled from her eyes and she dabbed them away impatiently. 'It's pulmonary oedema. The doctor told him if he doesn't go to hospital tonight he's likely to die.'

'Why won't he go?'

'He told me if he *is* dying, he wants to die at home.' Marie's body began to shake with sobs. She could barely get the words out. 'The worst thing is I had to tell him that the young couple who've been renting his house want to buy it. They've made an incredible offer.'

'How did he take the news?'

Marie laughed through her sobs. 'Better than I expected. The one thing about getting old is that you've already had plenty of practice dealing with bad news. Do you know what he said?' Hattie shook her head. 'After all his protests, after all the fuss about going home once he'd passed his scooter test, he said it didn't matter anymore. It was time for the house to find a new family. He told me *this* is his home now.' She looked around incredulously. 'This place. *Woodlands*.'

Hattie's thoughts returned to her bare garden, the orangutan-orange front door and the majestic Angophora tree now reduced to mulch, her beloved owls gone. It was as alien to her as Woodlands was familiar. Was the cottage still her home if it no longer looked or felt like one? What made a place home?

'Is he in any pain?'

'No.' Marie braved a smile. 'The doctor's given him some morphine and he looks very peaceful. She also gave him a shot of Lasix to clear the fluid and put a nitrate patch on his chest to open up the blood vessels in his heart. She said it was worth a try. She's coming back in the morning.'

'Can I see him?'

'Of course. He's a bit drowsy but I'm sure he'd like to see you.' She gave Hattie a knowing look.

They sat on opposite sides of the bed watching Walter breathe, his lungs full of the fluid his huge weak heart couldn't clear. But then, she'd heard drowning wasn't a bad way to go. Like falling asleep under water and never waking up.

Marie yawned and glanced at her watch.

'Why don't you go home, Marie? The night staff can call you if anything changes.'

Marie stretched her arms above her head and yawned again. 'I should stay,' she said. 'I don't want him to be alone.'

'I'll stay with him,' said Hattie.

'But you need your sleep too.'

'Not as much as you do. You have a son to look after, and a husband who'll be wondering where you are. You'll need to keep your strength up.'

Marie considered the offer. She looked dead on her feet. 'Okay,' she said. 'But I'll be back early tomorrow morning. I'm in bed by nine but I wake at five every morning, regular as clockwork. Always have done.'

Hattie smiled. 'That's because you're a lark, my dear. Good job I'm a night owl.'

In evolutionary terms, it made sense for there to be both, she explained. That way there's always someone awake to protect the tribe and ensure the survival of the species. It wasn't possible to turn a lark into a night owl. Nor the other way around. And no pressure sensor or mattress on the floor could keep someone in bed when their body clock was wide awake. Sister Bronwyn knew that.

Rising wearily from the chair, Marie paused for a moment. 'About the thing with Murray,' she said. 'Stealing the minibus and taking him home on his birthday.'

'Yes?' Hattie braced herself for the admonishment.

'Let's just say that nothing surprises me about my father,' said Marie. 'Behind all the bravado, he's a very kind and generous man. He might have some ideas that would make a Neanderthal look enlightened, and we don't always see eye to eye, but I'm proud of him. He is a good father, and was, whatever he thinks, a good husband to my mother. He's also the funniest man I've ever known. And not for the reason he thinks he is. Let's face it, Dad's jokes are terrible.' She leaned over and kissed Walter on his forehead. 'See you in the morning, Miss Bloom.'

'Bright and early,' replied Hattie.

Alone with Walter, Hattie dimmed the lights and made herself comfortable. It was going to be a long night but she would not leave his side. He would get better. He would. She would not fall asleep this time.

Hattie's eyelids were leaden. Every now and again Walter's arms twitched but he didn't stir. A dream, or the morphine? His breathing was still frothy and laboured, but it hadn't got any worse. She looked at his hand and wanted to touch it. Something held her back. She couldn't risk it.

'Miss Bloom?'

Hattie jerked upright on hearing her name and swivelled round to see who it was. A soft silhouette in the doorway.

'Sister Bronwyn. I didn't hear you coming,' said Hattie.

'I arrived by stealth.' Sister Bronwyn was all smiles. 'Brought in a can of WD40 and fixed that squeaky wheel at last,' she said.

'Is that allowed? Don't you have to go on a training course for that?' Hattie kept a straight face.

'Shush, don't tell anyone.' Sister Bronwyn tapped the side of her nose.

'I won't if you won't.' Health and safety wouldn't allow a resident to sit all night by the bed of another resident either. It was probably clearly stated in the rules and regulations. But then, Sister Bronwyn had her own way of getting around such pesky details. It was called common sense.

She took Walter's pulse and rearranged the bedclothes. Satisfied, Sister Bronwyn sat in the spare chair and pulled out a bag of boiled sweets. 'Want one?'

Hattie shook her head. 'We missed you.'

'I missed you too.' Sister Bronwyn sucked on the sweet and chased it round the inside of her mouth thoughtfully. 'It wasn't all wasted time,' she said. 'Queenie and I spent some quality girl time together, drinking tea and peeing in the bushes.' She chuckled.

'Where is Queenie?'

'She's here, doing her rounds. The good news is that when the DON phoned me this afternoon to ask me to come back at short notice to cover tonight's shift, she agreed that Queenie could come too. Strictly no toy geese allowed. It turns out she's known all along about The Night Owls. She told me she wants me to put together a manual for the other staff, ideas for improving the quality of care for our residents at night. I think it's a sign the industry is finally waking up, if you'll excuse the pun. We're the ones who need to adjust, not the other way round.'

'So,' said Hattie with a crooked grin. 'Queenie's official at last?'

'She's a member of staff now, yes.' Sister Bronwyn's vast bosom swelled with pride.

'Mr Clements is rather fond of that dog. Do bring her in to say hello to him, won't you?' Hello? Or goodbye?

'I will,' Sister Bronwyn said with a nod, then stood. 'Well, I'd better go and finish my round. I'll be back with more morphine in two hours. In the meantime, if you need anything, you know where to find me.'

'In the day room?'

'Cocktails and canapés at midnight.'

'I've thought of something I might like to do,' Hattie called after her. 'My Night Owls job.'

'Do tell,' said Sister Bronwyn, pausing at the door.

'I'm going to propose a column for the Woodlands newsletter. I could interview the residents about interesting aspects of their lives. They could share memories, and suggestions about the catering. It would be by the residents, for the residents.'

'I think that's an excellent idea. What are you going to call this column of yours?'

'I was thinking, "In Cahoots".'

Hattie remembered what Charles Darwin had purportedly said about evolution. It wasn't always the most intelligent species that survived, but the one most capable of change and adaptation to its environment. The owls would simply move on, find another ancient hollow and build another nest.

After Sister Bronwyn had gone, Hattie took Walter's clammy hand in hers. His fingers flickered and for a moment she stiffened. Then Hattie breathed in and let the cool fingers close around hers. She stroked his thick white hair gently with her spare hand and finally, against every instinct that had kept her apart from other people all her life, she leaned over and touched her lips to his forehead.

52

Walter

IN THE SAME WAY THAT HE HAD RELIED ON TICKING BOXES to coordinate Sylvia's care in her final days, Walter found comfort in busying himself with the arrangements after she died.

'Everyone copes differently,' the counsellor had reassured him. 'When it comes to grieving, there's no right or wrong way. There's no timetable either. It takes as long as it takes.'

Marie had organised the grief counsellor, worried that her father was coping too well. He'd maintained that his coping strategy – the one that he was apparently perfectly entitled to – involved ticking boxes. While he had boxes to tick, he had a tool, but it was when he started to run out of boxes that things went awry.

What Walter was really doing was postponing the inevitable last tick. He had hung on to Sylvia's clothes as long as possible. When he asked the counsellor what would be a suitable time to leave them hanging in the wardrobe, she replied, as she always replied, that there was no right or wrong.

'Whenever you feel ready, Walter.'

Eventually, Marie's offers to help had become so repetitive that Walter decided now was as good a time as any. She had approached the task, as she had approached every other as far as her mother was concerned, with grim resolve and what Walter took to be secret resentment.

'What a shame she won't get to wear this again,' or 'What a shame this lovely coat is going to waste.'

Somehow it was her father's fault that these items were hanging redundant on the rack, even the pieces Sylvia hadn't worn in decades. When Walter suggested they donate everything to charity, Marie had spiralled.

'Take what you want,' Walter had told her. 'I'll donate the rest to a good cause.' Sylvia had always believed in good causes.

Together, he and Marie had sorted out the wardrobe, dragging each item from its hanger and folding it into one of the waiting plastic bags. Walter had tried to lighten the mood with a few quips, warning her not to throw out any of his designer gear by mistake.

'You don't have any designer gear, Dad.'

Pulling out a khaki camouflage shirt he used to wear to do the gardening, he said, 'I'll have you know this is from the Armani surplus store.'

He hadn't seen her smile in months. It pained him to see his child suffering. Worse, his adult daughter had begun to infantilise him, inquiring regularly if he'd remembered to wash his sheets and change his underwear.

The final tick couldn't go into the box until the bags were physically disposed of. As a rule he avoided charity shops. They made him uncomfortable. Whether it was the frosty reception from the volunteers as they wearily added his bags of discarded items to the mountain of similar bags in the back room, or the smell of air freshener, Walter wasn't sure. He suspected they received more donations than they could ever hope to sell.

The alternative to the face-to-face guilt trip of donating without buying anything in return was to place the bags into the large metal collection bins in the car park. This strategy had the advantage of anonymity and avoided the judgement, but he'd heard that many of the items ended up as industrial rags and he couldn't bear to think of Sylvia's things covered in oil on the floor of some mechanic's workshop.

The final option was a compromise and saw Walter heading very early to the Red Cross store, where he planned to pull up at the back, unload his bags and be gone again before it opened. It was a short drive, a familiar route and one he knew well enough to let down his guard. Having hung onto Sylvia's things for so long, he wanted to get this over with. Taking his eyes off the road, he noticed a small rip in one of the bags in the passenger-side foot well. Poking through was a piece of blue checked fabric. Instantly, he recognised it as Sylvia's favourite picnic dress, the one she wore on their first date and countless others during their courtship. This was the Sylvia he wanted to remember; the young and vibrant woman he married, the one he made laugh, the one he fell in love with. The one who had loved him in return.

Reaching down, Walter tugged at the dress until the rip in the bag suddenly gave and the dress was free. The fabric was faded from so many washes, and mildewed around the hem, and suddenly Walter wondered why his wife had kept it all these years when she'd bought and worn and recycled so many other dresses. She could have parted with it, but she chose not to. He had been searching for the one thing that would hold her memory forever – and here it was. Walter brought the soft blue material to his face and inhaled.

He tried to open his eyes but there was nothing to see. A cool hand stroked his forehead.

'Don't try to move,' a woman's voice said. 'Everything is going to be all right.'

He stopped fighting then and lay back, sinking into the blackness. There was no pain, only the fight for each breath. He didn't recall the moment of impact. The last thing he saw was the telegraph pole, so solid and so final coming towards him. He remembered at that moment not caring whether he lived or died. He was so tired; all he wanted to do was sleep. The fight was over and everything was serene at last. He'd ticked his last box and it was time to hang up his clipboard for good.

53

Hattie

WHEN HATTIE OPENED HER EYES IT WAS LIGHT. IT TOOK A moment to orientate herself to the room that was not hers. Golfing trophies arranged on a low table. A rural landscape tilted against the wall. A crocheted blanket on the bed. She rubbed the sleep from her eyes and remembered where she was. Whitechapel Road.

'They never put enough butter in these things.'

Hattie shuffled to the edge of the reclining chair and watched Walter excavate the small plastic container with the tip of his knife. He turned to her and winked. Marie was sitting in the other chair.

'Morning, Miss Bloom,' she said.

Hattie yawned. 'Have you been here long?' What time was it? Eight? Nine o'clock?

'A while. I've been catching up on my book.' She lifted a dog-eared paperback for Hattie to see. 'And playing chaperone, of course.' She smiled at Walter. 'Protecting the young and innocent from my rogue of a father.'

'Now, now Marie,' Walter chimed in. 'Don't give Miss Bloom the wrong impression. I am a gentleman.'

'How are you feeling?' Hattie stood up to get a closer look. Was this really the same man?

'I've been peeing like a Shire horse all night, but otherwise, never better.'

'Dad!'

'I'm surprised you managed to sleep through all that flushing,' added Walter.

'You looked so peaceful, we agreed not to wake you,' said Marie gently.

'I wasn't asleep. Only resting my eyes.' Hattie was annoyed with herself. Had she really slept all this time? She remembered checking the clock at quarter to one, then nothing after that. Nearly eight hours. It was the longest she'd slept in a long, long time.

The colour had returned to Walter's cheeks this morning. He looked thinner around the face; in fact, his entire body seemed to have shrunk overnight.

As if reading her thoughts, Walter said, 'That injection the doctor gave me has worked wonders. I'm half the man I used to be, and for once that's a blessing!' He laughed at his own joke. Marie laughed too and Hattie couldn't help but smile.

The smile faded from Walter's face and he put his toast down on the plate. 'I can't believe Murray has gone.' His eyes swam behind man-sized tears and his voice cracked. 'I'm going to miss him.'

'Oh Dad.' Marie put her arm around him and squeezed him into a hug. 'What you and Miss Bloom did for Murray was very special. You were a good friend to him. A real mate, and I'm proud of you.'

Walter kissed his daughter's cheek. 'Be a good girl and get your old dad a fresh cup of tea, would you? This one's like dishwater.'

Marie took his half-empty cup from his hands. 'Be back in a tick,' she said. 'I'll fetch one for you too, Miss Bloom.'

When she was gone, Hattie said, 'You'll be pleased to hear, Sister Bronwyn is back. Queenie's back too, on probation.'

'Excellent news.'

'It's funny,' she continued, 'but we don't really think about how the staff must feel when a resident dies, do we? I mean, they spend all this time with someone, performing intimate tasks as well as getting to know them, listening to their fears, their worries. And then they have to say goodbye. It must be like losing friend after friend. That has to take its toll.'

Walter nodded. 'That's what makes Sister Bronwyn different. You get the feeling it's more than a job to her.'

Hattie hung her head and reflected on what Joyce had said. *Bronwyn is more than a nurse to us, she's like family.*

In the time it took for Marie to track down two cups of hot tea, Dr Wilson had popped in, taken Walter's blood pressure, listened to his heart and lungs, and declared him a miracle.

When Marie returned, Walter repeated what the doctor had said and added, 'Walter Clements defends his one hundred percent record.' He sounded like a sports commentator, making them smile. 'Even the girls pass with Walter.' Marie pursed her lips and folded her arms in mock indignation. Walter winked at Hattie.

～

Later, sitting in the big PVC chair in the treatment room, Hattie held her breath as Dr Robin Sparrow instructed the nurse to remove the dressing. Slowly and carefully she unwound the bandage as if unwrapping an ancient mummy. Layer after layer, a pass-the-parcel of potential badness. For once neither nurse nor doctor recoiled. The whiff had disappeared.

Dr Sparrow viewed Hattie's leg through his bifocals, moving them up and down his nose until he appeared satisfied.

'Well?' Hattie shifted in the chair with a loud squeak against the plastic covering. 'Is it getting better?'

'It certainly looks . . .' The doctor leaned down again for a second look. 'Much—'

'It's healing beautifully, Miss Bloom,' said the nurse. 'Look at all that beautiful new skin, all pink and shiny.' She looked genuinely pleased with what science or nature had done with Hattie's horrible ulcer. The uncommon bacteria had moved on, found another wound to inhabit.

'I think we could get away with a . . .' Dr Sparrow drew a rectangle with his fingers. 'No need for . . .' He mimed a winding motion.

'I think you're finally ready.' The nurse removed the backing paper from a woven dressing and stuck it to Hattie's leg.

'Ready? Ready for what?'

'To go home.'

Dr Sparrow nodded in agreement. 'I can arrange for community—'

'Nurses,' continued the beaming staff nurse. 'They can come in every morning and help you with your medication and check the leg.'

'Are you sure?' Hattie ran her fingers over her pale shin, her skin ultra sensitive where it had been hidden beneath weeks of bandaging. 'Are you sure it's healed sufficiently? What if it opens up again once I get home?'

'As I said, the nurses will—'

'Check.'

'Wouldn't it be better for me to stay a bit longer?' Hattie was getting desperate. 'Just to be safe?'

The nurse frowned. Dr Sparrow raked his hair, his fingers leaving it standing on end like a mad professor.

'I thought you wanted to go home,' said the nurse. 'All the renovations are finished.'

'But what about, you know, health and safety?'

'I think—'

'The occupational therapist has arranged for railings in the shower and non-slip mats on the floors. She's ordered a Vital Call buzzer and a weekly cleaner.'

There was an awkward silence while Dr Sparrow removed his glasses and pinched the bridge of his nose. His was the casting vote. The nurse tore off her latex gloves and dropped them into a pedal bin.

'If you'd let me finish,' said Dr Sparrow, 'I was going to say that I think you should do what *you* feel is best. Best for *you*.'

'He's right,' said the nurse, softening. 'It's up to you, Miss Bloom. It's time for you to decide whether to stay at Woodlands or go home. Give it some thought and let us know, so we can make the necessary arrangements.'

This was the moment she had been waiting for. Her entire life had been hanging in limbo. Her time was up now, she had served her sentence and at last she was free to make her own decisions.

54

Walter

IT WAS A PACKED HOUSE FOR MURRAY'S MEMORIAL SERVICE. Some of his former students turned up with anecdotes about the geography teacher who had opened their eyes to the world. Residents from Woodlands too, though Walter suspected that many of them had only come for the buffet.

The day room felt more like a greenhouse with Murray's botanical collection taking up just about every horizontal surface. The dusty plastic palms had since been consigned to the industrial bins by the back door. Even the vase of twigs that had doubled as a tripod for James's phone was gone, a luscious green peace lily having taken its place at the nurses' station. The foliage softened the day room, and with every resident now officially assigned their own plant to water and care for, there was an element of competition over which had the shiniest leaves or the most promising buds.

Joyce turned and waved from the front row. She was flanked by two very tall, slim women who couldn't have been anyone other than Murray's daughters, and a pair of flaxen-haired teenagers. Murray's young grand-Vikings. Projected onto the wall above all their heads, a photo of Murray in his garden, hosepipe in one hand, mug in the other, reminded them why they were all there.

The crowd was growing restless as the activities staff adjusted then readjusted the microphone and lectern. The service had been scheduled to start ten minutes ago and it wouldn't be long before the singing and chanting began. Led by Eileen, the ladies had gone on to form their own choir, and what they lacked in musical accuracy they made up for in sheer exuberance. Their performances were surprisingly effective when it came to getting what they wanted, too. It had only taken two verses and a chorus of Kylie Minogue's 'I'm Spinning Around' to get the DON to agree to pineapple rings.

'Ladies and gentlemen, may I have your attention, please?' The lifestyle coordinator waited for the chatter to die away. 'We'll be starting the memorial service very soon. Unfortunately, Reverend Richards is running late. He phoned to let us know he'll be with us as soon as he's parked his car. In the meantime, Margery has kindly offered to do the rounds with a plate of cheese straws.' The chatter resumed. 'But please remember to observe the usual rule of one straw per head so we don't run out.'

'What is this, 1949? I bet Eileen has been saving up her coupons especially.'

Walter turned as Miss Bloom settled into the empty chair next to him. He didn't need to look; he'd already felt her presence, as soon as she walked in.

'Miss Bloom,' he said, feigning surprise. 'How lovely to see you.'

'Were you saving this seat for anyone in particular?'

'No, feel free,' he said. In reality he'd been guarding it like a Rottweiler, snarling at anyone who dared to come near.

To Walter's relief, she hadn't changed a bit. But then, it had only been a matter of days since she'd gone home. He imagined she had looked the same for years. Miss Bloom was peculiarly ageless.

Their knees were almost touching in the cramped row of chairs. So far Miss Bloom hadn't moved hers away. 'Sister Bronwyn is here,' she said, leaning even closer. 'I spotted her and Queenie keeping a low profile at the back.'

Reverend Richards had arrived. He'd worked up quite a sweat considering he'd come straight from the car park. Walter watched him mop his brow with a handkerchief and loosen his dog collar.

'I had to park up by the school,' Walter heard him say.

'That's strange,' said the lifestyle coordinator. 'We reserved you a space right outside. Didn't you get the message?'

'I got the message all right. It's just that someone has left a dark blue mobility scooter parked outside.'

Walter treated the offender – a youngster in his mid-eighties who'd moved into Mayfair after Laurel Baker transferred to another facility – to a look of disapproval. He was going to have to say something. The newcomer was behaving like he was cock of the walk, hogging the red wine at dinner and hooning around the corridors like a lunatic on his top-of-the-range scooter. Somehow he had convinced Andrea that he was safe to drive the thing, while Walter's own test wouldn't happen until the day after tomorrow. This time, Walter had written it on the calendar himself. In capitals. It pained him to admit that since Dr What's-her-name had persuaded him to take his tablets, he'd never felt better. What a pity she hadn't insisted before.

Murray's daughters had put together a video tribute to their father. Walter watched the slideshow with what felt like a cheese straw stuck in his throat as Murray grew from a bald, sepia baby into a young man with thick hair, then a father with less hair and finally a balding grandfather. He'd ripened with age, as they all had. Were people most like themselves at the end of their lives? Were these the selves we could most trust?

The final photo of Murray was taken in his last days, in his room at Woodlands, surrounded by his beloved plants. Next to him sat a Tupperware container of Joyce's famous rock cakes, untouched. And a secret he would take to the grave.

When the formalities were over, Margery peeled back the cling wrap from the sandwiches and there was a rush to the buffet table. The first of the champagne corks popped to a round of applause and the party began. Walter was looking forward to a drink, the first since his secret supplier had found himself a steady girlfriend – one who no doubt admired his designer stubble – and quit his job at Woodlands. One glass would be sufficient. He didn't need more. For some reason he'd been sleeping so well of late.

Joyce noticed Walter standing with Miss Bloom and suddenly animated like a child noticing a puppy in a pet shop window, dragged her entourage to meet them.

'Thank you so much for coming,' she said. 'It would have meant the world to Murray.'

She introduced her daughters. One tanned from the African sun, the other daughter pale from the Arctic Circle.

'These are your grandad's dear friends Miss Bloom and Mr Clements,' said Joyce to the two grand-Vikings, a boy and a girl in their late teens. They looked so tired and a little awkward amid so many strangers. So many old people. How sad they had travelled all this way for a funeral.

Murray had been so proud of his family and all their accomplishments, and deservedly so. What a shame he couldn't be here in person to show them off. Walter realised, not for the first time, how lucky he was that Marie and James visited so often. They might have their differences, but they always came. In time, Marie would let go of her resentment and come to accept her mother's death and her father's transition to aged care, as he had. In time, the guilt would ease. As the counsellor Walter still maintained he'd never needed had said, 'There's no right or wrong way. There's no timetable either. It takes as long as it takes.'

'We've heard so much about you all,' said Miss Bloom. *We.*

Next, Joyce led the grand-Vikings over to meet the DON and Reverend Richards, leaving Walter and Miss Bloom alone.

'I thought once you escaped we wouldn't see you again,' said Walter. *We? I?*

'I wouldn't have missed Murray's memorial service.'

'Tell the truth, Miss Bloom, you only came for the cheese straws.'

She smiled. 'Is it that obvious?'

'So, how is life on the outside?'

Miss Bloom paused, her thoughts far away. 'Not quite as I remembered it.'

Queenie appeared, wagging her tail furiously in recognition when she saw them. When Walter bent to stroke her head, the dog moved away, glancing back as if beckoning him to follow. At the foot of Icarus's cage she sat to attention, tail flicking impatiently until they joined her. The cage door was ajar and Icarus was nowhere to be seen.

'Sister Bronwyn,' said Walter.

'Not guilty this time.' He turned and saw Sister Bronwyn standing behind him.

'Who, then?' said Miss Bloom, looking around for either the missing bird or the real culprit.

'I have my suspicions,' said Sister Bronwyn.

There was something different inside the cage. Queenie had noticed it too. Something out of place. The mirror that had previously hung from the wire was gone and in its place was what looked like a medal, dark and brassy on a faded red-and-yellow ribbon. A strange thing to leave in a birdcage, and far too heavy for the bird to have carried. Icarus must have had an ally. Reaching in through the open door, Sister Bronwyn retrieved the medal and inspected it, turning it over in her palm.

'It's some kind of war medal, by the look of it.' She held it in her palm for Walter and Miss Bloom to see.

Walter read out the inscription. '*Haakon VII, ALT FOR NORGE*. What do you think that means?'

'*Norge* is Norway, isn't it?' said Sister Bronwyn. 'All for Norway?'

'Wait here, I know someone who can translate for us.' Walter returned a few moments later with one of the grand-Vikings. His name was Henrik and his accent fell halfway between that of his Australian mother and Scandinavian father. His eyes widened when he saw the medal.

'Oh, wow,' he said, 'this is the Norwegian War Medal. It was awarded by King Haakon for service during the Second World War. The red and yellow ribbon is the king's standard.' He shrugged modestly. 'We did it in school last year. I did a project on the Norwegian Resistance – you know, about the civil disobedience, unarmed resistance and sabotage they carried out under cover. They used to wear paperclips on their lapels as a symbol of solidarity, and red bobble hats.'

Walter, Miss Bloom and Sister Bronwyn all looked at each other in surprise and recognition.

Miss Bloom turned to Henrik and dropped her voice. 'Who is Viga Ossicker? Was she a member of the resistance?'

'*Vi ga oss ikke?* It's not a name, it means "We did not give up". You know, no surrender.'

No surrender.

So, she hadn't given up. She had not surrendered to whatever horrors had put this bravery medal into her hands. She was still fighting, still struggling. The evasive Fanny Olsen was still waging her own silent war of resistance.

With the party slowly winding down, Walter offered to walk Miss Bloom to reception.

'Sally can order you a taxi,' he said.

'That won't be necessary,' she replied.

'It's a long walk, Miss Bloom.'

She smiled and her eyes crinkled at the edges. 'Not so far. Along to the end of the corridor, turn right at Piccadilly and it's just before Liverpool Street Station.'

Bond Street. Murray's old room.

55

Hattie

BOND STREET WAS DEFINITELY A STEP UP FROM OLD KENT Road. Her father had given her Monopoly one Christmas, several years after her mother died, but Hattie could only ever remember playing alone. She'd had a good imagination, conjuring the friends she never made in real life, and together they spent many happy hours buying houses and hotels, turning CHANCE cards and collecting imaginary rents. And now here she was, arranging her books and other paltry belongings around one of the board game's most valuable pieces of real estate.

In truth, she nearly hadn't made it back to Woodlands at all.

'You're too fit for a nursing home, Miss Bloom,' the social worker who'd been sent to assess her had said. Perplexed, she'd added, 'Most people are desperate to get out rather than in a hurry to get in.'

On the spot, Hattie had turned to an unexpected role model in Laurel Baker and drawn what she hoped was a convincing picture of a frail, helpless woman. 'But I've had a fall,' she protested. 'You should have seen me, I went flying. The surgeon said mine was the worst hip fracture he'd ever seen. It's a miracle my leg is still attached. My bones are hollow, you see.' *Like a bird's.*

It had worked. If the social worker had seen through the melodrama, she didn't let on, or at least hadn't been brave enough to deny Hattie the necessary paperwork.

Joyce had insisted that Murray's beloved plants – the ones that hadn't already found new homes in the day room – should remain with the room.

'There are plenty more where they came from,' she'd promised on a brief visit the day after the memorial service to check Hattie was settling in all right. She'd left a dozen rock cakes behind, so Icarus, who was still at large within Woodlands, would be happy too.

From the window, Hattie had a view over the garden that ran down the north side of the nursing home, and more importantly, a view of the untouched bushland beyond where the mature gum trees seemed to go on forever. Even with her window open a health-and-safety inch, she could lie in bed and listen to the owls and tawny frogmouths, and in the mornings, the tuning up of the native-bird orchestra: kookaburras followed by the cockatoos followed by the magpies.

The only downside was Bond Street's limited shelf space, nowhere near enough for her collection of books and bound manuscripts. The DON had told her she was welcome to use the shelves in the book corner outside her old room. Moving the dusty old paperbacks to one side, Hattie had found plenty of space for her books. Following her hasty departure, Laurel Baker had left behind a small coffee table and it found a new home in the book corner along with a couple of comfy chairs that had come from Walter Clements' house. The quiet corner gathered the morning sun and had become Hattie's private sanctuary.

Two days after Murray's memorial service, she decided to rehome a Boston fern that needed more light. It would do well on the coffee table, she'd thought. Hattie was surprised, and a little disappointed, to see a woman sitting reading a book. On seeing Hattie, the woman stood and introduced herself. She had a no-nonsense demeanour and the most extraordinary nose. It was all Hattie could do not to stare at the appendage that was shaped like a parrot's beak.

'Cynthia Parmington,' she said, offering her hand. 'I've recently moved into Old Kent Road but I like to keep myself to myself.'

Hattie shook her hand and introduced herself. 'That was my old room.'

'Damn silly notion, if you ask me,' said Cynthia. 'Naming all the rooms after a board game.'

'I think the idea was to give the place more character. To make it feel less . . . institutional.'

Cynthia harrumphed. 'I would have preferred something a little more upmarket, Leicester Square or Coventry Street at the minimum. Thankfully I'm not staying long.' Hattie smiled to herself. *Not In Jail. Just Visiting.*

The woman who kept herself to herself continued, drawing Hattie into a discussion of the various shortcomings Woodlands had to offer.

'It's so bloody noisy,' she said. 'All those squeaky wheels on the trolleys, doors slamming, cars coming and going at all hours.'

'You'll get used to it.'

'And why they call it Woodlands, I don't know. All I can see from my window is concrete. How ironic is that?'

Old age *was* a wonderful source of irony if nothing else. 'It helps to have a good imagination,' said Hattie.

'My son and daughter-in-law took me to see a place called *Ambrosia*. That means "food of the gods".'

'What was wrong with it?'

'They showed us around at lunchtime.'

Hattie smiled in recognition. 'The food's not bad in here,' she said. 'It's a lot easier than shopping and cooking for one.'

She debated warning Cynthia Parmington about the ladies and Walter Clements but decided she would let her make up her own mind about them. Cynthia Parmington returned her book to the shelf and ran her finger along the spines until it came to rest on volume one of *Guide to Bird Behaviour* by H. Bloom. She hooked it out of its spot and began to leaf through the pages.

'Do you like birds?' Hattie asked.

'My husband was a twitcher, God rest his soul. Spent most of our marriage peering through his binoculars. I went along with it because I didn't want to be left behind. Sometimes I thought he preferred birds to people. The birds seemed to flock around him too. It was like they had some special bond.' She closed the book and looked at the title. 'Perhaps this might help me understand a little better.'

Hattie disguised a smile, deciding not to reveal herself as the author. There was so much more left to learn about human behaviour, and anonymity was her only camouflage.

'Do you sleep?' she asked.

'I haven't slept a wink since I arrived.' Cynthia Parmington slumped back into the comfy chair and put her feet up on the coffee table. 'The worst thing is that during the day I can't keep my eyes open.'

'In that case, I'll introduce you to Queenie,' said Hattie.

56

Walter

'Good morning, Andrea,' said Walter. 'May I say how lovely you're looking today?'

'I'd rather you didn't, Mr Clements.'

Walter was quietly confident about his test. With all that had been going on, Walter's test had been postponed, but the day was finally here. If that young upstart with the dark blue scooter could pass, so could he. He rubbed his hands together in anticipation.

A stickler for procedure, Andrea insisted on doing the entire assessment again from the beginning, including the physical examination. Walter could barely contain his delight when she informed him that he had lost four kilos. He was surprised it wasn't more. The new water pills the doctor insisted he take were working wonders; his constant to-ing and fro-ing from the en-suite was keeping him fit as well as optimally dehydrated. He'd even ditched his walking frame. Walter felt the best he had in years.

'How's the foot?' he asked while she was flicking through the paperwork.

'It's getting better,' she said, looking up. 'Thank you for asking.'

'Don't you worry, love, I'll be on my best behaviour this time.'

'I'd prefer Andrea, if you don't mind.'

'Sorry, Andrea.'

Walter was so confident about today's performance that he'd even invited an audience. Marie had taken a day off from her career, and young James, who'd come from having braces fitted, was having the day off school. Luckily his sore teeth didn't stop him grinning a mouth full of expensive metal when he saw his grandfather polishing his electric scooter.

Shiny and impatient, the Tesla sprang to life as Walter turned the key. To his relief, Andrea kept her feet away from his wheels and he managed to exit Whitechapel Road with only a minor scrape of the doorjamb. Fortunately, Andrea was too busy checking for oncoming traffic to notice.

The course was straightforward. Once again, it was a slalom of dining chairs followed by a U-turn between two parallel tables. Marie was keeping a discreet distance but James had his mobile out ready to film. The police had confiscated the original phone, for evidence. Once the authorities had lost interest, the phone had been returned whereupon Walter had hidden it in the old shoebox after Marie, none the wiser and feeling responsible for mislaying her son's phone, bought him a new one.

The chairs were easy and Walter negotiated them without a hitch. So far, so good.

'Now the U-turn, Mr Clements,' shouted the OT.

Releasing the brake handle, Walter nudged forward. Nudge, brake. Nudge, brake. The Tesla was a good deal more manoeuvrable than the minibus but it was a tight squeeze between two dining tables so Walter took his time. Soon he was accelerating towards the waiting OT with a triumphant grin.

'Just the three-point turn now.'

Walter winked when he passed James, remembering not to take his hands off the handlebars. He gripped the rubber and turned the wheels. Checking the wing mirrors, as he'd always drummed into his pupils, Walter selected reverse and with the handlebars in the opposite direction, eased the Tesla backwards in another perfect arc. His neck creaked as he turned to make sure the coast was clear before accelerating forward, ending up a perfect one hundred and eighty degrees from where he started. He narrowly missed the antique hall table that had been clumsily mended. Even at this speed Walter could clearly see the drips of glue from the handyman's bodged job. The statue was still missing, however, presumably beyond the capabilities of that young idiot. It had been replaced instead by a display of pamphlets.

Working towards 100% Health and Safety at Woodlands. Your role.

On the final straight, Walter dialled up the speed towards the finish line. Out of the corner of his eye he saw Judy, Eileen and Ada heading for morning tea. He'd better hurry if he wanted a chocolate brownie. He also noticed Miss Bloom, and the new lady, Mrs Parmington, watching from the comfy chairs in the corner. They were an unlikely pair, rarely uttering a word to each other and yet seemingly inseparable.

'Remember, Mr Clements,' Andrea called, 'slow and steady wins the race.'

Said who? *Said no one.* Walter let out the throttle, his smile widening as the Tesla gathered speed, Andrea and her final tick box now firmly in his sights.

At the imaginary finish line, Walter brought the Tesla to a controlled stop, inches from Andrea's toes. She ticked the final box and signed her name.

'Congratulations, Mr Clements, you passed.'

Walter's chest swelled with pride. He had done it. Walter Clements still had a one hundred percent pass rate. Even with the girls.

'I'll let Peter know,' said Marie, kissing her father on the cheek. She seemed happier recently and had even brought him a tin of biscuits, albeit low-sugar ones. She'd softened somehow; in less of a rush on her last couple of visits. Best of all, it had been a whole week since she'd brought in new socks. Though, with his ankles looking so slim and trim these days he fancied showing them off. Patterned socks would be just the ticket, like the ones he used to wear for golf, the ones with the diamonds up the side. Dare he ask?

Andrea disappeared to file a copy of her report in Walter's notes and Marie went off to phone All-Electric Scooters to deliver the good news.

'That was sick, Grandpa,' said James when they were alone. He looked older, no longer the little boy who'd bravely fought back the tears at his grandmother's funeral only a year ago. How quickly they grew up.

'Thanks, James,' said Walter. He tried to swallow. For once he was sick and it was something to be proud of. He took the compliment, for he had received precious few in his lifetime. Aside from his undisputed skill behind the wheel, Walter had always considered himself an average man, an average father, an average husband. A good-enough man, according to Murray. He hoped that in time, James would surpass his grandfather's mediocrity and become impressive in his own right. Marie simply needed to give him the space to be himself.

'Fancy a spin?'

James's eyes widened. 'For real?'

Walter looked around. The coast was clear. He dismounted from the deluxe rotating seat with the adjustable headrest and flip armrests. 'She's all yours, mate.'

'What will Mum say?'

'Who cares? Live a little dangerously.' He rested a hand on the boy's shoulder. 'Want me to demonstrate the controls for you?'

'No need,' said James. 'It's like playing Fortnite. Only more exciting.' With that, he was off, his grin widening as he picked up speed.

Seeing the Tesla from the rear, it occurred to Walter that the walking-stick holder on the back would be the perfect spot for his golf clubs. After all, now he'd passed his test and there was nothing stopping him from popping down to the club for a quick round, maybe even invite the new bloke along. Home along the footpath too, evading the breathalysers. He could drive when it suited him and ride when it suited him even better.

James giggled as he snaked and weaved down the empty corridor, giving himself a running commentary.

The beep of the horn preceded the crashing sound by a fraction of a second. Walter looked up from his reverie to see a red bobble hat and Fanny Olsen sidestep to the left as James swerved to avoid her. To give the lad his due, he did a good job of not running her over. Unfortunately, the front wheel clipped the recently repaired leg of the antique table and it came crashing down, scattering health-and-safety leaflets everywhere.

Walter's heart skipped a single beat then returned to its steady fifty-six beats a minute, thanks to his new heart pills. He slapped his hands against his thighs and laughed. His chest tightened, the next breath trapped inside. Air gushed from Walter in a great guffaw. For once he was grateful that his record-breaking prostate was acting like a cork. James, on the other hand, looked petrified, his face drained of colour.

'Don't worry, son,' said Walter, clapping him on the back. 'Park the Tesla over there and pick up that lot while I fix the table.'

James obliged, scooping up armfuls of leaflets. Meanwhile, Walter propped the severed leg back under the corner of the righted table. It was wobbly but no one would be any the wiser. With any luck, one of the ladies would clip it with their walker and the handyman would get the kick up the arse he deserved.

'Fist bump, Grandpa,' said James.

It was a new thing the youngsters did, the modern equivalent of a firm handshake. Proving that he could move with the times, Walter touched his clenched fist to James's and they fell into a hug. A round of applause erupted from the comfy chairs. Walter sucked in his stomach and bowed to his adoring audience. Unless he was very much mistaken, Miss Bloom was smiling as she clapped. It was a smile that could melt a man's heart. Even one as large as Walter's.

57

Hattie

HE WAS NORMALLY SO CONFIDENT, THAT THE SIGHT OF Walter Clements perspiring beside her made Hattie worry there might be something seriously wrong with him again. He'd been rehearsing for days.

'Chest pain?'

He shook his head but loosened his collar. The bow tie had been a present from his daughter, he'd told her. One of the many Marie had started to buy him. Apparently he had quite a collection now, though he admitted it made a pleasant change from socks.

In the chair on Hattie's other side was Mrs Parmington, who, in spite of her reassurances that she always kept herself to herself had stuck to her like gumtree sap since she arrived. Not that Hattie minded too much. Unlike the ladies, she didn't gossip, and unlike Walter Clements, appeared blissfully at ease with silence.

'You've nothing to worry about, Mr Clements,' said Hattie. 'You'll be fine once you get started.' Unfortunately her well-intentioned reassurance fell flat and he began to flick through his notebook yet again, muttering under his breath.

Queenie was on her best behaviour. She was allowed to wander but not chase toys, and treats were now strictly rationed. It hadn't taken her long to work out who were The Night Owls' softest touches. Fanny Olsen was always a good bet, and always had some tasty morsel secreted somewhere on her person. Ada too, as long as Judy wasn't looking.

It was as if Sister Bronwyn had never been away. It was none of their business whether she had ever confessed to Brendan about her brief absence, whether he had ever guessed that his wife had spent several nights in a parked car pretending to be at work. Her secret would always be safe with The Night Owls. From the brief conversation they'd had, however, Hattie gleaned that she and Brendan still hadn't found a place to rent. And then it struck her: the perfect solution had been staring her in the face the whole time. Somehow Hattie needed to find the extortionate fees to pay for Woodlands. Angophora Cottage was modest, ideal for a couple, particularly if they didn't mind a bit of renovation, and best of all it had a large fenced backyard. A large, fenced, dog-proof backyard. There was no need to mention next door's new baby that cried all night, nor the ginger tomcat that treated Hattie's place as his own. Apparently Queenie loved barking at cats.

The stage was almost ready. Sameera had strung fairy lights between the paintings and across the ceiling to the chandelier. She'd also made use of a tinsel curtain she'd come across in the Christmas box and fashioned it into a backdrop. With the examination lamp from the treatment room in place, Sister Bronwyn called for everyone's attention.

'Ladies and gentlemen,' she said, 'our next act needs no introduction. Please put your hands together for . . . Walter Clements.'

The applause was ample for Walter to take his place in the centre of the stage. He squinted into the spotlight, and Hattie held her breath. There was a time when she had never wanted to see this man again. Now, her fingers were crossed so hard she developed cramps. He was a proud man, a relic of a bygone era really, but this was his big moment. Every dog had its day, and this was his.

Walter's voice cracked and he cleared his throat, tugged at his collar, and checked his notes. Hattie exchanged anxious looks with Sister Bronwyn. This wasn't exactly the Royal Variety Performance, but it mattered.

'My doctor told me that drinking would shorten my life. But how many old doctors have you seen compared to old drunks?' Judy, who had become a born-again insomniac – mostly because she didn't want to miss out on the nocturnal activities – was chatting with Ada and Eileen. Fanny had fallen asleep, red bobble hat askew and a can of fake snow also from the Christmas decoration box about to slip out of her hand. Even Queenie was lying on her side, paws flickering in some imagined canine adventure.

Walter consulted his notebook once more.

'A man was showing off his new hearing aid, boasting it was the highest tech model on the market. His friend asked him how much he'd paid for it. "Half past nine," he replied.'

Nothing. Not a snigger, apart from Sister Bronwyn whose hammed-up laughter was so exaggerated Hattie feared she might do herself an injury. Hattie wanted to laugh, she really did, but some vital connection was missing. The match was damp and simply wouldn't spark.

Undeterred, the comedian continued, but as his next couple of jokes fell flat his eyes were almost pleading for a response. Hattie picked at her fingers in her lap. After she'd cajoled him and encouraged him to take a chance, the entire act was proving an unmitigated disaster.

Ever the optimist, Walter Clements gave it one last try. 'I took my wife to the doctor the other day because she was a bit off colour. The doctor recommended sex three times a week to perk her up. "Which days, doctor?" I asked him. He suggested Monday, Wednesday and Friday. I replied, "I can bring her in Monday and Wednesday, but I play golf on Fridays, so she'll have to catch the bus."'

Ada adjusted her hearing aid then turned to Judy and before Sister Bronwyn could fill the awkward silence, said, 'Did he say sex three times a week?'

Judy replied, 'It was a joke, Ada. Nobody has sex three times a week.'

'Harold and I always did,' said Ada, taken aback. 'He was a voracious lover, you know, quite insatiable in fact, and I certainly wasn't complaining.'

Walter Clements' eyes were as wide as two saucers. It was too much for Judy. Her cheeks turned scarlet and she leaned so far away from Ada that Hattie was worried she might fall off her chair.

No one recalled who was the first to crack, but a beat later they were all in stitches. Sister Bronwyn was soon helpless with laughter. The ladies guffawed, waking Fanny with such a start that her hand clenched around the aerosol releasing a blizzard of fake snow. Queenie struggled to her feet and snapped her jaws at the frothy white flakes falling to the carpet. Even Mrs Parmington was helpless, rolling around in the armchair beside Hattie. Above them, Icarus swooped from the top of a lampshade to the string of fairy lights where he hung upside down by his feet like an acrobat. His feathers were beginning to grow back, Hattie noticed. He really was a handsome little bird, and he knew it.

With the audience well and truly warmed up, Walter's next jokes were greeted with hoots of laughter. The ladies were soon hungry for more. The more risqué the gag, the louder the whoops. But it was the look on Walter's face that made Hattie smile. It was an expression of raw, unbridled joy. Joy and relief. It lasted until a wide unabashed grin took over. He bowed, nodding his head in modest appreciation, giving the audience a little clap himself in return before shuffling sideways from the makeshift stage like a crab. At this, Hattie let go. And laughed.

Walter was a man renewed. It was written all over his face. It was in his stride and the swing of his arms, the way he carried his head a little higher, and in his shoulders now a fraction less hunched. To the casual observer he was still an old man but Hattie knew what this had meant to him. She was different too: the staleness flushed from her and her entire body energised. Her stomach and cheeks ached from laughing and her lips refused to close around her teeth. There were some things that were almost impossible to experience alone. Laughter was one of them.

'Bravo, Mr Clements,' she said.

'Thank you, Miss Bloom,' he replied and held her gaze. All that was too awkward for them to say would always remain unsaid, but understood. The moment passed as swiftly as it had arrived

On the stroke of midnight, Sister Bronwyn popped the cork from a bottle of real champagne and Sameera handed round the plastic cups.

'Tonight is a special night,' said Sister Bronwyn, holding her champagne aloft. 'It marks the return of The Night Owls, a very special group, a unique exclusive collection of elite individuals. Ladies and gentlemen, you are why we come to work every night. You are the reason Sameera and I battle our body clocks, and the reason I don't have a body like Elle Macpherson. Cheers to you all, old friends and new.'

'Here's to absent friends too,' said Hattie as she clinked plastic cups with Walter.

'Absent friends,' he echoed. 'I miss him, you know.' His eyes glazed for a moment then he said more brightly, 'I hear the new fellow in Mayfair has paid for a Netflix subscription. I might pay him a visit one night.'

The champagne seemed to go straight to Walter's head, soft snores soon reverberating from the back of his throat as he slept with arms folded across his soft belly. Hattie noticed Fanny hovering next to the open door of Icarus's cage and when she thought no one was watching, slip the war medal that had been hanging in place of the little round mirror, into her pocket. Where it belonged. With an unknown number of final warnings up their sleeves, Sister Bronwyn and Sameera cleaned away the cups and empty bottles. Around the day room, heads were beginning to nod. Late night had eased into early morning, and outside, the silver glow of the new day had already cast the first silhouettes.

People claimed the darkest hour was the one before dawn. Something to do with holding on to hope, she supposed. Birds and humans alike needed to believe that things would always get better.

Only Icarus noticed Hattie open the big French windows that overlooked the courtyard. The air conditioning would battle on for several minutes trying to keep Woodlands at a steady twenty-three degrees. Perched on the top of his Crystal Palace, the tiny bird eyed Hattie, his blue head bobbing back and forth until he had the full measure of her. In a silent flutter of coloured feathers, Icarus was gone, soaring out through the open window and up towards the last of the stars.

Author's note

ONE OF THE GREATEST PRIVILEGES AS A DOCTOR IS CARING for someone approaching the end of a long life. My nursing home visits have been one of the most rewarding – and occasionally entertaining – aspects of my career in general practice. I have seen many frail older people thrive in stimulating and caring environments, regain their health and strength, and embrace a whole new community of friends. I have also seen countless people for whom the loss of independence in transitioning to care has not been easy, and several who, with varying degrees of success, have attempted to 'escape'. While Woodlands Nursing Home, all its staff and residents are fictional, the obstacles facing the characters in this book, and the aged-care sector as a whole, are all too real.

One particular challenge faced by all aged-care facilities, one I frequently witnessed during my after-hours visits, is in meeting the needs of residents at night. Older people rarely sleep continuously during the hours of darkness. Fear, anxiety and disorientation often leave residents, many of whom live with dementia, wandering the corridors at a time when staffing levels are at their minimum. Although the idea of Sister Bronwyn's 'Night Owls' is an unconventional and somewhat romanticised answer, the aged-care sector should be encouraged and supported to find its own creative solutions to this issue and in doing so hopefully reduce the overreliance on chemical restraints.

In this novel, I deliberately wanted to tell the story from the point of view of those who are so often left 'out of sight, out of mind', and highlight the paradoxical demands of keeping vulnerable people safe while accommodating the right of an individual to maintain their independence. While not wanting to sugar-coat life in a nursing home, I hope that by focusing on the positives – love, laughter and human connection – this book will provide some solace where it is needed. I particularly wanted to draw attention to the countless dedicated staff who deliver high quality, individualised care with kindness, compassion and dedication. I would also like to acknowledge the many excellent providers who create the kind of home that, like Woodlands, I could envisage myself living in. It begs the question, why can't this be the norm?

In October 2019, the Royal Commission into Aged Care Quality and Safety delivered its interim report, describing Australia's aged-care system as a 'shocking tale of neglect'. It concluded: 'A fundamental overhaul of the design, objectives, regulation and funding of aged care in Australia is required.' While I acknowledge the shortcomings that have dominated the headlines recently, I remain overwhelmingly optimistic for the future for aged care.

In time, I hope that we can move away from referring to the ageing population as a 'burden' on society and instead focus on designing an aged-care system that meets the needs of all older people. We owe it to our loved ones, to our future selves, and to the generations to come.

Acknowledgements

MY HEARTFELT THANKS TO THE WONDERFUL TEAM AT Hachette and the many skilled hands my manuscript passed through on its way to becoming this book. Thank you especially to Rebecca Saunders, whose enthusiasm for my unconventional heroes was obvious from the start. Thanks also to the fairy godmother of editors, Karen Ward, who, along with Julia Stiles and Claire de Medici, waved her magic wand over my pumpkin. A big shout out to Sarah Holmes and Eliza Thompson in marketing, Jemma Rowe in publicity, and the all-important sales team, Dan Pilkington, Chris Sims and Sean Cotcher, for their various roles in spreading the word. Thank you also to Christa Moffitt at Christabella Designs for the fantastic cover and for giving Queenie a new lease of life! I'm enormously grateful to Thorne Ryan and the team at Hodder & Stoughton for sharing Hattie and Walter with UK readers.

THE GREAT ESCAPE FROM WOODLANDS NURSING HOME

To my agent Haylee Nash: as always, my gratitude for your wise counsel in all things, and for paving another smooth path to publication.

A special thank you to my writers' group – my 'Inkies' – namely Pamela Cook, Michelle Barraclough, Laura Boon, Terri-Ann Green, Penelope Janu, Angella Whitton – for all your advice, support and friendship. You ladies are my writing world and so much more.

I am deeply indebted to the following people who helped with my research: to Ann and Philip Watson, for allowing me to test-drive the 'Tesla'; to the three NSW police officers who kept straight faces when approached with a hypothetical query about a hijacked minibus; and to Donna Westlake for responding to my out-of-the-blue email. Although the seed of an idea for setting a novel inside a nursing home had been planted long ago, it was reading *Providing Good Care at Night for Older People: Practical Approaches For Use in Nursing and Care Homes* by Heather Wilkinson and Diana Kerr (Jessica Kingsley Publishers, 2011) that proved the inspiration for Sister Bronwyn and 'The Night Owls'.

To David B, thank you for allowing me to repurpose a favourite family anecdote.

I will be forever grateful to my father for passing on not only his love of birds but also a wider appreciation for the natural world. I would like to offer special thanks to Beth Mott at BirdLife Australia's Powerful Owl Project for introducing me to this majestic species, the country's largest – and now sadly threatened – owl. *Your Backyard Birds* by Grainne Cleary (Allen & Unwin, 2019) was also invaluable in researching the novel, not to mention a thoroughly enjoyable read.

Finally, it's no exaggeration to say that I could not have written this book without the love, patience, support and continued good humour of my beautiful family, John, William, Charlotte, and of course, Margot the dog.